PRAISE FOR *A BUSTLE IN THE HEDGEROW*

"This nail-biter teems with suspense and competently manages two murder mysteries in one… An unrelenting debut thriller that reads like the work of a pro."

-Kirkus Reviews

"I highly recommend *A Bustle in the Hedgerow* to any fan of intelligent thrillers. I could not put [it] down. An amazing first novel by an author who crafted a complex and unfortunately believable mystery/thriller that I will not soon forget."

-Peter Haywood Shaw, author of *Teeth of the Fog*

"*A Bustle in the Hedgerow* starts out deceptively simple, but gets more complex and interesting as the mystery deepens. Characters are three-dimensional and multifaceted…a good psychological thriller."

-Catherine Langrehr, *IndieReader*

"Lots of twists and turns, manipulation and red herrings mean this is a book that will stay with you long after you finish it. You many also want to give your children a tighter hug this evening."

- Julie Ryan, author of *Jenna's Journey, allthingsbookie.com*

A Bustle in the Hedgerow

A Novel

By Ben Miller

A Bustle in the Hedgerow

By Ben Miller

ISBN-13: 978-1494403720
ISBN-10: 1494403722

www.benmillerbooks.com

Published by Krac Publishing
Mars, PA

Lyrics from "Family Snapshot"
Written by Peter Gabriel
Published by Real World Music Ltd
Courtesy of petergabriel.com
Reprinted by permission. International Copyright secured.

Cover art by Beyond Book Covers
www.beyondbookcovers.com

INTRODUCTION:
THE FBI AND CASMIRC

The Federal Bureau of Investigation was not included in the
original design of The United States of America. The delegates at the
Second Continental Congress in the 1770s did not incorporate any
federal law-enforcement agencies into their plan. The first such
agency was the Department of Justice, established nearly a century
later in 1870. Up until and even including that time, federal crimes
were rare. Only those crimes that occurred on federal government
reservations or that crossed state lines were considered "federal." As
such, the Department of Justice did not feel the need to hire its own
investigative staff. Rather, on those exceedingly infrequent occasions
that federal crimes happened, the DOJ would hire freelance private
detectives to investigate. Around the turn of the Twentieth Century,
the DOJ began soliciting the services of other government agencies,
most often the Secret Service, to helm any inquiries. However, these
agents then would report to the Director of the Secret Service, not the
DOJ or its director, the Attorney General, creating an inherent
problem in this configuration. This could lead to massive amounts of
confusion and lost information, not to mention a potential conflict of
interest, depending on the type of case.

During Theodore Roosevelt's second term in office, his
Attorney General Charles Bonaparte voiced frustration regarding this
system. He shared Roosevelt's "Progressive" political bend, favoring
more federal government involvement in an ever increasingly

industrialized world. As such, he wanted his own team of investigators that reported directly to him. In May 1908, Congress heard his plea and outlawed the use of Secret Service Agents by the Department of Justice. Within the next two months, Bonaparte compiled thirty-four "Special Agents of the Department of Justice" – ten former Secret Service agents and twenty-four Department of Justice employees. On July 26, 1908, he ordered them to take a meeting with Chief Examiner Stanley W. Finch. Historians regard this meeting as the birth of the Federal Bureau of Investigation, even though the name was not applied until a year later by Bonaparte's successor, Attorney General George Wickersham.

The FBI spent much of the next several decades fighting against organized crime while also assisting local authorities with any investigative effort. In the early 1980's, the focus of the FBI expanded to include counter-terrorism, partly in anticipation of the 1984 Olympic Games in Los Angeles and the desire to avoid any situation similar to Munich in 1972. Despite this intense focus on potential international crime, in June 1984, at the suggestion of the Criminal Personality Research Project of 1982, President Ronald Reagan announced the creation of the National Center for the Analysis of Violent Crime, or NCAVC. The FBI training headquarters in Quantico, Virginia became the home for NCAVC, which, among other things, encompasses the Behavioral Analysis Unit.

In October, 1998, Congress passed the Protection of Children from Sexual Predators Act. In it, a new division of the NCAVC was established: the Morgan P. Hardiman Child Abduction and Serial Murder Investigative Resource Center, or CASMIRC. Today, local authorities can enlist the services of CASMIRC for any suspected or actual violent crime committed against a child, which includes abduction, molestation, rape, and murder.

DAY ONE: MONDAY

1

By the age of nine years, Adrianna Cottrell had concluded that a clear line exists between Good People and Bad People. Everyone lived on one side of the line or the other, and no one ever crossed the line. The two groups' memberships were mutually exclusive. Of course, she belonged with the Good People. She smiled politely and spoke with kindness and respect. She took out the garbage when asked, made her bed most of the time, and often volunteered to help out with her little sister. She still picked her nose, like many people, but she would never eat the boogers, mostly in fear that this might disqualify her from the ranks of the Good. In fact, she had never done anything to suggest that she fit in with the Bad People; thus, by her reasoning, she didn't deserve for anything bad to happen to her. Certainly she didn't deserve to get murdered four months shy of her tenth birthday. Unfortunately for Adrianna the Bad People don't seem to care about *deserves*.

Her warm body lay in the midst of last autumn's slimy, decaying leaves and the early sprouts of this spring's weeds. Jed Thompson, the school's gym teacher, discovered her, on the far side of a row of hedges, behind the tennis courts at the back of the playground. From his knees, with a faint plume of steam rising from the fresh pool of his vomit in front of him, Jed wondered how she had gotten on the other side of the hedges. He noticed no broken branches in the sturdy shrubbery, and surely this little third-grader couldn't have done the Fosbury Flop over them. The thought quickly faded as he called 9-1-1.

It took about eight minutes for the first responding police officer, Nat Fordham, to arrive. Like Jed, Nat had never seen a dead body before. Unlike Jed, Nat didn't puke. Instead, he found himself transfixed on the glassy, lifeless eyes of the young girl. Along with her curly auburn hair, her green eyes had been Adrianna's proudest and most distinguishing feature.

Nat had served on the force a mere seven months. The following day he asked for a two-week leave-of-absence, which he received, but he never actually came back. It equaled the second-shortest stint ever with the York Police Force. Nat eventually went back to school, got a Master's degree in accounting, and finished out his days as a CPA, but a week never passed that he didn't think about that little girl lying in that bed of old leaves, her mouth turned down in a confused frown, her greenish eyes staring endlessly into the woods.

2

The lights emanated a tremendous amount of heat. He should have remembered how hot they were. He had sat here before, right in this same chair, in this same situation. He could feel tiny beads of sweat forming at the top of his forehead. He tried not to focus on the lights or their heat. Like all of the men in his family, once he got a true sweat going, Jackson Byrne would need sixty minutes and a cool towel to make it stop. This propensity toward profuse perspiration was perhaps the sole curse of being a Byrne Man.

Why had he not remembered this detail of sitting here before? Given his history of copious perspiration, it seemed significant. Jack suddenly experienced a rare moment of insight: how was it that he possessed such skill in noticing the details of other people's lives—or, more accurately, their deaths—yet he could easily forget an important aspect of his own experiences? He didn't dwell on the thought for long, as he got distracted by the change in focus of the other people in the expansive studio.

Caleb Goodnight came onto the stage, entering the glow of those bright lights. He had an innate way of garnering attention just by entering a room. He was not tall, nor exceedingly handsome, nor especially bright. Nevertheless, he commanded a presence, for he possessed seemingly supernatural charisma. For anyone who knew him well, this seemed the case for all of his 42 years. Unlike some of his talk-show counterparts, Caleb did not put up a façade. Genuinely personable and equally likable, he was kind to his friends, and he treated his guests like friends.

A BUSTLE IN THE HEDGEROW

In addition to his distinctive personality, Caleb had a signature look: his navy sport coat over an argyle sweater, his light-brown neatly-trimmed goatee, and his thin, dark-rimmed rectangular glasses. It was akin to Larry King's suspenders and large spectacles, but more contemporary, and somehow more earnest.

Caleb approached Jack with his right hand outstretched. "Hi, Jack."

Jack stood up and grasped Caleb's hand. "Hi, Caleb. Good to be here."

They released hands as each sat down in the upholstered chairs angled towards each other in the center of the stage.

"How have you been?" Caleb asked.

"Busy. I never realized how much work it would be to write a book," Jack replied with a raise of his eyebrows.

Caleb gave a small nod in agreement. He had written two fact-based books himself, one of which became a national best-seller. "Fascinating, by the way. I think it's probably the best piece of literature offering insight into how minds like yours work, how detectives think about solving crimes. And I'm not just saying that because you're my friend." True to form, though he had a variety of guests on his show with a variety of accomplishments, Caleb never offered false praise. If he didn't like someone's work, he may have him on his show, but he wouldn't shower him with insincere flattery.

Knowing this about Caleb, Jack accepted the kudos sincerely. "Thanks."

"And that next-to-last chapter blew me away. I had no idea things had gotten so bad in this country, the laws so circumspect. I

7

think that's why it has struck a chord with so many people: anybody who has kids, works with kids, ever was a kid."

Jack offered a subtle nod. "I just wish we had a better solution."

Caleb opened his mouth to respond but he got interrupted. A man who had previously introduced himself to Jack as Tim the Producer raised a hand to signify his importance. "Thirty seconds to go, people."

"Ready?" Caleb queried.

"Yep. I think if I said 'no,' though, it wouldn't make much of a difference to Tim the Producer."

"You're a quick study." Caleb leaned to his right, a little closer to Jack. He said in a low whisper, "He has the personality of a toad, but he puts together a great finished product."

Jack stifled a smile as he motioned to his wireless microphone clipped to his lapel. "Aren't these mikes on?"

Caleb smirked wryly and nodded.

Tim the Producer pushed an open palm towards the men on the stage. "And in five, four ..." He stopped saying the numbers, but continued counting down on his fingers. *Why do they always do that?* Jack wondered. *Why not say 3, 2, or 1?*

Caleb turned to face the camera. "Good evening and welcome. I'm Caleb Goodnight, and this is The Goodnight Hour." He always opened every show with the same two sentences, spoken with the exact same intonation. Simple, most definitely, but over his six-year run as a late-night cable talk show host, it had become a staple in the Zeitgeist.

A BUSTLE IN THE HEDGEROW

"Tonight my guest is Special Agent Jackson Byrne of the FBI." Caleb rotated his head to face Jack. "Jack, welcome back to the show."

"Thanks, Caleb. It's good to be here."

3

Randall stared at the TV. *The Goodnight Hour* ended twenty-seven minutes ago, but his thoughts still lingered on that show. He had watched it religiously for years. He believed in Caleb Goodnight— one of the few TV personalities that Randall felt he could trust.

Jackson Byrne was back. Back on *The Goodnight Hour*. Back where it all began. When Randall first conceptualized his Work. When he got reborn.

Randall thought about his last victim. From local media outlets in York, he had learned her name: Adrianna Cottrell. She had a mother, a father, and a 4-year-old sister, all of whom missed her very much, according to the local papers. A gruesome tragedy, they called it.

With this, Randall agreed. It was very sad that she had to die. But she did, unfortunately. Well, Adrianna didn't, but somebody did. His Work dictated it. And she served as well as anyone.

Randall suddenly felt the need to be faster. Not with his thinking, God no. He already possessed greater intelligence and faster cognitive processing than anyone else on the planet. He wanted to move quickly, like a cheetah, a lynx, or a jaguar.

Adrianna's family pleaded with their community to help them find out who had committed such an awful crime. Local authorities apparently worked "around the clock" to solve it.

But they wouldn't. Randall knew this as well as he knew his own name.

A BUSTLE IN THE HEDGEROW

Fast like a greyhound, or an ostrich—he felt compelled to break up the feline theme. He despised monotony almost as much as banality.

He stopped thinking about Adrianna Cottrell, Jackson Byrne, and Caleb Goodnight all at the same time. He put on his running shoes and went outside for a run. Not a jog, a run. He needed to be faster.

4

The waitress arrived with the two draft beers on her tray. She set the drinks down in front of Jack and Caleb and lingered there for a moment. "I'm a really big fan," she said to Caleb, batting her eyelashes.

"Oh, thank you," Caleb politely responded.

"The worst part about this job is that I miss your show like four nights a week. I have it on DVR, but it's just not the same as watching it live, you know?"

"That's very nice support, thank you. I'm glad you enjoy the show."

She smiled awkwardly and walked back toward the bar.

The hotel bar had very little activity this time of night on a Monday. Besides Jack and Caleb, there were only about three other parties there, all of them small groups conversing softly. The bartender, a young, short, athletic-looking man with a pencil-thin beard, spent twice as much time watching an NBA playoff game on the TV than he did pouring drinks. Jack and Caleb's waitress, the only one still working, set her tray down on the bar and looked at the TV with only the slightest amount of interest.

Jack raised his glass and took a sip. "Thanks again for having me back. I love coming to New York, even for a short trip like this one."

"Are you heading back to Virginia tomorrow?"

"Yeah. I'm meeting an old family friend for a late lunch. Then Vicki and I are going to a school thing for Jonah, like a little play. Something about safari animals or something." He smirked and shrugged. "$14,000 a year to learn how to paint whiskers on his face and sew a lion costume."

Caleb gave Jack a knowing smile. "All part of the program, my friend."

Caleb always acted cordially towards his guests, but he seldom considered them friends outside of the studio. Sometimes it had to do with differences in background or philosophy. But more commonly it was due to the fact that Caleb just didn't like what fame—in any measure of the word—did to people. Even the 15-minute variety could alter the simplest of lives. A few weeks ago, he had as his guest an eleven-year-old girl who had become famous for her appearances in a series of wireless phone commercials. From that she had garnered the distinction of having the most rapid increase of followers on her Twitter account since the technology's inception. *Fame sure chooses some strange passengers*, he remembered thinking at the time. That certainly would not be the last time this concept would enter his consciousness.

During his first encounter with Jack, Caleb recognized instantly that fame had touched him differently. Jack hardly shied away from his newfound celebrity; in fact, he embraced it. However, it didn't seem to change the way he saw the world. Partly because of this, partly because of shared interests, and partly because of good chemistry—which exists even in the most platonic of relationships, even if most men wouldn't admit it—Caleb and Jack had become friends.

Caleb took another large sip of his stout and licked the tan foam from his upper lip. "So anything exciting going on in the job?"

13

"No, not now. I've actually been busier doing book signings than anything else recently. My literary agent is working me like a dog."

Caleb smiled. "Do you like it?"

Jack shrugged. "Not really. The most interesting thing is watching the sorts of people who come out to a book signing. I've convinced myself that sometime, somewhere, at least one person I meet will turn out to be a serial killer, kidnapper, or rapist himself. To keep my mind occupied during these excruciating days, I try to figure out which one it's going to be."

"Think you've met him?"

"My internal Psychopath Alarm hasn't gone off too loudly yet, no."

Caleb considered this concept briefly. "Boy, wouldn't that make police work a lot simpler." He held his hands aloft, outlining an imaginary marquee. "The Psychopath Alarm, retails for $49.99, available at Wal-Mart."

Jack smiled. "That would pretty quickly put me out of a job."

"You say that as if it might be a good thing."

"Well, I don't know." Jack's expression became somewhat pensive. "I don't think I'd complain too much, no."

DAY TWO: TUESDAY

5

Because of the cool temperature, the eerie silence, or the constant characteristic smell—something of a mix between kerosene, sulfur, and cheap perfume—most of the other detectives in the York County Homicide Division hated going to the morgue, but Kenneth Howard didn't mind it. He actually found the quiet, chilly atmosphere peaceful, and he had suffered a number of mild concussions while playing football through high school and college that left him with a diminished sense of smell.

He walked into the small, square office of the York County Coroner, Dr. Krishnavilli. His first name started with an R and was followed by a bunch of a's and consonants. Howard knew he would mispronounce it, so he had never even tried. Krishnavilli, a humorless man, possessed poor social skills and a detail-oriented personality that would easily meet the diagnosis of Asperger Syndrome, if he had ever spent the time to see a therapist and get a diagnosis. Howard—and everyone else in Homicide—thought Krishnavilli had found his true calling as a forensic pathologist.

"Hey, Doc," Howard said as he knocked on the open wooden door of the office.

BEN MILLER

Krishnavilli barely glanced up from his desk. "Hello, Officer. Come in." He continued typing on the laptop on the left side of his desk.

Howard had worked in Homicide for over 6 years. Despite losing nearly 60 pounds since his playing days—starting center at Villanova his sophomore through senior years— he still possessed great size at 6'3" and 235 pounds. Plus, he was the only African-American in the Homicide Division. His face and his frame were unmistakable. Though he had worked with Krishnavilli on at least a half-dozen cases, he was pretty sure that Krishnavilli did not know his name.

"What can you tell me about Adrianna Cottrell?" Howard asked.

Without making eye contact, Krishnavilli reached to the center of his desk and tapped a manila folder with his right index finger. He went back to typing away on the laptop.

Howard walked over to the desk and picked up the folder. He had forgotten how desolate this office felt. The walls were barren except for the empty bulletin board hanging on the wall behind Krishnavilli's desk.

"Anything interesting?" Even though Krishnavilli had a relatively thick Indian accent, Howard found it much easier—and quicker—if he could get the highlights verbally rather than sift through the report.

Again, Krishnavilli spoke without raising his eyes from the computer. "COD strangulation. No prints. Post-mortem trauma to the sternum and ribcage, including four rib fractures."

A BUSTLE IN THE HEDGEROW

Howard had always found Krishnavilli's monotone delivery unnerving, especially when referring to autopsy details. "What do you think that means?"

Krishnavilli shrugged. "You're the detective."

Howard nodded. He should have predicted that response. He would have to remember to stop asking such silly questions.

"Clothing and personal items?"

"Gail has them." Gail, the filing clerk, sat at a counter a little farther down the hall.

"Anything interesting there?" Howard asked, skeptical that he would receive an informative response.

Krishnavilli shook his head and continued typing.

Having his notion confirmed, Howard turned to leave the office. Shockingly, Krishnavilli spoke just as Howard had reached the door. "There was a love note or something in her front pocket. At first I just thought they were scribbles, but I think it actually has some meaning. It may be some kind of code the children were using."

The phrase "the children" nearly turned Howard's stomach. Of course he realized that he was investigating the murder of a 9-year-old girl, but thinking about her and her peer group as "children" made the murder all the more horrifying.

6

After arriving home from the airport earlier that morning, Jack had just had enough time to read the newspaper before he had to leave for his lunch with Philip Prince. Vicki had already left for work, dropping Jonah off at school on her way. They had left him a note on the kitchen island welcoming him home. Jonah's portion of the note included a smiley face in red crayon. In this age of cell phones, texting, Face Timing, and Skyping, Jack found it so refreshing and endearing that Vicki still took the time to write out a note commemorating his return from a day-trip to New York City. That was one of the things that he loved most about his wife.

Jack stuck Vicki and Jonah's note into his pocket as he walked into the garage. He had left himself 45 minutes to make it to the restaurant, predicting that traffic shouldn't hold him up too much at this time on a Tuesday. The Byrnes owned a modest four-bedroom house nestled in a family-friendly community in Lake Ridge, Virginia. Situated about 25 miles southwest of Washington, DC and 18 miles north of Quantico, Virginia, Lake Ridge was ideally located for a manageable commute to either one. He got behind the wheel of his black Ford Taurus and started the engine.

While en route he wondered about the reason for this rendezvous today. Prince had called him late last week and asked if he could take Jack out for a meal. "Let's meet for a friendly lunch to discuss a business matter." He wouldn't offer anything more specific than that. As Jack had the talk show obligation in New York yesterday, but they did not expect him back at work until tomorrow, he and Prince had settled on today.

18

A BUSTLE IN THE HEDGEROW

Philip Prince was the former Lieutenant Governor of Maryland and still held a place of significant prominence within the Democratic Party. He had gone to law school with Jack's father, Anthony Byrne, who had been the long-time District Attorney for the District of Columbia.

Anthony Byrne passed away three years ago from pancreatic cancer, only about eight months after he had learned of the diagnosis. This rapid decline spoke much more to the nature of pancreatic cancer than it did to the medical care Anthony Byrne received. "Cancer is never really good," Jack's father had bluntly explained to him, not long after his initial meeting with his oncologist. "But apparently there are some 'good cancers' and some 'bad cancers.' Pancreatic cancer is possibly the worst of the bad." Despite this ominous prognosis, Anthony kept a very positive attitude throughout his initial treatments and through his palliative care as well. He died in his home at the age of 69. Jack's sister Jody, a divorced nurse practitioner, had taken a sabbatical from her academic position at the University of Maryland to care for him at home. Both Jack and Jody felt that serving as nursemaid to her dying husband was not a role that fit their mother Florence very well. They much preferred that she spend her final days with her husband as a partner, not a servant. To this day Jack still felt a debt of gratitude towards his sister for providing their mother with that gift.

Jack had not been particularly close with his father as a young child growing up. Toiling in an extremely demanding job, Jack's father spent very little time at home, and, even when present, his father did not like to spend time with childish things. He never actually stated this overtly, but, in retrospect, Jack surmised this from

19

looking back at his father's attitude towards some of his childhood endeavors. Anthony failed to see the appeal in Star Wars action figures, skateboards, or Atari video games.

When Jack entered middle school and became active in sports, he and his father began to get along much better. Anthony greatly encouraged excellence, and what better way to show one's excellence than to best the other pre-adolescents in the 100-meter breast stroke? His father became his biggest supporter, often rearranging meetings and, once, a court date, to attend Jack's swim meets throughout high school. Anthony nearly beamed with pride when Jack got a full scholarship to swim at the University of Virginia—not because this eased a financial burden, but rather because it served as an evident display of excellence.

Jack remained close with his father throughout adulthood. He often wondered how much influence his father had on his decision to go to law school. Outwardly he steadfastly denied that going to law school at the University of Michigan reflected a desire to please his father; inwardly, when honest with himself, he wasn't sure. His father never pushed him toward one profession over another. He simply tried to instill in his children that they should always strive to achieve their greatest potential, which in his mind, of course, never stopped short of excellence.

As he crossed the Williams Memorial Bridge over the Potomac, Jack pondered how his father would react to his recent success if he were still alive today. *It depends on how many details of my success he knows,* Jack thought before dismissing that line of thinking. Attempting to intuit the opinions of the dead would surely end as a fruitless endeavor; he would not spend any more mental energy with such a query.

Jack's focus returned to the matter at hand: today's meeting. As one of Anthony Byrne's dearest and oldest friends, Philip Prince had kept in touch with Jack periodically in the three years since his father's death. Philip and his wife Reba played bridge with Anthony and Florence Byrne at least four or five times per year for two decades. Even when Reba died of breast cancer almost ten years ago, they continued to play with regularity. Often they would find a fourth to sub in; less often they would play three-handed bridge. Prior to last week, Jack had not talked to Prince in almost a year. At that time Prince had called to congratulate Jack on his success in his last case, the one on which Jack had based his book, the one that had made him a national house-hold name, if only for a few days.

Because Prince still remained very active in the Democratic Party, Jack's initial thought was that he wanted Jack to speak at a local convention. He had been asked to speak at numerous venues in the last seven months, but he had been very selective about his appearances. Miles Agostino, Jack's literary agent, also served as his booking agent. Although Jack had an aptitude for public speaking, he did not enjoy doing it. However, he (and Miles) did enjoy the extra revenue generated from his few speaking gigs.

Often skeptical, even without provocation— a prerequisite for any good detective— Jack considered that Prince could be asking for a favor. With the constant stream of politicians in murky waters from a variety of misadventures, perhaps Prince wanted some inside information regarding what the FBI knew about some of his fellow Democrats. Worse, maybe Prince wanted dirt on some Republicans.

Jack figured that Prince had to know that, first, Jack wasn't privy to this kind of investigation, and, second, even if he were, he would not divulge such information to Prince. Of course Prince wouldn't ask him for something like this. *Right?*

Jack decided that if Prince asked him to speak at a convention or some other gathering, he would do it, mostly out of gratitude and respect for Prince's relationship with Anthony Byrne. For all other requests, his answer would have to be no.

7

Philip Prince had already been seated at a table near the back of the restaurant when Jack arrived at The Palm. A steakhouse in northern Washington situated mere blocks from the White House and a short cab ride from The Capitol, The Palm had become known as a preferred site for power lunches in DC. The maître d' pointed towards Prince's table, and Jack raised a hand in recognition. He headed back, dodging between tables. Prince stood up to great him.

"Hello, Jack. It's wonderful to see you."

"Always good to see you too, Philip." The two shook hands. Prince gestured to the seat opposite his, and Jack sat down.

"How are Vicki and Jonah?"

"Good," Jack replied. "Things have been busy for Vicki at work, as usual. Jonah is doing great. He has a little play tonight through his school."

"Aw, that sounds sweet," Prince said in return, though Jack got the sense that he really didn't care too much. Prince clearly had other business on his mind more important than small talk.

He looks old, Jack thought. He did some quick math in his head. *He's got to be 73 or 74 now, but he looks at least a decade older than when I saw him last, just three years ago.* Jack was also reminded of how Prince often looked somewhat slovenly. He remembered leaning over to his sister at his father's viewing and saying, "Philip Prince is the only man I know who can make a four-thousand dollar suit look like it came off the rack at TJ Maxx."

"How has life been treating you?" Jack asked.

Prince opened his mouth to answer when the waiter appeared. "Can I get you gentlemen something to drink?" the bow-tied man asked the pair.

"Water for me," Prince answered. "Jack?"

"Water's fine." Jack felt some relief that Prince didn't order an alcoholic drink. With a few exceptions— when on vacation, on the golf course, or at an afternoon ballgame— it always bothered him when people drank at lunch.

"Shall I give you a few moments to look the menu over, then?" the waiter offered.

Prince ordered ahi tuna, rare, while Jack surveyed the menu. Jack settled on a chicken sandwich, with mayonnaise on the side. The waiter didn't write down either's order, which Jack always found intriguing, almost troubling. *Who's he trying to impress with his short-term memory skills? I don't give a shit if he can recite the Declaration of Independence from memory, I want to make sure I get my chicken sandwich with the mayonnaise on the side.*

"Life has been treating me pretty well, Jack," Prince said as he leaned forward in his chair to place all of his attention on his younger lunch companion. It took Jack a brief second to realize that Prince answered the question he had asked him prior to the waiter's arrival.

"Good." Jack was quite curious about the reason for this meeting—*Please no dirt-digging expeditions...*-- but he didn't want to be the one to bring it up. Knowing Prince, Jack thought he wouldn't beat around the bush too much.

"You're probably wondering why I asked you to join me for lunch," Prince offered after a brief pause.

Bingo.

24

"Yes, to be honest." Jack knew that Prince possessed a finely-tuned Bullshit Meter; to feign disinterest when genuinely curious would serve no purpose.

"Jack, a week hasn't gone by since your father died that I don't think about him. He was a strong man, of great character and integrity. And he was well-known and respected throughout this community."

"That's nice to know," Jack said. He noticed that Prince's intonation sounded slightly flat, as if he had rehearsed this little speech.

"And you have created your own warm spot on the radar screen recently. With your fine work of the Hollows Case, your book coming out, your TV appearances, your local speaking engagements…"

He's really been paying attention, Jack thought.

"…You have become a familiar face and an honorable name in many households."

Prince paused to study Jack's face. He thought that Jack seemed neither markedly proud of these accomplishments nor embarrassed at their mention. For the briefest of moments, Prince sensed that Jack was trying to hide something. He decided to sit quietly to see how Jack would respond. After several seconds, the silence became somewhat uncomfortable.

"Thank you, Philip. That means a lot. I wish my father could be around to witness some of this." Jack guessed that Philip would bring Anthony Byrne back into the conversation next, so he took the opportunity to beat him to it. Jack often created competition in even mundane occurrences, like a conversation over lunch.

25

"I know. I've thought of that too." Prince paused again, presumably out of respect for the elder Byrne. "Jack, sometimes when the stars align"— he made an open-handed gesture in the air above eye level, then brought his hands together with his fingers interlaced— "like this, one needs to take the fullest advantage of it."

Prince stopped and looked at Jack. Clearly he was waiting for a response.

"Okay." Jack knew that served as a poor excuse for a response, but it would have to do. Often these conversational competitions involved refusing to give the "opponent" the satisfaction of having the conversation go his or her way. The tendency to fight the natural course of a conversation often irritated those around Jack. Even Jack found it annoying sometimes, yet he chose not to stop himself from doing it.

Prince lowered his eyes and began arranging his silverware at the side of his place setting. "As you surely know, one of Virginia's Senate seats is currently occupied by a man named Rupert Schultz, a Democrat."

Prince looked at Jack, who slowly nodded. "I saw on the news that he got pulled over for DUI the other week."

Prince nodded. "Unfortunately the young Senator Schultz was not alone when he was pulled over. Now, Schultz is a bachelor, so there's no crime in driving with a companion."

"As long as you're sober," Jack footnoted.

Prince chuckled. "Yes. Well, as it turns out, Schulz was not sober, and this was not just any companion. It was his sister-in-law, his brother's wife. His brother, Dashiel, serves as Rupert's campaign manager and his top aide. Well, *served*, that is, until 10 days ago when Rupert was pulled over, driving drunk, with Dashiel's wife, with whom he had been having an affair for the last 2 years."

"Oops," Jack responded. Suddenly the conversation seemed more comfortable. Jack sat back and spread his napkin out on his lap.

The waiter approached with their lunch, and set the two plates down in front of Jack and Prince.

"Thank you," Prince said to the waiter as he grabbed the steak knife beside the plate and began cutting into his ahi. The waiter nodded and left.

Jack studied his plate: chicken sandwich, mayonnaise on the side. He tilted his head in an unnoticed gesture of respect to the waiter and his impeccable memory, a little pissed that the douche bag actually impressed him with his parlor trick. Jack spread a small amount of mayonnaise on his top bun and began to eat his sandwich.

"Oops is right. We've learned that Dashiel will be announcing his resignation sometime this week, leaving Rupert without a campaign manager or top aide. News of Rupert's adultery will surface shortly after that. When we put these elements together in the world of political chemistry, a mini-explosion is likely headed for the Schultz camp in the coming weeks." Prince took a bite of his tuna, and he let out a small "Mmmmm." He pointed down at the dish with his knife. "That's good," he said, with his mouth still a quarter full. He set his knife down and took a sip of his water. He finished chewing and swallowed down the bite.

Then Prince looked Jackson Byrne square in the eyes. "Which brings us to you, dear Jack."

Well, this definitely is not about a speaking engagement, Jack thought.

BEN MILLER

"I think you would be a perfect candidate to replace Senator Shultz as the next U.S. Senator from Virginia."

8

"Did you like the show, Daddy?" Jonah asked for the fourth time, sitting on the couch beside his father, finishing the last few bites of his hot fudge sundae.

"It was really good, Jonah," Jack reaffirmed.

Jack looked over at his son. A huge smile covered Jack's face as he noticed the faint black "whiskers" still drawn on Jonah's face and the streaks of hot fudge caked on both his upper and lower lips.

"And did you find me believable as the lion?"

Jack laughed out loud. "Believable?" He turned to Vicki, who watched this exchange from behind the kitchen bar that overlooked the family room. "Where does a five-year-old come up with this stuff?"

"Well?" Jonah insisted.

"Oh, most definitely. I never doubted for a minute that that was a real lion up there on stage."

"Oh, Daddy, you knew it was me, right?" Jonah flashed his adorable grin.

"I thought it was you, but sometimes it looked so much like a lion that I had to do a double take." Jack looked directly at Jonah then imitated an overly dramatic, wide-eyed double take with a sweeping turn of his neck. Jonah giggled, producing Jack's favorite, most delightful sound in the entire world.

Two hours, a bubble bath, and a bedtime story later, Jack quietly closed Jonah's bedroom door behind him. He walked down the hall and into his and Vicki's bedroom. Vicki sat on the bed leaning back against the headboard. She was wearing her typical bedclothes: a plain T-shirt and sweatpants. On the TV Caleb Goodnight interviewed Robert Redford. She looked up at Jack as she turned off the TV.

"Well?"

"*Corduroy*," Jack replied.

"Again? That must be the fourth night in a row."

Jack shrugged. "It's his new favorite book." He began to undress.

"Clearly." Vicki scooted over to sit on the edge of the bed as Jack went into the walk-in closet. "So, how was your lunch with Philip Prince?"

Jack walked out of the closet as he finished unbuttoning his shirt. "Interesting."

As he finished getting undressed, slipped into his typical bedclothes—a pair of running shorts—and brushed his teeth, Jack told Vicki of his lunchtime conversation with Philip Prince, culminating in Prince's proposal to run for the Senate.

"Wow," Vicki responded initially. "That is interesting." She concentrated on Jack's countenance for a few seconds. "You don't seem flabbergasted by this."

Jack looked at her as he walked around to his side of the bed. "Flabbergasted? No, I guess not."

"What was your initial impression, your first thought when Philip presented the idea?"

Vicki had always been talented at helping Jack to make good decisions. She helped him gain perspective and look at situations from various angles. Sometimes she would go through a "pro vs. con" exercise, while other times she would encourage him to rely on his "gut feeling." By himself Jack admittedly did not possess a significant alacrity for introspection. In fact, it seemed that the majority of bad decisions he had made since meeting Vicki—including his absolute worst decision— had occurred in her absence.

"It seemed like Prince had come to a logical conclusion." Jack responded after considering her question for several seconds.

"What do you mean by that?" Vicki prodded.

Jack considered his wording for a brief moment. "I mean that my 'star'…" Jack made air quotes—and rolled his eyes, because he usually had a distaste for people who made air quotes, and Vicki knew it—"…is rising, and, with my pedigree and my background, I would be a logical choice to run for some political office. With Schultz's career in disarray, why not the U.S. Senate?"

"Okay." Vicki shuffled back in the bed and lay on her side facing Jack. "And what are your thoughts now?"

"I'm not sure." Jack sighed. He thought about his last case, the murder of Lamaya Hollows, and the many steps that led up to the resolution of that case. Though it led to his current popularity and fame, overall, deep down, Jack was not proud of how he had gone about solving that crime. "Maybe this would be a good time to get out of the Bureau and move onto something different."

"And what if you did, and you lost the election?" Vicki challenged. She knew he would not have considered this line of thinking yet, nor would he find it a comfortable thought. But she also knew that it was an extremely important consideration.

"Huh." Jack seemed a little startled. He often, but not always, let down his adversarial conversation guard with Vicki. Sometimes he paid for it. "Do you think I would lose?"

"Absolutely not. But it's a possibility. Anything's possible, right?"

"I suppose, yeah," Jack acquiesced. "I don't know. There's a ton to be made in consultation work in the private sector. I could freelance for a while, see if I like that. I would probably end up making a lot more money for a lot less work."

"That sounds attractive," Vicki said as she leaned over to kiss him on the cheek. "You know we'd love to have more of our Jack around here."

Jack smiled and turned to face her. He gave her a kiss on the lips. "Thanks, Vic."

"What's the timetable on this? When do you have to let Philip know?" Vicki had grown up with three very outgoing, athletically-gifted brothers, none of whom were particularly bright. Her parents didn't possess the greatest intellectual prowess either, for that matter. As such, she often had to ask the same question twice with different verbiage. It served two purposes: she had a better chance of her busy, boisterous family hearing her, having said it twice; and she had a better chance of their understanding her by saying the same thing two different ways. It had become ingrained in her as a natural speaking pattern, so she never consciously realized that she did it. She and Jack had been together long enough that even he didn't notice any more.

"I told him I would get back to him by the end of the week."

Vicki nodded. "Well, sleep on it. Let me know if you want to spend some time talking through it." She craned her neck to kiss him on the lips again. "Goodnight. Love you."

"Love you too," Jack said. He rolled over and turned out the bedside lamp.

9

Jack and Vicki met fourteen years ago. He was 26, she 24. He had just moved back to Maryland from law school and was living at his parents' house temporarily while studying for the Maryland Bar exam. She was working full-time as a flight attendant and had just started going to business school at night for her MBA. Neither of them liked studying at home (a little too many distractions) nor in libraries (a little too quiet). Their paths crossed in Barb's Beans & Bakery, a quiet corner coffee shop that, coincidentally, both of them found conducive to studying. The coffee shop was quaint and simply decorated, with a dozen small pastel-colored tables arranged throughout the floor plan. The previous owner, before the eponymous Barb, had renovated a split-level office building, so the coffee shop actually sat about four feet below street level. One entered through a glass door onto a small landing before walking down five steps to the main level. Large plate-glass windows comprised the entirety of the two outside walls— except, obviously, for the four feet that were underground— exposing the two intersecting streets and their respective sidewalks.

Jack first noticed Vicki during his second time in Barb's. She sat by a window drinking a cappuccino with her nose in one of her textbooks. Jack had sat down at the other end of the shop, his window at a 90° angle to hers. Vicki initially stuck out to Jack with her natural beauty. She had relatively plain features, with dark brown eyes, slightly lighter hair, and a flawless complexion. She did not wear any make-up because she didn't need to. Jack contemplated approaching her, but instead decided to sit down and start studying.

Not much later Vicki looked up from her text. She widened and blinked her eyes for a moment to give them a rest. She looked around the shop and noticed Jack several tables away. He had a handsome profile, with angular cheekbones and a rugged five o'clock shadow. Before she could conclude whether or not she found him handsome, she noticed a small puppy on the sidewalk just on the other side of the window behind Jack. The puppy continually licked the sidewalk, lapping up the remains of a partially spilled gourmet coffee. His owner stood about ten feet away, engrossed in conversation with an acquaintance, oblivious to his dog's doings. Vicki realized that a few other people in the coffee shop also noticed the puppy and were grinning uncontrollably. Within less than a minute, the adorable puppy drew every pair of eyes in the shop, with more than one person uttering an "Awww!"

Every pair or eyes, that is, except Jack's. He focused deeply on the workbook in front of him. The attention of every patron and employee in Barb's Beans & Bakery focused on the puppy no more than four feet away from Jack's head, and Jack's gaze could not leave the page.

Soon, because now he became the oddity, people began focusing on him. Spectators speculated that he must not have a soul; how else could someone ignore something so close by that was so undeniably adorable?

Vicki, however, did not think Jack heartless. Quite the opposite, she found his focus on his work endearing, and hence instantly found him attractive.

A BUSTLE IN THE HEDGEROW

After another twenty seconds, Jack suddenly felt all those pairs of eyes on him. He looked up from his book to see everyone staring at him, many in disbelief. He was still unaware of the dog, so, naturally, he could not understand why everyone looked at him. Moreover, he couldn't understand why most of them gawked at him as if he had two heads.

As he looked around the room, trying to make some sense of his surroundings, he noticed that one face did not have a frown, but rather a huge smile—the attractive girl at the other window. Finding her smile open and friendly, he met her eyes, furrowed his brow and shrugged as if to say, *What is going on here?* She laughed as she pointed her index finger in the air, swirling it in a circle. *Turn around.*

Jack looked quizzically behind him and saw the puppy, finished its morning coffee. He laughed to himself and turned back around to face Vicki, who began another bout of laughing. He shut his workbook, grabbed his coffee, and went over to her table.

"How long was that going on before I noticed?" Jack asked, still with a slight grin.

She shook her head, minimizing. "Only about ten minutes."

He laughed and then extended his hand. "I'm Jack."

She shook his hand with an adequately firm grip. Jack was immediately impressed—most women don't have such a confident handshake. He liked her.

"I'm Vicki. It's nice to meet you, Jack."

She ended up inviting him to sit down. Uncharacteristically, he did. Normally Jack's mind would have been too focused on his studies to take a break and sit down. They shared about a twenty-minute conversation, mostly the getting-to-know-you variety. At the

35

time Jack did not share with her that he technically still had a relationship from law school with his girlfriend Danielle. She lived in Pittsburgh, where she had gotten a job in a medium-sized law firm. They had thus far succeeded in maintaining a long-distance relationship. Two weeks after Jack met Vicki, though, he and Danielle broke up.

Jack and Vicki started dating shortly thereafter. They naturally fell into a model relationship—both very much in love with each other, enjoying each other's company, but still maintaining their own individual interests and endeavors. Vicki still spent quite a bit of time on the road— or, more accurately, in the air—in the first two years of their relationship. She mainly flew three routes, two of them to-and-from Florida—Orlando and Tampa— the other to-and-from Dallas. When she wasn't on the road, she split time between being with Jack and her MBA classes. Jack had taken a job with a large law firm in Bethesda, which he quickly grew to hate.

The next year she completed her graduate degree, he took a job as an Assistant District Attorney for Montgomery County in Rockville, MD, and they got married. The following year Vicki applied for an administrative job within her airline and easily won the promotion. Now that she could stay in one place, they decided to start a family.

Unfortunately, their first attempts ended in a late miscarriage, around twelve weeks after conception. Vicki took it quite hard, and Jack promised patience and understanding. He provided the former— they shared limited physical contact for almost a year— but he never could fully comprehend how deeply and emotionally scarred the experience had left Vicki.

During that time Jack felt increasingly unfulfilled in his job. He decided that if he were to continue to spend over eighty hours per week at a job, it needed to provide him with a sense of accomplishment. Less than six months after Vicki's miscarriage, Jack applied for a position with the Federal Bureau of Investigation as an investigator in the Criminal Division of the Washington Field Office, which he got.

About two years later, after playing a large role in the apprehension of a serial molester in southern Maryland, Jack took a brief meeting with FBI Director Robert Mueller, III and a man named Dylan Harringer, the Special Agent in Charge of CASMIRC, or the Child Abduction and Serial Murder Investigative Resource Center. Mueller and Harringer asked Jack to move permanently to CASMIRC, located in Quantico, VA. A relatively small but prestigious division, CASMIRC would offer Jack more opportunities for advancement and a wider range of potentially important cases, with its jurisdiction spanning the entire country. He accepted on the spot.

By spring of that year he and Vicki moved to Lake Ridge. One month later, Vicki became pregnant with Jonah. She was 33 when she had Jonah and 35 before they decided to try again. After another 18 months, and her 37th birthday, they decided that Jonah would be their only child rather than risk a pregnancy in her late 30's. Despite their difficulty in coming to such a tough decision, both seemed very content with their small family and their wonderful son.

DAY THREE:
WEDNESDAY

10

Early the next morning, Kenneth Howard stared at the scrap of paper enshrined in a plastic bag in front of him. He had been through all of the crime scene photographs, the autopsy report, the crime scene analysis, and all of the other victim's belongings. Nothing intrigued him as much as this 1" by 4" piece of paper. It had been folded in half once horizontally and slid into the front pocket of Adrianna Cottrell's jeans. It had the following script, written in black ink:

ฉันต้องการใคร

Howard had no idea what it meant. He needed someone proficient in linguistics to analyze this. He had a strong feeling that he currently held in his hands the most important piece of evidence in his case.

He set the plastic bag down and looked through his Rolodex. Despite storing hundreds of phone numbers in his cell phone, Howard still felt the need to have a Rolodex on his desk. He found the number he needed, picked up the phone, and dialed.

11

Jack was the first to arrive in the conference room shortly before 9:00 am. He had gotten to work a little after 7:00 that morning, earlier than usual. He knew he would have several things to take care of—forms to sign, secure e-mails to return, etc.—as it was his first day back in the office for almost a month. He had received a special leave in order to promote his book. Apparently the Powers-That-Be felt that his book and his presence on the talk-show and book-signing trails provided good—and free—PR, which outweighed the downside of being short one senior investigator for several weeks. The most recent e-mail he had received, which announced this current meeting, came from Dylan Harringer, who still served as CASMIRC's Special Agent in Charge, or SAC.

Jack always arrived early for meetings. He felt that as the first person present he would have the opportunity to observe others as they arrived. He also valued punctuality. Punctuality projected a sense of seriousness. Jack could use his charm and sense of humor to put others at ease, but he always wanted them to know that he meant business.

Dylan Harringer had served as the head of CASMIRC for the last nine years. Due to his short stature (Jack had always assumed, at least), Harringer had grown up spending most of his free time in the gym. He became a competitive weight-lifter in high school and still, at the age of 53, spent a minimum of ninety minutes per day working out. He wore snugly fit yet impeccably stylish suits which emphasized his massive arms and V-shaped frame.

Harringer arrived not too long after Jack, at 8:59 am. *Typical Dylan*, Jack thought, *right on time.*

Harringer looked up to see Jack already seated in the conference room, half-smiling. *Typical Jack,* Harringer thought.

"Hello, Jack. Welcome back."

"Thanks, Dylan. Did I miss anything exciting?"

Harringer shook his head. "Nothing outside the usual." He started laying down some files on the front table. "This one should catch your eye, though."

Dylan Harringer served as an excellent SAC. He knew well the strengths and weaknesses of his team members. More often than not, he got the most out of the men and women who worked for him. Though he lacked Jack's charisma and likability—and certainly his recent fame— he was very well respected in this office and throughout the Bureau, more so for his commendable leadership skills than for the rippling muscles underneath his finely-tailored clothing.

"Oh, yeah?" Jack replied. He felt an unfamiliar sense of unease. After his conversation with Philip Prince yesterday, and with Vicki last night, he wasn't sure he was ready to take on a new case. Unfortunately, as he well knew, malfeasants rarely consider the preferences of law enforcement officials when committing their crimes.

Two more agents entered the room, Heath Reilly and Camilla Vanderbilt, followed shortly by Amanda Lundquist and then Charlie Shaver, the agents comprising the rest of the team. Most of them greeted Jack back amongst them with honest appreciation. They all took seats in chairs aligned in two rows, facing the front of the room, where Harringer stood behind a plain table, his files piled neatly on top. Harringer signaled to Reilly, who stood up and plugged a flash drive into the computer on the far end of the front table.

Harringer unceremoniously launched into the meeting. "This morning Heath took a phone call from a homicide detective in York, PA, about a murder earlier this week of a nine-year-old girl."

Jack's heart sank. Immediately a vision of Lamaya Hollows popped into his head. He could feel that others in the room had similar reactions.

"Last month we also received word of a similar homicide in Frederick, Maryland. Another nine-year-old girl. Both girls were strangled by hand, both in late afternoon. Both bodies were found near playgrounds. No eye witnesses, no fingerprints, no DNA."

"Sexual assault?" Camilla Vanderbilt asked.

"No," Harringer answered curtly.

Camilla was in her mid-thirties, married, no kids. She had earned the reputation of a tenacious investigator. She never missed a detail in a witness' story and poured over evidence item by item, line by line. Jack found her to be a very strong asset to the team.

Since high school Jack created nicknames for many of those around him, as an unofficial sign of admiration and respect. Soon after meeting her, he began calling Camilla Vanderbilt "Camilla Commodore," after the mascot of Vanderbilt University. Within a few weeks, this shortened to "C.C."

Reilly's flash drive had connected to the conference room computer. Soon two photographs appeared on the screen in front of them: a pigtailed redhead's fourth grade picture, and a crime scene photo of her lifeless body. Reilly took over the debriefing.

41

"This is Adrianna Cottrell. She was found dead in York, PA on Monday. This morning the homicide detective…" He consulted his notes on his handheld device. "…Officer Ken Howard called me about some oddities in the investigation."

Jack had a quizzical smirk on his face that Harringer noticed. "What is it, Jack?" he asked.

Jack blinked and shook his head. "Nothing important. Ken Howard is the name of an actor. He was The White Shadow— remember that TV show from the late 70's?"

The White Shadow?" Harringer asked.

"Yeah."

"No," Harringer said, matter-of-factly. Jack often made pop-cultural references, but usually not in team meetings like this one. Harringer generally found it annoying, even more so in the middle of a debriefing.

"I remember that," Reilly offered. He really didn't, but he always took advantage of any opportunity to get on Jackson Byrne's good side. He saw Jack as the future of this division and assumed that his best chance of ascending through the ranks of the Bureau would be riding on Jack's coattails. Unfortunately for him, he did not realize that Jack saw through his sycophantism and actually didn't care much for Heath Reilly. Jack had no nickname for him.

"Great," Harringer uttered. "Continue please, Heath."

Reilly refocused on his presentation. "Yeah, so, the oddities in the York murder. There were several post-mortem rib fractures and some bruising to the sternum. In addition, there was a slip of paper in her front jeans pocket with unrecognizable script on it."

42

Despite Jack's initial hesitancy to get involved in another investigation, his brain couldn't resist processing the information, formulating a question, and forcing it out through his vocal cords.

"Unrecognizable to whom?"

"To Detective Howard. The main reason he called was for linguistics help. Because of the nature of the crime, the phone call came to us," Reilly explained. He clicked the mouse and two more photographs came up on the screen.

"And this is Stephanie McBurney from Frederick. She was found three weeks ago. She had virtually identical post-mortem injuries to her chest and a slip of paper in her pocket. This one we've had for a while." He clicked the mouse again. On the screen came a scanned image of the message found on Stephanie McBurney's body:

Ја стварно не те мрзе

Confusion fell across the agents' faces. No one said a word, until a melodic voice like that of a radio host announced, "It's Serbian."

Everyone turned to face the tall, lanky man standing in the back of the room. He had slipped in unnoticed after everyone else had been seated. He wore a suede jacket over a collared shirt with jeans and had wavy gray hair with a salt-and-pepper beard. His circular dark-rimmed glasses seemed to accentuate his long, thin face.

"Yes," Reilly said, almost amazed.

Harringer pointed to the mysterious man. "Everyone, this is Terrence Friesz. He's a linguistics expert from the DC Field Office, and he will be joining us for this investigation. It seems as though his services will come in handy."

Friesz raised a hand to the group. "Hello, everyone. Call me Terry, please. It's a pleasure." He pointed towards the screen to redirect their attention. "It roughly translates, 'I do not really hate you.'"

"In Serbian?" Camilla reiterated.

Friesz nodded, but then realized that no one saw his gesture because they all had turned back to the screen. "Yes."

Camilla turned her attention to Reilly. "Is the message from Monday also in Serbian?"

"I don't know, but I don't think so. By Officer White Shadow's description..." Reilly smirked, but Harringer did not seem amused. "...It sounds more like a Middle-Eastern or Asian language. It didn't share any recognizable characters with our alphabet."

"Do we have a copy of it yet?" Camilla asked.

CC's really starting to sink her teeth into this one, Jack thought with admiration.

Harringer fielded this one. "No. Officer Howard is going to scan it and e-mail it this morning, right Heath?"

"Correct," Heath said as he pulled his iPhone out of its belt holder. He checked to see if he had gotten any new e-mails, but he hadn't.

Jack looked back at the screen. "I do not really hate you," he repeated aloud, mostly for himself. "It looks like it came from a printer."

"Yes," Reilly replied. "Based on analysis of the ink, typeface, et cetera, it most likely came from an HP Photosmart printer, which is one of the most popular printers sold in the U.S."

Harringer stood up, placed his hands on his hips, and said, "All right." This was his usual method of beginning a summative statement at the end of a meeting. "Clearly this has the look of a serial child killer. For right now, Heath and Camilla are going to go to York to speak with Officer Howard and investigate the scene.

"Jack, I want you and Charlie to gather and summarize the findings from the McBurney murder in Frederick." Harringer held his hand out with only his index finger and pinky extended—a common gesture of Texas Longhorn fans—pointing one stubby, muscular finger at Jack and the other at Charlie Shaver. Shaver, a single man in his mid-forties, had been with the FBI for over a decade, but only recently moved to CASMIRC.

Shaver nodded. Jack gave little response. Harringer placed his hand back on his hip.

"Amanda…" this time Harringer just nodded his head in Amanda Lundquist's direction. She was the most junior of the team, having only been at the CASMIRC for 5 months. "I would like you to search databases in the tri-state area, and even expand to North Carolina, Delaware, and West Virginia, to try to find any other similar cases of strangulation of young girls. Make sure to look at both solved and unsolved, and attempted murder as well."

Lundquist jotted down this assignment in her pocket notepad, then looked back up and nodded once.

"Please try to have all this info in to me by 1:00 today. Heath will distribute the cryptic note from the York murder to Terry and the rest of us as soon as possible. He and Camilla will then report in from York by tonight. Terry, let us know your translation after you get the message.

"Questions?" Harringer finished his plan as he began it: per routine. No one voiced a query, and a quick glance around the room revealed no raised hands.

"Let's get to it, folks." Harringer dropped his hands from his hips and exited the room. The rest of the team gathered themselves and followed out, all taking one last look at the odd text on the screen in front.

12

Jack sat at his desk, flipping a pencil in his right hand. He sensed an emotion that he didn't think he had ever felt before.

Insecurity?

No, he had felt insecure before, back in his teenage years. Granted it was a rare occurrence, as an intelligent, athletic, likable person, but he surmised that everyone felt insecure at least once during adolescence.

Fear?

Not even close. He knew fear. Not terribly intimately, but he had certainly made fear's acquaintance on more than one occasion. For Jack, fear was that neighbor that lived six houses down, whose name he knew, whom he waved to when driving by, and with whom he might exchange pleasantries at the local grocery store. They weren't tight, but familiar enough to recognize.

He looked at the photo of Vicki and Jonah on his desk. The unfamiliar emotion didn't swell, nor did it dissipate.

He turned his head to the left, peering through the glass wall that led into Dylan Harringer's office. His eyes moved back to the desk in front of him.

Uncertainty.

Bingo.

At first, he could not recall ever feeling this way. He certainly had not experienced this in his professional life. He had felt discontent, accompanied by the urgency to escape his current position, when working at the law firm in Bethesda. But he had never felt uncertain, unsure of which path to take.

Unexpectedly, an emotion began to swell, bubbling up from some deep, dark, forgotten place, shooting to the surface like boiling water from some subterranean geyser. He suddenly remembered uncertainty. The first piece of the memory came—as it does for many people—in the form of a scent. He remembered what it smelled like in that moment almost thirty-five years ago: dirt. Wet, cold dirt. He had positioned his sleeping bag inside his tent with his head toward the zippered entryway. It had been raining most of the night, soaking the mossy soil around him. He had drifted in and out of sleep most of the night, in part due to the noise of the rain and in part due to the hard ground underneath him. He had just closed his eyes again when Uncle Ned, his mother's sister's husband, unzipped the flap in front of Jack's face and scooted into the tent. He swiftly yanked the zipper back down.

"It's nasty out there," Uncle Ned whispered, running his hand through his sopping wet hair. Jack didn't respond. He felt confused. He couldn't understand why Uncle Ned had come into Jack's one-person tent. Uncle Ned had his own two-person tent just a few yards away, with Jack's cousin Greg. Why would he be coming in here?

"You warm enough?" Uncle Ned asked.

"Yeah," Jack lied, his teeth nearly audibly chattering.

"Are you sure?" Uncle Ned seemed disappointed, as if he wanted Jack to feel cold.

"Yeah." He didn't quite know why, but Jack felt scared.

"Here," Uncle Ned said, deciding that he knew better than Jack how to handle the temperature. He lay down beside Jack on the ground and put an arm around him, squeezing him gently. "Is that better?"

Jack could feel Uncle Ned's warm breath on the nape of his neck. "No," the young Jack said timidly.

"Oh." Again Jack sensed disappointment in Uncle Ned's voice. "How 'bout I just crawl in there with you. That's a pretty big sleeping bag." Uncle Ned began to slip his right arm into the top of the sleeping bag, curling it around Jack's torso.

Jack's eyes widened in the dark, his pupils saucers. He knew this was wrong. "No. No, no, no, no. No!"

Uncle Ned took his arm from around Jack. "Ok! Keep it down, ok? I was just trying to help."

They both sat there silently, inches from each other but not touching, for several minutes. Uncle Ned shuffled his feet under him and got into a crouch. He reached for the zipper on the tent. "You shouldn't tell your mom or your dad about this, ok, Jack? You wouldn't want to look silly."

Jack didn't know how to respond. He did feel embarrassed, but he didn't quite know why.

"Don't look silly, ok, Jack? There's no need for that. Ok?"

"Ok," Jack finally said.

Uncle Ned left the tent as abruptly as he had arrived.

After the zipper closed, Jack wondered briefly if that had actually happened. Jack, ever the thoughtful boy, lay awake all night, unsure of what to do. Should he say something to his parents? Or maybe to cousin Greg? Was this really as weird as it felt, or did he imagine that disturbing feeling? Maybe it was just the cold, damp night that made him feel so creepy. Maybe he should have let Uncle

Ned— with his supposedly forthright, innocent intentions—try to keep him warm. Eventually, after his head hurt from hours of consternation and lack of sleep, he decided to forget that it ever happened.

He never said a word to his parents. He actually had never mentioned that night to anyone, not even to Vicki. Not even to his psychological analyst during his entrance exams into the FBI. Uncle Ned never touched him again, not even to shake his hand. About ten years later, and only about three months after cousin Greg's suicide, Uncle Ned drunkenly drove his Honda Civic into a river and drowned. Jack presumed that Uncle Ned took the events of that camping trip to his grave, and, for reasons he couldn't fully understand—or, in truth, didn't want to— Jack intended to as well.

He hadn't thought of that night in decades. He also had never pondered the seemingly obvious influence of that experience on his life's career path.

Now, in his cubicle at CASMIRC, Jack had to rub his eyes to clear his thoughts, like a windshield wiper cleaning the run-off sprayed by the preceding pick-up's tires. He found himself in another quagmire, a crossroads, and he needed to focus. He surmised that the decisions he made in the next few days would likely shape the rest of his life.

He got up from his desk and went to Harringer's office. Jack rapped his knuckles on the open door.

Harringer looked up from his desk. "Yeah, Jack."

"Do you have a sec?"

Harringer looked a little confused. It struck him as odd that Jack received an assignment twenty minutes ago and hadn't already immersed himself in it. "Sure." He gestured to one of the chairs opposite his desk.

Jack closed the door behind him before he sat down. "This one feels bad."

Again, Harringer seemed confused, now obvious on his pursed face. "Don't they all? On some level, they all feel bad."

Jack nodded in acquiescence more than agreement. "This one seems different." He scratched his chin. "Maybe it's me."

"What do you mean?"

Jack shook his head, as if attempting to deny his thoughts and the words about to come out of his mouth. "Maybe I'm not ready to come back just yet."

Harringer raised his eyebrows. "Did you get bitten by the literary bug? Or maybe the Hollywood lifestyle? Traveling around, talking on talk shows, drinking cocktails..." He said this last comment in an attempt at light humor, trying to get some emotion out of Jack. No success.

"I think I just have a few things going on that I need to sort out. And I'm pretty sure that if I get involved in this case, it will... cloud my judgment. Make it more difficult to sort them out."

Harringer considered this, then got hit with an apparent epiphany. "Have you gotten some kind of job offer? You're not going to go private on us, are you?"

"No, no," Jack said. Technically he had not received a job *offer*; no one *offered* him the job of US Senator. Jack felt better about relying on technicalities to avoid lying. "I just have a few personal things that need some attention."

"How long do you think you'll need? This is an important case for us, Jack. And for those families in York and Frederick." Harringer hoped that playing a sympathy card might work with Jack. Despite Jack's hard exterior, Harringer knew that he was a family man, and that he often developed close bonds with victims and their families. That was part of what made him so successful as an investigator. Finally, Harringer reached back and threw a fastball down the middle with all he had. "And for the family of the next victim if we don't get this guy."

"I know. A couple of days. I'll be ready by the end of the week." Jack didn't take a swing at Harringer's juicy pitch.

Harringer seemed a little disappointed. He contemplated Jack's proposal. "All right. Come in early on Friday. I'll meet you here and debrief you on everything we have until that point."

"OK," Jack said, knowing that there was a good chance he would not be coming in on Friday. "Thanks, Dylan."

Harringer nodded. "Be ready by then, though, OK? Be fresh."

Jack nodded reassuringly as he left the office, leaving the door ajar behind him.

13

Heath and Camilla landed at Hostetter Airport outside of York, PA around 11:20 that morning. A uniformed police officer met them at the airport. As per Heath's suggestion on the phone earlier, the officer drove them to the scene of Adrianna Cottrell's murder, where Ken Howard met them shortly before noon. They exchanged handshakes and introductions. Howard then walked them around to the playground along the side of the Grove Street Elementary School.

"Anyone ever say anything to you about The White Shadow?" Heath asked the large, chiseled African-American police officer.

Camilla rolled her eyes. She perceived Heath as an intelligent agent with good work ethic and diligence, who often lacked appropriate social skills. He reminded her of that awkward but well-meaning kid in middle school who spoke out of turn during class, trying to be funny, only to receive groans from his classmates and scorn from his teachers. Though she didn't exactly enjoy working with him directly, she had always found it tolerable. Sometimes, though, he really pushed the boundaries of her tolerance. Like now.

"Excuse me?" Howard replied, his voice deeper than a few seconds ago.

Already Heath wished he had not said anything. "Uh, The White Shadow. It was a TV show about a white NBA player who coached at a mostly…ethnic…inner city high school after his retirement. The actor who played him was named Ken Howard." Heath had read up on Wikipedia from his iPhone on their way to the airport in Quantico.

"Never heard of it," Howard muttered. His mood lightened slightly, "But I did see *1776* like ten times when I was a kid. My parents used to make us watch it every year on the 3rd of July, to get us in the mood, you know? Ken Howard played Thomas Jefferson."

"OK," Heath said, now feeling that he and Howard had formed a bond.

"Jefferson has been my favorite president ever since."

"Cool." Heath nodded in approval, happy with the exchange. He suddenly felt the urge to choose his own favorite president.

Howard stopped walking at the corner of three tennis courts, with a twelve-foot high fence running around the perimeter. In front of them stretched an 8-feet wide grass walkway between the fence on the right and a waist-high hedgerow on the left. A strand of yellow "Crime Scene" tape ran between the fence post to their right and a tree on their left, about ten feet behind the hedgerow. "This is it," Howard declared. He lifted up the tape and Camilla and Heath ducked underneath and walked through.

They looked around them, at the green grass, the burgeoning hedgerow, and the scraggly grass, weeds, and leaves behind it. A mix of pine trees, hemlocks, and tall oaks thickened the brush substantially about fifteen feet behind the hedges. They all stood in silence for a good minute, ostensibly out of respect for the deceased. Camilla realized this quietness must be tough for Heath; she gained a little more respect for him as he remained silent with the other two of them.

Howard was the one who broke the silence. He began to walk forward and point behind the hedgerow as he spoke. "The body was found here." He stopped walking about 40 feet down the grass path. Both Camilla and Heath had been following, but their attention diverged. Heath's gaze followed Howard's pointing right hand, but Camilla spent her time surveying the surrounding area.

"She was face up, her head here," he pointed to his left, towards the direction they had come from, "and her feet this way." His right hand fanned out, palm down.

Even though it was only mid-April, the hedges had filled in nicely. They would have provided cover for the body, and the murderous act that created it.

"Who found her?" Heath asked.

"A teacher, Jed Thompson. It was at the end of the school day. The kids will often play outside for ten to thirty minutes while they wait for their parents to pick them up. In addition to Mr. Thompson, one other teacher was assigned After School Duty to keep watch out here while waiting for parents to come by. Mrs. Orlovski, fifth grade teacher, was the one here on Monday."

Camilla interrupted her survey of the perimeter to look at Howard. She noticed that he did not have a notebook in his hand, and this impressed her. Officer Howard recited all of these details from memory.

"Where was she? And where was Mr. Thompson?" Heath inquired.

"Mr. Thompson spent the entire time after school around the front of the building, near where we parked." Howard pointed back in that direction. "As you can see, from where we are here, all the way over to there...." He turned to point to the opposite corner of the tennis courts. "...is obscured from the front of the building."

"And the other teacher?" Camilla reminded.

"She spent the time walking back and forth along the side of the school."

About forty yards separated the school from the tennis courts. Swing sets, slides, monkey bars, and other traditional playground equipment populated the northern half of this area, nearer to the parking lot. A bed of pavement covered the southern half, with a small baseball diamond painted on it, as well as a hopscotch board, a four-square court, and a shuffleboard court.

"She said she never saw anything over this direction. Her attention was focused on the playground in between. In fact, she never even saw Adrianna come this way."

"How many children were playing out here that day?" Camilla seemed to take charge of the questioning.

"We estimate about seventy-five. Of course, the numbers continually diminish as parents arrive to pick up their kids. No one ever takes attendance, but the average start is usually around seventy-five." Howard continued, as if anticipating the next question. "Adrianna was apparently known to sometimes wander off on her own. Her parents both said that they often lost track of her—on days at the park, at the mall, what have you. She would say she was off 'imagining.'"

The corners of Camilla's mouth turned downward in sadness. *Surely she never "imagined" anything like this,* she thought.

"The last anyone saw her alive, she was walking-slash-skipping on the opposite side of the tennis courts away from the school, her head bobbing from one shoulder to the other."

"Who saw her?" Heath chimed in.

"Two of the other children and Mrs. Orlovski."

A BUSTLE IN THE HEDGEROW

Howard turned his gaze down to the ground where Adrianna Cottrell's body had been found. "Adrianna was car-pooling with one of the other children, Amelia Schwab. Amelia's mother was running a little late that day, showed up at about 4:05, twenty-five minutes after school let out. There were 14 children left here at that time, Amelia being one of them. When they couldn't find Adrianna, Mrs. Schwab, Amelia, and the two teachers went looking for her. Mr. Thompson found her."

Howard held his hand out palm down, at an angle parallel to the ground, on the other side of the hedges. "You can see that the ground here slopes away toward the trees. We've had an unseasonably dry April so far, and any rain we get would have mostly run down that way, toward the trees. So, no footprints anywhere around to speak of."

"Witnesses?" Camilla queried.

"No one. Hard to believe, I know, but..." Howard shook his head. "Nothing."

He turned and began walking away from them, opposite from the direction they had come. He kept his head turned back over his right shoulder and gestured with his right hand to follow him. As they neared the end of the fence at the far side of the last tennis court, Howard pointed ahead of him. "You can see that the tennis courts are on an elevation, and the ground slopes down about fifteen to twenty feet to Orchard Street below."

Heath and Camilla could now see the street. On the other side was a stone wall standing about six feet high that spanned the entire city block. From their elevated vantage point, they could see the desolate cemetery beyond the wall.

57

Howard turned back to face them. "No passers-by have come forward, so, for now, I assume there were none. But we continue to put our contact info in the paper and on the news." He turned to his left, looking south along Orchard Street. A few relatively dense rows of maple trees stood behind a chain-link fence on the far side of the tennis courts, and Howard indicated them by raising his left hand.

"On the other side of that tree line are a few houses. Only one person was home at the time, three houses down. Mrs. Ulbright, 72, retired widow. She was watching TV in the back room of her house, didn't see a thing."

Howard turned back toward them and pointed at the street with his right hand. He was a very demonstrative person, Camilla noticed. *He would make a great tour guide*, she thought sincerely.

"My theory is that the perp parked somewhere here along Orchard Street and came up here." He started walking back along the grass pathway, crouched slightly as if re-enacting the murderer's trek.

"He probably hid over here…," He leapt over the hedgerow in one quick, steady step, displaying unusual agility for a man his size. "…On this side of the hedgerow, and waited for Adrianna to come by."

"But how would he know she would?" Heath asked.

Howard tilted his head. "Both her teachers and her classmates said she sometimes skipped around the tennis courts, singing to herself. Not every day, but often enough that anyone watching for a week or two might notice."

"So you think the perp was stalking her?"

Howard nodded. "In my theory."

Camilla asked, "What about her parents?"

"Both at work at the time. Father is an accountant and had a 4 pm meeting with a client, who verifies. Mother is part-owner of a floral shop downtown, and it was her night to work until closing, which is usually 5 pm. When she got the phone call from our department, several customers were in the store and heard her shriek."

"Phone call?" Heath asked, somewhat derisively.

For the first time, Howard looked slightly embarrassed. The look didn't fit him. "Yeah. It wasn't me. It was one of our newer officers. He has since been reprimanded." This was a bit of a lie, though Howard didn't really know that. Nat Fordham had self-imposed his leave of absence and would never return to the force.

"Family had no known enemies, no recent threats. They've never noticed anyone suspicious around their house or in the neighborhood. There is a 4-year-old sister who was in day care at the time."

"We would like to question the family," Camilla stated.

"Of course. They've been very helpful so far. Devastated, understandably, but willing to help. When we're done here, I'll try to reach them to set something up," Howard said.

Heath gestured back to the ground where her body had been. "And you said over the phone that there was no blood, fingerprints, or foreign DNA found anywhere on or around the body."

Howard looked up from the ground into Heath's eyes. "That's right. We have a pretty good forensics unit; I trust them."

"Remind me of some of the oddities with the autopsy?" Camilla asked. She remembered the details from the debriefing that morning, but she wanted to hear them from Howard. Maybe something had been omitted between his first phone conversation with Heath and their morning meeting.

"Yeah. I'll get you a copy of the full report. I think that's where the money is. That, and the note. COD was asphyxiation from strangulation. Significant bruising of the anterior throat. But she had several post-mortem lateral rib fractures, as well as sternal bruising. As if something heavy had been dropped on her chest shortly after strangulation."

Camilla bent her knees into a crouch and looked at the dense trees in front of her. She then looked back to her right, toward Orchard Street.

"He had to have come and gone from that direction." She pointed back toward Orchard Street.

Heath concurred. "The trees would have created too slow a getaway."

Camilla looked up at him. "And too noisy. The ground in there is covered with dried leaves."

She turned herself around, still crouched, to look at the hedgerow. After studying it carefully for several seconds, she shifted her gaze up to Howard. "Any evidence of damage to the hedges? Any broken branches, anything that might leave a trace of him behind?"

Howard again shook his head, "Nothing. While forensics was here, I myself crawled along both sides of these hedges. Nothing was out of place."

Camilla stood up and took a deep breath. She blew it out in a huff and turned to Heath. "Anything else you want to see here?"

Heath contemplated briefly. "Nope."

Camilla nodded as she turned to Howard. "All right. Let's get to know more about poor little Miss Adrianna."

14

Jack took his Bluetooth out of his right ear and placed it back into the console between the front seats of his car. He firmly believed in using hands-free devices while driving-- even before it became a law-- but he hated those pretentious assholes that walked around with their Bluetoothes in their ears. (*Or is it Blue Teeth?*) Once Jack had completed his conversation, the hands-free device went back to its rightful resting place. He tapped one of the sound system buttons on his steering wheel to restart his iPod where it had left off before the phone call: about halfway through the Arcade Fire album *The Suburbs*. Jack had always followed music slightly off the mainstream. He became a big fan of the eclectic Canadian group after their 2004 debut *Funeral*.

He was almost home, and it was only 12:40. He had just gotten off the phone with Philip Prince; they had set up another lunch meeting tomorrow. Philip seemed as delighted as the over-privileged pre-teen girl who gets a pony for her birthday. Jack couldn't remember ever hearing Prince sound so excited. It struck him a bit odd.

As the brief conversation wound down, Prince had asked for Jack's permission to invite another friend to join them the following day.

"Who did you have in mind?" Jack had asked.

Prince paused for effect. It wasn't lost on Jack. "Montgomery Johnson would like to meet you."

"Really?" Jack replied. For the second time this week, Prince had shocked Jack.

The current Senate Majority Leader, Montgomery Johnson was serving his fourth consecutive term as a Democratic Senator from Alabama. His Party had selected him as the Majority Leader at the end of his previous term. Jack did not know much about him personally—or professionally, for that matter—but he knew his name carried a lot of weight on The Hill. By bringing Johnson along, Prince emphasized the seriousness of his proposal. Jack surmised that this was the political equivalent of a full-court press.

Jack told Prince that he had no objections to Johnson coming to lunch. He knew now how he would spend the rest of the afternoon. As soon as he got home, Jack got on the laptop to begin researching Johnson, Rupert Schulz, the current political tone in the Commonwealth of Virginia, and as much as he could about the US Senate.

15

Just like the first debriefing earlier that day, Terry Friesz was the last to arrive in the conference room, shortly after 4:00 pm. Dylan Harringer sat in the middle of the front row, facing the screen in front of them, with Amanda Lundquist on his left and Charlie Shaver flanking him on the right. Heath Reilly and Camilla Vanderbilt were projected onto the screen in front of them via Skype.

"Hi, everyone. Sorry I'm late," Terry said, though he didn't feel late. To him, arriving within ten minutes either way of the start of a meeting did not qualify as late or early.

Amanda turned her head to face him. No one else budged or said a word. Amanda flashed a nervous smile, her eyes motioning towards Harringer. *It's OK*, her eyes said, *but around here, Harringer likes things to start on time.* That facial gesture signaled to Friesz that not all members of the group disagreed with his sense of punctuality, but the most important person did. Friesz noted this, but doubted that this would affect how he approached his job in the future. After a long career in academia, with the pressures of fighting for grants and publishing papers, Friesz did not want to let this second career apply any more strain than was inherently present in working for the FBI. He slipped into the second row of seats, spread his arms out on the backs of the chairs beside him, and crossed his legs, apparently quite comfortable with his tardiness.

"We'll start by hearing from Amanda about any similar cases that may need to be lumped into this investigation," Harringer announced.

Amanda nodded and looked down at her laptop. "I performed a pretty exhaustive—"

"Wait," Heath interrupted via satellite. "Where's Jack?"

Amanda looked up from her laptop, and looked at Harringer. Everyone else looked around and also noted Jack's absence.

"He's working on something else for a few days. I expect him to rejoin this investigation later this week," Harringer explained.

"OK," Heath replied, as if anyone cared that he found this acceptable.

"Sorry for the interruption, Amanda." Only because she currently sat beside him, Camilla felt that she should apologize for Heath. She remembered what it felt like being the newest investigator with CASMIRC. This occasionally awkward, ostracized feeling seemed exaggerated as a female. Men still dominated the world of the FBI, especially at the rank of special agent. When she remembered to, Camilla tried to go out of her way to make Amanda feel comfortable.

"No, that's fine," Amanda replied. She easily transitioned her focus back to the laptop. "In the last twelve months, only two female children were killed by strangulation throughout the mid-Atlantic. Both were teenagers, one 16 and one 14, and both by their boyfriends. The 16-year-old's 19 year-old boyfriend was recently convicted in West Virginia for her murder, and the younger girl's 16 year-old boyfriend confessed shortly after the crime. Both boys— or, men, I guess— are currently incarcerated. There were no records of successful or attempted murder by strangulation of any girls in the same age range as our two victims."

"What about boys?" Harringer asked.

Amanda nodded again, having anticipated this question. "There were six cases of attempted strangulation in older teenage boys, no murders. All of them were by similar aged boys as part of a physical altercation, and all but one involved alcohol or other drugs.

"And then there were eleven other cases of domestic child abuse that, at least in part, involved strangulation or suffocation. One case last summer of homicide by suffocation of a 17-month-old male toddler by his mother's boyfriend in southern Maryland. He is also currently incarcerated. Of the other ten cases, five had offenders that went to trial, four convicted and now serving sentences."

"So that leaves six cases in which we have no convictions?" Harringer calculated.

"Yes. I spent the last two hours delving into two of them. Both were young toddlers—one boy and one girl—who were found to have evidence of multiple injuries. Both are too young to testify, though. So even though law enforcement had suspicions, no convictions could be made."

"OK," Harringer said. "Try to finish up looking into those other cases for us by the end of the day tomorrow, but I'm guessing they'll end up with similar stories—mostly domestic."

"I don't think we should discount these, though, sir, just because they are domestic cases. Most violent people start being violent at home before they branch out to others," Camilla argued.

Harringer held up his hand and nodded. "Agreed. We need to investigate these cases thoroughly. I didn't mean we should disregard them. One of these cases may indeed turn out to involve our un-sub. Any questions for Amanda?"

Harringer looked at the others in the room and the agents projected on screen in front of him. They shook their heads.

"Yes, sorry," Friesz said from behind them, unafraid of asking the proverbial stupid question. "Un-sub?"

Amanda turned to face him. "Unknown subject. Perpetrator."

Friesz nodded in understanding. "Thank you."

"OK." Harringer turned his shoulders slightly to his right to face Charlie. "Charlie, what did you find out about the McBurney murder?"

Charlie pulled out his notebook and flipped back the flimsy cardboard cover. He felt comfortable using most of the tools of modern technology but still preferred writing out his investigative notes by hand. He found it much more conducive to contemplating facts as he collected them, rather than simply recording them.

"Stephanie McBurney, nine years old," Charlie began. He always gave his investigative presentations in the same manner: through brief, informative, fact-filled sentences. His language contained no fluff. As long as his listeners could maintain their attention despite his staccato, monotone delivery, they would get all the necessary information.

"Found on the afternoon of March 25th in some weeds on the periphery of a playground beside her family's home in Frederick, Maryland. She lived with her mother, step-father, and five month-old half brother. Her mother, Jennifer Cugino, had been watching her on the swing set through their window. Around 4:30 pm the infant brother began to cry. Mrs. Cugino got up to get the baby and a bottle. When she came back to look out the window, about six minutes later, Stephanie was out of sight. She assumed Stephanie was on her way inside, so she sat down to give the baby his bottle. This took twelve minutes. A few minutes into the feeding, she realized that Stephanie wasn't home, and assumed she had just missed seeing her during her last survey of the playground. At the end of the feed she got up to look out the window, but again did not see Stephanie. She put the baby in his swing seat and went outside to look for Stephanie. At 4:50 she found the body on the northwest corner of the playground, opposite the street and farthest from their house. She ran back into the house and called 9-1-1. The call was received at 4:52 pm.

"Stephanie had been strangled by hand, no ligature marks. No evidence of blunt force trauma, except soft-tissue bruising around the breastbone and three lateral rib fractures, very similar to what we heard this morning about the second victim."

He looked up from his notepad and paused briefly, leaving a few seconds for questions. No one offered any, so he continued. "No DNA at the crime scene or on the body. No evidence of sexual assault. No fingerprints anywhere. Negative toxicology report. We all saw the note in her front right pocket this morning, a Serbian saying that translated into, 'I do not hate you really.'

"No witnesses. There are two houses on the opposite side of the street from the playground, but no one was home at the time of the murder. No passers-by on foot or by car that saw anything. Local police have interviewed nearly 200 people without getting any info."

"Suspects?" Harringer asked.

"None at this point. The biological father, Andrew McBurney, still had partial custody and had seen her the weekend before. He also lives in Frederick and works at a local auto parts store. He was at work all day with numerous people to support his alibi. The step-father, Mario Cugino, was at work. He is a pharmaceutical sales rep and had paid his last visit of the day at a doctor's office in Breezewood, PA, some 40 miles away. He had left that office at 4:25, corroborated by several office staff. After several interviews, the mother has been eliminated as a suspect at this point, though she has no one to corroborate her story.

"No known family enemies. There are eighteen registered sex offenders that live in a 25 mile radius. Two were convicted of crimes against children, but both have been eliminated as suspects based on alibis." Charlie flipped his notebook closed, which signaled the end of his presentation.

"Questions from anyone at this point?" Harringer asked.

Camilla had one. "Charlie, do you know anything about the landscaping or terrain around the playground?"

"No. Why?"

Everyone turned their focus to Camilla. "Because of the topography of our crime scene. We think the killer could have used it to his or her advantage as a shield from witnesses."

"I don't know. I reviewed several crime scene photos, but none of the surroundings."

Harringer interjected. "Call the local PD tomorrow and ask them to send us photos of the surrounding areas, making sure they illustrate the topography of the area."

"Got it," Charlie noted as he flipped his notebook back open to jot down his instructions.

Then Harringer turned to face the screen in front of them. "Your turn," he said, as he gestured to Camilla and Heath.

Heath began by describing the crime scene. He then continued into the scenario that led up to Adrianna Cottrell's disappearance, the discovery of her body, and the subsequent investigation. Camilla talked about their interviews that afternoon with the family and the inspection of their home, including Adrianna's bedroom. These examinations revealed no new relevant information and supported the local investigator's theory that the family was not involved. She then moved on to discuss the autopsy findings, finishing with the note found in Adrianna's front pocket.

Harringer pulled out a copy of the fax Camilla had sent earlier which contained the image of the note. He turned around to face Friesz for the first time this entire meeting. "Terry, did you have a chance to look at this yet?" He passed the fax over his shoulder to Friesz, clearly with a slight modicum of disdain. *If he can't come to the meeting on time, surely he hasn't looked at this assignment ahead of time*, Harringer's body language stated to Friesz.

Friesz held up his hand, refusing the paper.

"I did look at it." He stood up and moved to the front of the conference room. On the right side stood an easel supporting a large dry-erase board with a small shelf below with several colored markers. He moved the board closer to the center of the room, angling it towards the laptop in front so that Camilla and Heath could see it as well as the others in the room. He picked up a blue marker and wrote the phrase found on the piece of paper from memory:

ฉันต้องการใคร

70

A BUSTLE IN THE HEDGEROW

Everyone watching, even Harringer, was impressed by Friesz's presentation. He had not lost his classroom presence as a college professor.

"It's Thai," Friesz declared.

"Thai?" Harringer asked.

Friesz nodded. "Thai."

"Well, what does it mean?" Camilla voiced, though everyone else also sat on the edge of their seats, dying to know. Most FBI agents don't care much for the dramatic flairs of former college professors.

Friesz looked at her, at Heath, and then met the eyes of each member in the conference room. He was milking the limelight, and he loved it. His eyes came back and met Harringer's before he offered the translation. "It means, 'I want to be somebody.'"

Harringer looked pensive for a moment, his investigative mind chewing this new morsel of information. After a barely discernible glimmer of realization in his eye, his gaze dropped down from Friesz's face slowly to the floor.

Friesz became concerned over the change in Harringer's body language. "What is it?" he asked.

Without looking up Harringer responded. "A message like this may suggest that we are dealing with a killer who will continue killing children for the purpose of achieving infamy." He finally raised his vision to look at Friesz and the other agents in the room. "His accomplishment, or, more accurately, his goal, is not the murder itself. It's the attention that follows. And as he continues killing, especially child victims, the attention will become greater and greater.

His accomplishments then only continue to fuel further and further killing."

A somber mood fell over the agents. They seemed to tacitly agree upon Harringer's interpretation of this most recent message from their killer. Camilla nodded, with expressions of recognition and despondence coming over her face simultaneously. "I wrote a thesis on such perpetrators back in undergrad. For these killers, it doesn't matter who the victims are. It's not about killing *them*. It's just about killing *somebody*."

Harringer completed the thought. "Making it very difficult to predict where the killer will strike again."

16

When Vicki and Jonah got home that afternoon, Jack had just finished reading an essay written by Montgomery Johnson in the late 90's about the President Clinton/Monica Lewinsky affair. Johnson had admonished his fellow Democrat, but he also spent much of the article examining the scandal-hungry American culture. He compared and contrasted Clinton and John F. Kennedy, not in political terms, but more in social and interpersonal ways. Johnson displayed a knack for discussing political themes within American culture while remaining relatively politically neutral. Jack admired his writing skills and already looked forward to meeting him tomorrow.

Jonah ran into the living room where Jack sat with his Dell on his lap and jumped up onto the couch beside him. "Hey, Daddy!"

"Hey, Jonah!" Jack imitated with equal enthusiasm.

"Whatcha doing?" Jonah asked.

"Excuse me?" Jack replied in an exaggeratedly inquisitive tone.

"Sorry," Jonah said deliberately. "What ARE you doing?"

Jonah previously had some difficulty saying the letter "R", as did most toddlers, so he learned to avoid saying words with "R" as much as he could. Recently, though, Jack and Vicki enlisted the assistance of a speech therapist through Jonah's school. After Johan sat through only a handful of sessions with her, his "R's" improved significantly. However, he often still subconsciously reverted back to avoiding "R" words, and Jack and Vicki had vowed to each other to correct him at every opportunity.

"Oh, yes," Jack said, pretending that only now did he understand Jonah's question. "I just finished reading an article online."

"Uh-huh," Jonah replied. "What was it about?"

"Well," Jack answered, as he looked up at Vicki to see if she were also listening. "It was written by a man whom I am meeting for lunch tomorrow."

"Really?!" Jonah responded, evidently impressed that his father was going to meet someone who had written an article posted on The Internet.

"Yep. His name is Montgomery Johnson."

Vicki's eyebrows raised and she smiled; now she too was impressed.

"He's an important senator from Alabama," Jack finished.

"Alabama?!" Jonah answered, though he had no idea where that was or what it really meant.

"Yes, sir," Jack said.

"Yes, sir," Jonah repeated.

Vicki walked into the living room from the kitchen and leaned against the threshold separating the two. "Jonah, why don't you go upstairs, put your school stuff in your room, and go to the bathroom before we go get Grandma for dinner."

"OK," Jonah exclaimed as he jumped off the couch. He ran back into the kitchen to pick up a small workbook from school then headed upstairs.

"Don't forget to wash your hands," Vicki called after him as she walked into the room and sat down on the couch beside her husband. She leaned over and they exchanged a kiss. "Senate Majority Leader Montgomery Johnson, huh?"

Jack nodded. "Yeah. I called Philip today to tell him I was interested in taking another meeting."

"So you've decided to pursue this," Vicki said, more in the form or a statement rather than a question.

"For now, yeah." Jack took the computer from his lap and set it on the couch beside him, opposite Vicki. He shifted his weight to face her. "Dylan began presenting a new case today. Looks like a serial killer."

Vicki groaned.

Jack nodded in agreement. "Yeah, groan. I just didn't have the...I don't know... fortitude, I guess?... to delve into another case right now. I felt like it was my subconscious trying to tell me something. I felt uneasy and uncertain, and it didn't feel good."

Vicki smiled and took his hand. "Well, I think then it's wise to meet with Philip and see where this takes you."

Jack smiled. Moments like this always reminded him of how much he loved his wife.
"Thanks," he said.

Vicki nodded and stood up. "I'm going to go change."

"OK. Where are we going tonight?"

Ever since Anthony Byrne died, every Wednesday they all went out to eat with Jack's mother Florence. They rotated through three different restaurants that she called her "favorites," though they all knew that she called them "favorites" because they were very child-friendly and Jonah loved them. What Jack and Vicki never knew is that Florence also chose these places because she had never been there with Anthony. Thus they offered no memories of him. She did not habitually avoid places that provided memories of Anthony; she just

75

preferred to go to those places alone. Wednesday evenings were a time for Jonah, for innocence, and for happiness, not for Anthony, for longing, or for sadness.

Because of speaking engagements and book signings, Jack had missed the majority of these Wednesday dinners of the past few months. He therefore could not keep track of where they stood in the rotation.

"Pirate Pete's," Vicki answered.

"Arrr!" Jack growled like a pirate, with more than a hint of genuine excitement. "I never thought in my adult life I would get excited about going out to a restaurant whose most famous dish is the Bucket O' Fish."

Vicki smiled in agreement as she turned to head for the stairs. She called behind her toward Jack, "Just one more reason to love parenthood."

17

Randall sat at his desktop computer, surfing the internet, conducting both research and reconnaissance. Dave Brubeck's classic genre-crossing album *Time Out* played on the turntable. Randall had recently replaced the needle to the beginning of the A side, "Blue Rondo a la Turk."

Behind him, in the makeshift living room, the TV showed the denouement of the latest iteration of a forensic crime scene investigation show, the volume turned down low but not completely off. Turns out the not-yet-fully-out-of-the-closet gay husband's male lover killed the unsuspecting wife. Never saw that coming.

Randall had arguably the best album collection anywhere in the world. Not CDs. Vinyl. And not best as in most, but best as in best quality. He believed listening on the turntable was the purest way to experience the music as the artist had intended. He had jazz, blues, heavy metal, new wave, punk, funk, bluegrass, hard rock, rap. Tonight felt like a jazz night, at least for now. Hence the Brubeck.

CNN.com did not have anything exciting, nor did Reuters. He went to the website of WHTM, the local TV station that covered York, PA. He scrolled down, found a story on Adrianna Cottrell, clicked on it.

He didn't like disco, and he didn't like modern pop. That included most modern country and hip-hop, which was just a marketing guru's method of trying to repackage old familiar music under different, usually inane lyrics. Other than that, Randall would give a listen to just about anything.

The TV went quiet before leading into the opening music of *The Goodnight Hour*. Randall turned to look at the TV. Caleb Goodnight, sitting in his arm-chair, went into his familiar introduction, "Good evening and welcome. I'm Caleb Goodnight, and this is The Goodnight Hour."

Randall turned back to the computer monitor, looked at the digital clock in the lower right corner.

10:00 already? he thought. *Huh.*

The online article about Adrianna Cottrell discussed the brief press conference held by the local police that evening. After skimming the article, Randall concluded that it did not reveal anything exciting. The photo at the top showed a healthy-looking African-American man behind a microphone. His name was Officer Kenneth Howard, according to the caption.

"Tonight my guests are country music superstar couple Tim McGraw and Faith Hill," Caleb Goodnight said. Randall lost interest.

He focused on the photograph in front of him. In the background stood a plain-faced man wearing a plain suit. Though the man's face was out of focus, Randall felt that he recognized him.

Randall swiveled his chair to the right and grabbed a tattered book from the bookshelf beside him. Though the book had been published merely two months ago, it appeared decades old—its pages crinkled, dog-eared, scribbled on, highlighted. Randall opened the book to the middle section that contained several color photographs. He flipped past the photograph of Lamaya Hollows with her parents, and one of the crime scene. A few pages later he landed on the one he had been looking for. Again the man stood not in the foreground of the photo, but in the background. But, in this photo, the blurry man was properly identified.

Heath Reilly.

CASMIRC.

No Jackson Byrne yet, but it was a start.

Randall knew that he must allow for some degree of variation, even if that felt uncomfortable to him. But, so far, his Work proceeded as planned.

18

About thirty miles away, in her cubicle at *The Washington Post*, Corinne O'Loughlin looked at the same website. A couple of hours earlier she had submitted her latest piece on the investigation into a hit-and-run in Georgetown. A popular female lacrosse player for the Hoyas had been struck by a Chevy sedan in the early hours of Sunday morning, almost four days ago now. She remained in critical condition at Georgetown University Hospital. Corinne had been covering the story all week for *The Post*. It provided little excitement for her (and her readers, to be honest), but it kept her writing, and it kept her editor off her back.

Now she had been scanning the World Wide Web for something else to pique her interest. She had nothing in particular to get home to, except an empty loft apartment. Besides, the speed of the internet service in her office far surpassed even the DSL hook-up she had at home.

She remembered hearing about Adrianna Cottrell on Monday; she made a mental note at that point to continue keeping tabs on the investigation. York, PA sat outside of the area of interest for her readership, but, if a story turns juicy enough, everyone will want to read about it. With the sudden murder of a child, this story had started off quite piquant. It had potential.

Plus, though her hard exterior would never admit it, Corinne had identified with the victim. The photo that had been in the local papers, the posed school portrait, easily could have passed for Corinne's third-grade photo. They had the same curly, orange-red hair and pale, freckled skin. They shared the same innocent, child-like appearance as well. At 32, despite working at *The Post* for nearly a decade, Corinne still was often mistaken for a high-school or college intern by new-comers.

Until they met her, that is.

A former editor had once described her—to her face—as "acerbic." She took it as a compliment. She thought harshness, aggressiveness, and biting honesty were pre-requisites for investigative reporters. Well, good investigative reporters, anyway. She never apologized for her tenacity or her frankness. She felt very comfortable in her own pasty skin; she didn't care if others didn't like her.

She finished reading the article on the WHTM website, then went back to the caption. She too recognized Heath Reilly. She had reported on the Lamaya Hollows murder from the beginning and had met Heath through Jackson Byrne.

She instinctively swallowed hard to suppress the bile suddenly accumulating in her stomach.

Like most people, Corinne had liked Jack Byrne the minute she met him. She found him handsome, charming, and very intelligent. She continued to enjoy seeing him throughout the case, as he treated her with respect. In Corinne's experience many members of law enforcement see the press as the enemy, always trying to hinder *their* investigation. She felt that Jack saw her, and her colleagues, as a resource. Information often flowed bi-directionally, as they each tried to help the other further understand the case.

But then he solved the case, blowing everything wide open. As Corinne struggled to put all of the pieces together, Jack met with a retired editor and they took the story to a national publishing house. The Hollows case should have been her big break, catapulting her into the national spotlight: a full-length book, the talk-shows, the prolonged interviews during an episode of *Dateline* dedicated to the case. She had anticipated a subsequent move to one of the national weekly magazines afterwards.

But Jack Byrne beat her to it.

Corinne O'Loughlin was no stranger to ill will. As a first generation Irish-American, it seemed that at least some degree of bitterness ran through her veins. But this acrimony towards Jack stood in such contrast to her initial sentiments about him that it actually bothered her. Upon further introspection, the fact that her resentment bothered her caused her even more resentment. It could quickly turn into a vicious spiral.

She tried to forget about Jackson Byrne and continue about her tasks. And, as per usual, she accomplished this with aplomb.

Reilly's presence in York surely signaled that CASMIRC had been enlisted to assist with the Cottrell murder. This seemed slightly odd to Corinne, as she would not expect CASMIRC to get involved necessarily in a single, relatively low-profile homicide. On a hunch, she launched an internet search on child strangulation. Within a few minutes, she found herself reading about the Stephanie McBurney murder.

Consider her interest adequately piqued.

Corinne spent the next few hours compiling information about both murders. When her eyes finally began to feel heavy, she checked the time on the corner of her monitor. 2:18 am. She saved a notepad document to her flash drive and shut down the computer. She then made a mental note to call Jack Byrne tomorrow. She surmised that very little happened within CASMIRC without his knowledge. He must have an inside scoop on this case.

If she could swallow her pride long enough to get some information from Byrne—and, to reach a goal, Corinne O'Loughlin could muster the strength to do just about anything— perhaps she still had a chance to create her big break after all.

DAY FOUR:
THURSDAY

19

Jack's morning had not started off well.

He left the house in a bit of a hurry that morning. He had planned on meeting Prince and Senator Johnson for lunch at 1:00 pm, until Prince called him shortly after 7:00 that morning. Jack hadn't yet finished his first cup of coffee of the day, and he certainly hadn't showered. Vicki had left to take Jonah to school about five minutes earlier.

"Good morning, Jack. I hope I didn't wake you," Prince had said after Jack answered his cell on the second ring.

"I wish, actually. I haven't slept past seven since Jonah was born," Jack replied.

"Slight change in plans, my boy," Prince had said jovially. "Lunch wasn't going to work so well for Senator Johnson, so he suggested we reschedule."

"Oh," Jack said casually, careful not to reveal his disappointment. He knew this meeting was pivotal for him to make his decision, and he did not want to put if off any further.

"Can you do a 9 am? At the Senator's office?" Prince posed.

"Whoa, uh—," Jack looked at the clock: 7:14. It would take him well over an hour to get into downtown Washington at this time of day, and he hadn't even showered yet. "If I hurry."

"Well, hurry then. I'll see you in a little bit," Prince instructed, then hung up.

Jack threw his cell phone on the bed, turned on the shower, and stepped in with the water still lukewarm. He shampooed his hair, lathered soap on his hairier body parts, rinsed off, shaved, toweled dry, brushed his teeth, and got dressed in one of his finer suits. His first attempt at tying his tie ended with the long end halfway down his crotch, so he had to tie it a second time. Albeit minor, this served as the only setback in his whirlwind preparation before leaving the house at 7:41.

He felt underprepared for this meeting. He had planned on spending the better half of the morning continuing his preparation. After returning from dinner with his mother, Jack played checkers with Jonah for a while—Jonah didn't quite understand all of the rules, but he loved sitting down with his father to play a "serious game"— before bathing him and reading a bedtime story together. (*Corduroy* again.) Then he had done some additional research on the laptop for about thirty minutes, sitting in bed with Vicki before turning out the light.

Now he regretted not spending some more time with it last night. Jack rarely got nervous, but his career could hinge on this meeting. He felt as if he were on his way to the bar exam without having studied. He hated that feeling.

Jack arrived at the Hart Senate Office building on Constitution Avenue at 8:59, after parking in a garage on the opposite block. By the time he took the elevator to the fifth floor and walked down to Senator Johnson's office, his watch read 9:02. He hated being late almost as much as he hated being underprepared.

This morning had not started off well at all.

The outer door to the office stood ajar, so Jack poked his head in. A young woman with dark hair pulled back in a bun sat at the front desk. She looked up and smiled at Jack, her teeth crammed together at odd angles, as if she either had more of them than the average person, or her mouth was just too small to house the normal number. Either way, she could have benefitted from some orthodontic work earlier in life, Jack thought. Though he disliked such judgmental sentiments bubbling from his subconscious, this one did seem to lighten his mood a bit, providing much–needed internal levity.

"I am Ana Gorczyka, Senator Johnson's assistant," she said, standing up and walking around the desk as she extended her right hand. She had an Eastern European accent, but the English flowed off her tongue quite naturally. Her friendly voice automatically made her seem more attractive than her appearance. "And you are Special Agent Jackson Byrne."

"Yes." Jack shook her hand, impressed with the firmness of her grip. "Nice to meet you."

"And you too, sir, of course. I read your book when I learned of this meeting, and I enjoyed it immensely. I found it very insightful." She turned to lead him to an anteroom separating her entry office from the Senator's. "Right this way, Special Agent Byrne."

Jack followed, initially flattered by her compliment until the former portion of her comment settled in. *She read my book since learning of this meeting?* His book was no great tome, by any stretch, but it measured just under 300 pages. *Either she's a very fast reader, or this meeting's been planned longer than I've known about it.*

Before he could ponder this thought any longer, Ana opened the door to Senator Johnson's office and announced his arrival. "Senator Johnson and Mr. Prince, Special Agent Byrne is here."

"Jackson Byrne!" a rotund African-American man said as he stood up from his large mahogany desk and walked around to the front of it to greet his visitor. Though Jack had seen Montgomery Johnson before, in print and on television, it took meeting him in person for Jack to realize that Johnson reminded him of James Earl Jones, circa *Field of Dreams* era. Even his voice shared similar characteristics, though not quite as booming. Jack hoped to one day hear Johnson give a "Luke, I am your father," but he decided not to request that on his first visit.

"Senator Johnson, it's a pleasure to meet you," Jack said as he shook the Senator's hand. *Not quite as firm as his assistant's,* Jack thought, *but still very respectable.*

"Please, call me Monty," the Senator replied in his slow, genteel drawl. Jack surmised that most people in the Senator's life called him Monty. He possessed a welcoming air that fit such an amiable nickname.

Jack turned to his right to face Prince, who had also stood. "Philip, nice to see you again," he said as they exchanged a shake.

"Indeed," Prince concurred. "Twice in one week."

"Can I get anyone something to drink?" Ana asked from the doorway. "Coffee? Tea? Water?"

Both guests declined politely.

"OK. Well, thank you, Ana," Johnson said, dismissing her.

"I'll be at my desk, sir, if you need anything," Ana said as she bowed out of the room.

Johnson signaled for Jack to sit in one of the leather armchairs behind him. Jack eased into the luxurious chair and absorbed the otherwise plainly-decorated room around him. It emanated a warm ambience, all burgundies and browns, oak and leather. Despite the two large windows behind Johnson's sizable desk, with thick fabric shades held open by tasseled gold rope, the room still seemed preternaturally dark. It reminded Jack of a sitting room, or, more likely, a smoking room, in one of those Old Boys' Clubs.

Johnson sat down in a chair beside Prince, both of them facing Jack. Johnson placed his elbows on the chair's arms and folded his hands in his lap. Suddenly the entire scene reminded Jack of the 80's film *Trading Places*: Johnson and Prince as the Ralph Bellamy and Don Ameche characters (*Wasn't one of them even named Montgomery!?*), sitting in their executives' club, making a wager about the ruination of the Dan Aykroyd character and the ascension of the Eddie Murphy character. Though he had a pretty good idea—at least he hoped he did—Jack wasn't yet sure which character he would represent.

Johnson nodded his head toward the door where Ana had recently stood. "Nice girl. Very smart and very motivated. I think she'll do well in this town." He leaned forward, as if telling a little secret. "She is very excited and a little nervous about this meeting this morning." He smiled as he leaned back.

Jack seemed outwardly a little confused by this. "Really?" Inwardly, this comment did not surprise him. He had seen the animation in her eyes when she spoke about his book earlier.

Johnson nodded, and Prince just smiled. Jack sensed that they might share an additional secret, one he was not yet privy to.

Johnson sat back in his chair, projecting a relaxed air. "So tell me about yourself, Jack."

Jack leaned forward with his elbows on the armrests. "Well, I was born in Florida but grew up just south of Chevy Chase…"

Johnson began shaking his head and held up his hand, flashing the international sign for "stop." He spoke in a very deliberate yet relaxed manner. "Not a history lesson, Jack. I know all about that: son of a District Attorney—whom I knew and liked very much, by the way— UVA undergrad, Michigan Law, so on and some such. I don't mean any offense."

He looked at Jack, who shook his head. "None taken," Jack replied.

"I've read your book. Skimmed it, to be honest, but I was fascinated by what I read. I would like to hear about you, who you are now. I know that we have approached you about this opportunity, not the other way around. But you're pursuing it this far. Why?"

Johnson's directness caught Jack a little off guard. He felt prepared to answer this question; he just didn't think it would come so early in the conversation in such a straightforward manner. "Well, sir—"

Johnson cut him off again with a raise of his hand. "Monty, please."

BEN MILLER

If Johnson didn't come across as so likable, Jack would be getting pretty pissed by now about the repeated interruptions.

"Monty," Jack continued. "To be honest—which seems to be a theme here today—being a Senator has always been a dream of mine. It's one of the main reasons I decided to go to law school years ago. I ended up in corporate law for a short time out after graduation, mainly because that's what everybody did. It's what I felt most comfortable with given my training at Michigan. But I hated it, for a variety of reasons that I won't bore you with now.

"When I got into law enforcement with the Bureau it felt like a great fit. I possess certain talents and attention to detail that enabled me to excel. Solving crimes, particularly those against children, and bringing justice to families and communities has offered me great satisfaction. But over the past few years I've sensed an urge to contribute more. That was the main motivation for writing my book. In solving the Hollows case, we discovered so many injustices within the system. Essentially, as you know, I feel that that was a preventable crime, like countless others in our society. As a Senator, if I can help put better legal parameters in place—and help provide the means to uphold them—I can work to prevent crimes before they happen instead of solve them after the fact."

Jack noticed that Prince's face lit up, like a valedictorian's proud parent on graduation day. Johnson smiled too.

"Sorry, I don't mean to sound preachy," Jack apologized, but he knew he had said what they wanted to hear. Yes, he had rehearsed his brief a couple of times, but that did not make it any less earnest.

"No, not at all." Johnson crossed his legs, still emanating repose. "There's your platform, Jack. It's that motivation and that character that will win you a seat in the Senate."

Prince spoke for the first time since they all sat down. "How committed are you to this, Jack?"

"Quite, I suppose. But, my biggest concern is not knowing where to go from here, what lies ahead."

Johnson opened his mouth to speak, when a knock came at his office door. He closed his mouth and smiled a knowing smile. He glanced down at his wristwatch as he pushed himself to a stand. Jack looked at the small mahogany mantle clock that sat on the front edge of Johnson's desk. 9:10.

"I hope you don't mind, but I've asked someone else to join us briefly." Johnson moved toward the door.

Prince stood up and straightened his jacket before buttoning the top button. He looked at Jack, scrunched his face with a smile, and flapped his fingers upward into the palm of his hand. *Stand up*, the flapping fingers told him.

Jack stood up as Johnson got to the door and swung it inward halfway, such that Jack couldn't yet see the guest.

Johnson shot his right hand into the threshold. "Hello, sir. Thank you so much for coming this morning."

Jack could hear the visitor's voice as their hands clasped together in greeting. "Senator, my pleasure. Nice to see you."

Jack thought he recognized the voice. Within an instant he suddenly placed it. A stunned look appeared on his face, revealing his astonishment.

Johnson opened the door all the way as the guest stepped inside. Johnson announced, "Mr. President, I'd like you to meet Jackson Byrne."

20

Corinne had set her alarm for 9:00, but hit snooze on the first pass. She turned it off on the second beeping—*What an inhumane sound*, she thought, as she did on almost a daily basis—but stayed in bed for another few minutes. She eventually got up and walked over to her desk in the corner of her bedroom, unceremoniously picking a wedgie from her underwear on the way. She picked up her cell phone, unplugged it from the charger, and walked back over to sit on the edge of her bed. She tapped the touch screen to open up her contacts. She typed "J," and Jackson Byrne's cell phone appeared as the first number on her list.

She stared at the digits displayed on the phone. She felt far less resentment than she had the night before, likely the product of several hours of cooling off and a good night's sleep. She knew that she couldn't really justify her acrimony; Jack had never done anything to personally harm, defame, ridicule, or insult her. He had simply written a book, a book that he felt was important to write. He hadn't known that Corinne had also begun to write a nearly identical book about the sensationalized murder case. At least, she was pretty sure he hadn't. This acknowledgment made her feel better, but it didn't completely erase her bitterness.

"Nobody's perfect," she said aloud to her empty apartment. If someone else had been there, with knowledge of her thoughts, this hypothetical insider would wonder if she were referring to herself, with her unreasonable grudge, or to Jackson Byrne, who had unknowingly robbed her of a perceived opportunity.

She hit SEND and put the phone up to her ear. The line rang once before going straight to voice mail. *"Hello, this is Jackson Byrne with the FBI. Please leave your name, number, and the reason for your call, and I will return it as soon as I can."* Beep.

Corinne opened her mouth to speak, but then didn't know what to say. She didn't even know how to begin. "Jack" might come off as a little too familiar, yet "Special Agent Byrne" felt too formal. He had introduced himself as Jack, which is how she referred to him throughout the Hollows case. After several silent, awkward seconds, she hit END.

She hated that she had hung up, and that she was now spending so much time thinking about this. "Fuck it," she mumbled, again to no one, and hit SEND again to redial.

21

"Harrison Sullivan." The tall, slender, confidently-dressed Most Powerful Man in the World introduced himself as he shook Jack's hand. Surely The President knew that Jack recognized him. Jack concluded that The President introduced himself in this unpretentious manner to help put his company at ease. It worked.

A former Senator from the state of Washington, Harrison Sullivan neared the end of his first term in office. Three years ago he earned the Democratic Party nomination on a platform of radical change in an otherwise stagnant political climate. The momentum from that race carried him through the Presidential Election toward a stunning victory over the heavily favored Republican incumbent. However, he quickly realized the difficulties of working with the multitude of tired curmudgeons that populated Capitol Hill. By the time he found his footing and began to accomplish only a few of the ambitious goals that highlighted his original campaign, he needed to turn his focus to his re-election.

"Jackson Byrne, Mr. President," Jack said as he shook the man's hand. "It is very much an honor to meet you."

"You look surprised," The President noted. "They didn't tell you I would drop by, did they?"

Jack began shaking his head when Johnson spoke. "Where's the fun in that, sir?"

The President shook his head, feigning disapproval. He turned to face Prince. "Philip Prince, how are you doing these days?"

Prince shook his hand. "Quite well, sir. It's a pleasure to see you, as always."

The President turned to Jack, pointing a finger back at Prince. "Philip here was one of the first people I met in DC. A wet-behind-the-ears crusader fresh off my Senatorial election, I hadn't even unpacked all of my boxes in my office, just across the street..." He pointed out the window. "Philip shows up with a bottle of wine to welcome me to the city."

Prince nods and utters a gruff chuckle.

"Won't you sit down, Mr. President?" Johnson asked as he closed the office door and motioned toward the leather armchair beside where Jack had been sitting.

"You know I really can't stay long. I just wanted to meet you, Jack. I read your book and found it very insightful. And troubling, frankly. Monty probably told you that he read it too, but I'm guessing he just skimmed it."

Jack laughed at The President's honesty. "He admitted to skimming."

The President looked back at Johnson, raising his eyebrows in pleasant surprise. He turned his attention back to Jack. "Well, your book points out several flaws in our government's efforts, and I'm excited to hear that you're considering running for political office. You have my full support." He extended his hand again, and Jack shook it again.

"Thank you, sir. That really means a lot."

"You'll meet a lot of people in the next several months, many of whom will make promises they won't keep. But I am serious, Jack. You let me know if there's anything you need. You can always get in touch with me through either of these gentlemen." He alternated his thumb between Prince and Johnson.

"Thank you. Again." Jack felt he was running out of things to say, other than expressing gratitude.

"Philip tells me you're quite the hockey fan," The President probed.

"Big Caps fan," Jack replied. Now the conversation moved a little closer to his wheelhouse. He could talk politics with intelligence, but, in this company, he feared that eventually he would find himself in over his head. He could wax about sports and hold his own with anyone.

"Growing up, everyone around me loved the Canucks, even through those many down years, but I just couldn't pull for a Canadian team. I grew up a huge Gretzky fan, so when Edmonton traded him to LA, I instantly became a Kings fan. Tell you what, Jack. If the Caps and the Kings meet in the Stanley Cup Finals, I'll make sure to get you a spot in my box to go see one of the games."

Jack contained his excitement as best as he could. "That would be awesome," he said, deciding immediately after the words left his mouth that he must have sounded like a 15-year-old. Too late to take it back, though, so he hoped his juvenile vocabulary came off as enthusiasm rather than immaturity.

"All right," The President nodded. "I have to run."

Immaturity, Jack thought. *He thinks I'm a complete tool.*

"Again, Jack, nice meeting you," The President said. They shook hands for a third time as Jack agreed, and thanked The President for the umpteenth time. The President turned to Johnson and Prince, shaking each of their hands in turn. "Gentlemen, a pleasure, as always."

"Thanks so much for coming by, sir," Philip said. Johnson opened the door as The President waved a hand while exiting. Johnson closed the door behind him. The energy in the room suddenly seemed different to Jack, diminished from mere seconds ago.

Johnson turned back to face them and then walked back to his chair. "He is such an inspirational man," he said. Prince nodded in agreement as the two of them sat down.

Jack felt speechless, a disquieting sensation for him. He did not think of himself as someone who would get star struck, but he guessed the term adequately described his current state. He also still felt a little embarrassed. *Awesome?* The word repeated in his head. He decided he would leave out that part when retelling his story of The Time I Met The President.

"So, where were we?" Johnson posed to the group.

Prince answered quickly, as if he made a point of remembering from the beginning of their diversion. "We were going to explain to Jack what happens from here, now that he has decided to run for office. Right, Jack?"

Jack considered this for a brief moment. *Is he asking me if this is the point at which the conversation had halted, or if I had truly decided to run in the election?* Jack decided it was both, but more the latter than the former. "Right."

Johnson responded. "Well, let me tell you where things are on our end." He cleared his throat and shifted in his seat. "And, it pains me to say this, as I know you are a trustworthy man, Jack, but, given my position and my personal history, I feel I must: What we say here should go no further than this room."

Jack never broke eye contact. "Of course."

Johnson nodded, instantly seeming more relaxed again. "Philip told me that he discussed Rupert Schultz with you."

"Briefly," Prince interjected again.

"Briefly," Jack concurred.

Johnson continued. "Senator Schultz won his election four-and-a-half years ago on a fairly typical, mostly liberal Democratic platform. But, in his years in Congress, he has become more conservative in his politics and more liberal in his personal life. Downright cavalier, actually. This recent DUI is not his first blemish, by any means. His personal record is tainted by several, shall we say, unbecoming events. When we put this together with his changing politics, Mr. Schultz has turned into a bit of a disgrace for the Democratic Party. The American People don't stand for disgraceful people serving in public office—nor should they— and we as a Party do not either."

Johnson smiled and looked directly at Jack. "You're married, right Jack?" His tone had quickly changed from a didactic one back to a conversational one. Good politicians could do this effortlessly. As Jack quickly realized, Montgomery Johnson was a great politician.

"Yes. Vicki and I have been married for almost eleven years now," Jack replied. He didn't like where this conversation was heading.

Johnson nodded, already knowing the answer. "Surely you dated in your younger days. A man like you— good-looking, athletic, intelligent— must have had his share of girls knocking at your door at some point, yes?"

Jack tried to seem convivial, but he was losing patience with this line of seemingly rhetorical questions. "I went on some dates back in my day, sure, but not more than the average guy. I was more of a 'serial monogamist,' I suppose."

Johnson's eyes widened, and he smiled. "'Serial monogamy,' yes! So, tell me, Jack, when you broke up with one girlfriend, wasn't it always more comforting to have another girl in mind, waiting in the wings? I'm not saying that you would jump right into bed with her, but knowing that you had another prospect waiting always made a break-up much easier, didn't it?"

"Sure," Jack complied.

"Well, Jack, in that same vein, I plan on holding a meeting with Rupert Shultz in the very near future to ask him to resign as Senator. That is, if you will commit to running for his spot this fall."

"How soon do you need an answer?" Jack asked.

"Now," Johnson replied without missing a beat. "Now would be good." For such a kind man, he could really apply a lot of pressure.

"Well, what about my current job?"

"Of course, you would need to resign from the FBI," Johnson answered.

"What about income? Benefits? Health insurance?" Jack asked matter-of-factly.

Johnson waved at this notion, as if it were a gnat floating by his face. "We have several funds to help support you financially during your campaign. That won't be a problem. The only problem arises in the unlikely event that you lose the election."

Prince jumped in. "It should go without saying that the Democratic Party will offer its full support of your campaign. However, we won't be able to support you following the election should you lose."

Jack nodded in understanding.

"But we don't expect you to lose, Jack," Johnson added. "You're our ace-in-the-hole, our next-girlfriend-in-waiting. We would never give up a seat in the Senate—even though it's currently occupied by a buffoon— if we didn't have full confidence that we would get it right back."

"When would I have to resign?" Jack queried.

"If we move ahead on his, Schultz will resign before the end of the month. There would be an emergency primary, perhaps as soon as next month, which will be a breeze; we would not officially nominate anyone else from the Democratic Party," Johnson assured him.

"So…?" Jack asked; Johnson had not really answered his question.

Prince jumped in. "This is really going to be a full-time job by the beginning of next month. It's going to be important for you to find staffers, meet backers, lobbyists, and so on in the coming weeks before going into your full-blown campaign. The actual election will likely be held this November. So, you would need to resign from CASMIRC… now."

"So you see why we need an answer now. We have an unusually rapid timetable on this, Jack," Johnson added.

"You were born for greatness, Jack," Prince stated. "This is the appropriate next step for you."

Jack nodded. He knew that Prince was right. Despite some doubts about leaving CASMIRC, he had more important items on his agenda now. Finally, Jack said confidently, "I really feel that my heart is in this. I want this."

"Then let's make it happen," Johnson said convincingly.

The meeting ended a few minutes later, and Jack thanked them both. He and Prince rode the elevator down to the first floor together and exited the building.

"I'm proud of you, Jack" Prince said, squinting into the mid-morning sun as he pulled on his overcoat. Though still a bit chilly, even for April, Jack left his overcoat slung over his left arm.

"Thanks, Philip. I think I am too," Jack replied.

"You should be. And, I don't want to sound too clichéd, here, but..." Prince began.

Jack's head gave a slow nod, as he turned from Prince to also face the sunlight. "I know..."

"He would be, Jack. He would be very proud."

22

A short while later, Jack stared at the reflection of the great obelisk as it bounced off the water in front of him. *What a strange way to memorialize someone?* he thought. He had read the Dan Brown book some years back, the one that put forth the hypothesis about the Obelisk being an important symbol to the alleged Mason George Washington. He couldn't remember which of Brown's novels had theorized this particular conspiracy theory. *They were all basically the same, anyway.* Still, even if one bought this theory, isn't it odd to erect a huge phallus in honor of one of your country's patriarchs? Why not a bust, or a full-bodied statue like Lincoln or Jefferson?

He sat on the third row of steps of the Lincoln Memorial, drinking his Grande Starbucks coffee. He left the house in such a hurry that morning that he didn't have the chance to savor his morning brew. Jack recognized very well the cliché that he had come here—to the Reflecting Pool— to reflect. But this was one of his favorite spots in the city, and he couldn't deny the calming effect this place always had on him.

He thought about his time with the FBI, and with CASMIRC specifically. In a relatively short time—seven years total—he had played a role in over fifty investigations, the vast majority of which had led to successful convictions. He felt proud of his work, but he also had grown tired of it. His speech for Johnson and Prince was not insincere. He had always dreamt of serving in the Senate; he did want to do more with his professional life on a policy level. He purposefully left out of his monologue, though, that recently he felt more and more defeated by the horrors of his current job. The various crimes that he encountered through CASMIRC had always sickened him, but he always found a way to put that nausea aside. He focused on the details—the forensics, the pathology, motive, means, opportunity. He had become quite adept at profiling, trying to think like the killer, the kidnapper, the pornographer, or the pedophile. He could accomplish this comfortably because he was nothing like those people; he had learned to *think* like them without *associating* with them.

On the other hand, he struggled with the victimology— trying to understand how a person becomes a victim. Jack had much difficulty fathoming how children could play a role in their own victimization. With few exceptions, they are all so innocent. As Jonah got older— developing from an adorable novelty into a unique little person, full of hopes and dreams, flaws and weaknesses— victimology became even harder for Jack, a near impossibility. He could not *think* about the victims without *associating* with them. Though Jack occasionally lacked insight, that morning at the Reflecting Pool, he possessed enough to recognize this growing inability to think about child victims as a harbinger for his resignation from CASMIRC. It served as much of a motivating factor as did his desire to run for the Senate.

With that thought he took the final sip of coffee from his Styrofoam cup. He reached to his belt and took out his Blackberry, turned it on. He had one voicemail.

"Hi, Jackson Byrne, this is Corinne O'Loughlin. I am doing some investigating into a new case and was hoping to discuss it with you. Please call me back when you can..." And she left her cell and

office numbers, which Jack did not write down. He knew he had kept both numbers stored in his phone.

Wartime, he thought. *What's she looking into?*

Jack remembered Corinne very well, a talented and tenacious investigative reporter. He had met her in the early stages of the Hollows investigation. He first remembered seeing her at the crime scene, though they did not speak. He had already been working the case as a Missing Person/Possible Abduction, so he was one of the first on the scene when Lamaya Hollows' body was discovered. Though it was an unusually chilly and windy May morning, Corinne wore only a light sweater to the crime scene. No jacket, wind-breaker, or even a scarf. Her wavy red hair had been pulled back in a pony-tail, offering no relief to her nape from the cutting spring wind.

The following day, while Jack exited the home of the victim's famous father, Lamond Hollows, Corinne approached him to ask some questions. She didn't come armed with a microphone or recorder aimed at his face, just with a notebook and a seriousness that struck him immediately. He felt she could be an ally, if utilized properly, and he had been right.

"Special Agent Byrne, I'm Corinne O'Loughlin from *The Washington Post*," she had said, extending her hand. Jack shook it, then stuffed his hands into his pants pockets as he turned to lean against the door of his car. Again, though the weather has eased up some, Corinne seemed underdressed for the conditions. Jack noticed that she had straightened her hair, put it back in a clip near the crown of her head, with strands falling down on either side.

"Hello, Miss O'Loughlin. What can I do for you?" Jack replied. He, like Corinne, had found that most law enforcement officials treated the media with disdain. He always made a concerted effort not to, which he found much more productive.

"You can call me Corinne, please, for starters," she replied with a forced smile. Jack sensed that she flashed this disingenuous grin with some frequency, used more as a tool for camaraderie than to express emotion. "I was wondering if you have any suspects at this time."

Jack paused. Though he remained cordial yet casual with the press, he always chose his words carefully. "We are exploring many leads right now, but we have no main suspects."

"Are Mr. or Mrs. Hollows considered suspects at this time?"

She went there quickly, Jack thought. He knew this would be a huge case from the minute it came to CASMIRC. Not Lindberg Baby huge, but almost in that category, all because of Lamaya Hollows' parents.

Lamond Hollows played wide receiver for the Washington Redskins. He had grown up in the greater DC area before going to the University of Georgia on a full scholarship. Hollows stood 6'5" tall, weighed 230 pounds, and possessed natural gifts of stunning speed and exceptional hands. After his junior year, when he was undisputedly the best player on the team which lost the BCS National Championship Game to Oklahoma, he got drafted in the first round by the 'Skins. Since then, over the last decade, he has put up very consistent statistics, averaging just over 1000 yards per season. He was widely considered one of the most dependable receivers in the league.

His behavior off the field had been every bit as erratic as his play on the field had been consistent. At the end of his rookie year has was arrested for DUI. At the time he was dating a former Playboy Playmate, who was found passed out in the passenger seat. She was taken to a local hospital, where her blood alcohol level was 0.2 and her toxicology screen revealed a veritable cornucopia of pharmaceuticals: Ecstasy, cocaine, marijuana, and oxycodone. She required an overnight hospitalization; Hollows was imprisoned overnight for DUI and released the following day on bail. He had a few other minor run-ins with the law, including a call for a domestic disturbance when the aforementioned former Playmate threatened him with a knife.

At the beginning of his second season in the NFL, Hollows' coach encouraged him to spend some time doing charity work. While spending time with some patients at Children's National Hospital, Hollows met Melissa Tidgewell, a former Miss Virginia and Miss America finalist, who subsequently had launched a moderately successful career in modeling. This encounter turned out to be the biggest influence in Hollows' personal and professional life. He had no further encounters with the law, and his play on the field improved even further, mostly through better chemistry with his socially uptight Southern Baptist quarterback and even other less conservative teammates.

Hollows and Melissa began dating the week after they met at Children's National. Nine months later they discovered that she was pregnant. A few months after the birth of their daughter Lamaya, Lamond Hollows and Melissa Tidgewell got married in a small summer ceremony in the humble church in rural Virginia where Melissa grew up.

"Both Lamond and Melissa Hollows have firm alibis for the day and time of Lamaya's disappearance," Jack replied to Corinne's question. "While we remain open to all lines of investigation, at this point they are not considered suspects."

Corinne nodded and glanced down briefly at her notepad. "There are rumors that Lamaya was sexually assaulted. Can you confirm this?"

Jack shook his head with an apologetic look on his face. "I can't comment on that at this time." Both knew he couldn't and wouldn't answer the question, but both understood Corinne's need to ask it.

Corinne nodded and let her arm fall down to her side. Her tone of voice changed, softened, from that of a calculated, information-gathering reporter to that of a caring citizen, concerned about the shortened life of a young girl. "Do you have any good leads at all at this point, Special Agent?"

Jack looked into her green eyes and read the emotion there, genuine empathy. Subconsciously, his tone of voice changed too, more conversational, more personal. "Not really. And you can call me Jack, by the way. We still have a lot of people to question. And we're still waiting on final autopsy reports. Hopefully we'll find some DNA that will be extremely helpful."

Corinne's eyes dropped, then turned to look at Lamond Hollows' expansive home behind them. "How are they holding up?"

"Honestly," Jack shrugged, "I never know how to answer a question like that. How is someone supposed to handle something like this? They don't seem suicidal, I don't think, which I guess is the best one could hope for."

Corinne pursed her lips and nodded slowly again. "Thanks for your time."

"Any time," he said.

As he walked around to the driver's side door, Corinne approached the curb near the passenger's door. Still in her conversational manner, she asked, "So, if you're waiting to try to find DNA, does that mean there was a sexual assault?"

Jack stopped at his door and put his hands on top of the car. *She's good,* he thought, and smiled at her. Corinne smiled back. Jack reached down and opened up his door. "Your hair's different," he said.

Corinne got a quizzical look on her face. His comment completely took her by surprise. In that instant she realized what a wily adversary, or potential ally, Jack could be. "Excuse me?" she replied, trying consciously not to blush (which, of course, never works).

"At the crime scene, when the body was discovered, you wore you hair curly, tied back in a pony tail. Today it's straight but pulled back in a clip."

She looked down at the car window in front of her to see her reflection, as if she had forgotten how she had done her hair and didn't believe Jack's description. Jack was instantly reminded of a line from one of his favorite songs, "Life During Wartime" by Talking Heads, about refugee renegades; the narrator claims to have altered his hair style so often that he wouldn't even recognize himself.

Corinne looked back from her reflection in the window to Jack. "You're very perceptive, Special Agent Byrne."

"Jack," he reminded her. "Thanks. It's kinda in the job description." He opened up his door and got in. He put the keys in the ignition and started the car. Corinne took a step back from the curb until Jack opened up the power window on the passenger's door. He reached across to hand her a business card.

"Here," he said loudly, over the hum of the car's engine. Corinne leaned in and took the card. "If you think of other questions, or you get any information that you think will aid the investigation, please call me. My cell is on the back."

"Thanks," Corinne said. She suddenly felt the need to reciprocate, so, as he was putting the car in gear, she reached into a pocket on the covering of her notebook and pulled out a card. He began to pull away. "Jack!" she called after him, and he stopped. She took a few steps forward to hand him her card through the still-open window. "Same deal, OK?" she said.

Jack took the card and regarded it in his hand for a brief moment. He looked back at her. "Ok, Corinne. It was nice meeting you."

"You too," she said, as she leaned back out of the car before he drove away.

Since that first meeting, Jack had always thought of Corinne as "Wartime." He hadn't used the term in front of her, and only rarely referred to her as that around CASMIRC. Jack found that she possessed an assertive, borderline aggressive method of acquiring information for her articles. Adding that to the esoteric song reference made "Wartime" a fitting nickname.

Still sitting there, overlooking the Reflecting Pond, Jack decided to return Corinne's call a little later. He needed to get back to CASMIRC and have a talk with Dylan.

A BUSTLE IN THE HEDGEROW

As Jack stood up to head to his car, he recalled his Trading Places analogy from the beginning of his morning meeting. Though he never pictured himself in an Eddie Murphy role, that certainly was the one Johnson and Prince—Mortimer and Winston (*Mortimer, not Montgomery!* Jack remembered)— had thrust him into. Rupert Schultz would get cast as the Dan Akroyd character. *At least he'll get to whore around with a hot Jamie Lee Curtis,* Jack thought, *before she needed the yogurt to maintain regular bowels,* his mind added, amusing himself. Little did he know that Rupert Schultz would indeed spend the rest of his short life whoring around, mostly with women far less hot than Jamie Lee Curtis.

23

"Your co-pay today is five dollars," the receptionist told Vicki.

Vicki reached in her wallet, pulled out a five-dollar bill, and handed it to the spritely receptionist behind the desk. While having a husband employed by the FBI had its many disadvantages, it did provide reliable and very affordable health insurance, which had always pleased Vicki.

Jonah had developed some significant seasonal allergies. He actually had one previous episode a little over a year ago where his allergies moved into his lungs, causing him to have wheezing and such severe breathing difficulties that he required several hours of aerosolized breathing treatments in their local emergency department. He still had an albuterol inhaler at home to use in case of emergency, but luckily he hadn't needed it since that episode. As a result, though, he's been coming to see his pediatric allergist Dr. Franklin every four months for the past fifteen months.

The receptionist took the cash, filed it in her drawer, and typed a few short bursts into her keyboard in front of her. "While your receipt prints, would you like to schedule Jonah's next appointment?"

"Sure," Vicki replied. She had seen this receptionist for every visit, but did not know her name. She sneaked a peak at her name tag. "APRIL," it said, in all caps. In smaller font below it read "Reception." *Fitting name*, Vicki thought. *April. Springy.*

"So…." April began, scanning through the computerized scheduling program. "Three months from now would be July. How does the 20th sound? It's a Tuesday."

"Perfect," Vicki replied. Jonah stood quietly at her side, trying to read the "Patient's Bill of Rights" sign posted on the wall beside April's counter. Vicki surmised that he could only get maybe a quarter of the words, but she reveled in his inquisitive mind's efforts to try to read the document.

The receptionist handed Vicki her receipt and an appointment card. "There you go. See you in July."

"Thanks," Vicki said.

"Bye, Jonah," April said, peeking over her counter to wave at him.

Jonah looked up from his reading, smiled, and waved back. "Bye, April!" he said with enthusiasm.

Vicki tried not to look astonished. *How did Jonah remember her name?* she thought. *Smart kid....*

Dr. Franklin's office was near the end of a strip mall with a large parking lot. As they opened the glass door and walked outside, Vicki and Jonah nearly bumped into someone walking down the sidewalk in a bit of a hurry.

"Oh, excuse me," Vicki said.

The tall, gangly man wearing jeans and a hideously ugly sweater slowed his rapid pace to face Vicki. "No worries, ma'm," the man said. He then nodded and proceeded into the storefront beside the allergist's. The sign hanging in front of the store read "Family Snapshot" in fancy script, with "Portrait Studio" underneath in a more traditional font. Vicki remembered that this unit had previously housed a sewing shop, offering both tailoring and other amendments, as well as sewing and knitting supplies. The last time Vick brought Jonah here, "Needles and Such" had closed and the space was undergoing renovations; this was the first time she had seen it open. Intrigued, she decided to walk in and pick up a brochure before driving home.

24

After grabbing a turkey wrap for lunch at his favorite deli, Jack got back to CASMIRC shortly after 2:00. He'd had ample time to gather his thoughts in preparation for his meeting with Harringer. He dropped off his suit jacket at his desk and went to Harringer's office. Through the window that overlooked the rest of the department, Jack could see Harringer busily writing notes on a yellow legal pad to the right of his computer.

When Jack knocked on the door, Harringer looked up over the rims of his reading glasses. He deliberately focused his attention back to the computer and continued to write. "One second, Jack," he said slowly. Harringer hoped to convey a sense that—for him, at least—the investigation into these children's murders took precedence over Jack's personal life. If Jack hadn't perceived this message initially, it became clear after Harringer let him stand there for almost two minutes in silence.

Finally, Harringer put down his felt-tip pen, took off his glasses, and rotated in his chair to face Jack at the threshold. He held out his hand toward one of the chairs in front of his desk. "Have a seat," he said impatiently, as if Jack should have seated himself sooner.

He's not in a good mood, and it may be because of me, Jack thought. He had known Harringer long enough to recognize his mood swings. *This won't be easy.* Jack entered the office and sat down. He looked up and met Harringer's eyes.

"Dylan, I need to talk to you about a unique opportunity that has come my way," Jack began. With that, Harringer leaned back in his chair and tilted his head, emanating disapproval. Yet he remained silent.

"It's a once-in-a-lifetime opportunity, really," Jack continued. He had already deviated from the script he had lain out in his head earlier today. "I have been approached by relatively high-ranking members of the Democratic Party..." He paused briefly, thinking of meeting The President earlier that day, but refraining from name-dropping. "...To run for a position in the U.S. Congress." He didn't want to specifically mention Schultz or the actual position he would seek. Though he knew he could trust Harringer, he felt it was still too premature to offer specifics regarding the privileged information from his morning meeting.

Harringer tilted his head to the other side and briefly raised his eyebrows, but still he said nothing. Jack could not discern if this last statement had impressed him or bored him.

"The campaign will not kick off in earnest for a few weeks, but, as you know, once you get embroiled in a case, it's pretty difficult to extricate yourself out of it."

Harringer broke his silence. "Embroiled and then extricated, huh?"

Jack recognized that Harringer was making fun of him, but he let it go. Perhaps he should not have spent so much time thinking about what he would say. "So, I would like to put in my two-weeks' notice and would prefer to work on some back logs and finishing up other business rather than get...embroiled... in this new case."

Harringer didn't flinch. Not one muscle on his taut face moved. For a second Jack thought he had blacked out briefly and Harringer had been replaced by a wax statue of himself. *With remarkable detail,* Jack thought.

Jack remained silent as well. He had said what he needed to say. Harringer would respond eventually. In time. Soon, probably. *I would hate to be interrogated by him,* Jack thought. *He could get someone to confess just by staring at him.*

Finally Harringer sat forward in his chair, his muscular hands clasped together in front of him. He looked at Jack inquisitively. "Rupert Schulz?" he asked.

This was not the response Jack had expected, but he tried not to act startled. He quickly gathered himself and nodded. "Yes."

"That guy's been a fuck-up since he was old enough to drive. How he ever got elected is beyond me," Harringer mumbled, mostly to himself. He sat up straighter and addressed Jack more properly. "Well, Jack… I'm saddened by this. I think that you are a great investigator and you possess natural talents that, frankly, we won't replace any time soon. We've had a number of cases over the last several years that I fear would not have been solved, at least not as quickly, had you not been here."

Jack realized that Harringer again attempted to apply a guilt trip, his second in two days. He foresaw something like this, though, and had prepared himself to withstand it in silence. Yet it started to work anyway. Jack began to feel guilty about abandoning his post. Surely Harringer and his crew would thrive without him, but he couldn't help feeling remorseful about leaving.

Harringer knew that lingering on this sentiment only made the effort more transparent, so he continued. "But, I know you feel that you have bigger fish to fry, and I wish you luck with these endeavors. 'Senator Byrne' does have a nice ring to it." With this, Harringer smiled for the first time since Jack knocked on his door. "Take your two weeks to finalize stuff that needs finalizing. Just submit your formal letter of resignation to me by tomorrow. From there we'll start the exit interview process, probably early next week."

"Yes, sir. Thanks, Dylan."

"Of course, Jack." Harringer stood up and extended his hand. "Congratulations. I hope everything works out great for you. You'll have my vote, by the way."

Jack smiled as he shook hands with his now-former boss. "I hope to serve you well," was the best thing he could think to say.

25

On his way home from the office, Jack remembered to call Corinne O'Loughlin. He put in his Bluetooth, found her cell in his contact list, and called her back. She answered on the third ring.

"Special Agent Byrne," she answered.

"Hello, Corinne. And it's Jack, remember?" he responded.

"I remember," she replied. *Was that... angst in her voice?* he thought. He quickly tried to think about why she would be angry with him but came up empty. He made a mental note to contemplate this further after the phone conversation.

"How have you been?" Jack asked cordially.

"Quite well. How about you?"

"Well, too. Busy."

"Yeah, I saw you making some appearances about your book. Congratulations on that."

"Thanks. Have you read it?"

Pretentious ass, she thought. *I have better things to do than read your self-serving book* was what she wanted to say. But, as it turns out, she had read his book, cover-to-cover, in the first week after its release. "No, I haven't gotten around to it yet."

"Oh. If you ever get the chance, I would love to hear your opinion on it."

"Fair enough," Corinne replied, hoping this would kill the subject. "I called you this morning to ask you about the murder of Adrianna Cottrell in York, PA."

"Ah," Jack grunted. He didn't want to divulge anything about his personal situation or the investigation—not that he knew much about the investigation to divulge. Unlike his open confidence in Dylan Harringer, Jack had more limited trust in Corinne, despite their working well together on the Hollows case; she was still a member of the press, after all. "Actually, Corinne, I'm not working that case right now."

"You're not?" She seemed shocked.

"No. Our SAC Dylan Harringer is overseeing everything, and Heath Reilly has taken lead on that one, I believe."

"Huh," Corinne said. Clearly she hadn't expected this.

"I think you know Heath, right?"

"Yes, we met during the Hollows case."

"Right," Jack said. "Tell you what—I'll pass your number along to him and recommend that he give you a call. He's a good investigator, and I'm sure he would appreciate having you on board as well."

"Sure, that would be fine," Corinne said, without really listening.

"Great. Well, I'm glad things are going well for you, Corinne. Take care."

"Thanks, Jack, you too," she said and hung up.

Jack Byrne not working on a sure-to-become-high-profile case? This didn't make much sense. Something seemed awry within the ranks at CASMIRC, and Corinne resolved to get to the bottom of it.

26

Heath Reilly had no sooner hung up his cell phone talking with Jack when it rang again. He looked at the number of the incoming call and did not recognize it initially, though something about it looked familiar. As he swiped his screen to answer the call, he looked down at his hand-written scrawl on a scrap of paper on his desk: Corinne O'Loughlin's name and cell number. That's where he had seen this number, mere seconds before.

"Special Agent Reilly," he answered.

"Hello, Special Agent Reilly, this is Corinne O'Loughlin, with the Washington Post. We met last year during the Lamaya Hollows case."

"Yes, of course. Jack Byrne just called me and gave me your number to call. I literally just got off the phone with him."

"Oh, yeah. He had suggested that we speak. I had contacted him about the Adrianna Cottrell case, and he referred me to you."

"OK. How can I help you, Corinne?" For the time being, he decided to defer questioning her about how she got his private cell number. Jack had specifically told him that he hadn't given it to her. He surmised simply that, as a talented investigative reporter, she had found a source with his cell number.

"What can you tell me about the investigation so far?" she asked.

"On the record, not much at this point."

"What about off the record?" By the slight change in her voice, he could tell she was smiling on the other end of the line.

Heath didn't know if all people could hear facial expressions over the phone, but he knew that he could.

"Not much at this point," he repeated, coyly.

"OK," she said. The smile had disappeared. "How about I tell you what I know, and if you can confirm and/or elaborate, that would be fantastic?"

"We can try that." Heath remembered Corinne from the Hollows case very well, though he had officially met her only once and spoke to her one other time. He recalled watching her have conversations with Jackson Byrne and feeling a little jealous. He liked her feisty attitude, and he loved her curly red hair and pale freckled skin. His first girlfriend in high school was a redhead. They dated for two years, did a lot of "stuff," but never had sex. This fact still struck Heath as one of his greatest regrets. He had dated dozens of women since then, had sex with nine of them—he kept count, not surprisingly— but he never had the unbridled passion for any of them like he had for Darla Wright, that high-school sweetheart.

Corinne went through some details of the Cottrell murder, all of which had already been published in the local media: the strangulation at the playground, discovery of the body, no known suspects, family distraught, etc. She did not mention the autopsy findings of the post-mortem trauma nor the note found in Adrianna's pocket; neither of these pieces of information had gotten out to the media. Heath hummed an "Mmm-hmm" whenever she took a brief pause, confirming her facts. When she finished she took a somewhat longer pause, likely waiting for Heath to speak, but he remained silent. Corinne decided to try her next tactic, a little surprise attack.

"And, what about the Stephanie McBurney murder?" she asked.

This did indeed catch Heath off guard, so he didn't say anything at first. No one from The Bureau or from the York or Frederick police departments had issued any statements about the likely link between the two murders. Either she was better than he thought and had made the connection herself, or she had received inside information. *Does she know someone on the inside?* he thought anxiously. He tried to dismiss the thought. *If she did, then why would she need to come to me with all of these questions?*

Based on Heath's silence, Corinne deduced that her mini-ambush had succeeded. She hoped that his daze would lead him to disclose some more information than he normally would.

"Which one now?" Heath said, trying to act cool, but failing, as usual.

"Stephanie McBurney, from Frederick, Maryland. She was strangled last month, also at a playground, also during the light of day, also without any witnesses. Ring a bell?"

Heath did not know how to respond. If he confirms that they highly suspect that these crimes are linked, Corinne runs the story with CASMIRC attached. He needed a moment to think this through, measure pros and cons, before responding.

"Hey, Corinne, sorry, but I have another call coming in. Can I call you back to discuss this further?"

"Sure. But, just so you know, I've made this connection and I'm working on my story to run in tomorrow's edition whether you confirm or not."

"Got it, thanks," he said and then hung up.

Corinne, sitting in her cubicle, hung up shortly afterwards and placed her cell phone on her desk. Success. She had flustered him, not quite enough into making an admission of the connection, but sufficiently to make him run and hide for a minute to collect his thoughts. She felt confident that he would call back. She went back to her computer to read through her story again.

27

Back at his desk in Quantico, Heath stared at his phone, his mind racing. If he plays this right, this could present a huge break for him. He might get named Lead on this investigation, which could end up twice as huge as the Hollows case, depending on how far it goes. Unfortunately for him, he had no idea how to play this right.

His initial instinct told him to go discuss this matter with Harringer. As the SAC Harringer still stood as the head of this investigation. Everyone assumed that Harringer would hand it off to Jack and step back into a supervisory role soon. But Jack wasn't around, and based on his phone conversation with him today, Heath guessed that Jack had other things going on and would not be a part of this investigation.

On the other hand, if Heath decided to discuss the case with Corinne, putting his name all over the article in *The Post*, Harringer might have no choice but to make him Lead. Or he could get chastised and taken off the case entirely.

Heath could not decide, but deep down he knew that he should follow his instinct; it told him to follow proper protocol, which, in this situation, could never serve him wrong.

He got up and went to Harringer's office, where the door stood open, as usual. He knocked anyway, remaining just outside the door.

Harringer looked up from his computer. "Reilly. What is it?"

Heath stepped into the office, but did not sit; Harringer had not motioned for him to do so yet. "I just received a phone call from Corinne O'Loughlin, a reporter at *The Post.*"

"I remember her. She wrote a lot about the Hollows case," Harringer said. "What did Jack always call her?"

"I believe it was 'Wartime'," Heath answered.

Harringer smirked, a rather unusual sight in his CASMIRC office. "Yeah, that's it. Fiery little gal. What did she want?"

Heath recounted his phone conversation with Corinne O'Loughlin, concluding with her inquiring about Stephanie McBurney.

Harringer raised his eyebrows suspiciously. "And what did you tell her?"

"Nothing. I told her I had another call coming in and I'd call her back. Then I came in here."

"Aha, retreat. Not always a bad tactic." Harringer extended his hand towards one of the chairs in front of his desk, and Heath took a seat.

"So?" Harringer asked.

Heath stared at him, not quite sure what he was asking. Harringer seemed a bit disappointed.

"So how do we handle this, Reilly?" Harringer clarified.

Heath had thought about this on his walk to Harringer's office. He came upon a solution that might bolster his positioning in CASMIRC and also potentially help the investigation. Though he tried to deny it internally, Heath knew that the former held more importance to him than the latter.

126

"We confirm the connection. In doing so, we might accomplish three things. First, this may help get the word out to other precincts and lay people. Someone might make a connection to a third case that has eluded us thus far."

"OK, go on."

"Second, it helps get the word out to families. I'm guessing that every parent in Frederick and York are acting a little more vigilant about keeping an eye on their kids, but if people knew that these murders have happened in two different communities, it might heighten awareness in a number of surrounding areas in several states."

"As long as those people read *The Post*. Two for two, continue."

"We let the killer know that we have made this connection. As long as he reads *The Post*," he conceded. "This might make him more careful in the future, possibly even deciding to stop killing altogether."

"Possibly, but I disagree," Harringer replied. Recently Harringer had found himself annoyed by Heath Reilly more often than not. This conversation had reminded him of the redeeming qualities that had drawn him to Reilly when he brought him into CASMIRC two years ago. "What do we know about our unknown subject so far?"

Heath contemplated this for a moment. He found profiling difficult, so as a result he doubted the validity of the discipline. In his experience profilers created accurate depictions of un-subs less than 50% of the time. "We think it's a man working alone. He's likely trained in many languages. Perhaps he has some deep-rooted issues from his childhood…" Heath felt himself fishing, especially with this last piece of bullshit, just hoping something would match what Harringer wanted to hear. Then suddenly Heath remembered the translation of the note found on Adrianna Cottrell, and Harringer's question made much more sense. "And he 'wants to be somebody.' He thrives on media attention."

"Exactly," Harringer replied with satisfaction, though he found it a little disappointing that it took Heath so long to get there. "So, I think we can look at this one of two ways: either we try to block the story altogether, thus avoiding feeding his fire for the time being—"

"I don't think that will work," Heath interrupted. "Corinne told me that she would run the story with or without our cooperation."

"She could be bluffing. Or, I'm sure she could be persuaded to delay things indefinitely if we give her a little something in return. Inside access, for example."

"You would do that?" Heath asked.

Harringer leaned forward. "I would *say* that I would give her inside info."

"OK. You said two ways. What's the second?"

"We use the media to our advantage, with or without Corinne O'Loughlin's knowledge."

"How would we do that?"

Harringer looked at his watch. "How long do you have to get back to her?"

"I didn't give any set time, but I think I shouldn't take too long."

"We don't want to be too hasty or too brazen, but I think we can come up with something in a short amount of time that might be advantageous to our cause. Let's get everyone together to brainstorm."

Before Heath could agree, Harringer picked up his phone and started dialing.

28

From inside the garage, Jack could smell dinner. He had forgotten that today Jonah had his appointment with Dr. Franklin. Whenever he had these appointments, Vicki would take a half-day off of work, come home early with Jonah, and bake a pot roast— Jack's favorite meal. The aroma of the tender beef filled the house and would linger for several mouth-watering days.

He opened the door from the garage into the kitchen. Vicki stood at the kitchen sink, cleaning a head of romaine for the salad. In the adjoining family room, Jonah knelt in front of the couch, carefully staying between the lines in his favorite coloring book.

"Hi guys!" Jack exclaimed.

Vicki turned from the sink. "Daddy's home!" she called with enthusiasm.

"Daddy's home!" Jonah echoed.

Jack walked over to Vicki, who turned her head to kiss him. He then walked into the family room. "High five!" he said, as he held up his hand. Jonah looked up, his eyes huge and his tongue sticking out of the side of his mouth slightly, and slapped his father's palm with his own. Jack sat down on the couch beside his son and mussed his son's hair with his hand.

"How was your appointment with Dr. Franklin?"

"Goo-ood," Jonah replied in sing-song.

"Did you get a sticker today?"

A BUSTLE IN THE HEDGEROW

Jonah flipped over the back flap of his coloring book to reveal his Buzz Lightyear sticker on the table beneath. Without looking, he handed it over his shoulder to his father.

"Buzz Lightyear. Cool," Jack said as he leaned forward to put the sticker back on the table.

"Yep," Jonah replied.

Jack ran his hand over Jonah's hair one more time before standing up and walking back out to the kitchen. "How was old J.R.?" he asked his wife.

"Fine," she answered. "Odd, as usual."

"He always was a bit of an odd duck," Jack said.

"J.R." had been Jack's nickname for Franklin back in high school. He had moved to Jack's school in 11th grade and joined the swim team. Though only a sophomore at the time, Jack had already solidified his spot as probably the best athlete on the team and one of the leaders. From their first meeting, he had found Franklin to be awkward, and always very serious. Hence, Jack nicknamed him "J.R." after the Larry Hagman character from "Dallas." (He admittedly had never watched "Dallas," but from the ubiquitous previews and articles in *TV Guide*, Jack had surmised that J.R. was a pretty humorless, business-first kind of character.) The nickname stuck among the members of the swim team. In fact, to this day Jack couldn't remember Franklin's actual first name. Not unexpectedly, he had lost track of Franklin after they graduated high school.

Then, a little over a year ago, the impersonal but not unfriendly pair shared a reunion when Vicki and Jack showed up in Dr. Franklin's office for Jonah's first visit. They recognized each other immediately and exchanged pleasantries before the awkward but

131

cordial Dr. Franklin turned his attention to Jonah. Though they weren't crazy about Dr. Franklin's lackluster bedside manner, Jack and Vicki never could complain about the medical care he provided to Jonah.

Jack moved in behind Vicki to put his arms around her waist. He kissed the side of her neck, which always tickled her. She gently and playfully nudged her elbow into his ribs. "Thank you for making pot roast," he whispered.

"We can't stray from tradition," she said. She finished cleaning the last leaf of romaine, put it in the colander, and turned to face Jack. "How was your day? How was your meeting this morning?"

Jack recounted the details of his meeting with Johnson and Prince, including the surprise visit from The Commander in Chief, which produced a wide-eyed, mouth-agape response from Vicki, who mouthed, "Holy shit." He then told her of his meeting with Harringer, and his final decision to pursue the Senate seat.

"Wow," she said. She smiled and shook her head in amazement and excitement. "So you're going to run for the U.S. Senate?!"

"It appears that way," Jack smiled.

"Then we need to celebrate!" she exclaimed.

Jack shook his head. "How about we all just sit down together for a pot roast dinner? There's really nothing to celebrate yet."

"OK," she conceded. She went to the fridge to retrieve a tomato and brought it back to the island in the center of the kitchen, where a cutting board awaited her.

"How can I help?" Jack asked as he hung his suit jacket over the back of one of the kitchen chairs.

"You want to cut up one of the green peppers for the salad?"

"Love to." Jack got a pepper out of the fridge. After finding the second cutting board and a knife, he positioned himself alongside his wife at the island and began dicing the pepper.

"Oooh," Vicki said, as she put down her knife to turn to face Jack. "I know how we can celebrate." She went over to the kitchen table and pulled the brochure from Family Snapshot out of her purse. She held it up in front of her to display it to Jack. "We schedule a family portrait." Her eyes stayed bright, hoping for Jack's approval of the idea.

One of the things Jack still loved most about his wife was her excitability. He always found it endearing, and could not deny her such a simple request. "Sounds like fun. I think my schedule should be pretty flexible for the next few weeks, so why don't you take a look at your schedule and make an appointment."

She smiled, put the brochure down on the kitchen table, walked over to her husband, and threw her arms around his neck. She planted a firm kiss on his lips. "I love you," she said. "And I am so proud of you."

He put his arms around her waist and kissed her back.

29

Corinne put her cell phone down on the desk beside her and pressed STOP on her handheld tape recorder. She had made a habit of recording interviews and other important conversations, though, at this stage in her career, she rarely used the tapes; most of what she used in her writing—even direct quotes— came from her memory.

Heath Reilly had given her some great material and an even better promise. Well, maybe *deal* was a better term than *promise*. In return for using their language—to a certain extent—in her articles about The Playground Predator, Reilly and CASMIRC would supply her with inside information. Much of this would have to stay off the record for now, but this could prove to be invaluable information in compiling research for a book. Fuck the Lamaya Hollows book— this could be her big break.

She knew part of this first interaction served as a test. She needed to carefully include what Reilly had suggested, but do it in such a way that seemed natural. This would likely require her to go back and rewrite nearly the entire article, but she felt it would eventually pay large dividends. If she passed their test by complying with their requests, the information floodgates could and should open up for her.

The first part of their deal upset her the most, for admittedly quite selfish reasons: She could not apply a nickname to the killer. "The Playground Predator" had come to her almost immediately upon sitting down to write the article, and she loved it. She felt certain that this name would stick, both in the press and in her readers' minds. The Playground Predator would become a media icon. She thought, as a nickname, it packed more punch that The Boston Strangler, The Zodiac Killer, and Son of Sam combined. It couldn't measure up to Jack the Ripper, perhaps, but what nickname could. Of course, with a tally of only two murders, The Playground Predator would have to chalk up several more victims to reach the aforementioned killers' status in infamy. But with a nickname like that, he definitely had an edge. As Corinne well knew, the more iconic the subject, the more sales in the true crime volume chronicling his exploits. For now, in order to honor the deal, she would put the nickname on the back burner. Eventually she would find a way to use it, just not now.

She understood the reasons behind this first stipulation, which Reilly had shared with her. CASMIRC thought that their killer had a thirst for fame. Giving him a name only fed this desire. They wanted to make the killer as anonymous as possible and asked Corinne to spend most of her time in the article discussing the victims. When referring to the unknown killer, Reilly had fed her some quotes that she actually liked. Following this aspect of the deal would be no problem.

Much to Corinne's pleasure, the topic of Jackson Byrne's involvement in this investigation— or, more appropriately, lack thereof— remained fair game. She had asked Reilly about Jack's involvement, to which he replied, "At this time Special Agent Byrne is not involved in this investigation." When pressed further, Reilly would not comment.

What did this mean? she wondered. Clearly Jack hadn't done anything to warrant dismissal from CASMIRC. *Had he?* She felt confident that Jack wouldn't give her a straight answer. She couldn't spend much more time contemplating this minor aspect of her story, as she knew she had to get to work on her article; press time stood a mere four hours away.

Corinne reminded herself that a good reporter knows how to use her resources. So she sent an e-mail out to all of her colleagues at *The Post*, asking if anyone had any information about Jackson Byrne. He had enjoyed some minor celebrity recently, so perhaps his visage would show up on someone's radar. At this point, it seemed worth a shot.

After this she got to work on her article, beginning by painfully erasing "The Playground Predator" from her headline.

DAY FIVE:
FRIDAY

30

Jack awoke early Friday morning, as usual, though he really had nothing specifically to do today. He planned on going into his office in Quantico to work on getting his personal belongings out of his desk and continuing to tie up loose ends. First, though, he helped Jonah get ready for school, then left to drive him there at the same time as Vicki left for work. On his way home, his Blackberry vibrated, signaling that he had received a text message. As a responsible driver, he waited until after he had parked back in his garage to open the text as he got out of the car.

It was from Philip Prince. *Really?* Jack thought. *That old coot is sending text messages? The world never ceases to amaze me.*

He opened the text:

U read The Post 2day? Looks liked youve been outed.

At first Jack had no idea what this meant. He initially paid less attention to the content than he did to the lack of correct grammar and punctuation. Even Philip Prince lost his etiquette when communicating via text. He read the message again, then went into their study on the first floor, where the laptop sat on top of the desk.

Outed? he thought. *What could that possibly mean? I'm not gay. Right?*

Once the computer had gotten into Windows, he went straight to TheWashingtonPost.com. He scrolled down the page, but didn't find anything that grabbed his eye immediately. Reluctantly, he typed his name into the search bar in the upper right corner of the page. Within seconds the site returned his search results. He didn't need to look past the first headline; he knew he had found the one Prince referred to in his text.

31

For the second night in a row, Randall hadn't slept at all. He didn't feel the least bit tired, though. He didn't need sleep. Not when he felt like this.

He needed to continue preparing his Work. He had gone to Best Buy the day before to get supplies. On his way home he stopped by his favorite record store. He found a copy of the album "Elephant" by The White Stripes. He had listened to both sides of the album nine times overnight.

He went to his computer to perform his daily online search for articles about his Work. He went to Google.com and typed in Adrianna Cottrell.

He hated how people used the word "google" as a verb. The online search engine got its name from the term "googol," which is the number 10 to the power of 100, presumably because the search engine provides a very large number of responses to a search request. Randall had used the term googol on more than one occasion during his days training as a mathematical and electrical engineer, mostly in the abstract, of course. But he had never used it as a verb. He refused to use the name of the search engine in any capacity other than the name of a search engine.

The first few entries in his search results represented sites he had visited before. They bore the color purple rather than blue. The third link down corresponded to a new one. From *The Washington Post.*

BEN MILLER

Randall felt a chill of excitement. *The Post* certainly signalled a step up from WHTM.com out of York, PA.

He clicked on the link.

The White Stripes' track "Seven Nation Army" kept playing over and over in his head. Randall had heard the song dozens of times, even before last night, but it never got old for him. He considered it their opus. Jack White's voice both haunted and enchanted him, as always.

The title at the top of the page brought a huge smile to Randall's face:

FBI CONNECTS CHILD MURDERS IN TWO STATES *by Corinne O Loughlin, Staff Writer*

He recognized the name Corinne O'Loughlin. She had followed the Hollows murder for *The Post*, and she appeared a few times in Jack Byrne's book. This was huge. This was *The Post*.

He began reading the article, savoring every word, every letter even, as if each character on the screen were a tiny morsel of delicious food, settling on his tongue as he extracted every last bit of taste. He had read about his Work before, of course, but up to this point nothing equaled this sensation. Reading about his work in *The Post* was a thick juicy filet mignon, compared to the McDonald's hamburger of WHTM.

The article began by introducing Stephanie McBurney. Apparently she liked to go skiing, both water and snow. She had a new baby brother at home. She liked school, especially science class.

140

Then the article jumped into the life of Adrianna Cottrell. She mostly kept to herself, though she had some friends at school. She loved to read, and had even written a few short stories about a little girl growing up in a small town.

Though this part of the article made Randall a bit uncomfortable, he continued to read carefully, not missing a word. He didn't like thinking about the girls or the families they left behind. Not that he felt remorse, and certainly not regret; he would just rather move on to more exciting reading.

Then there it began:

Other than being nine years old, what do these two girls, living in small cities 65 miles apart, have in common?

Both were murdered. Both in the last month, both by strangulation, both within the seemingly safe and friendly confines of their favorite playground. According to the FBI, both likely by the same killer.

"We are currently assisting local authorities in both York and Frederick to investigate these crimes," said Special Agent Heath Reilly of the Child Abduction and Serial Murder Investigative Resource Center, or CASMIRC, a special division of the FBI headquartered in Quantico, Va. "At this point we are working under the assumption that these horrible crimes are the work of one person: a nameless, faceless killer preying on defenseless young children."

Reilly further commented that, at this point, they do not believe there are more murders connected to this killer.

"Based on the unskilled and somewhat clumsy nature of these murders, we do not think our killer has struck before," Reilly said in an exclusive interview.

Randall stopped reading for a moment. Suddenly this didn't feel as exhilarating as it had before.

Why were Reilly's words co cruel? And why was Reilly the one giving a quote to this cunt reporter? Where is Jack Byrne?

He took a deep breath and continued reading:

Currently, details of the crimes are limited.

Randall paused again, reconsidering his first question. He went back to the preceding paragraphs, focusing on the words "nameless" and "faceless," "unskilled" and "clumsy."

He jumped back into the article where he had left off. O'Loughlin recounts the details of the crime scenes, circumstances, lack of witnesses, etc.

No mention of the notes.

Randall's last note had read, in Thai, "I want to be somebody."

CASMIRC had, to an extent, misinterpreted his last note. Of course, Randall had anticipated that they would make that interpretation, at least for now. Reilly had used specific language to try to insult him, to try to make him feel like a "nobody" when, ostensibly, he had expressed his desire to be "somebody."

Perfect. All continued to go as planned.

But where's Byrne?

142

Both local authorities in York and Frederick stated that they have no suspects right now, confirmed by CASMIRC.

CASMIRC was made famous approximately one year ago for its involvement in the investigation of the Lamaya Hollows murder. The lead investigator Special Agent Jackson Byrne attained subsequent greater fame and minor celebrity status for his book *Class Dismissed*, chronicling the investigation and highlighting the systematic flaws that led up to the Hollows murder.

According to Special Agent Reilly, however, Byrne is not currently involved in this investigation. Reilly refused to comment further. Sources within *The Washington Post* state that Byrne held a meeting yesterday with Democratic Senate Majority Leader Montgomery Johnson. Pundits speculate that Byrne may be considering running for political office.

For the McBurney and Cottrell families, all agencies have assured that they will continue to work together to solve these crimes before the killer can strike again.

Randall's gaze despondently fell from the screen down to his keyboard.

"Motherfucker," he muttered aloud to the empty room.

No Jack Byrne. Nor his minor celebrity status.

For a moment, Randall couldn't think. His mind filled with rage. Red, hot, blinding rage.

Byrne played an integral role in Randall's Work. He had to have him. Could his Work still function without Jack?

No, he thought immediately. *No.*

He brought his hand to his face, rubbed his forehead. He reconsidered, contemplated his Work. *Well, yes, it could still be done. Somehow.*

His Work was nothing short of genius, the birth child of a brilliant mind. He could adjust it, tweak it, find another way to fulfill his Destiny.

But I don't want it to.

I must find a way to adjust the path of my Work to reach the same conclusion, the same breath-taking climax.

He hated that many writers used the word "climax" synonymously with "orgasm." He always used "climax" in the literary sense, and any other use bothered him. The world was so obsessed with sex it often sickened him.

He looked over at his bookshelf and once again pulled down his tattered copy of *Class Dismissed.* He hoped to find inspiration within its pages, a spark to ignite the now necessary change in his Work.

Within minutes an epiphany struck him like a bolt of lightning, as epiphanies often do.

He turned his attention back to the computer. He had some research to do, but he knew as well as he knew his own name that this new plan would succeed.

His Work was back on track.

32

"I'm just kind of surprised that I find out about my son's huge career change – into politics, no less—by reading the morning paper."

"Sorry, Mom. Things have been moving a little fast lately," Jack countered through his Bluetooth. His mother had called on his cell five minutes after he'd left the house. He pressed lightly on the brake as traffic slowed ahead of him. Rain fell hard onto the tarmac, which always slowed down his commute. "I just had that meeting yesterday morning, and talks with Philip and some other people are still in the works. I had no idea anything would show up in the morning *Post.*"

"So it's true?" Florence Byrne asked. Jack couldn't tell if he sensed sadness or exhilaration in his mother's voice, but if he had to bet, he'd say the former.

"I'm pretty sure, yes," he replied. "But, as I said, things still need to be ironed out."

"Is it in place of that jackass Schultz?" His mother always had a way of getting right to the point.

Jack chuckled. "Yes, Rupert Schultz. I guess he has been too much of a jackass, even for Capitol Hill."

"Well, just be careful. You know what they say: 'Politics makes for strange bedfellows.'"

What an odd thing to say, Jack thought. "Got it, Mom. I'm on my way to work. I'll talk to you over the weekend, OK?"

"OK. Be careful—it's raining."

Jack regarded the deluge around him. "Thanks. Bye, Mom."

"Bye, Son."

Jack tapped on his Bluetooth to end the call. Before he could remove the device from his ear, though, it signaled that he had another incoming call. He glanced down at his Blackberry in the console to see the caller ID: Caleb Goodnight. He pressed the center of his ear piece once again.

"Hello, Caleb."

"Hello, Jack. Have I caught you at a bad time?"

"No, not really. I'm just driving into the office in the middle of a glorious mid-Atlantic rainstorm. How are you doing?"

"I'm doing well. The real question is: How are you doing, my friend?"

"Good." Jack's reply was purposefully terse. He felt sure that Corinne's article prompted Caleb's call also, but he decided to wait to have Caleb bring it up.

"And what's this I hear about quitting your job and running for office? Have you become smitten with the public spotlight?"

"Something like that," Jack acquiesced. Traffic slowed to a crawl. "How did you hear about it?"

"I read *The Post* most every day. I'm one of the few New Yorkers who believes that accomplished journalism does exist outside of *The New York Times*."

"Right. No, this unique opportunity has presented itself, and I feel I could really try to accomplish some important things."

"Oh, yeah," Caleb replied. "Such as?"

Jack paused. "Is this an interview?"

"No, of course not, Jack. I'm just curious. But mostly I'm excited for you."

"Thanks." Jack sensed the genuineness in Caleb's enthusiasm. Traffic in Jack's middle lane began to pick up.

"Speaking of interview, though…" Caleb began, smiling. "I think having you back on the show—maybe in a couple of months— could be a good opportunity for you."

"Maybe."

"And for me, of course. I'm not completely altruistic," Caleb admitted.

"Of course." Already Jack felt himself grow weary of talking on this subject. Just then a blue Camry pulled out in front of Jack from the slower right lane. Jack had to hit his brakes pretty hard. "Asshole," he mumbled.

"Oh, sorry, Jack, I didn't mean anything…" Caleb began apologizing.

"No," Jack laughed, "not you, Caleb. I was referring to the asshole who just cut me off in order to go about three miles per hour faster."

"Oh, that asshole."

"Yeah. Hey, how about I call you back sometime in the next few weeks, Caleb. I still need to get a lot of the details of this stuff straightened out."

"Sure, Jack. I hope it all goes well—that's the purpose of my call. I'll be pulling for you."

"Thanks. That means a lot," Jack said, matching the earnestness of his friend.

"OK. Cheers, then," Caleb signed off.

"Yeah, cheers," Jack echoed reluctantly. He disliked using the popular British phrase "cheers" to close a conversation; to him it

147

seemed a bit pretentious when used by Americans. Somehow, though, Caleb Goodnight could make it sound sincere.

As the rain began to ease up, traffic thankfully moved a little more quickly. Jack did not have any pressing business awaiting him at the office, yet he still felt anxious to get there.

He reminded himself how quickly news travels, especially in the era of online newspapers, text messages, etc. He appreciated Caleb's— and, to a lesser extent, his mother's—call, but it unnerved him a little that so many people now knew about such a personal matter. He made a mental note to call Corinne O'Loughlin later, but he wanted to gather his thoughts first. His main question remained why a crime reporter decided to write about a political topic. It seemed a little outside her purview, and it seemed a little personal.

He arrived at work a short while later, went through the main secure entrance, and up to the third floor. No sooner had he gotten to his desk when his Blackberry began vibrating on his belt. He looked at the display: Melissa Hollows.

Melissa? he thought. He assumed she was calling to comment on this morning's article as well, but still it struck him as odd. He had not spoken to her in eight or nine months. Perhaps she wanted to plead with him to reconsider this pending career change, due to his involvement in solving her daughter's murder. Or, perhaps the opposite: to congratulate him on catapulting himself onto the political stage. But deep down he knew these weren't correct. Regardless, he didn't want to speak with her right now. He didn't feel like talking to anyone about this topic anymore, especially not Melissa Hollows.

A BUSTLE IN THE HEDGEROW

He let it go to voicemail and holstered his phone back on his hip. He decided he would listen to the voicemail later; he had other work to do now and didn't want to get distracted.

Weeks, months, and even years later, Jack would wonder how the trajectory of his life—and the lives of countless others— might have differed if he had taken that call.

33

Lamaya Hollows went missing on Monday, April 30, 2012. The NFL Draft had been held the weekend before, so she didn't see much of her father. He spent Thursday night, Friday night, and all day Saturday with his teammates, watching to see who their Redskins would claim from the ranks of college hopefuls for the upcoming season. Therefore Lamaya spent most of the weekend with her mother, which didn't bother her one bit. They had gone shopping all the way downtown at Georgetown Park, her mother's favorite place to shop. Lamaya found it more appropriate for grown-ups than kids—they didn't even have a good toy store!—but she enjoyed it nevertheless because her mother had enjoyed it so much. Plus she got some new summer clothes, which was pretty awesome.

Monday morning she went to school as usual. Her mother dropped her off, with her father scheduled to pick her up at the end of the day. After school she called him to ask if she could walk home. She and her friend Jennifer, who lived six houses down from them, wanted to enjoy the warm spring day. Besides, it was one of the few days that they didn't have field hockey practice, so she hoped to get some exercise. As added pressure, Lamaya shared that Jennifer's parents had already agreed to the idea.

Lamond Hollows considered this reasoning. They lived just a little over a mile-and-a-half from Washington Country Day School, and all the connecting neighborhoods seemed very safe. She had walked home a few dozen times before, so Lamond didn't feel that he needed to give it much thought. He said sure, and the girls began their walk.

A BUSTLE IN THE HEDGEROW

Jennifer arrived home safely at 3:43 in the afternoon. Her mother greeted her at the door and waved at Lamaya, who waved back as she continued walking down the sidewalk. The two of them were the last two people to see Lamaya Hollows that day. She never showed up at her home.

At 4:21 pm, Lamond Hollows called Jennifer Horowitz's house and spoke to her mother, who informed him of Jennifer's uneventful, safe return from school, and of having seen Lamaya trek past on her seemingly uneventful way home. Though they lived in an upper-class suburb with large estates, surely it shouldn't take her over half-an-hour to walk six houses. Five minutes later, Melissa Hollows returned home from the grocery store. Lamond met her in the garage and shared the news of their daughter's late return. At the end of his discourse, both immediately and instinctively turned their eyes to the back of the garage; her bicycle stood in its usual spot, leaning on its kickstand. Without unloading the groceries, she set out in her Escalade and he in his Mercedes to troll the neighborhood looking for their child.

With a speed limit of 20 miles per hour, it took approximately twelve minutes to drive through every loop, street, and cul-de-sac in their subdivision. They each drove the circuit twice, going slower than the posted limit as they called out to their daughter, scanned the sidewalks, driveways, gardens, and bushes. They returned home within a minute of each other. Melissa decided that she would call 9-1-1 and stay at home, in case Lamaya returned. Lamond would go out on foot into the neighborhood. Both retained a calm exterior, but inside they each filled with dread.

151

BEN MILLER

The call came into the 9-1-1 operator at 4:59 pm. By 5:12 pm the state police posted the reflexive Amber Alert, and at 5:14 the first police officers arrived at the Hollows' home. Detective Greta Wegener from the Missing Persons Division in Montgomery County arrived at the home shortly before half-past five. With only about two hours of daylight remaining, she quickly organized a search of the entire neighborhood, all surrounding neighborhoods, and the spaces in between. All teams were equipped with police-grade flashlights, so the search continued into the evening, and then into the night. At 11:30 pm, Detective Wegener halted the search until daybreak. She had seen group exhaustion set in before, so she didn't want to risk even one search party member losing focus; this could be the difference between finding crucial clues and walking right past them.

Greta Wegener knew well that about half of all kidnapping cases are perpetrated by family members. Therefore, shortly after the area search commenced, she and her partner John Min questioned Mr. and Mrs. Hollows for almost ninety minutes. Lamond had not left the house all afternoon. Though alone at home, he spent most of the last hour before calling the Horowitz home on the phone with his agent. Both the agent and cell phone records would later corroborate this. Melissa had been to the grocery store after getting her weekly manicure and pedicure. Her manicurist, her pedicurist—two different people working in the same salon—the grocery store clerk, and grocery store video surveillance would later corroborate this. Wegener and Min then interviewed Mr. and Mrs. Hollows separately, and neither parent suspected that the other had anything to do with their daughter's disappearance. Their individual descriptions of their relationship matched nearly verbatim: Not a perfect marriage, but certainly better than most. They loved each other, and they both loved their daughter.

Initially, neither parent could think of anyone who would want to do harm to their family. They had no known enemies and no significant debts. Of course, Lamond's career as a professional athlete and their combined celebrity status served as a wild card in this initial investigation. Wegener, however, went with her instinct at the onset to treat this as a typical missing child case; if this yielded little to nothing, she would deal with the possible obsessed-celebrity-fanatic angle secondarily.

Detective Min continued with the Hollows while Wegener went to talk to the Horowitz family. They, and the dozens of neighbors interviewed later that evening and in the following days, shed no new light onto the case. They did not see anyone or anything suspicious. They confirmed the timeline established by the Hollows' story. They all found Lamaya Hollows and her parents to be perfectly well-meaning people and pleasant neighborhood citizens (though two separate interviewees did complain briefly about Lamond's holding penalty in the Wild Card round of the playoffs two years ago, which negated a 46-yard touchdown run and, in their eyes, resulted in the Redskins' loss).

Miraculously, though the Amber Alert became a topic in the 11 o-clock news that night, the significance that it was Lamond Hollows' child who had gone missing did not hit the local news until the 12 pm news broadcast the following day. One neighbor had called ESPN the night before to spread the word of Hollows' daughter's disappearance, but, with Lamond Hollows and his agent not answering calls and the Redskins' office refusing to comment, the

153

cable giant did not run the story until it could be confirmed the following day.

By that next evening, a media frenzy had begun. The story ran on regular news shows, (CNN, Headline News, etc.), sports news (ESPN, NFL Network, etc.), and entertainment news (Inside Edition, Entertainment Tonight, etc.). Various speculations came from a variety of sources, most of which the investigative team could quickly dismiss. One theory from FoxSports.com implicated one of Lamond Hollows' teammates, DeJuan Masters. Masters, the Redskins' starting Pro Bowl center, had recently been accused of domestic violence against his girlfriend, a 19-year-old high school dropout. Given the alleged history of violence against women, this assertion had to be investigated fully, which Wegener herself completed quickly: Masters had an airtight alibi (with his 19-year-old girlfriend, no less, who had found it in her heart to forgive him and had previously dropped the charges). It was later discovered that this theory had originated from a FoxSports staffer who was a rabid New York Giants fan, trying to bring ruination to the Redskins. The network promptly fired him.

Due to the high-profile nature of the case, and the quick decline in incoming information, Wegener enlisted the assistance of the FBI by contacting CASMIRC. Jackson Byrne arrived with his team the following morning, 64 hours after Lamaya Hollows had gone missing. Officially the investigation still bore the label of a Missing Persons case, but most involved felt that, at this point, they were most likely looking for a body. Nearly ninety per cent of missing persons not found in the first 48 hours were never found alive.

Shortly after 11 am on the morning of Thursday, May 3, Lamond and Melissa Hollows held a press conference to beg for the safe return of their daughter. Her school photo was shown for what had to be the hundredth time on national TV. The phone number of a toll-free hotline scrolled across the bottom of the screen repeatedly.

That afternoon they received a phone call from the kidnapper, demanding a ransom of $65,000. They traced the call to a home in southern New Jersey. Local FBI agents raided the home less than two hours after the call, and found a 43-year-old schizophrenic who had compiled $55,000 of gambling debts. He later claimed the extra $10,000 he asked for would serve as his "nest egg," declining to further elucidate the meaning behind this.

FBI agents and local police questioned every registered sex offender in the area without garnering any compelling suspects. Given that the disappearance occurred during the end of a traditional work day, the majority of them had easily confirmed alibis. Those offenders without alibis complied with cursory searches of their homes without any suspicious findings.

Each member of the Washington Redskins organization agreed to an interview. All felt awful about the Hollows' situation. Daniel Snyder, the outspoken owner of the NFL franchise, offered a $250,000 reward for any information that led to the safe return of Lamaya Hollows and/or the arrest and conviction of the perpetrators of this crime. As expected, this brought in thousands of tips, none of which served useful.

The following week, while investigators resumed their questioning of all of the employees and parents associated with Lamaya's school, a call came into the local 9-1-1 center from a local waste removal employee named Eugene Kermichael. He phoned from the penultimate stop on their route, a dumpster behind a recently constructed strip mall— still only half occupied by retail stores— located less than five miles from the Hollows' home. He and his co-worker had found a body lying on the hillside behind the strip mall. Wrapped in a white sheet, the figure on the knoll resembled a childhood notion of an Egyptian mummy. Kermichael guessed it contained a child, based on the size and shape. His curiosity drove him to pull back the first layer of the cotton sheet, which confirmed his suspicion. Having watched the news—and having been a lifelong Redskins' fan—he knew the case of the missing Hollows girl well and quickly recognized her face.

As such, as silently but inevitably expected by many, on the afternoon of Monday, May 14, 2012, the Lamaya Hollows Missing Persons case turned into the Lamaya Hollows Abduction/Homicide.

34

Dylan Harringer had assembled his team in the conference room to discuss the Cottrell and McBurney murders. Normally these meetings took place at the end of the day, but, with the weekend coming up and Corinne O'Loughlin's piece in the paper that morning, Harringer wanted to get a jump on things. He stood in the front right corner of the room, the chair beside him angled so that, when seated, Harringer could see all his agents in the chairs to his left as well as the dry-erase board in the front. Heath Reilly stood at the ready beside the board, with a black marker in his right hand.

Reilly had taken the reins of this investigation so far. Though Harringer had not yet officially named anyone Lead Investigator, Reilly led the meeting yesterday when they discussed what information they wanted to leak to the media. Harringer had decided he would give Reilly a trial run at Lead over the next few days, but he silently reserved the right to name someone else if Reilly proved himself inefficient, or, more likely, a pain in the ass.

"I think we've had ample time to review the facts of the cases so far, so I wanted to spend some time delving into our un-sub. I want to generate some ideas about our killer and try to answer some questions that might help us see where to go next," Harringer said to commence the meeting. He sat down and opened a hand to Reilly at the front of the room. "Reilly…"

"Thanks, sir," Reilly began. "As you all know based on our meeting yesterday, we have developed a strategy for dealing with our un-sub through the media. One component of our strategy is to keep him feeling as anonymous as possible, hoping he will become offended and make a gesture, big or small, that might reveal his identity. That being said..." He turned his back to the group to face the board. In large letters he wrote across the top:

THE PLAYGROUND PREDATOR

"Corinne O'Loughlin from The Post mentioned this as the name she was going to use to refer to our un-sub, and I like it."

Harringer interrupted, with his bulky arms folded across his chest. "I think you all know how I feel about nicknames, but for those of you who don't..." He looked up, shooting daggers directly into Reilly's eyes. "I hate them."

Strike one, Harringer noted to himself.

"But," he continued, "since the cat's out of the bag and many of you will use this nickname informally anyway, I just want to remind you that this will strictly be for internal use only. I do not want to see this name showing up in the news media anywhere."

Camilla asked the obvious, "It came from O'Loughlin. How do we know she won't use it?"

"Pretty sure she won't," Reilly answered. "That's part of our deal for giving her exclusive quotes and a small amount of inside info. Only if it serves our purpose, that is. If she breaks her promise, we are done with her."

"OK," Camilla conceded.

Reilly had asked Harringer before the meeting if he could use the informal moniker during the investigation. Harringer had conceded, but he had an ulterior motive. He still had some fresh agents in his ranks, not to mention Terry Friesz from linguistics. His first SAC Ronald Van Wyk had taught him this trick early in his days with the Bureau: give innocuous yet "classified" terminology or information early in the investigation to see if anything leaked. If not, he could trust his people. If so, he would have issues.

"Our first topic is motive," Reilly said, as he wrote "**1. MOTIVE**" at the top left of the board under the title. "Based on the killer's communication so far, through the notes in the pockets, we are working under the assumption that infamy serves as his main motivation right now. Are there other thoughts?"

As expected, Camilla had already formed some theories of her own. "Hatred of women, or little girls," she postulated.

"OK." Reilly jotted this down on the board under "**INFAMY**." "Other thoughts?" He waited several seconds in silence before turning back to the board. "All righty then." Though in the past couple of years he had mustered the restraint to not say this phrase with Jim Carrey's Ace Ventura inflection, he couldn't help continuing to use the phrase. "The next thing to discuss is the notes themselves." He gave this topic its own title on the dry-erase board before turning back to face his audience. "Before we discuss content, let's ask about the languages. Why? Why does he use foreign languages?"

After a brief contemplative moment, Camilla asked, "So far we have Thai and Serbian, right?"

"Right," Reilly confirmed.

Camilla turned in her seat to look at Friesz, who, as per usual, sat in the second row. "Terry, do you give any significance to the use of those two languages?"

Friesz scratched his right temple as he pondered the question. "Not that I can think of. They are very dissimilar languages. They do not share common roots. Obviously Serbia has been notorious for civil war and much political unrest, but the same cannot be said of Thailand."

Amanda Lundquist spoke up from her spot in the far left of the front row. "Can we assume that our un-sub has a background in linguistics?"

Reilly nodded and turned to write this on the board.

"I doubt it," Friesz said, stopping Reilly before he wrote on the board. Reilly turned back around to face Friesz, as did everyone else in the room. However, Friesz offered nothing more.

Camilla remembered how much Friesz enjoyed the spotlight, as he waited for others to extract the information from him. It may have functioned as a successful teaching technique in his days as a professor, but, in The Bureau, it became tiresome quickly. She refrained from rolling her eyes, but she did throw a hint of sarcasm into her question. "Why, Professor?"

Friesz, apparently detecting her mockery, glanced at Camilla from the corner of his eye. "Both phrases are rather simple, with very literal translations. They do not display the subtlety of either language. A linguist, in my estimation, would relish the opportunity to use these languages to their fullest. It seems much more likely to me that the person who wrote these notes used a translation dictionary, or, more probably, an online translation application. There are dozens available for free, including Google, Yahoo!, and other popular search engines."

"If this were done online, then, could it be tracked?" Harringer said from his post at the front of the room.

"Unfortunately no," Friesz answered dismissively. "We've run into this issue with some other crimes before. If we had the individual's computer, we could trace back to find out the input into the websites. However, it's impossible for Yahoo! to search its output from its translator application, except by individual entry. In other words, we can't go to Yahoo! and ask them to search for which computer entered a search for 'I do not really hate you' into Serbian. All they can do is go through their output, one by one, to find which one it is. They get around half a million hits to their translator every day. Then there's Google, Bing, and other sites. So, even if you had someone working full time on this, it would be virtually impossible to find your guy this way."

The room fell quiet for a few moments, the collective excitement dying down from this lost potential lead. The silence broke when the laconic Charlie Shaver said in a low monotone, "What if it's not the phrases that's important?"

The group turned to face him, sitting on the far left end of the front row. A quizzical expression filled every face but his.

"We have been assuming that these phrases are meant to explain his motivation. But, what if it's code for something else? Or what if it's the original languages themselves that contain the message?" he continued, still in his usual droning delivery, looking down at his notebook in his lap, where he had written the phrases both in their original language and with their corresponding English translations.

After another pause, Harringer pressed. "Keep going."

Shaver finally looked up from his notebook at Harringer, then at the rest. He introduced some welcomed inflection into his voice. "I don't know."

Reilly walked over behind Harringer in the front right corner of the room, grabbed the easel they had used for previous meetings, and brought it over to the center of the room beside the dry erase board. He flipped back the cover page on the oversized tablet to reveal the Thai phrase that Friesz had written during their meeting two days earlier. He put two short dashes to the right of it and wrote, "**THAI**." Underneath the phrase he wrote the English translation, "**I WANT TO BE SOMEBODY**." Reilly flipped the page back to reveal a fresh blank one. He turned to face the others, holding the pen towards Friesz. "Terry, do you mind writing the first phrase?"

"Sure," Friesz said, as he stood and approached the easel. He took the pen from Reilly, and wrote the first phrase found on Stephanie McBurney on the sheet, again from memory. He followed Reilly's format by scribbling two dashes before the word "**Serbian**," and underneath the English translation, "**I do not really hate you**."

"So, this one was first, yeah?" Shaver asked.

"Right," Reilly replied.

"OK, so we have Serbian first, then Thai. Maybe he's writing a message with those, like the letters 'S' and 'T'. Maybe he's trying to spell a phrase. His name, maybe? Steve something?"

"Christ, I hope not," Harringer spouted. "That means he's planning on killing a lot more victims to spell out his entire name."

"Or could the phrases be code," Amanda posited. "Maybe we're supposed to crack some code that reveals a hidden meaning to the phrases."

Harringer shrugged, shaking his head a little. "I suppose that's possible, but why embed them in another code— a different language? That's seems like too many layers to be realistic to me."

"Maybe," Amanda admitted.

Reilly, who had been jotting down these thoughts in abbreviated sentences on the dry erase board, tried to bring the thinking back towards their original theory. "I feel that these messages carry so much meaning on their own that we don't necessarily need to think of them as code. Perhaps he used the foreign languages to show off how smart he is—or at least how smart he thinks he is."

Quietly sitting in her chair, taking this all in, Camilla finally spoke up. "What if it was just to get to us?"

Harringer turned his shoulder's to face her. He had always valued Camilla's contributions, so he felt excited to hear her hypothesis. "Explain."

"Local PD's don't have linguistics departments, and I doubt most state PD's do either. If our killer is smart or savvy enough to be aware of this, by using foreign languages to write his little notes, he basically insured that his case would get to the FBI. If he really does desire notoriety, getting the FBI involved in his case would seem to naturally escalate things on a broader level, right?"

Amanda's eyes lit up as she jumped on this bandwagon. "It would also create a quicker link between the two murders. If we hadn't gotten involved, I think it's unlikely that the detectives in York and Frederick would have linked the two so quickly."

"And it's that link that led to the article in *The Post* today, which presumably is exactly what he wanted," Camilla finished.

"Though I'm sure the content wasn't to his liking," Reilly chimed in proudly.

"This makes a lot of sense," Harringer declared. "OK, what about the timing of everything?" He wanted to move on, and he felt that Reilly was beginning to lose control of the tempo of the meeting.

"Well, they were both killed three weeks apart. He's not working on a lunar cycle or anything batshit like that," Reilly answered.

"They were both Mondays, right?" Shaver offered.

"OK. Why?" Harringer posed to the group. "Why Mondays? And why did it start now?"

"Maybe he has off work on Mondays," Amanda said.

"Does he work?" Reilly asked.

Amanda turned her hands up. "I don't know. Don't we assume he has some sort of income? We assume he has a car to get to the sites, he has internet access, the means to plan these acts out..."

"Perhaps he's independently wealthy," Reilly countered.

"Or recently laid off," Freisz said from the back of the room. In the current economic crisis, several of his former colleagues in Academia—along with thousands of other Americans—had lost their jobs as their employers favored less experienced, and thus less expensive, workers.

"Sure. Maybe that was the inciting event that sparked the killing spree," Shaver said. "Maybe he got caught looking at kiddie porn at work, got fired— on a Monday, no less— so now he's taking out his rage on little girls."

Reilly's eyes lit up at this new, seemingly cohesive theory, but Harringer could sense the facetiousness of Shaver's comment. "Charlie?" Harringer admonished.

Shaver sat up straight in his chair. "Sorry, sir, but I think we leave profiling to the BAU. We could sit here and imagine every possible scenario and create a profile of our un-sub with any number of characteristics based on little nuances of the case. But the reality is that it's all horseshit until we can put together the evidence that leads us to someone. It's one thing to review the evidence, like the notes, but I think now we're sailing without a compass."

"Your opinion is noted," Harringer said.

Reilly agreed. "But I think considering the timing could be important. Obviously we want to catch this guy before another kid ends up dead. If there is any pattern to the timing, then maybe we have some kind of a shot."

Now Camilla felt the team going off on an unproductive tangent. "But how can we get a pattern out of only two events? And with such disparate locations—York, PA and Frederick— how are we ever going to predict where he might strike next?"

Of course, they all had no way of knowing that their Predator had already struck again.

35

Outside the room and down the hall, Jack sat at his desk, presumably for one of the final times. Most of the files within his drawers and file cabinet would have to remain with CASMIRC, but he wanted to sort through them himself. When Harringer passed by earlier on his way to the meeting, Jack told him he was organizing them. He didn't share that he also took some pleasure in going over some of those memories, despite the grotesqueries of the cases. Jack often—but not always— found pride in their solution, or at least in his approach to finding one. Not surprisingly, the Lamaya Hollows case left him with the most complex mix of emotions of any case he had ever worked.

He leafed through the manila folder with photos of the site where the trash men discovered her body. He vividly recalled sitting in an interview with Lamaya's French teacher, Mrs. Smith—*What an oddly boring name for a French teacher,* he remembered thinking— when his cell phone rang with news of the body's discovery. While other agents interviewed parents and other school personnel, Jack assigned himself the duty of interviewing all of Lamaya's past and present teachers at the school. The mundane Mrs. Smith embodied his twelfth interview of the day, and he had begun to grow a little weary. After the brief and exhilarating phone call, he excused himself from the interview, which he never did complete, and drove to the crime scene.

Several local officers, including the soon-to-be-replaced lead investigators Detectives Wegener and Min from Missing Persons, had already arrived on the scene when Jack arrived. Local media had just begun to gather, and national media was not far behind. A forensics team of at least a dozen people stood and crouched in the perimeter around the body, still shrouded in white. Jack walked toward Wegener and Min, who stood speaking with two tall, well-dressed men in one corner of the driveway, about twenty feet from the corpse. The four stopped speaking and turned toward Jack; it was the first unspoken gesture signifying that this case belonged to him.

"Detectives," Jack said as he shook hands once again with Wegener and Min.

"Special Agent Byrne," Wegener said as she grasped his hand. "This is Detective Bennett McIlhenney and Detective Brian Minert from Homicide." She nodded to each of the two men in turn as she introduced them.

Jack shook their hands, trying surreptitiously to study their faces. They looked so much alike—both tall, thin, pale white men with short-cropped dark hair and long, flat faces— Jack predicted he would have difficulty telling them apart. "Call me Jack," he invited. "What do we know here?"

"OK, Jack. People call me Mac." McIlhenney spoke first, in one of the deepest bass voices Jack had ever heard. Jack's initial apprehension about confusing the two detectives immediately abated. "We have a positive ID on the body over there as Lamaya Hollows," McIlhenney began. "She was discovered shortly after eleven hundred this morning by sanitation workers who had come to empty this dumpster. The same two men had been here on Friday and did not see anything over there."

Jack turned to his right to look at the location of the body. "No way they'd have missed it."

"Exactly," McIlhenney bellowed. "One of the men pulled back the top layer of the sheet—wearing gloves, thank God—recognized the face, and called 9-1-1."

Jack turned to his left to look at the back of the strip mall. His eyes moved up to the top of the wall, and he scanned the entire façade from right to left.

McIlhenney witnessed this and confirmed Jack's observation. "No video surveillance in the back of the building."

Jack turned back to face the detectives. "What about the front of the building?"

"There's a small camera at the entrance of each store, but only 4 of the 8 cameras are activated because not all of the available spaces have been leased yet," McIlhenney answered.

"We don't think they'll be helpful, though," added Minert, his somewhat nasally baritone lacking the unique timbre of his partner's voice. "We looked at them real quick. They cover very little of the parking lot."

"We have officers interviewing all of the stores' employees right now," McIlhenney said. "So far, nothing."

As it turned out, the last employee to leave the strip mall the day before had left at 6 pm, though she left through the front. No one had come out of any of the back entrances of any of the stores since about 5:20 pm. That employee, one of the instructors from the Yoga studio, had thrown out some trash into the dumpster. She swore that she did not see anything in the hillside on the other side of the driveway. No one employed at the building admitted to seeing anything or anyone suspicious the entire day before.

Now at his desk, Jack flipped through the photos in the folder in his hands. With each snapshot of the scene, the memory of seeing it with his own eyes flashed in his mind. He could even recall the chemical odor coming from the dumpster, overpowering the freshness of the spring air.

Deeper into the folder, the autopsy photos followed the collection from behind the dumpster. This brought with it first the memory of a completely different smell, one all too familiar to Jack. As he thought about the experience now, he mostly recalled his struggles with writing about the autopsy findings in his book. He wanted to include sufficient detail to accurately and completely tell the story without providing so much detail that he would lose those readers with weak stomachs. He must have rewritten that section a dozen times, possibly the most of any section in the book. He spent so much time on it that he could nearly recall the passage verbatim.

The first thing apparent to any observer was how peaceful she looked. Her hands had been placed on her abdomen, the right over the left, and, if she weren't so ashen gray, it might appear as if she were sleeping. Along with the ceremonious wrapping in the white sheet, which was 700-count white Egyptian cotton, the careful placing of the hands indicated to me immediately that Lamaya Hollows' killer had known her personally. On some level, he had cared about her, though not enough to stop himself from killing her.

Her skin had a light white film over her entire body, accentuating how pale she looked, especially given the naturally darker tone of her skin. Technicians performed scraping and examination of the film, which turned out to be dried chlorine bleach. In an attempt to eliminate any trace of his DNA, the killer had bathed her in a diluted bleach solution prior to dumping her body.

At first inspection by the medical examiner, there were no obvious outward signs of trauma: no lacerations, no bruising, and no deformities. There was also no indication of any decomposition. As such, the medical examiner initially determined that, though she had gone missing 14 days prior to the discovery of her body, she had likely died within the previous 48 hours.

A more careful examination led to the discovery of a small puncture wound on the left side of her neck, likely the site of an injection into her left jugular vein. This led us to later assume that our killer was right-handed, as fluid distribution suggested she had been killed while lying supine on her back. Toxicology reports would later confirm the presence of formaldehyde, ethanol, methanol, and other chemicals in Lamaya's blood and tissues. The killer had prepared a homemade version of embalming fluid, and this injection had turned out to be the cause of death. This in turn created some equivocation about time of death, as the fluids may have kept her body preserved for longer than several days prior to its discovery.

Her stomach contents included partially-digested cheese and ham, along with pieces of almond and a chewed piece of gum. Her parents had documented that she had gone to school with a Ham and Cheese Lunchables on the day she had gone missing; her dessert had been a Hershey bar with almonds. This information changed the time of death determination significantly, suggesting that she likely had been killed merely hours after her disappearance.

During the autopsy, several areas of bruising were found. She had mild bruising and skin irritation at both her wrists and ankles. We surmised that this was caused by soft ligatures, such as a thick scarf or padded handcuffs, than had been used to tie her down in one place. She also had a very small amount of bleeding into the lower layers of the skin at the back of her scalp, indicating that her head had banged against a hard object. The absence of any brain injury or underlying bone contusions led us to believe that this injury may have been self-inflicted, as if she threw her head against a wall or headboard in an attempt to avoid her captor, or possibly to render herself unconscious.

The gynecological exam revealed tissue damage consistent with forcible rape. The pattern of blood pooling within the tissue suggested to the medical examiner that she had been raped several times while alive and likely also after her death. She also had small tears at the corners of her mouth indicating that she had been sodomized. No DNA could be recovered from her vagina or mouth, likely due to denaturing from the bleach bath; small traces of bleach were found in the vaginal opening and on her teeth.

The examiner searched for fingerprints on the body, including her fingernails, toenails, corneas, and teeth, but none were recovered. However, in sum the autopsy turned out to be extraordinarily helpful. The story it told us about our killer—a right-handed pedophile who knew Lamaya and had the intelligence and resources to make home-made embalming fluid and bathe his victim in bleach prior to leaving the body in an area in which her body would surely be discovered—turned out to paint a very accurate picture. At the time we felt very confident that these conclusions would lead us down the investigative path that would eventually end at the doorstep of our killer.

Jack placed the manila folder on his desk and leaned back in his chair, a vision of Mervin Young, Lamaya Hollows' murderer, filling his head. He had once heard the phrase "the banality of evil" to describe Ted Bundy and serial killers like him who blend in with the rest of us as seemingly normal people; whenever he thought of Mervin Young, he found himself reminded of this phrase.

36

Randall put on his turn signal as he approached the stop sign. He hated people who did not use their turn signals. How much effort does it take to use a fucking turn signal? It conveys vital information to the other drivers on the road. For Randall, lack of using turn-signals was one of the many harbingers of the downfall of mankind. He stopped his car, looked both ways, and then proceeded to the right, just as he had signaled.

Luckily for Randall, driving in this neighborhood had become a mindless task, as he had been here so many times. His thoughts therefore wandered, as they often do, to his Work. He had a very productive day and felt proud of his accomplishments. He had had to improvise, not one of his strengths, admittedly, but today he did so with aplomb. He had also done some reconnaissance work on his next sacrifice, which would come much sooner than expected due to his new accelerated schedule.

The White Stripes still echoed in his head, running over the lyrics from "Seven Nation Army" in a seemingly endless loop. Randall nearly slammed on the brakes, struck by an epiphany. Fortunately no car followed close behind him at the time. *I should go to Wichita!* he decided. *A sacrifice there would baffle them all. Take my Work across the country!*

His excitement burned out quickly, as he consciously restrained himself. He had already improvised enough. This was, after all, his carefully planned Work; it did not just fall together haphazardly. A great conductor does not change the symphony halfway through the performance, but rather he artfully lets the orchestration continue to play itself out.

His thoughts had wandered sufficiently that he almost missed his destination. He put on his turn signal and pulled into the driveway, obscured from the front of the house by a row of small pines. He coasted to the end of the driveway and parked the car in front of the large closed doors of the detached garage. He took a deep breath and looked at himself in the rearview mirror, preparing himself for what came next. Throughout recent days, getting out of his car to begin this routine seemed one of his most difficult tasks.

He closed the car door quietly behind him. This was a calm, peaceful neighborhood, in which something as seemingly hackneyed as the slamming of a car door might catch attention. He walked to the rear door of the house, which allowed entrance by way of a mud room off the back of the kitchen.

The door knob turned without resistance. Unlocked, as Randall knew it would be.

He stepped inside the house. The kitchen was mostly dark, but light from the living room in the front of the house projected in to provide some illumination. He slipped off his shoes as he closed the door behind him. He proceeded into the kitchen, his socks making no sound on the tile floor.

Carpet covered the staircase going to the second floor, ascending from the far end of the hall near the front door of the house. Despite the plush surface on the stairs, Randall could still hear footsteps rapidly descending. He turned to face the hallway, just as the young girl landed at the bottom of the stairs, having jumped down the last two steps. She turned toward the kitchen. Obviously not expecting to see Randall standing there, she startled, putting her hand over her heart like some Hollywood ingénue from an old black-and-white movie.

"Hello," Randall said flatly.

She squinted into the poorly lit kitchen as her hands dropped from her chest to hang back down by her sides. "Hey, Dad," she returned, equally flatly.

They stood there looking at each other for several seconds. More and more, Randall found himself unsure of exactly what to say to his seven-year-old daughter. He felt disconnected. Not that it bothered him all that much.

The exuberance that his daughter had demonstrated by leaping off the stairs vanished, snuffed out like a candle. She looked down to the floor, turned around and walked into the living room.

"What's for dinner?" he called after her.

She shrugged. Without turning around, head still angled toward the carpet, she suggested, "Ask mom."

Randall nodded his head and followed her down the hallway. As he approached the room, he could hear the din of the TV. He recognized the show from the voices: a *Friends* rerun. As Randall entered the room, on the TV screen in the opposite wall of the room he saw Matt LeBlanc's Joey, sitting on Monica and Chandler's couch, raising his hand in the air. "Ken Adams!" Joey exclaims. The episode with the backpacking-through-Western-Europe story. Classic.

Randall's wife sat slumped in the couch along the near wall. She stared straight ahead into the unlit fireplace, ignoring the hilarity on the TV. Randall stood and examined her. In addition to his daughter, he also seemed to have lost the ability—and the desire, quite frankly— to communicate with his wife in recent months. His wife turned her head in his direction without actually looking at him, as if merely a gesture to acknowledge his presence. She paused a second or two before she looked back to the cold hearth.

"Any dinner plans, Dear?" Randall asked with only a hint of facetiousness.

His wife shrugged. "Not really."

One fucking job, he thought. *She has one fucking job! I only ask for one goddamned thing a day and she can't even get that right!*

"OK," he replied, feigning nonchalance. "I'll warm up some chili, then, and take it out back."

She lifted her head slightly, seemingly the closest thing to a nod she can muster.

"You want some?" he asked, hoping for a negative reply.

She shook her head once back-and-forth, barely more demonstratively than her nod. "Nah," she uttered.

Randall raised his gaze across the room to his daughter, who had sunk into a bean bag in the corner of the room, playing on her PSP hand-held gaming device. "How 'bout you, Peggy Sue?" Randall asked her.

His daughter—whose name was Mary Beth— rolled her eyes, displaying wordless sarcasm well beyond her years. "What?" she asked in return.

"You want some chili?"

The young girl looked up at the ceiling, trying to imagine the taste of Sheila's two-day-old chili in her mouth. "No."

Eight months ago Randall would have replied with a "No, *what?*" attempting to teach his daughters some manners. But he had

177

given up on parenting. It didn't seem to matter anymore. "Okey-doke. Suit yourself." Randall turned back down the hall toward the kitchen.

From a large Tupperware container in the refrigerator, he ladled some chili into a bowl, then sprinkled shredded cheddar on top before placing it in the microwave. He studied the bowl intently, watching the cheese slowly melt on top. He held a Bachelor's degree in engineering, so he understood how microwaves worked. Plus he had used microwaves countless times in his life. Yet the technology never ceased to amaze him. Randall felt pity for people who lost their appreciation for things once they understood them. Once the quite dim-witted Dorothy—an allegorical character for the average middle-American— saw the frightened little man hiding behind the curtain, she lost sight of the fact that The Great and Powerful Oz still accomplished some pretty amazing things. To the contrary, Randall reveled in his ability to still feel awestruck by those things that he could comprehend on an intellectual level.

Randall knew someday people—many people, thousands, maybe millions—would try to understand his Work. He just hoped that—even if they somehow could mentally absorb it— this wouldn't make them lose their awe for it.

The microwave beeped, he grabbed his piping-hot chili, dunked a spoon it in, and went outside through the back door. He walked across the back end of the driveway to the garage. He opened up the unlocked door on the side of the garage and climbed the wooden staircase to his immediate right. Once at the top of the stairs, he pulled out his set of keys from his pocket. He first unlocked the deadbolt, then, switching to different key, the knob itself. He opened the door.

A BUSTLE IN THE HEDGEROW

His sanctuary. His Work space. He immediately felt a sense of calm, of relief. He spent the better part of his days wishing he could be here, dedicating himself wholly to his Work.

He set his chili down on the desk to his right, turned to close and lock the door behind him. He leaned over the desk to scoop some chili into his mouth, realizing too late that it was still too hot from the microwave. He scuffled double-time over to the mini-fridge, grabbed a bottled water, unscrewed the cap, and guzzled a mouthful. He swallowed the watered-down chili, then took in some more water.

He turned to the small table to the left of his desk and reached out to one of the bins that housed his record collection. He turned his face upward and closed his eyes as his fingers crawled across the top of the bin, flipping through the numerous cardboard album covers. This was how he "randomly" selected an album to listen to, but the process was hardly random. He had his albums alphabetized, of course, and he knew the collection by heart. Even if he consciously focused on not counting as his fingers scrolled through the library, he couldn't help knowing how far he had gotten through the collection when he "randomly" stopped.

He rubbed his tongue across the roof of his mouth, expecting to feel that sandpaper sensation indicative of a burned tongue. No such texture, though, so he considered himself lucky.

He removed the album, knowing without opening his eyes that he had likely selected something from Jethro Tull. Possibly Jefferson Airplane, but he felt pretty confident that he had passed through that section. He removed the vinyl from its sleeve, placed it on the turntable, flicked the switch, and lowered the needle, clenching his eyes shut all the while. He turned away before opening his eyes.

179

Within the first few picks of the guitar strings, he turned his head to the ceiling and let out a sigh. *Thick as a Brick.* He had not heard this album in several months, maybe a year. The brilliant concept album—intended as a satire of concept albums of the late 1960s— had been one of his favorites since his childhood. The copy now spinning on the table behind him had actually belonged to his father. Due to his and Randall's meticulous care over the years, it still did not bear a scratch.

He sat down at his computer as he grabbed the bowl of chili. He gave the next spoonful a blow before putting it into his mouth. It tasted a little bland, which reminded Randall that he had forgotten to add a little hot sauce. Oh, well, still edible.

He started up his computer and entered his password when prompted. He opened up the folder entitled "Work" while he waited for Explorer to open up a browser.

He had told his wife that he was working on an autobiographical novel. It served as a form of therapy, he had told her. A catharsis, of sorts.

He also had told her that he continued to take his Zyprexa daily, and she believed that too.

He clicked through a few folders until he found the Word file he wanted. He opened it up and stared at the screen. The document had only one sentence, yet gazing at it filled Randall with a sense of pride. He clicked on the printer icon on the toolbar.

After shoveling a little more chili into his mouth, he opened the top drawer of his desk to don his gloves. He never touched any of his printer paper without wearing the gloves. He had no intention of getting caught by the authorities on some stupid slip-up like leaving fingerprints on something. That would degrade his Work, and he refused to let that happen.

The printer hummed as it spit the top sheet back out at Randall. He held it up in wonderment, a chill of excitement shooting through his spine. He could not wait for the next lucky person to see this message.

الساعة رجل

37

Jack closed the lid of his trunk on the cardboard box containing his desk belongings. As he rounded the car to the driver's door, he remembered the missed call and subsequent voice mail from Melissa Hollows. He had never actually forgotten it; he had simply continued to put it to the back of his mind every time it came up, which turned out to be approximately every ninety seconds. Finally he reasoned that he had found an appropriate time to listen to it.

After he sat down in the car, he dialed up the voice mail. It began with a brief silence, and then he heard Melissa. Her effusive and seemingly uncontrollable sobbing muffled her voice, but he could make out the words. "We were made for each other, Jack. You and me." She sobbed louder before adding, "Me and you, me and you!" Quickly the recording stopped, and the delightful woman from his menu reminded him, "To delete this message, press seven..."

Jack, confused, stared at his phone, as if it might offer some explanation for the odd message. Instead, only the time of the phone call ticked away on the digital display. He pressed 4 to repeat the message, listening more intently this time.

The first several milliseconds did not actually contain silence; he could recognize Melissa's sobs and a brief sniffle. She had been crying for sufficient time to cause her nose to run. She said the first phrase very deliberately, almost robotically, through her crying. "We were made for each other, Jack. You and me." The tone changed for the next repeated phrase. It felt more hurried, as if she found something vile in those words and she tried to spit them out before they damaged her mouth. "Me and you, me and you!" Then silence.

182

A BUSTLE IN THE HEDGEROW

Through his professional life, and even in his personal life, Jack had witnessed the gamut of emotions: utter helplessness and desperation from parents of a missing child; distraught and disbelief from the spouse of a convicted child pornographer; ruthlessness and icy cunning of a murderer confessing to a crime as if reciting a cookie recipe. Jack immediately recognized the emotion from the other end of that voice mail.

Fear.

It wasn't hopelessness, or despair, or the wistfulness of the forlorn. Jack knew in his heart that, at that moment earlier in the day, Melissa Hollows felt afraid, perhaps even terrified.

He hung up his voice mail and searched his recent call log to find the recent incoming call from Melissa. He hit send. The line rang only once before going to voice mail. Having no idea what to say, Jack hung up rather than leave a message.

He put the phone down and thought for a moment. Images of Melissa raced through his mind. He searched at blinding speed through his memories of her—from when they first met until he heard this voice mail— for any tidbit that could explain the message, as it seemed so foreign to her personality. He hadn't spoken to her for nearly eight months. What had happened to her in that time?

He knew he would not be able to let this go. He put the car in gear, backed out of his parking spot, and sped off to Melissa's townhouse.

38

"You want a piece of gum?"

It seemed like such an innocuous question, without hidden meaning or ulterior underpinnings. Little did Jackson Byrne know at the time that it would change the course of his life.

About five weeks after the discovery of Lamaya Hollows' body, Melissa Hollows moved out of their spacious mansion in Potomac, Maryland into a townhouse in Georgetown. She told Jack that "life with Lamond had grown unlivable." Unfortunately, Jack had seen this too many times before: a marriage crumbling due to the unimaginable stress of losing a child. Melissa would later tell Jack that every time she looked at Lamond, and he at her, their hearts and minds overflowed with emotions: the crushing heartbreak of the death of their Lamaya, the accusation that the other one could have done something to prevent it, the guilt that they had not prevented it themselves, and countless others. They had come to the conclusion that a trial separation would be the only way they could survive, literally.

Almost two weeks later, Jack spent over two hours at Melissa's townhouse conducting a prolonged interview that included looking through dozens of photographs of registered sex offenders, none of whom Melissa recognized. When it became apparent that this line of investigation—searching through lists of known sexual criminals—would likely prove fruitless, Melissa began to cry. She mumbled through nearly unintelligible words about Lamaya and Lamond and the horrible, sick people in the world and little terrorized children. And her Lamaya, again and again her Lamaya. Jack, a veteran of witnessing meltdowns like this, usually felt uncomfortable during such an episode. Here, however, he felt at ease.

That night was the first time they slept together. It certainly had not been planned by either one of them. Melissa spontaneously initiated the first kiss, through a face full of tears, and Jack resisted at first. She backed away sheepishly, hiding her face and crying even harder. Jack felt guilty and even a little embarrassed, though he never really understood why. After a moment's pause, he went to her to hug her, to try to comfort her. She reciprocated the embrace, grabbing him tightly. Her hand moved up to the back of Jack's head, massaging his neck. She looked up to meet his eyes, and their second kiss was borne of mutual desire.

Later, in the aftermath, they lay side by side on the floor of Melissa's living room. After a few minutes of silently catching their breath, they discussed the initial mutual attraction upon meeting each other, that subconscious, uncontrollable feeling of desire for another person. But neither ever had any intentions of acting on it. In fact, the sentiment quickly dissipated for each of them as they worked together over the course of subsequent weeks to solve Lamaya's murder. Apparently the emotional charge of the night—and perhaps the cumulative emotional impact of the preceding several weeks—took over, and each participant succumbed to it.

Of course, this rationalization served to comfort both of their consciences. It seemed much easier to think of oneself as "succumbing to an uncontrollable desire" than as an adulterer. After they had fallen quiet, as Jack looked up at the swirled patterns in the plaster of the living room ceiling, he began to think about guilt. He had never cheated on Vicki before. He had cheated on other girlfriends in his youthful past, but never on his wife, never on the mother of his child. He knew that he should feel guilty, yet he didn't. He knew what he had done was wrong, but it remained an intellectual concept rather than an emotional response. He thought, *If Vicki doesn't find out about this, then no harm done.*

He raised his left arm up at the elbow and regarded his wedding band. "I'm... I'm married," he said. He turned his head to the right to look at Melissa as he opened his palm to her, displaying his ring.

She looked over at him, at the ring, then back at the ceiling. "I know," she replied, revealing little emotion. "So am I, technically," she shrugged. "Don't worry. I'm not going to tell anyone about this. This looks just as bad for me as it does for you."

Thus Jack felt comforted. It wasn't until after they had sex a second time, four nights later, that Jack possessed the insight to recognize that what he considered a natural consequence of undeniable mutual attraction was really just rationalization of abhorrent behavior. With this epiphany, this time looking up at the ceiling of Melissa's bedroom, guilt hit Jack like the proverbial ton of bricks. He felt nauseated. He didn't provide a reason for his hasty exit from Melissa's apartment that night, but the look of despair on his ashen, sullen face revealed to her his feeling of shame. Instantaneously, she felt guilty too. Since that moment, neither spoke of their brief relationship. They continued to interact during the investigation, but never alone, never again at her apartment.

Due to Lamond Hollows' fame and the ghoulishness of his daughter's murder, the case had become national news. As Jack descended the steps of her Brownstone that second night, a photographer from a national tabloid magazine snapped his photo. Luckily, he had taken the time to put his entire suit back on— tie and all—prior to his departure. This did not stop the tabloid from running the photo with an incendiary headline suggesting an affair between the FBI man and the estranged wife and mother. Both Jack and Melissa publicly and privately denied any relationship.

Vicki never saw the tabloid piece, but the rumor made its way back to her a few days later through one of her co-workers. Ever the trusting wife, she never even asked Jack about it. When Jack crawled into bed after another 16-hour day, she rolled over to give him a hug. "I'm glad you don't have to defend your work to me," she said softly.

Jack stiffened slightly, a shockwave of shame jolting through his body. "What do you mean?" he asked.

"You spend tireless hours trying to solve these awful crimes. I know you sometimes have to spend late hours, and sometimes even in the home of a former supermodel. I just want you to know that I'm proud of you, and that you don't have to defend any of your work to me."

Jack silently took a deep breath and held it, hoping this would stifle the wave of self-hatred that began to overtake him. "Thank you, baby," he said as he finally exhaled, kissing her on the top of her head. He also felt thankful that the lights in the room were turned out, or else his wife may have seen the tension in his face: his clenched jaw, furrowed brow, and intensely widened eyes. He rolled over and stared at the wall ahead of him.

He lay awake for over an hour, wondering how he could have been so weak, so gullible, to fall for the advances of another woman. Then he cursed himself for thinking of himself as weak, as if he were a victim. He actively and willingly participated, and he needed to take responsibility for his actions. He nearly rolled over to wake up Vicki and come clean. As he began to spin under the sheets, he halted. He needed to evaluate the potential consequences first. *What if Vicki left me?* An image of Jonah sprang into his mind. *What if Jonah found out? How would he react?*

He leaned back to his original position, away from Vicki. He forced himself to run through the events of those two nights. Those memories sifted through his mind like red-hot coals; he supposed that the painful shame of remembering his adultery could serve as part of his penance for committing such a reprehensible act.

He thought back to the beginning, to that first tear-soaked kiss. As Melissa had begun to cry, Jack tried a simple maneuver to distract her.

"You want a piece of gum?" he had asked. When he reflected on it, it seemed such a stupid thing to say, but it had worked once before with a distraught mother to make her stop crying. But it only made Melissa Hollows cry even harder, leading to their first embrace.

Later that night, as they got dressed, Jack tried to lighten the mood. "I had no idea that asking you to have a piece of gum could have such a dramatic effect."

Melissa looked at him sadly, but she did not cry again. "Sorry. Lamaya loved chewing gum. She always had a piece in her mouth. When you said that… it just made me sad, that's all."

Jack nodded understandingly, and he never brought it up again.

Lying in bed beside his wife several days later, he considered what might have happened had he never mentioned gum. Melissa wouldn't have cried harder, seeking comfort, and he wouldn't have felt obligated to provide it.

Gum.

Suddenly his eyes resembled saucers, his pupils dilated to within millimeters of the edge of his irises. He nearly leapt out of bed, startling Vicki, who quickly drifted back off to sleep. Jack went down the hall to his office, booted up the computer—which seemed to take an unbearably long time—and opened up his file on the Hollows murder. He pulled up the autopsy report, scanning it to about two-thirds of the way through: her stomach contents.

Gum.

The autopsy report had detailed injuries to Lamaya's mouth and throat, likely secondary to pre-mortem sodomy. Her post-mortem bleach bath had penetrated into her mouth and esophagus, so no sperm or other foreign DNA had been recovered. The natural acidity of the stomach always prevented recovery of DNA from any stomach contents… unless that DNA had been protected somehow. Such as by residing within a piece of chewing gum.

In numerous cases, DNA has been recovered from chewing gum. This usually occurs when investigators find gum left behind at a crime scene, and the forensics team can use the DNA held within to identify the perpetrator. However, if someone had gum in her mouth while exchanging saliva with another person, or, while gruesomely sodomized, the other person's DNA might also be preserved in the gum.

Jack looked at the clock on the lower corner of the computer screen: 2:25 am. Though he could hardly contain his excitement, he knew it was too early to call the medical examiner for a non-emergent matter. It could wait until the morning, though Jack knew he would get very little sleep between now and then.

39

As per usual in the late afternoon, traffic on I-95 North began to slow to a meander and then to a crawl as Jack approached the Beltway. As he stared at the red taillights ahead of him and his right foot reflexively alternated between the accelerator and the brake, his mind continued to race through possible scenarios that would have resulted in the phone call he had received from Melissa. He couldn't make sense of it. He also began to wonder if he had overreacted. What exactly had convinced him that something bad had happened? He could not deny the weirdness of the message, but this did not necessarily imply impending doom. Sometimes his experiencing extreme circumstances in his professional life— and subsequently reacting to them— would get the better of him when it came to dealing with the relatively mundane in his personal life.

He envisioned knocking on Melissa's townhouse door. What would she look like when opening it? Would she still be crying? How would he deal with that? He then considered an alternate scenario: What if she no longer lived at the same townhouse? She could have gotten back together with Lamond, or with someone else, or simply moved to another location. He had no way of knowing.

As he pondered these possibilities, his certainty about this current mission deteriorated. He snapped out of his semi-trance to look down at his watch: 5:38 pm. At this rate he wouldn't make it to Georgetown until close to 6:30. It would likely be nearly 8:00 by the time he got home, depending on how long he spent dealing with Melissa.

BEN MILLER

He glanced at his phone and decided to try calling Melissa again, and again it went straight to voice mail. A follow-up phone call tomorrow would surely suffice for someone he hadn't seen for the better part of a year.

He got off at the Springfield exit on Franconia Road, drove under the I-95 overpass, and turned onto the on-ramp for I-95 south. The heavy traffic moved even slower in that direction, but he still arrived home in Lake Ridge by 6:15.

DAY SIX:
SATURDAY

40

Randall stood squinting into the early afternoon sun. He wore a Virginia Tech baseball hat, but even this couldn't keep the bright day from affecting his eyes. He had forced himself to lie down for two hours last night, though he hadn't really slept. All day his apparently fatigued eyes belied his intense mental energy.

Despite the growing excitement of coming events, he remained calm. He always remained calm. His sangfroid was essential to completing his Work.

Since first encountering the word "sangfroid" in high school, it had become one of his favorite words. Whenever he used the word, he delightfully recalled an episode in college in which an especially pretentious classmate in a literature class tried to use the word in an effort to impress the rest of the class. During a discussion of Joseph Heller's post-modern masterpiece *Catch-22,* the classmate averred that the character Yossarian "demonstrated sangfroid in his response to the chaos around him." Though he expressed an arguably valid point, he made himself a fool by pronouncing the word phonetically—"sang-froyed"—rather than the correct French pronunciation—"sahn-frwa." While everyone else in the class let it slide, or perhaps didn't even recognize the gross mistake, Randall laughed out loud. He suggested that the classmate have a chicken salad "cross saint" for lunch, then proceeded to laugh even harder. Not only did his classmates fail to join him in his raucousness, but some of them also gave him dirty looks.

The memory of making fun of that douche bag brought a smile to his face. Quickly, though, the din of the cheering crowds and the excited voices of dozens of children brought him back to the present moment.

He looked out across the half-dozen or so soccer fields in front of him. As he compiled the research for his Work, he read about the soccer tournament taking place here this weekend. He had been here to Front Royal, Virginia, once before, almost two months ago, performing reconnaissance for his Work. He knew the terrain well, and his vision at that time of what the area would look like during a soccer tournament turned out to be quite accurate.

In the field in front of him, a preteen girl in a bright yellow T-shirt squeezed a shot just to the right of a diving goal keeper, scoring the first goal of the game. Randall pumped his fist in the air, feigning excitement for the Gold Team, or whatever they might be called. Their T-shirts only had numbers on them along with the name of their local sponsors, like "Bill's Meats" on the back of Number 2's shirt, and "Dunmire Lumber" on Number 8's.

As Randall had predicted, at any given time, there were nearly as many players not playing in games as there were playing. This left several dozen nine-to-twelve year-old girls wandering around with nothing to do but wait for their next game. Most of them sat with their teammates, gabbing about this or that. Some less fortunate children seemed forced to sit with their parents or coaches awaiting their turn on the playing field.

However, some other children stayed to themselves.

A smaller subset of these, amounting to only an unlucky few, ventured out away from the fields, away from the parking lots, apparently going for walks, exploring the surrounding trails.

Signage indicated that a pond existed a half a mile west of the soccer fields. From the corner of his eye, Randall spotted a young girl about ten years old wearing a hot pink and black striped shirt wander off in that direction. He casually turned and started back a nearby trail, one that he knew from his previous visit would intersect with the girl's trail prior to reaching the pond, while still covered in mostly dense coniferous foliage.

After he entered the trail, Randall looked over his shoulder to ensure that no one followed him. Satisfied that no one had, he reached into his pockets to pull out his leather gloves, which he then stretched onto his hands. He quickened his pace to a very brisk walk, just short of a jog. He would have to make up quite a bit of distance to meet the young girl before she got to the pond, where the trail opened up considerably, providing a view much too broad for him to perform any part of his Work. He surmised that she would keep the same meandering pace, which should allow him enough time to beat her to the spot .

As he neared the intersection, about ten yards from the mouth of the trail, he could see ahead down her trail as it opened up to the pond. He did not see the girl; either she had turned around or she had not yet reached this spot.

Randall slowed his pace to a more comfortable walk, and called out, "Chelsea!" in a sing-song manner. He looked around, swinging his head from left to right. As he reached the intersection, he sang again, "Chel-sea!" He turned right, toward the direction of the soccer fields.

The girl in the pink and black T walked down the middle of the trail about 15 yards ahead of him, looking down at a small fern she had picked along her stroll. She looked up at him quizzically.

Addressing the unsuspecting girl, Randall put his hands on his thighs, crouching down a little bit to make himself seem less imposing. "Hi. Do you know Chelsea Martin?"

The girl looked at him, unsure how to respond. She seemed frightened without knowing why, as if some part of her could sense an as-yet unrevealed danger. "No," she said, more like a question than an answer.

Randall shook his head lightly. "Darn. That's my daughter. She went for a walk out here and I'm not sure where she is. Her game starts in less than ten minutes!"

With this phrase the girl seemed to relax, her shoulders settling down from their tensed position near her ears.

Randall turned toward the pond, beginning to walk in that direction. "Chelsea!"

The girl jogged up to him, stopping about five feet away. He turned to face her.

"I can help you, sir," she offered.

Randall glanced over her shoulder, back down her trail, as well as down the trail from which he had come.

No one.

He looked at her cherubic face, her innocence on full display. Her eyes stared wide, eager to help a fellow human in need.

An image of Lily flashed in Randall's mind. Lily. His muse. For whom, of whom, and with whom he had created his Masterpiece.

"Yes," he said calmly to the girl. "I believe you can help me."

He quickly lunged at the girl, bringing both hands to her throat. He lifted her slightly off the ground by squeezing and using her lower jaw for leverage, and then he slammed her to the ground on her back, a few feet into the thick brush. This jolt essentially knocked the wind out of her, doubling the intensity, and also the futility, of trying to catch her breath. It happened so abruptly that she never had a chance to scream.

Randall ended up on one knee beside her, continuing to apply pressure to the front of her windpipe. She began to reach for his hands, but he brought his surprisingly powerful elbows down across the tops of her arms. Moving as agilely as a dancer, he swung one leg around her body and then brought both knees down on her elbows, trapping her arms and rendering them useless. Her legs thrashed about, but she could not move.

Though he hated doing it, Randall forced himself to look into her eyes. He knew it was the only way to really know when he had finished. Terror and shock filled those eyes for the next fifteen seconds, until the intensity of those emotions began to fade. He had cut off the blood supply to the brain through her carotid arteries. Within another twenty seconds her eyes slowly closed, as she passed out.

Amateurs might stop at this, thinking that they had completed the act. Randall knew better.

He continued to squeeze with as much force as he could muster for the next sixty seconds. She remained completely limp.

By this time Randall had grown accustomed to the brief period of sadness that accompanied this portion of his Work. The sensation shocked him a little with his first murder, as he had felt mostly numb through the entire planning process. Early on he quickly realized that his sadness had nothing to do with the victim. These deaths comprised the most vital part of his Work, making them both utterly necessary and unavoidable.

His sadness had everything to do with his Lily.

During his first murder, he was almost immobilized by the sadness. Luckily he had chosen a much more secluded spot for that act, or else someone might have spotted him. He stood over the first girl's body for what must have been nearly two minutes. He then fell to his knees hurriedly and tried to resuscitate the body with chest compressions, just like he had with his Lily. This went on for only about thirty seconds before he regained his composure and snapped back into the moment, back to focusing on his true Work.

He never allowed himself to feel shame for that previous lapse in dedication to his Work. He deemed it an understandable reaction to the situation. Each successive act, each piece in his Work, however, made him more resolute, more steadfast. Never again did he waver. In this he took pride.

He did perform chest compressions in his second act as well, but only to create as many similarities as possible to the first act. He did it not as an act of contrition or second-guessing, but rather as a purposeful gesture to link the second act to the first.

A successful plan, he reminded himself.

A BUSTLE IN THE HEDGEROW

At this point he had learned to allow the sadness to come over him, but for no more than ten seconds. It felt like an appropriate length of time. Therefore he incorporated it into the ritual.

After those ten seconds elapsed, he looked back down both trails. Still no one approached, but he knew he did not have much time. He reached into the back pocket of his jeans to remove a plastic sandwich bag containing the strip of the paper he had pulled off his printer the night before. He carefully opened the bag and removed the note with his gloved fingers. He could not find any pockets in the girl's soccer shorts, so he decided to stuff the note into the top of her rolled-down socks. He put the plastic bag back into his back pocket as he stood and began walking, this time away from the fields towards the pond. He had left his car on a side street less than a quarter of a mile from here. He hoped to be well on his way out of town before someone discovered the little girl's body.

41

A bead of sweat hung on the end of Heath Reilly's nose, swaying back and forth with each running step. He stuck out his lower lip and exhaled forcefully, blasting the salty drop into the air in front of him. He had been jogging in the neighborhood around his apartment for only about fifteen minutes, and the temperature barely reached 70 degrees, but Heath had already worked up quite a sweat. Clearly he wasn't in the best shape of his life, but his heavy breathing and profuse perspiration disappointed him. He supposed he hadn't been as active this winter and early spring as he should have. Today's jog simply marked the beginning of a healthy jump-start to the spring and summer, he reminded himself.

His mind then reverted back to thinking about Corinne O'Loughlin. He remembered feeling a physical attraction for her when he first met her during the Hollows investigation; after speaking with her on the phone at length two days ago, he felt an even stronger intellectual and emotional pull toward her. He liked her feisty nature and found her confidence very appealing. While he often chose women with less personality— the Wallflower Type, his mother liked to say in her trademarked polite yet condescending manner— he naturally felt drawn to strong, self-assure women, and Corinne definitely fit that archetype. His thinking about her early today had been the impetus to this jog; he wanted to get into better shape before asking her out. He knew enough about himself to know that he felt much more at ease in front of the fairer sex when he felt confident about his physical self. When he looked in the mirror at home last night, he perceived his insecurity. Within a couple weeks of jogging, sit-ups, and push-ups, he knew he could bolster himself sufficiently to approach her in a more personal setting.

After rounding a street corner, a beep from his iPhone broke his concentration. He pulled the phone off his hip as he slowed to a walk. The display told him he had an incoming call from the dispatcher at CASMIRC. He pulled off his head phones and slid his index finger across the screen to take the call.

"Special Agent Reilly," he answered, still quite short of breath.

"Hi, Special Agent Reilly, this is Lisa from dispatch. I have an Officer Hanley from the Sheriff's office in Warren County, Virginia on the line. He called asking to speak with you."

Reilly inhaled deeply and let out a slow exhale. He didn't want to seem out of breath when talking to Gomer Pyle (his adopted name for any member of local law enforcement). He didn't know exactly why, but he thought this would exude weakness. He finally responded, "OK, patch him through."

Reilly looked up at the sky as he waited a few seconds for the dispatcher to complete the connection. A few cumulus clouds dotted the blue expanse: a perfect spring day.

The faint hum of the static in Reilly's ear jumped. "This is Special Agent Reilly."

"Hello, Special Agent Reilly. This is Hank Hanley with the Sheriff's Department in Warren County."

"What can I do for you, officer?" Reilly tried not to sound annoyed, unsure of how successful he was.

"The body of a young girl was just discovered here. She was murdered along a hiking trail within the last two hours. I heard about your string of—"

201

"Wait!" Reilly's head snapped down from admiring the bright blue sky to stare at a tree trunk in front of him as he interrupted the man on the other end of the line. "Where are you?"

"I'm in Front Royal, Virginia. Warren County, about 75 miles west of D.C."

Reilly turned and began back towards his apartment at a brisk walk. "Rope off the entire area and don't let any piece of evidence out, including the body. I'll be there with my team in less than two hours. Please call back to our dispatcher, give her your exact location and your cell number. I will call you back when we are en route." He now had quickened to a light jog. "Do you understand?"

"Yes, sir," Hanley replied.

"Great," Reilly said as he hung up. He kept his iPhone in his right hand as he broke into a full sprint, which, despite his nearly six months of relative inactivity, he sustained most of the way back to his apartment.

42

Hank Hanley hung up his cell phone and put it back into the front pocket of his jeans. He surveyed the scene in front of him: two uniformed officers stood silently on either side of the entrance to the hiking trail from the soccer fields to the pond. Yellow tape marked this off and extended along the tree line in either direction. An ambulance sat idly in the grass just to the right of the trail entrance, its back doors ajar and its EMTs sitting on the back stoop, both looking at the ground.

He turned around to face the soccer fields, which had hosted several hundred playful young girls mere hours ago. Now these several hundred kids and their several hundred parents and coaches all sat huddled silently on the bleachers. Most had chosen to sit on the sides of the fields that faced away from the trail leading to the pond, away from the tragedy. Most parents still clutched their children tightly; most of those children contradicted their normal behavior by allowing it. Despite the mass of humanity, it seemed ghostly quiet. The only sounds came from the handful of police officers surrounding the crowd, occasionally making small talk amongst themselves or with the children, trying to perhaps lighten the mood. Earlier a few children had gotten bored and decided to kick a soccer ball around, but they went back to the sullen crowd after their parents chastised them.

Hank felt awkward wearing his street clothes at a crime scene, certainly one of this magnitude. He had a good excuse, though: he was technically off duty, attending his daughter's soccer tournament.

In fact, his daughter's team had been slated to play the missing girl's team when this awful turmoil commenced.

When Danielle Coulter didn't show up at her scheduled game time, no one seemed very surprised initially. Her coaches and most of her teammates knew that Danielle only played soccer because her parents made her. They thought that it would be a good way to socialize as well as get some exercise, both of which little Danielle lacked for most of her ten years. Unfortunately, though they encouraged her participation at home, neither her father nor her mother could be bothered to support her in person that Saturday.

After ten minutes passed, a handful of her teammates offered to go looking for her. She had shown up for the initial head count earlier in the day, so she couldn't have gone too far. Rather than hold up the game any further, two fathers of her teammates went out searching for Danielle, fully expecting to find her picking wildflowers or skipping stones on the pond. Only four minutes passed before one father, a balding man in a Nike jumpsuit, shrieked from within the woods between the fields and the pond.

Hank's daughter had just made an impressive pass across the field to an open teammate when the man's screams made everyone— players, parents, referees— stop in their tracks. They all turned toward the trail to see the cause of the crying. Though the action on all of the fields had already ceased, one referee inexplicably and unnecessarily blew his whistle. The man emerged from the mouth of the trail in a full sprint, his eyes wide, panting like a greyhound at the end of six furlongs.

Hank had leapt from his folding lawn chair at the first shriek and began to walk quickly toward the sound. When the man flew into daylight and Hank saw the expression on his face, he too began running headlong at the man. As they neared one another, Hank could see true terror in the man's eyes. He barely slowed as they approached, so Hank had to put out both hands and catch the man's by his arms. They nearly both fell down due to the man's speed prior to the collision.

"What?! What?!" the man screamed.

"Sir! Sir!" Hank tried to center the man, holding both upper arms firmly and looking into his eyes.

"She's… Oh, fuck. Oh, God—" Before he could put the "d" on "God," the man vomited.

By now that vomit had time to dry on the left sleeve of Hank's sweatshirt. He needed to decide what to do next while waiting for Special Agent Reilly and his FBI team. He had called the dispatcher back and provided the information as instructed. He supposed he would walk back into the woods to oversee the goings-on, making sure that everyone understood the explicit instructions to leave the crime scene as undisturbed as possible.

First, however, he decided to walk to his car in the parking lot, where he removed his soiled sweatshirt and placed it in the trunk. The day had turned warm enough that he shouldn't need it anyway.

43

Corinne O'Loughlin shifted in the uncomfortable vinyl chair in the waiting room outside of the ICU at Georgetown University Hospital; her left butt cheek had fallen numb. She stared at her Droid phone in the palm of her hand, only half paying attention to the word-finding game on the display. She found that this helped pass the time idly while her mind could wander to more important things.

About an hour ago she got a phone call from one of the staff nurses in the ICU. The nurse informed Corinne that the parents of Allison Branford, the Georgetown Lacrosse player and hit-and-run victim from almost a week ago, decided to withdraw life-support. Unfortunately, Allison's tests run by her team of doctors the past two days had shown that she had no brain activity left. Her parents called in her extended friends and family to say their final goodbyes this morning. After the parade of loved ones came through, Dean and Eleanor Branford sat alone with their only child and asked that the doctors remove the breathing tube connecting her to the ventilator.

Corinne had arrived shortly after that. According to her nurse contact—whom she paid fifty bucks for her helpful information— Allison took a few shallow breaths on her own, but then stopped. Two minutes later she was pulseless. She died in the arms of both of her parents.

Over the course of following this story, Corinne had become familiar with the Branfords and had actually grown quite fond of them. They expressed great appreciation for her journalistic efforts, fighting on their daughter's behalf to publicize the accident in hopes of catching the hit-and-run perpetrator. The things she learned about

Allison by talking with friends and classmates seemed too good to be true. Numerous times in her work Corinne has observed this "positive recall bias"— people tend to remember only the good things about victims of tragedies. However, after spending time with the genuine and truly nice Dean and Eleanor Branford, she began to believe what she had heard about their daughter. Their kindness had drawn her to the hospital this Saturday. She could write about Allison's death from home; she came to offer condolences to her family in person.

Corinne had gone through three games on her phone when the Branfords emerged from the ICU doors into the hallway that joins the waiting room, their faces pale and their eyes puffy, haggardly bloodshot. Friends and family flooded them immediately. Eleanor, the more outspoken of the two, swam through the crowd to make a beeline towards Corinne. Corinne, surprised, put her phone down and hurriedly stood up. She opened her arms and began to lean in to hug her.

"Eleanor, I am so—" she began, but Eleanor interrupted the hug by grabbing her by both shoulders and gripping her tightly. She looked straight into Corinne's eyes intensely, her pupils fully dilated.

"You find him," she commanded. A previously shed tear escaped the well of her left lower eyelid and streamed down her face. "You find the son-of-a-bitch who did this to our daughter."

Corinne tried to meet her eyes, but it felt like staring straight into the sun. She instead looked at the wet vertical track down Eleanor's left cheek that the tear had created. She nodded and opened her mouth to speak. On the chair behind her, her cell phone rang, but she focused on the shattered woman in front of her. "I will," Corinne confirmed through the din of her phone.

Eleanor's eyes never left Corinne's. She squinted, as if focusing her vision could help discern the veracity of Corinne's assertion. She began a barely perceptible nod, almost like a fine tremor.

The phone rang a second time. Eleanor then relaxed her grip and pulled Corinne in tightly for a hug. Corinne shared the embrace. "Thank you," Eleanor said, a little too loudly for the close proximity of her mouth to Corinne's ear. "Thank you."

Eleanor stepped back and put her hands back on Corinne's upper arms, much more lightly than seconds before. Her face had softened and even offered a small smile. She dropped her arms and walked back to her husband and their group, who enveloped her with open arms.

Corinne watched her walk back then sat back down. She let out a deep sigh, realizing how much that short conversation had drained her emotionally. She then picked up her phone and navigated to her missed calls, finding the most recent name on the list: Heath Reilly. Corinne felt a bolt of excitement shoot to her toes. Her mental energy returned just as quickly as it had been sapped by Allison's bereaving mother.

As per their phone conversation two days ago, Reilly and Corinne agreed to share information about the Playground Predator case. (Though she couldn't use the moniker in print, she still gave the case this label in her mind as well as her document files.) His call likely signaled a breakthrough in the case. At least she hoped it did. She picked up her laptop bag, threw her phone in the side pocket, and quietly exited the waiting room. She took the elevator downstairs, paid for her parking (and asked for a receipt—she full expected reimbursement for this as a job expense) and walked to her car. She drove out of the parking garage and then parked on the street, leaving her car idling as she called her voicemail to retrieve Reilly's message.

44

Reilly sat in the passenger seat of their black Ford Expedition. He had met Camilla in Quantico; she drove to Front Royal due to his need to make phone calls. They had just merged onto highway 66 West, only about thirty-five more miles to Front Royal.

After he had left Corinne a voicemail, Reilly called Lisa at dispatch, who connected him to Officer Hank Hanley in Front Royal. He barked instructions to Hanley, most of which Hanley had already accomplished. Halfway through the conversation, Corinne beeped in, but Reilly waited until completing his call with Hanley before returning hers. He filled her in on his limited knowledge of the findings in Front Royal, and then he finished the call by suggesting that she drive over there to report directly from the scene. After he hung up, he looked over at Camilla, who briefly broke her intense focus on the road in front of them to shoot him a sardonic glance. He caught a glimpse of it.

"What?" he asked.

Camilla shrugged. "What?" she replied in turn.

"What did I do?"

She shook her head and looked back at the road. "Nothing."

Reilly wasn't satisfied. "Really, what?"

Camilla knew Reilly well enough to know that he likely would not let this go, much like a three-year-old who needs to know why he's not allowed to go outside to play in the rain. She took a breath, pausing to choose her words carefully. "You spoke very differently during those two conversations."

"What do you mean?" Reilly leaned forward, as if in an interrogation. He glared at her, but she didn't look away from the road again.

"When you spoke with the officer from the crime scene, you spoke in a very... commanding manner. Very business-like. And a little condescending, to be honest."

"And in the second?"

"More like... you were talking to a friend," Camilla said, though she held back what she had wanted to say: that he spoke as if he were wooing a woman. She decided to throw in a little jab that might hint toward her true observation. "Except your voice was a little higher."

"My voice was higher?" Reilly repeated, consciously lowering the register of his voice, trying his best to land in bass but still ending up in mid-baritone.

"Yes. Like... you're talking to a child, trying to get him to climb down out of a tree," she answered. *That should keep him guessing*, she thought, *and to think twice before asking me these kinds of questions again.*

Neither of them spoke for the rest of the short drive. Camilla did not use her emergency lights, but she maintained a speed between 80 and 85 miles per hour while on the highway. Their dashboard navigation system guided them straight to the soccer field complex on the west side of Front Royal.

As the Expedition pulled into view of the soccer field, Reilly and Camilla could see the two sets of bleachers filled with people. They stared sullenly at the Expedition, their heads turning in unison to follow the oversized vehicle as it passed by, as if watching a tennis match in super slow-motion. Farther down the fields, between the bleachers and the bordering woods on the west end, a muscular man in a white T-shirt and jeans with a polished badge on his belt walked toward their car. He signaled for them to park at the curb in front of him, at the south end of the soccer complex. Camilla eased the large SUV to the designated spot. The plain-clothed cop stood watching them with his hands on his hips, accentuating his angular physique. Both Reilly and Camilla got out of the car and walked toward the man at the edge of the fields.

The man extended his hand to Reilly. "Special Agent Reilly?"

Reilly grasped his hand and shook it gently. "Yes," he replied, almost as more of a question than an answer.

"Hank Hanley, Warren County Sheriff. We spoke on the phone," Hank replied, releasing the weak grip of the FBI man. He turned toward Camilla and also offered her his right hand.

"Special Agent Camilla Vanderbilt," she said as she firmly took his hand and gave it three confident pumps. "Nice to meet you, Sheriff."

"Call me Hank, please." He turned his shoulders slightly as to face both of them. He sensed that Reilly was in charge, but his early impression of the two made him prefer Camilla. He wanted to include both in this brief orientation. "We have all of the potential witnesses over there—," he pointed to the sets of bleachers in the distance to his left, "—and have begun questioning them as you had asked."

"OK," Reilly nodded.

Hank then pointed to his right, toward a break in the tree line less than twenty yards away. "The body is back this trail. It was discovered at 12:52 pm today." He began walking in that direction, expecting the pair of FBI agents to follow. Camilla came with him, but Reilly instead turned to face the crowd of spectators and soccer players.

"How do you know the perp isn't sitting in that crowd?" Reilly posited.

Hank stopped and walked back toward Reilly, leaning in because he hadn't heard the question. "Excuse me, sir?"

Camilla stayed back where she was. She had heard the question the first time and considered it an honest possibility. She also knew Reilly well enough to assume that he had posited the question only to regain control of the situation: he would go to see the crime scene when he felt ready, not when a local sheriff told him to.

Reilly turned to face Hank once he came even with him. "How do you know that this little girl's killer isn't sitting on those bleachers over there?" he repeated.

Hank pondered this question genuinely for several seconds. "I guess I don't," he shrugged. "But that's one of the reasons I've kept them all here." He looked up to meet Reilly's eyes. Satisfied that he had given a sufficient answer, Hank turned back toward the trail. When he met up with Camilla, she began walking with him.

Hank began telling her the story of Danielle Coulter's brief stint as a missing person and her discovery by the Nike track suit guy, who turned out to be a struggling realtor named Timothy Yongauer. Hank had questioned him personally before an ambulance took him to the local hospital; Yongauer continued vomiting so much that he began to feel light-headed. An officer stayed with him in the Emergency Department and had phoned in minutes ago to inform Hank that Mr. Yongauer felt much better after getting an injection of an anti-nausea medication and a liter of IV fluid. Reilly caught up with them a few yards into the trail, about halfway through the story.

"I get the impression that you don't think this Yongauer had anything to do with the murder?" Reilly asked.

"Absolutely not," Hank replied without hesitation. He looked sideways at Reilly without ever breaking stride. "I saw the terror in his eyes first hand. That man won't sleep for a week." He looked back toward the trail ahead of them.

"Any clues or leads thus far?" Camilla asked him. She possessed much more faith in the ability of local police officials to conduct investigations than Reilly did.

"Maybe." Hank stopped in his tracks, and the other two followed suit. "Let me be very honest and apologize to you folks up front: this has not been an easy crime scene to control. News of this spread fast. Within twenty minutes we had over two dozen officers here, both local and county. Staties came fifteen minutes later. We quickly roped off the area, but we probably had five-to-ten officers down these various trails—myself included—in the first thirty minutes. Now, no one's removed any evidence. But identifying footprints, broken branches, so-on, so-forth... that might be a significant challenge."

Camilla nodded understandingly; Reilly briefly shook his head with pursed lips, as if trying unsuccessfully to hide his disgust.

Hank took a few steps forward until he had to duck under the strip of yellow tape strung across the trail. Camilla and Reilly shuffled under the tape as well, and stopped on the other side along with Hank.

214

Hank pointed to the ground beside Camilla. "That's just how I found her."

Camilla looked down to the ground on her immediate left. Startled by the site of the dead body up close so suddenly, she exhaled forcefully, almost a grunt. Reilly leaned forward to glance at the corpse.

"Over here....," Hank pointed to the ground to his right, about a foot-and-a-half away from the girl's outstretched legs. Three small yellow flags stuck out of the mud. "And over here..." He pointed to the left of the body, where another three flags had been planted. "...We found footprints that we think belong to the perpetrator. Yongauer swore that he never got within a yard of her body, which checks out." Hank pointed to the ground immediately in front of the three of them; a clear half-footprint was visible with the trademark Nike Swoosh.

"After Yongauer, I was the first on the scene. I noticed those footprints on my arrival, and tried to avoid them as best as I could. I crouched down beside the girl on her left to feel for a carotid pulse."

"Which way did those footprints come in, and how did they leave?" Reilly asked.

"And how did you get here so fast?" Camilla asked, somewhat pointedly.

Hank answered Camilla's query first. "My daughter participated in the soccer tournaments this morning. I was technically off duty."

He looked up at Reilly and signaled for them to walk a few steps further down the trail, careful to take a wide berth around the corpse. He pointed down a trail on the other side of Danielle's body.

"We found two partial footprints heading this direction on this trail, so I assume that's how the perp got here. We haven't found any that point away from the scene." He swept his hands in front of him, motioning to bordering trees and weeds in all directions. "We carefully surveyed the brush and didn't find any sizable disturbances." Hank then turned and pointed a hand down the continuing trail, toward the pond. "My best guess is that he left in this direction."

"What's in that direction?" Reilly asked.

"There's a small pond just to the northwest, but there's also several short trails that lead to side streets."

"Have you questioned the people living on those side streets? Maybe you have witnesses there," Reilly pointed out.

"I have about a half-dozen officers in the process of going door-to-door right now." Hank lowered his head for a brief moment before looking back up, almost apologetically. "Problem is this damn soccer tournament. We have well over two hundred out-of-towners sitting out there, not to mention the several dozen locals. People parked their cars all over these side streets because parking here at the fields was limited to buses only. Asking people to remember if they saw any strangers today won't be too helpful."

"But remembering any strangers who drove off in a hurry between 12:30 and 1 certainly would be," Camilla offered.

"Right," Hank agreed. "So, we're going through the motions. I'm hopeful, I guess. Just being realistic."

They turned back around and came back towards the body. Reilly pointed down the trail to their right, the one Hank indicated earlier had brought the killer to the scene. "Where does that trail go?"

216

"It starts at the corner of the soccer fields, about twenty-five yards south of the entrance to this trail." Hank pointed to the trail on their left, the one they had walked down a few minutes earlier.

Without saying anything, Reilly walked quickly down that trail, paying attention to avoid the yellow flags in the mud marking the suspicious footprints. Camilla and Hank shared a glance before following him. They caught up to him at the mouth of the trail, where he has stopped to look out at the fields.

"He stood here," Reilly declared. He turned toward Hank and Camilla to further elucidate. "He stood here where he could watch the games, looking like an average spectator. He even probably picked a team to cheer for, trying to blend in. Then he saw the victim walk down that trail by herself, probably the first one to go down there in a while." Reilly turned back down the trail they had just traversed. "He hustled down this trail to head her off at the pass."

"Makes sense," Hank agreed.

Camilla looked back out at the fields, then down the trail behind them. "He knows this place." Both men turned to face her as she continued. "He's been here before, studied the trails. He knows this layout well."

Hank nodded. "And he probably knew that the side streets would be filled with cars, making his escape much less noticeable."

Reilly squinted, considering the possible implications of this hypothesis. "Are we dealing with a local?"

Camilla began shaking her head. "I don't know." She wiped her face, as if trying to manually clear away the confusion. "I don't think so. Why would he strike as far away as York and Frederick only to then murder someone in his own back yard?"

217

"Drawing us in?" Heath suggested.

Camilla looked at him quizzically, indicating her need for clarification. Hank became more confused as the conversation progressed, but he kept quiet.

"Something hasn't felt right this entire time. He obviously wants something greater than just to kill. He has some kind of message…" His voice trailed off, and his eyes met Camilla's. Almost simultaneously they began running back down the trail, toward the body. Hank followed not far behind them, having no idea why they were running.

Upon arriving back at the crime scene, Reilly knelt down beside an open CSI kit and pulled out four latex gloves. Still kneeling, he turned to face the Hank Hanley as he put on his gloves and extended the other two to Camilla.

"Is your investigative team done with the body? Photographs, et cetera?"

Hank looked at the group of officers standing nearby. One man came forward, holding a sophisticated digital camera. "I think so," said the middle-aged officer without much confidence. He turned a knob on the camera, switching to "view" mode rather than "camera" mode, then handed it to Reilly. In one fluid motion, Reilly took the camera from the officer and passed it to Camilla. She quickly scrolled through the nearly three dozen photos and nodded to Reilly. "Looks adequate."

Reilly nodded in return and moved forward toward the body, staying hunched over to kneel easily again once beside the dead little girl. He palpated the front of her shorts, but found no pockets. He visually surveyed her top, looking for a breast pocket in her T-shirt, finding none. He looked back a Camilla.

"Back pockets," she said, as she knelt down beside him. She slid her hands under the girl's left shoulder and Reilly cupped his under her hip, and they rolled the body onto its side. Rigor mortis had not yet set in, so this task proved more difficult than they had expected.

"Nope," Reilly announced. They gently let the body rest back on the ground. Reilly began looking around the body in concentric circles, beginning to branch out to survey the ground surrounding her. As he did this, Camilla scuffled down to the girl's right ankle, reaching into her sock. Her eyes lit up as she extracted the piece of paper and held it up in front of her face.

"Bag," she commanded, not lifting her eyes from the clue that dangled in front of them. A younger officer who stood beside the camera man scurried over to the CSI kit and removed a plastic evidence bag. He handed it to Camilla, who placed the slip inside of it.

She looked at Reilly with a hint of sadness. Though they both obviously suspected as much, this scrap of paper confirmed that this little girl had fallen victim to their killer, The Playground Predator, now having struck for the third time. Reilly concurrently made the same revelation, but he returned her glance with the wide-open eyes of an excited little boy.

45

Jackson Byrne had spent much of that afternoon working outside in the yard. Jonah had come out for almost two hours to help his daddy. His "help" mostly consisted of kneeling beside Jack in the grass, staging an innocent little inquisition with a barrage of mundane questions, as Jack painstakingly removed one weed after another from his lawn. Despite spreading granulated lawn treatments with some regularity, he could never seem to eradicate all of the dandelions and other photosynthetic vermin from his property. Jack professed this as a source of much frustration in his life, though in actuality he found all aspects of yard work—even pulling weeds with a spade—a nice break from his often stressful days.

Earlier that morning, while Jonah watched cartoons and Vicki closed herself off in the spare bedroom to do a little Yoga, Jack had tried once again to return Melissa Hollows' phone call. Again it went straight to voicemail, and again Jack did not leave a message.

After he pulled enough weeds to satisfy his perfectionism, Jack had mowed the lawn and spread yet another lawn treatment. He had showered off the dirt from his knees and under his fingernails, and now he stood out on the back deck, drinking a bottle of beer and waiting for the grill to warm up. He looked out over their modest-sized property, silently admiring his day's work.

Jack set his bottle of beer down on the railing beside the grill and went inside to get the burgers from the kitchen. Jonah knelt on a stool at the island as he tore leaves of romaine lettuce into small pieces and put them into a large serving bowl. "Careful there, Tiger," Jack warned to his son.

"Tiger?" Jonah asked, looking somewhat disappointed.

"Yeah." He looked at Jonah and read the expression on his face. "What's wrong with 'Tiger'?"

Jonah hung his head dejectedly. "Daddy... I was a lion, not a tiger."

Jack tried to hide his smile, remembering Jonah's proud performance in the school play this past week. "I know you were, buddy. 'Tiger' is just a nickname. Tiger. Sport. Champ."

Jonah looked up at him with his puppy dog eyes. "Can 'Lion' be a nickname?"

Jack smiled the endearing smile of a proud, loving father. "Sure it can." He turned around and walked back outside. As soon as the screen door closed, Jack twirled 180 degrees and came back through the door into the kitchen. He looked at Jonah, and, trying to use the exact some intonation as he had one minute ago, said, "Careful there, Lion."

Jonah grinned from ear to ear. He then deliberately pulled his knees a little closer together to firm his balance on top of the stool. "Yes, Daddy."

Jack walked over to the refrigerator and removed the plate of freshly made hamburger patties covered in plastic wrap. He glanced at the small TV in the corner of the countertop, which played the local news. He put his free hand around Vicki's waist and gave her a kiss on the cheek as he passed by. She smiled.

He went back out on the deck. As he placed the last burger on the grill, Vicki called out from the kitchen. "Jack?"

"Yeah?" he replied.

221

Vicki had walked over to the door to talk to Jack through the screen. "Heath Reilly is on the news."

Jack turned to face her with a puzzled look on his face.

"Yep," Vicki confirmed as she turned back to the TV.

Jack followed her inside, looking across the room to the small flat screen. He could make out Heath's image with a few microphones in front of him. Jack moved into the nearby living room and turned on their large flat screen, quickly navigating to the same channel then turning up the volume.

"...Likely the same perpetrator of the two murders in York, Pennsylvania, and Frederick, Maryland, that the FBI is currently investigating," Reilly said into the microphones. A text banner across the bottom of the screen identified Special Agent Heath Reilly, FBI; below that, in a smaller font, it revealed Front Royal, Virginia, as the locale. Jack could also see half of Camilla Vanderbilt's face in the background.

The news then cut to another taped interview, this one of a thirty-something woman in a windbreaker. "It was terrifying," she proclaimed. "They kept us all on the bleachers for, like, ever, until they could talk to each one of us. Meanwhile, my kids are scared out of their minds, and I'm trying to keep them calm. We just came here to play a soccer tournament!"

Then the broadcast cut to a live shot of the reporter on the scene, a confident, fast-speaking Latina woman, standing in front of a tree line decorated with yellow police tape in the waning sunlight. "The identity of today's victim is still being withheld by police until all family can be notified, though authorities confirm that she was a nine-year old girl, just like the other two victims in York and Frederick that

Agent Reilly mentioned. Police are not releasing any other
information tonight. However, it seems clear that The Playground
Predator has struck again, and he remains at large."

Jack turned back to the kitchen. "The Playground Predator,"
he muttered.

"Catchy," Vicki commented. "Do you know anything about
this one? Did you work on this at all?"

"Yeah. Info about the first two came in this week. I sat in on
the first debriefing on Wednesday. Pretty awful stuff."

"It's all pretty awful stuff, Jack," Vicki reminded him.

"Yeah," Jack agreed somberly.

Vicki studied his face. "Do you miss it? Do you wish that
you were there?"

"No," he answered quickly, more because he knew it was the
answer he needed to say than because it was the truth. He didn't want
to take the time to think about how he felt; that seemed moot given
that he had essentially resigned. Jack had never found offering second
guesses very productive.

He looked down at the remote to hit the Power button, when
Vicki said, "Oh my gosh, look." He looked up at her to see her
pointing at the little TV across the kitchen. He then turned his
attention to the screen in front of him to see a photo of Melissa
Hollows in the upper right corner behind the news anchor.

"Melissa Hollows, a former model and ex-wife of Washington
Redskins wide receiver Lamond Hollows, was found dead in her
Georgetown home today of an apparent suicide," the anchor
announced.

Jack's face went white.

223

BEN MILLER

The newscast cut to a uniformed man behind a podium, identified by text as Justin Jones, Chief of Police, District of Columbia. "Nine-one-one received a call at 2:48 this afternoon from a friend of Ms. Hollows, who came by the home when Ms. Hollows failed to meet her for a scheduled racquetball game early this morning. She likely died sometime yesterday afternoon. At this point, her death is still under investigation, though it does appear that she may have taken her own life."

Back in the studio, the anchor continued the story. "Ms. Hollows first entered the national spotlight when she married the NFL star, who at the time had a reputation as a partying playboy, among other things. Of course, she is most famous as the mother of Lamaya Hollows, who was abducted from their affluent DC neighborhood last spring and found murdered several days later. Lamond Hollows' publicist has denied any comment at this time. Melissa Hollows was thirty-six years old."

"Oh my God," Vicki said as she turned to face Jack. Dazed, he slowly met her eyes. "That poor woman," Vicki lamented.

Jack blinked, but didn't say anything initially. He didn't know what to say. After several seconds he broke his silence, speaking deliberately. "She called me."

"What?" Vicki asked. "When?"

"Yesterday," Jack answered. "She left me a very odd message. I was cleaning my stuff out at the office, so I didn't take the call." Jack knew that, if authorities truly planned on a full investigation, her phone records would be checked, and her phone call to an FBI agent on the day she died surely would get noticed. He found no sense in hiding it from Vicki now.

224

"What did she say? Did you save the message?"

He looked down at his phone, trying to decide if he would play the message for Vicki. Before he settled on a response, his phone began to ring. He looked at the display: Philip Prince. Jack looked perplexed yet again.

"Who is it?" Vicki asked.

"Philip Prince," Jack replied as he answered the call.

He put the phone to his ear. "Hello, Philip," he said as he walked back onto the back deck.

"Hello, Jack. Have you seen the news about Melissa Hollows?" Prince spoke briskly, pressured, almost irritated.

"Yes, I just saw it on the news."

"Did you have sex with that woman, Jack?"

"What?" Jack responded, truly offended. Though Prince's accusation hit the mark precisely, Jack felt insulted that Prince would even ask.

"Did you fuck Melissa Hollows? I saw the tabloids last year, and I ignored them at the time because it was none of my business. But that has now changed. Now it is my business. No judgment here, Jack. I love Vicki and I know that you love Vicki. That has nothing to do with this. I just need to hear the truth. From you."

"No," Jack lied. "No I did not."

Prince paused, and Jack offered nothing more. He sensed Prince trying to evaluate the truthfulness of his statement over the phone line. Finally, apparently satisfied, Prince said, "OK. I'm sorry to be blunt, but I'm sure you understand why I ask."

Given the Rupert Schultz debacle which opened the political door for him, Jack understood exactly why Prince felt the need to know this information. Jack knew he might face an uphill battle to keep his brief but secretive affair with Melissa under wraps, but he also felt compelled to fight that battle. "I do, I suppose," Jack admitted. "But it doesn't mean I'm not offended."

"Please accept my apologies," Prince replied. "In this line of work, though, I suggest you get used to people caring a lot more about the details of your personal life than they ever have before."

"I suppose that's true," Jack conceded.

"OK. Sorry to bother you. Back to your weekend, Jack, my boy. I'll speak with you on Monday," Prince said, then promptly hung up

"OK," Jack said into an empty line.

"Daddy," Jonah said behind him.

Jack took his phone from his ear and looked down at it, still reeling a bit from the events of the last ten minutes.

"Daddy," Jonah repeated from behind the screen door.

Jack snapped into the present moment and turned around to face his son. "Yeah, buddy?"

Jonah pointed at the grill. Smoke poured from the borders of the closed lid.

"Shit!" Jack exclaimed, then quickly correcting himself with, "Shoot!"—which really did not make much sense, as Jonah clearly had already heard him swear. Jack darted to the grill and pulled back the lid to reveal small black orbs on the surface of the grill, more resembling charcoal than hamburgers at this point.

Jack turned back to the screen door, where now Vicki stood behind Jonah, both of them looking at him. "How does pizza sound?" he asked, deflated.

226

46

"Thanks for getting dinner."

Heath Reilly sat in the desk chair of his hotel room, his foot-long turkey sub sitting on its paper wrapper in front of him.

"Sure," Camilla replied, her voice muffled by the big bite of meatball-with-marinara sub in her mouth. She sat opposite him, on the armchair he had pulled over to the desk. After she swallowed the bolus down with the assistance of a gulp of Diet Coke, she said, "Thanks for getting the rooms."

Reilly pointed to the end of the long dresser, beside the outdated tube television set. "There are your keys. You're right next door, in 215." Her small rolling suitcase sat on the floor just beside the dresser.

"Great, thanks," she mumbled; she had already taken another bite.

Reilly felt famished earlier, but the sensation had passed, at least for now. "Beyond hungry" his mother used to call it. He grabbed a notebook from the outside pocket of his rolling tote bag and slapped it on the desk. He looked up at Camilla, who had almost finished half of her sub.

She returned his gaze, then let her eyes drop down a bit sheepishly. She grabbed a napkin as she finished chewing her most recent bite. "Sorry," she said with an empty mouth, as she wiped around her lips. "I was starving."

"No worries," Reilly returned.

"Are you going to eat?"

Reilly looked back down at his sandwich, getting colder by the minute. After several more seconds, he answered her. "Yeah," he said as he picked half of his sub.

"Something wrong?" Camilla asked.

"No," he replied quickly, but then reconsidered. "I don't know. Maybe I'm starting to feel the pressure of being lead on this investigation. This could get huge."

Camilla had just picked up the second half of her sub, but she promptly put it back down. She got a determined look on her face, like a coach building up her trailing team at halftime. "First of all," she put her elbow up on the table and stuck out her thumb, "you haven't officially been named Lead on this yet."

Reilly shot a very hurt look at her.

"But I'm sure that you will soon, especially after today," she encouraged. "Second of all," her index finger popped out from her curled fingers, "this is already huge. And if we don't start getting some answers, it's just going to get bigger. There are three little kids dead in three states, all during the light of day and all seemingly random. This is going to start terrorizing people through the mid-Atlantic.

"Third," she extended her middle finger to join her thumb and forefinger, "this is such a huge opportunity for you. Look what happened to Jack with one high-profile case. Not that I'm saying that you're Jackson Byrne, but you could really make a name for yourself within the Bureau."

Reilly, responding appropriately to this pep talk, began to look a little more animated.

"What did happen to Jack, by the way?" Camilla asked, breaking character for a minute with an intrigued look on her face. "Do you think he really is going to run for some kind of public office?" She knew that Reilly had read the article from *The Post*— probably a hundred times, since he had been quoted in several spots.

"Yeah, I don't know. It doesn't really seem like him, though, does it?"

"I don't know. I could see it."

"All I know for sure is that Harringer just said that Jack wouldn't be working on this case," Reilly said.

"Yeah. And he never said why."

"No," Reilly reflected. "And I guess I have been so excited to be driving this thing that I never really stopped to ask."

"Weird," Camilla said, contemplatively. She put her elbow back in her lap and picked up her sandwich. "Do you want to finish eating before we call Harringer?"

"Sure," he agreed. They both ate quickly and silently. Camilla drew the last of her Diet Coke through a straw before it started slurping.

"Ready?" Reilly asked as he reached for his phone.

"Yeah," Camilla answered as she turned to get her notebook out of her shoulder bag.

Reilly placed his phone in the center of the table and called Harringer's cell phone. Reilly tapped the icon for speaker phone.

After two rings, Harringer picked up on the other end and offered his usual greeting. "Harringer," he said.

"Hi, Dylan, it's Heath and Camilla," Reilly said.

There was a brief pause, as they could hear a door closing in the background. "Ok, get me up to speed," Harringer ordered.

They offered a brief overview of the events in Front Royal and the direct link to their killer, with Reilly doing most of the talking.

"Witnesses?" Harringer asked.

"No one reliable so far, sir," Reilly replied. "It was a tough scene to control, but the local PD felt pretty confident that no witnesses got out without being questioned first."

"We're working on the surrounding neighborhoods right now, with locals going door-to-door," Camilla explained further.

"OK. And the shoeprint?"

"I already e-mailed all of the photos back to Erikson in forensics," Heath said. Glenn Erikson worked in their forensics lab in Quantico and was an up-and-coming expert in the field of shoeprint forensics, among other things. "I spoke to him on the phone, and he said he should have some info for us by tomorrow."

"And the note?"

"That's been a little tougher, sir," Reilly admitted. "We have forensic photos of it, but I can't get a hold of Friesz. I tried his cell, and Lisa in dispatch even connected me to his home phone—no answer."

"Hmm," Harringer uttered, his tone revealing neither disappointment nor confusion.

After a pause, Reilly continued, "My plan is to try him again later. If I haven't heard from him by tomorrow, I'll contact the field office in DC about getting another linguistics consultant."

"Sounds fair," Harringer commented.

After another brief pause, Camilla chimed in. "Dylan, one conclusion that we speculated today is that our killer had to know this area pretty well. He had to have surveyed these trails before today to know his best area for attack and to have an established escape route."

"Makes sense," Harringer conceded.

"And, in retrospect, we got the same feeling from the previous two murders," Camilla continued. "Our un-sub definitely did re-con in York, knowing exactly how to come and go from that playground without being spotted. The same is probably true of Frederick, though neither of us have seen that crime scene first hand."

"Right," Harringer said. "Shaver should be able to give us more on that, hopefully by tomorrow." Yesterday Harringer had sent Charlie Shaver to Frederick to investigate that crime scene, as well as to interview Stephanie McBurney's family and any possible witnesses.

"Right," Reilly and Camilla said in unison, then shared a look of surprise. Camilla went on. "So we think we should entertain the idea that something other than killing has brought our un-sub to these places. I am going to look into conventions, festivals, road shows, and so on that may have passed through these three towns in the last few months."

"Good idea," Harringer said.

Reilly drew a deep breath. "And I would like to try to get a subpoena for hotel records from all three towns as well. If we can find one person who booked or paid for a hotel room in each of these three towns in the last few months, that could be a great lead."

"How many hotels and motels do you think we're talking about here?"

231

Reilly paused and looked to Camilla. "There were... about seven hotel choices around Front Royal here. I would expect maybe the same around Frederick, maybe a few more in York?" Reilly guessed.

Harringer paused on the other end, which left Reilly's heart hanging in his throat. This felt like his first major contribution to the investigation, other than gathering existing data, and he craved acceptance of his idea. Finally, after about fifteen seconds—which felt like fifteen minutes—Harringer responded. "I think that's a great idea." Reilly breathed an inaudible sigh of relief while Harringer continued. "But it's going to be a tough sell. Getting records from two to three dozen places over a—what?—two month span? Four month span? Plus we're going to need a federal judge— we're dealing with three states." He paused again, contemplating the suggestion. "Let me make some phone calls tomorrow and see if I can get anything done. It'll be Sunday, but I could find someone who will listen."

Reilly, feeling vindicated, shot a genuinely proud smile at Camilla. He looked like a fifth grader who had just successfully spelled "onomatopoeia" in the spelling bee. Ever the loyal partner, she offered an approving smile back at him. As much as she sometimes disliked working with Reilly, for his often childish, stubborn behavior, his awkward, insecure interactions, and his feigned arrogance, she still felt herself rooting for him to succeed.

"What else?" Harringer queried.

Reilly shrugged and looked at Camilla, as if to say, *I'm done.*

Camilla, however, was not. "I'm going to attend the autopsy tomorrow morning. Based on what we saw at the scene, though, I'm not expecting anything different from the other two."

"Yep," Harringer agreed. "Don't mention anything about the sternal bruising or the fractured ribs, at least until the end. See if they pick up on that subtlety on their own. Keep in mind that we still haven't leaked that to anyone, and we don't plan to."

"Yes, sir," Camilla complied.

"While we're on the subject of leaks..." Harringer paused for effect. Reilly and Camilla could hear him shifting in his seat. When he came back in, his voice was louder; he must have pulled his phone closer to his face. "Tell me how 'The Playground Predator' got out."

Reilly and Camilla exchanged a surprised glance. Reilly broke the silence. "I... we didn't know that it had."

"On the news tonight, during your little press conference. A field reporter for a local station used it. Then the networks followed. I've seen it in half-a-dozen headlines on the net and heard it on every news network in the last hour." Harringer sounded annoyed, as expected.

"I don't know, sir," Reilly admitted.

"Camilla?" Harringer inquired.

"No, sir. I didn't mention it to anyone."

"All right," Harringer said. "What about your little red-headed reporter friend?"

"I... don't know," Reilly responded. "I was very clear on our agreement. I'll touch base with her to get her story."

Camilla rolled her eyes, but it went unnoticed by Reilly.

"OK." The tone in Harringer's voice had changed, from mildly accusatory back to collegial. It also had the tone of a denouement; Camilla could almost picture him putting his hands on his hips. "I'll touch base with you two tomorrow. Keep trying to reach Friesz."

"Will do. Thanks, sir. Have a good night," Reilly concluded.

"Yep." Harringer replied. Then he hung up.

47

About an hour later Reilly sat by himself at a table beside the bar in Trendsetters, a local TGI Friday's knock-off. He mostly kept his eyes on the door, but occasionally he would look down at his quarter-empty bottle of Michelob Ultra and peel back the label a little further. He had spoken to Corinne O'Loughlin about thirty minutes ago and asked her to meet him here. She had just checked into her hotel, so she asked for about a half an hour to get oriented.

Reilly looked down at his watch. The half hour had elapsed four minutes ago.

He knew why he felt nervous, as he was immensely attracted to Corinne, but he genuinely had business to discuss with her. So this really did not constitute a social gathering whatsoever, he convinced himself. Once again he mentally went through his list of topics to discuss with her, chief among which was the moniker of The Playground Predator.

He looked back up at the entrance and caught a glimpse of her curly red locks, most of which she had pulled back in a pony tail, with a few stragglers purposefully left behind to dangled over the right side of her face. He felt his heartbeat accelerate and quickly looked away, back down at his beer. He suddenly felt embarrassed and a little stupid.

She approached his table, and he looked up surprised, as if he hadn't seen her come in.

"Hey!" Corinne said.

"Hey," Reilly said as he stood up impulsively. It felt like the gentlemanly thing to do.

235

She signaled to the bar on her right. "Are they coming to the table, or should I get a drink at the bar?"

"I've seen a waitress or two roaming around, but I think you're better off going straight up."

She nodded and turned to go to the bar. She whirled back in his direction and looked down at his beer. "You need another?"

Reilly looked down at the bottle in his hands—still three-quarters full. "No, I'm good." He sat back down as she walked over to the bar. It took her all of ten seconds to get the young male bartender's attention. She leaned over to place her order amidst the raucousness of four college-aged men beside her. Reilly's gaze moved down to examine her ass. Again his pulse quickened slightly. He quickly looked away to avoid getting caught, and then he took a deep breath to try to refocus. *Professional*, he reminded himself.

Corinne came back over to the table a couple of minutes later, carrying three bottles of Michelob Ultra. She slid one over in front of him and kept the other two for herself. "I thought I'd save us a trip in a few minutes," she explained.

"Oh, thanks," Reilly responded sheepishly. He had hoped to buy her a drink.

"I ordered some nachos too—I'm starving."

"Yeah, fine."

"Did you eat?" Corinne took a swig of her beer.

Reilly nodded. "Subway."

"Ooh, a gourmet. Well, you can still have some of my nachos. I probably won't eat them all." She looked over both shoulders and leaned into the table, speaking in a somewhat lower tone. She was a ball of energy. "So, number three, huh?"

236

Reilly nodded slowly, almost sadly. "Number three."

"So it's definitely linked to our killer?" she asked.

Reilly began to nod. Then he recognized an opening. "You mean the Playground Predator?"

"Yeah?" she replied, obviously not understanding why his tone had changed.

He studied her for a moment, trying to discern the veracity of her response. "Apparently a reporter used that term during a broadcast tonight."

Corinne looked shocked. "What?! Who?!"

Reilly's eyebrows rose up his forehead; he had not expected this response.

"That name was my idea!" she said. "That motherfucker stole it from me!"

"How do you suppose they did that? Have you used it with anyone?"

"No one, I swear," she promised. Reilly intuitively believed her. "I was waiting for the go-ahead from you to use it. Fuck!"

Reilly hadn't expected such profanity, especially during their first real meeting in person. He liked her fieriness. He wondered if she had that much passion with everything she did. "You're taking this pretty hard?"

"Hell yeah!" She took a deep breath and exhaled through her bottom lip, blowing those hanging strands of hair away from her forehead. "Sorry, I'm not mad at you, Heath."

She used my first name, he thought, trying hard to keep his best poker face and not reveal that he had noticed.

"I just…I don't know," Corinne tried to explain. "It's…"

Heath guessed that she rarely found herself at a loss for words. However, her struggle ended abruptly, as she rapidly shook her head with a few small oscillations and smiled.

"Whatever. It's not important." She took a fierce swig of her beer, swallowed it down, and took a deep breath. "So, what are you thinking now?"

Reilly recounted the details about the time leading up to Danielle Coulter's disappearance, her discovery, and the likely exit route. He explained their next few steps, about continuing to search for any witnesses that may have seen the un-sub. He had to be careful not to divulge too much, so he kept it simple. He did share his idea about the likelihood of the killer's preceding reconnaissance missions to each site.

"That makes sense," Corinne concurred. "Clearly he's not a local at any of these places, right? And he had to pick out his locations carefully, know the ins and outs. You can't explain his lack of being sighted at any of these scenes as simple luck."

"Exactly." Reilly took another sip of his beer. He was nearly two-thirds through his first bottle. He looked across the table as Corinne tipped hers back to polish off her first.

"So what does your day look like tomorrow?" she asked.

"My day?"

"Yeah. What's next for you in your part of this investigation? I assume you're hanging around here?"

"Yep. Camilla and I—"

"Vanderbilt?" she interrupted.

"Yeah. She came up with me today."

"You two work together a lot?" She took the first tug from her second beer.

"I guess. She's a good partner. Not that we are really assigned partners, per se. But we tend to get sent on assignments together often." As he said this, Reilly couldn't help wondering why she seemed so interested in how much he worked with Camilla. *Was she jealous?* he hoped. He swallowed down some more of his beer.

"Sorry, you were saying what you're doing tomorrow when I interrupted you."

"Oh, yeah. We need to go talk to the little girl's family tomorrow. We're all under the assumption that this is a random killing, just like the other two, but we can't leave any stone unturned. Perhaps these are all related in some way that we just can see yet."

She narrowed her eyes and studied him. "Do you think that's possible?"

"No," he answered quickly. "But we have to consider it."

She nodded. "You don't seem real enthused about doing that interview."

Reilly paused to finish his beer. He regarded her question, trying to decide how much to share. "It's obvious, huh?"

She nodded with an understanding curl to her lips.

"I hate it. It's the part of this job that I hate the most. By far. These people are going through the worst experience imaginable. Actually, it's so bad it's *un*imaginable. No one should be able to imagine what that is like. More often than not, they're so fucked up that they can't even think straight. And here I come along to ask them questions—sometimes very personal questions—to try to find the person who attacked their child. I try to stay compassionate, you know, but sometimes they stagger and stammer and can't give a straight answer because their heads are so jumbled. It becomes frustrating. But I can't get frustrated, because these people are going through such a fucking awful time." He waved his hands in front of him. "Sorry. TMI, huh?"

"No. I asked the question," she reassured him.

A muscular forearm with wristbands suddenly held a plate of nachos in between them. "Nachos?" the food-runner asked.

Corinne looked up at him. "That's us."

"Careful, plate's hot," the surely future body-builder said as he set the plate down in the middle of the table. He put a small plate in front of each of them and a short stack of napkins on the edge of the table. "You need anything else?" he asked, his tone clearly indicating that he didn't care.

"Nope, we're good," Corinne replied. Corinne began to pull tortilla chips off the pile and pop them into her mouth, disregarding the appetizer plate in front of her. "Help yourself," she reminded Reilly.

"Thanks, I'm good."

"Ok," she said, continuing to eat the smothered chips. "So," she began with her mouth still half-full. She took a swig of her beer to help her wash down the nachos. "It seems that talking with victims' families would constitute a decent proportion of your job. Am I right?"

Reilly nodded. "Ah, yeah, I suppose."

"If you hate that so much, do you hate your job?"

"No. Not at all. I kind of love my job."

"So all the other aspects are just that much better?" Before Reilly could answer, she fired another question his way. "I mean, why... why are you in this job? Why the FBI? Why CASMIRC specifically?"

Reilly took a deep breath and held it, not saying anything. He slowly let it out. He grabbed a cheese-laden chip from his end of the plate and popped it in his mouth. As he chewed he raised his eyebrows and nodded approvingly. He grabbed his beer and swallowed some, trying to nullify the sting of the jalapeno pepper that found its way onto his bite. He took another swallow.

Finally, he looked Corinne square in the eye, fully intending to answer her question honestly. She stared back at him with her striking green eyes, having taken a break from inhaling nachos. Reilly broke his gaze from their locked eyes and reached for another chip.

"You know, we've been talking a lot about me here. How about you tell me what your thoughts are on this case?"

His refusal to answer her question was obvious to both of them. Corinne decided to let it go—for now—and answered his question.

48

Jack lay in bed, staring at the ceiling. The warmth of the day had lasted into the evening, so Jack and Vicki turned on their ceiling fan on its lowest setting prior to going to bed. The glow from their bedside alarm clock cast looping shadows across the ceiling; Jack's eyes continuously followed the shadow of one blade as it went from short and stubby on the near side to a long, slender one on the far side.

His thoughts bounced back and forth between the two momentous pieces of news from that day. A third child murdered, and The Playground Predator surely the culprit. He hated the name, he thought to himself. Having a media moniker seemed to play right into his hands, to build his fantasy. He had spent too much of his time in the past wondering how much the mass media, in all its iterations, altered the course of police investigations in this society. He decided long ago to lament this no more, accept it as part of the job, and move past it. Hell, as a published author on the topic of a sensationalized crime, he now could lump himself into the media heap. He didn't like thinking about that very much at all.

He wondered if this third victim came with another message, embedded in a foreign language. Surely it had; the killer would have no reason to stray from his MO at this point. What did it say? What did it all mean? And, of course, the biggest question of them all, why kill innocent little girls? And why now?

And why—*Dear God, why*—would Melissa Hollows take her own life? She had been through some horrible things, worst of which losing a child. Her marriage had crumbled. She had slept with a married man. But she had always seemed so strong, so self-assured. Suicide did not make any sense to Jack.

But he knew that it must; he must somehow make sense of it. She had called him yesterday for a reason. He replayed her voicemail again in his head. It certainly had romantic undertones, but it didn't sound romantic at all, not in the way that she had said it—sobbing, nearly hysterical. Her delivery took a possibly endearing message and made it almost scary.

Did she want him to feel guilty? Was this about him? He already felt tremendous guilt, every day. But for Vicki, not for Melissa.

But what if he had answered his phone yesterday instead of letting it go to voicemail? Could he have prevented this? The thought hadn't crossed his mind before now, and it terrified him. Perhaps Melissa was reaching out for help, and, for some reason, he served as her last lifeline. Had he answered his phone, would she still be alive? He quickly shoved this idea out of his head; his mind couldn't bear to contemplate that much responsibility right now. Not for this.

He tried to refocus his thoughts on his current project: his political platform. He had a great base, as he had spent almost an entire chapter in his book discussing child protection laws. Since his book, they had become a hot topic in social circles and around Capitol Hill. He knew the current laws' shortcomings inside and out. Now he needed to find a solution, a proposal to propel his campaign. A vague outline could suffice for now, but eventually he needed to conjure up something concrete, something that would work. He had no intentions of someday getting elected to public office only to fall short of his campaign promises. He saw this as the bane of our current political system.

Suddenly his thoughts shifted back to Melissa's voicemail. With the ferocity and abruptness of a thunderclap, a thought rose to his consciousness: her message seemed familiar. He pored through his interactions with her— despite how ashamed some of those now made him feel— trying to remember the details of their conversations. After several minutes he felt almost certain that she had never uttered those words to him before. Still, he couldn't shake the feeling that he had somehow heard that phrase from her voicemail sometime before.

As he pondered this topic, he found that he could no longer follow the shadow of a single ceiling fan blade in its oblong path. His eyes felt heavy, so he decided to let them close.

49

The morning after Jack had sex with Melissa Hollows for the second and final time he got out of bed shortly after 5:00 am. He hadn't slept much at all, thoughts of Lamaya Hollows' killer's DNA spiraling through his head. He quietly rolled off his side of the mattress, showered, and dressed, all without waking Vicki. As he silently opened the bedroom door to leave, however, she stirred.

"Where are you off to?" She squinted at the digital clock on his nightstand. "It's so early."

"I know. I'm sorry," Jack said, apologizing for so much more than she knew. "I got a hunch last night. I couldn't sleep."

She nodded, her eyes still mostly closed, then rolled away from him. "Good luck, hon. Have a good day." She nearly slurred the last two words; she fell back asleep before he got to the kitchen.

Instead of going to his office at CASMIRC in Quantico, Jack drove straight to the police station in Potomac, Maryland. He arrived around 7:00 am. He parked in the mostly empty municipal lot adjacent to the station. He decided it was too early to call the Twin Towers McElhenny and Minert, so he chose to kill some time by walking half a block to the nearest Starbucks for his morning coffee. When he got back to the station, he sat for a minute on the front steps, checking his e-mail on his Blackberry and finding nothing of importance. He put the phone back on his belt.

He felt anxious, excited. He dug his thumb and forefinger into his eyes, rubbing deeply, before pinching the bridge of his nose. He surveyed the well-manicured lawn in the front of the police station.

The sun glinted off a dew drop, waiting to fall from the leaf of a rhododendron a few feet away.

His current state of anticipation conjured up one of his earliest memories: Christmas Eve, four or five years old. He had gone to bed as instructed around 9 o'clock and somehow managed to fall asleep, despite his excitement about the following morning. Some time later—now he couldn't remember, but he thought that he hadn't yet learned how to tell time—he awoke. His room remained pitch dark except for the glow of a street lamp emanating through the slit under his blinds. It was still nighttime, still too early to get up to open his presents. Santa may not have even had a chance to come to his house yet.

But what if he had come, and all of his presents—and Jody's presents too, of course—happened to just be sitting down there, waiting for him to play with them, ride them, toss them around? This thought bounced around his head, much like the oversized Superball he had gotten the Christmas before.

He sat up in bed and remained there, legs dangling over the side, listening intently. He could not hear any other noise in the house. Surely Mom and Dad had gone to bed by then. Surely everyone else lay fast asleep. After a few minutes, he could no longer resist the allure of the bounty that potentially already surrounded their Christmas tree. He slid out of bed, tip-toed to his bedroom door, twisted the knob slowly, and opened it inward. He knew of the characteristic creak that echoed down the upstairs hallway when his door reached the half-open point, so he stopped just short of it. He turned sideways and sidled out of his room into the hallway.

A BUSTLE IN THE HEDGEROW

Jody's door remained closed. Mom and Dad's door was closed too, and he couldn't see any light coming through underneath. They must be asleep. He continued down the hall, still on the tips of his toes, to the top of the stairs. A soft light bathed the staircase and spilled over to the end of the hall. He and Jody had insisted on keeping the living room table lamp lit to help Santa find his way around. Jack turned the corner at the end of the hall to look straight down the staircase. He climbed down the top two steps before pausing.

Did he really want to keep going? What if Santa had already come, and his presents really did sit down there? Could he still act surprised in the morning, when he and Jody ran down the stairs together to discover their haul?

He sat down on the steps to ponder his next move. His bravery had faltered, and now he contemplated retreating back to his room.

Just then he heard something: a clank. A single, solitary clank. It came from the living room. He racked his brain, trying to figure out what could have caused that sound. When he almost gave up, having convinced himself that he hadn't actually heard anything, another sound shot at him, again from the living room.

He froze. Someone was downstairs.

This second sound was different, higher pitched. This sound he recognized: a drinking glass being set down on a hard surface. An empty drinking glass. With this revelation he now understood the previous sound. He concluded that the first sound was that of an empty ceramic plate, coming to rest also on a hard surface. Such as

247

their brick hearth. The brick hearth in the living room where he and Jody had left a plate of cookies and a glass of milk for Santa Claus.

Santa Claus was in their house!

He didn't know what to do. He knew that Santa never came until after both he and his sister had fallen asleep. What would Santa do if he found out that one of them woke back up? He had heard from Aaron Turk, one of the other kids in preschool, that, if Santa ever sees a child awake, snooping around the house, he would take back all of the presents—even those for his sister—and he would probably skip over their house the following year. He wanted so badly to meet Santa. Jack would act very politely, of course, opening with a huge "thank you" for all of the presents, this and every year. Would his friendly greeting be enough to prevent Santa's disappointment, and the potential punishment that might ensue?

After several pensive seconds— always a thoughtful boy, that Jackson Byrne— he decided that he wouldn't take the risk. He quietly rose to his feet, walked back to his room, and crawled into bed. Amazingly, he willed himself to fall back asleep almost immediately.

Now Jack—who had turned into a thoughtful man— sat on these steps, feeling much like that little boy some thirty-five years ago: so eager to proceed, yet wary of the possible implications of his actions. He brimmed with both exhilaration and trepidation. He suddenly felt that so much rode on the next several hours, on the presence or absence of DNA in that piece of chewing gum recovered from Lamaya Hollows' stomach.

He twisted his wrist to read his watch. 7:46. It would have to do.

He stood up and walked inside. A young uniformed male officer sat behind thick glass at the front reception area. The officer, whose nametag read DENARDO, politely informed Special Agent Byrne that neither Detective McElhenney nor Detective Minert had reported in yet that morning. Luckily, Jack had their cell numbers in his phone. He chose to call McElhenney, the one with the deep bass voice. He walked back outside as he retrieved his cell phone.

McElhenney answered before the second ring.

"McElhenney."

"Hi, Mac, it's Jack Byrne."

"Jack, how are you? And what are you doing standing outside our police station?"

Flummoxed, Jack didn't reply. Something about McElhenney's deep voice made this sound unexpectedly accusatory. Before Jack could answer, or ask any questions of his own, McElhenney laughed and explained. "I just drove past. I'm in the parking lot. Be there in a minute."

Jack felt relieved, though he wasn't sure why he had briefly felt so anxious. He hung up his phone and put it away. Seconds later Bennett McElhenney entered his sightline, walking across the beautiful green grass of the station's lawn.

"Come on back to my office." McElhenney didn't stop moving; he just merely slowed down a little to exchange greetings. Jack followed him into the building, past Officer Denardo, who nodded knowingly, and into McElhenney's small office. McElhenney flashed an arm toward a chair inside the door as he walked around the metal desk and plopped down in his own chair. "What's up?" He jiggled the mouse on his desktop computer to awaken it from its overnight slumber.

Jack sat down and examined the office. The sheer number of personal items surprised him. He had been in a myriad detectives' offices over the years, and he didn't think he'd ever seen so much shit from someone's private life: at least two dozen photographs, all containing an image of McElhenney, often by himself; trophies on the bookshelf, most of which had either a basketball or an athletic-looking statuette holding a basketball on top; novelty coffee mugs with various expressions or worldwide locations printed on them. In the span of several seconds, Jack's impression of McElhenney swiftly changed; he now found him quite conceited. Jack doubted his own ability to work closely with someone so full of himself.

As he had no choice—at least not at this juncture—he decided to press on. He stopped scrutinizing the room and focused on McElhenney's eyes, which were looking at the computer screen in front of him. "The gum."

His attention successfully grabbed, McElhenney turned in his chair to face Jack. "Sorry? The gum?"

Jack nodded intently. "The gum found in Lamaya Hollows' stomach at autopsy. If she were sodomized, as the coroner's report suggests, and she still had that gum in her mouth at the time…"

"Sperm," McElhenney concluded. "DNA. Something."

"Yep," Jack concurred. "We need to get your path lab to cut into that gum ASAP, or, preferably—with your permission— get it down to one of my lab guys so they can run it. I think we could probably get results faster."

"No doubt," McElhenney agreed as he swiveled in his chair to pick up his phone. He looked at the clock on the edge of his desk. "It's after 8. Someone should be down there." He dialed the number from memory. He politely and cordially asked the assistant who answered the phone to go into the log and find the location of the stomach contents. After he hung up, preceded by a sincere "thanks so much for all your help," he swiveled again to face Jack fully. "Brilliant, man. This is brilliant."

Jack wondered if he had judged McElhenney too harshly earlier. He found himself beginning to like this guy a lot.

Within minutes, after Jack and McElhenney had a chance to rehash the known facts of the case to that point, the phone rang. McElhenney picked up the receiver and had a short conversation. Though McElhenney's portion of the conversation contained nothing more than three "yeses" and a "thank you," Jack concluded, mostly from McElhenney's bright-eyed smirk, that he spoke to the lab tech on the other end.

McElhenney led Jack past the elevator to a rubber-coated steel staircase at the end of the hallway, where they descended two stories to the medical examiner's office in the basement of the building. The lab tech already had the specimens packed up. Behind the counter sat a hand-held blue cooler—the type used by normal people to keep their six-pack chilled—which the clerk opened to show a smaller, white Styrofoam box with a sticker on top. The clerk used a small infrared gun to scan the barcode on the sticker; Jack could see the text below the barcode contained a series of digits, followed by "stomach contents," followed by the date of the autopsy. The clerk asked Jack to see his ID, which he slid through the side of the computer monitor like a credit card. He returned Jack's ID, then asked him to sign on a computer pad on the counter. Jack couldn't help getting the impression that he had just purchased a piece of jewelry at Macy's.

Jack picked up the pseudo-pen, but before signing, he asked the clerk, "What's your return policy?"

The clerk looked at him dryly. "It better come back in the same fuckin' condition that it left in. That's our return policy. Sir."

"OK," Jack said as he turned his attention to scrawling his name on the pad. "Not a new joke."

"Nope," affirmed the clerk.

"Lighten up, Paul, OK?" McElhenney pleaded.

Paul the Clerk reached down to rotate the top back onto the cooler. He grabbed it by the handle and put it on top of the counter for Jack to take. "C'mon," he replied to McElhenney, as if Jack had it coming. McElhenney shot him a glance, one a teacher might share with the student acting up in the front row while the principal visited the class. Paul rolled his eyes as he stepped away from the counter to continue cataloguing evidence entries.

Out in the parking lot, McElhenney apologized to Jack for Paul's behavior. "No worries, Mac," Jack assured. "Now I know why you're so nice to him on the phone."

"He can be a real pain in the ass if you get on his bad side."

"That sweetheart? Nah!" The two smiled as they shook hands. "I'll let you know as soon as I do," Jack said as he got into the driver's seat.

He took the small cooler containing its Styrofoam treasure straight to the FBI Forensics Complex in Quantico, a state-of-the-art facility housing numerous divisions that worked on specific aspects of forensic science. He had called ahead to the Nuclear DNA Unit, also known as the NDNAU—which Jack considered a silly acronym, as it barely saved any syllables over the actual name—so that they could expect him. Even though that office received dozens of samples per day, due to the high-profile nature of the Hollows case, the examination of— and potential extraction of DNA from— the gum in Lamaya Hollows' stomach took top priority.

Jack spent the rest of that day at the office looking through files, interview notes, photographs, and other pieces of evidence from the case. Or at least pretending to. He found it hard to focus, his attention alternating between the possibility of finding Lamaya Hollows' killer's DNA and trying to avoid the shameful, infuriating memories of his adulterous behavior over the past week. He left the office late, around 9:00, no longer able to tolerate sitting at his desk immersed in his thoughts. When he got home, Jonah had already gone to bed. Vicki lay in bed reading a novel. Luckily she appeared quite invested in her reading and didn't seem interested in talking too much. Jack did not feel up to talking with her right now, fearing that his self-hate and guilt might swell up and overwhelm him.

He awoke early the next day, having slept poorly once again. He was at his desk by 7:45, and the call came from NDNAU around 9:30. They had found usable DNA, distinct from Lamaya Hollows'. They should have it sequenced by the end of the day, when they would enter into CODIS to try to find a match. Jack reminded them unnecessarily that he should be the first phone call once they make the match.

He had been right. He had likely just solved this case.

Of course, the possibility existed that CODIS would not possess a copy of the killer's DNA, but Jack found this very unlikely. From the beginning of this case, he knew in his heart that this un-sub had struck before. Harringer had agreed; "This is not his first rodeo," he had said during one of their briefings. Jack got up to tell Harringer that NDNAU had recovered DNA.

As Jack approached the office, Heath Reilly rushed in to tell Harringer of a tip that had come through their 800-number. A woman from Arlington had called to offer information about a white minivan she spotted coming from behind the strip mall where they had found Lamaya's body early on the morning of the body's discovery. When Reilly briefly reviewed previous tips, he found one that referred to a white minivan in the Hollows' neighborhood on the day of the disappearance. This news excited Harringer, who assigned Reilly to cross-reference white minivans registered under the names of known sex offenders within a 500-mile radius and deployed Camilla Vanderbilt to Arlington to interview the woman in person.

Jack witnessed this all from just inside Harringer's office, where he stood, nonplussed. Harringer looked at him with a half-snarl, confused by Jack's silence. "This could be a big tip, Jack."

Jack could not match his exuberance, for a variety of reasons. "I suppose."

"You're distracted," Harringer observed. "What gives?"

"I found his DNA," Jack stated simply.

Harringer's face flattened, expressionless, before his eyebrows furrowed in a quizzical expression. Jack raised his eyebrows and nodded in confirmation. Harringer became anxious all of a sudden. "How?" he asked. Jack had never conducted an illegal investigation before—at least not that Harringer was aware of—but Harringer knew how important this case had become to Jack. He knew people sometimes did wacky things when pushed to the brink of their abilities.

"Bubble gum," Jack said.

Harringer put his palms in the air and shook his head. Jack's mild elusiveness began to irritate him.

"Her stomach contents. She had gum in there. I got the gum to NDNAU, and they found foreign DNA," Jack explained.

Harringer stood baffled. "How did...?" He couldn't finish his question, as the answer came to him before his mouth could spit out the words. "The bastard sodomized her, and she still had gum in her mouth."

Jack nodded sadly.

"Motherfuck." If this wasn't Harringer's favorite expletive, it certainly ranked somewhere in his top five.

"They should have it sequenced by tomorrow, and hopefully CODIS will spit out a match within 24 hours after that."

Harringer nodded resolutely, effectively putting behind him the awful thoughts of what their wanted man had done to that little girl. "Good. Great, Jack. But we still should follow-through on this white minivan thing."

"Definitely. I'll talk to a buddy at the DMV, see if anyone driving a white minivan had any traffic violations nearby that morning."

"Good." Harringer put his hands on his hips and turned to go back to his desk. He stopped and turned his shoulder around to face Jack. "I want to be your first phone call when you hear from CODIS."

"Of course."

Jack went back to his desk. An hour later he still hadn't made that phone call to the DMV. He knew this wild goose chase didn't matter; he would have a photo of the killer's driver's license in the next 48 hours, long before anything could pan out from the white minivan tips. Yet he also knew the importance of due diligence, of following orders, and chasing down every lead. So he finally placed the call. His contact told him he would look into it and get back to him, hopefully later in the day. Jack decided he would search the records himself instead, through the secure intranet in their office. By the end of the day, he had found one white minivan pulled over for running a red light at an intersection roughly four miles from that site. Leslie Concannon, a 38-year-old married mother of four running late to pick up her youngest from kindergarten, received a citation. No other white or grey minivans had been stopped for a traffic violation that day. About ninety minutes after Jack reached this conclusion, his DMV friend called to confirm this same result.

The rest of the day and night surprisingly passed quickly. Jack mustered the inner resolve to talk casually to Vicki that night, after finding time to play with Jonah a while before his bedtime. Jack began to feel more at ease in his own skin around his family. For the first time in the last two days, he thought that he and his marriage might survive his stumble.

He actually slept until the bludgeoning cacophony of his alarm at 7:00 the next morning. He got to work by 8:30, feeling somewhat refreshed. At 9:15, more due to lack of something better to do than any other reason, he called NDNAU. When he got connected to the forensic scientist whom he had spoken to yesterday, the man seemed surprised to hear from him.

"I was just about to call you," he said. His voice had the nasal, geeky intonation one might expect from a forensic scientist who spent all his working days in a laboratory. "We finished the sequence, and, within... oh... 35 minutes, I'd say...CODIS gave us a match."

Jack's heart raced. He had experienced the exhilaration of big breaks before, on other cases, but he couldn't remember feeling so electrified by it before. "Send it over. Please."

"Sure," the scientist replied. "Jackson Byrne..." he said aloud as he searched the e-mail directory for Jack address. "Here. Got it."

Jack could hear the guy tap his mouse with authority, likely as he hit "send." Jack maximized Outlook on his desktop. Within several seconds— that seemed more like days—a new e-mail popped into Jack's inbox. "Got it. Thanks," Jack said as he already began to remove the receiver from his face to place it back onto the phone.

He opened the e-mail and double-clicked on the attachment, a three-page document containing mostly a bunch of lines of code of a DNA sequence. But Jack focused solely on the very top of the first page: the driver's license. Melvin Andrew Young's driver's license.

Melvin Andrew Young.

The name meant nothing to Jack. He had never heard it before.

But he recognized the face.

I interviewed him.

Jack looked up at the ceiling, his mind racing through the mental pictures of all the people he had interviewed during this investigation, trying to remember where he had seen this man before.

He looked back down at the screen, studying the man's face. His eyes quickly scanned the rest of the document, stopping briefly to notice that Young's vehicle registration listed a black Toyota RAV 4 SUV, not a white minivan.

I told you so, he allowed himself to think smugly.

It seemed that this brief diversion provided what his brain needed to arrive at its epiphany.

The school. Melvin Young is a teacher at Lamaya Hollows' school.

But that teacher's name was not Melvin Young.

DAY SEVEN:
SUNDAY

50

Reilly awoke in a daze on Sunday morning, initially confused by his strange surroundings. Despite how frequently this happened to him when he slept in an unfamiliar place, it still produced a modicum of anxiety until he remembered: the hotel room in Front Royal. He looked at his wristwatch—he had always slept wearing his wristwatch—which read 7:50. He knew Camilla well, and knew she would be awake by now.

"Hello." Camilla sounded out of breath when she answered her phone.

"Hey, it's Heath."

"Hey... Sorry I'm... just finishing... a jog."

"No prob. Meet in the lobby in thirty?"

Camilla paused briefly on the other end. When she spoke again, she controlled her breath remarkably well. "Can do, but I'll still need to grab a quick breakfast."

"Me too. See you then."

Thirty-four minutes later, Reilly emerged from the elevator into the small lobby of the hotel. Camilla stood waiting for him. She pointed to the small café area that abutted the lobby. "Free continental breakfast?"

259

"Free food always tastes better," Reilly replied.

Reilly had a muffin, a banana, and a coffee; Camilla drank a bottle of water with her English muffin and grabbed an apple and another water to go. Camilla drove again. They sat quietly for the first few minutes, until Reilly broke the silence.

"I hate—HATE—this part of the job."

Camilla looked at him out of the corner of her eye. "You say that every time."

"Do I?" he asked, but he knew that he did.

Camilla nodded. "Yes."

"Maybe I'm hoping that if I complain enough about it someday you'll just offer to do this yourself."

"Fat chance." Camilla smiled at him. "We work well together. I spend so much effort trying to ask empathetic questions that I sometimes miss subtle stuff. You just sit there, looking like a stump, but you pick up on that stuff."

"Fair enough," Reilly said, appeased. In reality he had no idea how well Camilla knew him, and how well she could play his strings.

"How was your date last night?" Camilla asked playfully.

"C'mon."

"What?"

Reilly shook his head and took a deep breath. "She said she had no idea how 'The Playground Predator' got out. She actually seemed pretty pissed about it. I believe her."

"Really?"

"Yeah, I do."

"Shocker there."

"Come on!" Reilly now seemed to get a little upset, taking offense that he might let a possible attraction—to which he hadn't actually admitted yet—get in the way of his professional judgment.

"*Turn right onto South End Way,*" the pleasant, ostensibly British woman on the nav system instructed from the middle of the dashboard.

"Oh, please. I'm just teasing you," Camilla said with a chuckle as she turned the wheel. "And so what? There'd be nothing wrong with it. She's an attractive, single woman, you're a... single man..." She didn't want to stroke his ego too much, so she left out any complimentary adjectives.

"Well, at any rate," Reilly began, trying to change the subject. "She offered some interesting thoughts on the case."

Camilla's smile faded quickly, back to business. "Such as?"

"She pointed out that the three cities in which the murders have happened form an arc."

"An arc?"

Reilly brought up his right forefinger to draw a curved line in the air in front of him. "York, PA at the top, like 12 o'clock; Frederick just shy of 11; and Front Royal at about 9 o'clock."

"And DC in the middle," Camilla finished the thought.

Reilly brought his finger right in front of his chest, pointing directly outward, and thrust it forward into the middle of the imaginary circle he had begun drawing in the air. "DC in the middle."

"Hmmm," Camilla murmured with a hint of approval at Corinne O'Loughlin's investigative skills.

"Yeah. It may not amount to anything, but it gives us something to look into when we're done here."

BEN MILLER

"You don't think we're going to find anything useful here?"

Reilly took a deep breath, held it, and shook his head. He let out his breath in a soft sigh. "I don't. I think he's too good, at least at this point. We're going to have to find him; he's not going to offer himself up to us."

"Yeah," Camilla agreed.

"Arriving at 487 South End Way, on left."

Camilla guided the Expedition into an open spot on the street across from the Coulter family home. She recognized the unmarked police car across from them, parked at the curb in front of the home. She felt some relief that they wouldn't be the first investigators there that day. It somehow eased the burden of their impending mission.

The Coulters owned a modest home. The wood siding could have used a fresh coat of paint, but it otherwise stood in good repair. They shared a driveway with their neighbors to the right. Camilla and Reilly walked up the driveway, then along the curved sidewalk that led to the Coulters' front door. Before they reached the small front porch, a terrier abruptly appeared at the front window, barking annoyingly. It must have perched itself atop a couch or another piece of furniture on the other side. Camilla and Reilly paused simultaneously, both briefly taken aback by the canine. Camilla restarted up the steps of the porch first, followed by Reilly. When she rang the doorbell, the dog took a brief break from its yapping as it jumped off the couch and ran to greet them inside the screen door.

"Hazel, easy," a raspy man's voice called from inside the house. The dog stopped barking and looked behind her. "C'mere girl." Hazel looked back at Reilly and Camilla before jogging away, directly between the shins of Hank Hanley, walking toward the front screen door. He wore a jacket, tie, and neatly pressed slacks, in stark contrast to the T-shirt and jeans from yesterday.

"Hi, guys," Hank said. He pushed the metal release on the door and shoved it open. Reilly grabbed the door and signaled for Camilla to enter the home before him.

"Hi, Hank," Camilla said as she walked into the small living room.

"Hey," Reilly said before his lips pursed, preparing to put on his sympathetic face for the bereaved parents.

"Mr. and Mrs. Coulter are in here." Hank signaled to a room past the living room. Camilla followed his pointing hand, and Reilly trailed several steps behind.

When they turned the corner from the living room into the kitchen, they saw Mr. and Mrs. Coulter sitting at the circular pressed-wood kitchen table. At first they both stared at the coffee cups in front of them. As if following some unseen, predetermined cue, they both simultaneously raised their heads slowly to look at the two FBI agents. If there had ever been color in their expressionless faces, it had all drained away. The deep indigo circles under their eyes suggested they hadn't slept in days or even weeks, instead of just the one previous sleepless night. Reilly noticed that Hazel had curled up between them on the floor under the table, resting her head on her paws.

Camilla purposefully moved forward. "Mr. and Mrs. Coulter, I'm Special Agent Camilla Vanderbilt with the FBI. I'm so sorry for your loss."

As they dropped their eyes back down to the surely lukewarm coffee, they both nodded slowly; they had heard this a dozen times already, and it hadn't once meant anything to them.

"And I'm Special Agent Reilly," Heath said as he also moved forward, though still staying behind Camilla. Neither Coulter raised his or her gaze again to greet him. At this distance Reilly could notice the myriad tattoos covering most of the man's exposed skin: a Chinese symbol on the right side of his neck, barbed wire, flames, knives, and other various objects—including more symbols in foreign languages—up and down each arm. The woman's complexion, on the other hand, bore no memory of any blemishes. Even in her exhausted state, Reilly found her quite beautiful, with that girl-next-door kind of purity and simplicity. *What an odd couple*, he caught himself thinking. With the man's hands cupping the coffee mug, Reilly made note of a tattoo in the inside of his right wrist: a red heart with the name "Danielle" written in fancy script in the middle. A pang of sadness shot through Reilly, but he quickly forced it to pass. "We're with CASMIRC, a division of the FBI that investigates crimes against children."

The woman's head tilted to the right, like she heard a distant sound and waited for it to repeat itself. A second later her eyes narrowed, signaling that she had made some connection. "Jackson Byrne?"

Camilla and Reilly, somewhat startled, looked at each other. "Excuse me, ma'am?" Camilla said.

"I seen him on the TV, on the Goodnight Hour." She looked up at Camilla and Reilly, then at the empty space behind him, like she expected Jack to arrive at any second.

"Yes, Special Agent Byrne is with this division," Camilla responded. "Is it OK if I sit down?"

The man nodded, so Camilla pulled out a chair on the kitchen table and began to sit. The woman ignored the question. "Where is he?"

"Special Agent Byrne?" Camilla asked.

"Yeah. Jack Byrne. The guy on TV. The mastermind FBI guy."

"He's..." Camilla began.

Reilly stepped forward a little, sensing a time to show his authority in this investigation. "He's not an active part of this investigation. Special Agent Vanderbilt and I are—"

"What?! We're not good enough for him?!" Color began to rush back into her face as the woman quickly became much more animated. "We're not some fucking famous fucking football player, so he doesn't need to... *grace* us with his... his almighty fucking presence?!"

"Amy..." the man said, as he slowly reached out toward her arm.

She jerked her arm away before he could touch her. "What, Carl? Fuck!" She shot him an evil glare. She suddenly didn't seem quite so angelic in Reilly's eyes.

"I assure you, Mrs. Coulter, that we have all of our resources actively working on this case," Reilly offered. Her evil glare switched focus toward Reilly, who instinctively took a half-step back, which he immediately regretted.

"Whatever." Under her breath, but clearly still audible, she muttered, "Fucking ridiculous."

"Can we ask you a few questions about Danielle?" Camilla queried gently, seemingly unfazed by this outburst.

Both nodded slowly. The woman lazily rolled her eyes before retreating to her withdrawn state nearly as quickly as she had exploded.

Hank Hanley stepped forward, close to the kitchen table. "I'm going to excuse myself."

Lucky bastard, Reilly thought.

"I need to head back down to our office to meet up with some of my key people on this investigation," Hank continued. He turned to Camilla and Reilly. "Will you folks be joining us when you're done here?"

"Yes," Reilly replied.

"Great." Hank turned to face the Coulters. "Mr. and Mrs. Coulter, do you have any family coming in? Would you like me to talk with anyone else?"

Reilly's cynicism kicked in, internally questioning the genuineness of Hank Hanley's kindness.

Both Coulters shook their head slowly. Without looking up to make eye contact, Amy Coulter said, "His folks are both dead, and my folks are both assholes."

"My sister is coming in from Parsons. She'll be here later this morning," Carl Coulter mumbled without lifting his chin.

"Bawlin' like it's her child…" Amy Coulter muttered, then trailed off.

"OK. We'll send on officer by later to check on you, but you call me if you need anything or think of anything." Hank waited for a reply, but got none. He tapped the top of the table twice with his knuckles. "OK," he said again before turning and walking out of the kitchen. They could hear the screen door squeak open and closed as he left through the front door.

Camilla pulled a notebook out of her jacket pocket and opened it up on the table in front of her. "Can you think of anyone who would want to hurt Danielle?"

Both shook their heads. "No," Carl Coulter said softly.

"Have you seen anyone around lately, any strangers or anyone out of the ordinary?"

Heads shook, no. They clearly had been asked these questions innumerable times already.

"Had she ever mentioned seeing someone following her or threatening her?"

No.

"Do you have any friends or family in York, Pennsylvania, or Frederick, Maryland?"

Both Coulters met her eyes with blank stares. Camilla had asked this seemingly odd question deliberately, in part to see if they were still paying attention.

"No," the woman said with a sneer.

"Have you visited those places before, especially recently?"

"No." Amy Coulter began to seem annoyed again.

Keeping his distance, Reilly asked from his position behind Camilla, "What about Washington, DC?"

The woman directed her stabbing gaze toward Reilly. He had to fight the urge to look away or take another step backwards. After about ten seconds, she looked back at Camilla as she answered Reilly's question. "No. We don't travel much." She emphasized "travel" by separating the T, so it came out like "tuh-ravel." Reilly sensed that she intended to make a point that life had not afforded them the luxuries of such things as travelling, even if only one state away.

Camilla looked back down at her notebook. "OK..."

Reilly's phone rang, interrupting Camilla. *Thank Christ,* Reilly thought. He pulled his iPhone of its belt carrier. "Excuse me," he said to the Coulters as he stepped back out of the room. He looked down at the screen: Harringer. He walked back through the living room as he slid the bar on his phone's display to answer the call. Hazel trotted pleasantly after him. "Heath Reilly," he said into the phone as he opened up the screen door and walked out onto the front porch.

"Reilly, it's Harringer."

"Morning, sir." Reilly looked back at the screen door. Hazel stood there, her nose touching the wire mesh. She looked at him, almost longingly. He imagined that she implored him to take her with him, away from the misery inside that house.

"I wanted to let you know that I finally got a hold of Terry Friesz." Typical Harringer, going right to business. No need for pleasantries.

"Good. Where was he?"

"Out to dinner, I guess. He said that he doesn't typically work weekends, so he didn't realize the importance of answering calls or checking voicemails." Reilly clearly heard the disdain in Harringer's voice.

"He really hasn't been with the Bureau long, has he?"

268

"Guess not," Harringer said quickly, not caring to dissect the reasons for Friesz's misconduct. "You need to fax him a copy of the note found on your girl, and he'll get right on it."

"Can do." Reilly entered Friesz's fax number into his iPhone as Harringer read it off to him. He gave Harringer a quick run-down of their plan for the day, to which Harringer uttered a curt approval. They signed off and Reilly hung up.

He looked out over the Coulter's front yard, procrastinating. He had no desire to go back into that house. Almost on cue, the front screen door opened. Relieved, Reilly turned around, expecting to see Camilla emerging from the house. Instead, Carl Coulter walked through the door, onto the porch beside him. He pulled a pack of cigarettes from his pants pocket and removed one, which he fluidly placed between his lips. He held the pack forward towards Reilly and raised his eyebrows.

Reilly put up his hand. "No, thank you."

Carl nodded and put the pack back into his pocket, from which he removed a disposable lighter. He lit the cigarette, closed his eyes, and took a deep drag, holding his breath for several seconds. He opened his eyes and his mouth simultaneously, with gray puffs slowly billowing from both corners of his mouth. He leaned forward, placing his hands on the thin metal railing running across the porch, and joined Reilly in a visual survey of his front lawn. The two men stood silently for a few minutes. Despite never having met before, and the tension that had brewed earlier inside the home, Reilly never found that silence with Carl Coulter uncomfortable.

Carl put his hands to his mouth and inhaled the smoke again. "Quit ten months ago."

Reilly just looked at him, nearly startled by his speaking. "What's that?"

Carl removed the cigarette and put his hand back on the railing. He took a deep breath and coughed once as he exhaled. "I quit. Smoking." He held up the cigarette, offering Reilly a visual demonstration. "Danielle was on me for years, tellin' me I need to quit." He looked down at the cigarette, suddenly not knowing how to regard it. "Finally did, ten months ago. Almost eleven. She was so proud."

Reilly noticed tears welling up in the corner of Carl's eyes. "I'm so sorry," was all he could think to say.

Carl Coulter nodded without making eye contact. He swallowed hard, then sniffled abruptly, pulling back the moistness in his nostrils. He rubbed the cigarette against the top of the railing, extinguishing it. He then tossed it behind a shrub in front of the porch. He nodded again, as if in appreciation for Reilly's empathy, before he turned and went back inside. Hazel yipped once excitedly.

Reilly stayed in place, gazing at the door where Carl has just disappeared.

Back inside, Camilla had finished asking questions of Amy Coulter. The two of them had gone upstairs to examine Danielle's room. Amy stayed outside in the hallway; neither she nor Carl had entered Danielle's room since they learned of her murder. She had given Camilla carte blanche to look into whatever she needed to, but she watched Camilla closely for the entire seven minutes. Camilla didn't find anything of interest or importance, just a typically messy bedroom of a typical nine year old girl. No diary, no photo albums, nothing that might reveal secrets unbeknownst to her parents. They went back downstairs.

Carl Coulter stood idly in the living room, staring at the ceiling with his arms folded. He looked at his wife when she and Camilla came down the stairs. She went to stand beside him and rested her head on his upper arm.

Camilla supplied each of them with her business card that included her personal cell number. "Please call me anytime, day or night, if you think of anything that you want to tell me. Big or small. You never know what might tip the scales in an investigation like this."

Amy Coulter looked at the business card in her hand, then back up at Camilla. Her upper lip folded under the bottom one and she began to cry. "Why our baby?"

"We don't know. We think that a very sick person did this to your daughter. He picks on little girls, and we don't think there's any reason why he chooses them."

This explanation apparently sufficed, for Amy Coulter nodded.

Camilla walked over and shook each of their hands, which they participated in half-heartedly. "We'll be in touch if we find anything. And don't hesitate to call me."

With that, Camilla turned and walked out the front door. She noticed Reilly still standing on the porch and shot him a questioning and somewhat disgusted look. He shrugged self-effacingly and followed her off the porch down the sidewalk.

"Hey!" Amy Coulter called from behind them. They turned around to find her standing behind the closed screen door, her arms crossed in front of her chest. Tears stained her cheeks, but her voice came out clearly and confidently. "You find that fucker. You find him and you fucking bring him in. We don't need fucking... Jack... Fucking What's-His-Name. We need you. You do it. OK?"

Now Reilly and Camilla were the speechless ones. They simply nodded.

51

One of Vicki's best friends from college, Brenda, married a cop named Troy Scharf. Jack and Vicki had double-dated with the Scharfs on several occasions, and Jack quickly grew to enjoy their company. He found Troy earnest and genuine—a straight shooter, Anthony Byrne would have called him. Three years ago Troy moved from Narcotics to the Homicide Branch of the Criminal Investigation Unit in the District of Columbia Metropolitan Police Department (MPDC). In that time he and Jack had never officially worked together. However, like most people who share similar vocations, they often conversed about their individual cases during social gatherings. From those discussions Jack had developed an appreciation for the way Troy approached his job. He knew he could feel comfortable working with him if their professional paths would ever cross. Like today.

After making some pancakes for Jonah (and some for himself), Jack plopped his son down in the family room to enjoy some Sunday morning cartoons. Vicki currently indulged in one of her favorite weekend pleasures: she had slept late and now stayed in bed, reading the Sunday paper. Jack walked out onto the back deck for some privacy and called Troy. They had exchanged personal cell numbers several years back, intending to get together to play golf sometime. They never had hit the links; in fact, this marked the first time either one had used the other's number.

Troy answered after the first ring. After exchanging quick introductory pleasantries, suddenly Jack realized that he didn't know exactly what to say. He needed to tell him about the voice mail from

Melissa Hollows, but he didn't know how. An empty void filled the line.

Awkwardly, Troy finally broke the silence. "So... what's going on, Jack?"

"Yeah." Jack cleared his throat. "I saw on the news last night about Melissa Hollows."

"Oh, yeah—you knew her, right? From working on her daughter's case?"

"I did. Right." Jack paused briefly again. After the phone call ended, he would convince himself that he simply imagined it, but in the moment he felt as though Troy were judging him, now remembering the tabloid rumors about Jack's illicit affair with Melissa. Before he could let this settle in, though, he continued. "Did you get her case?"

"Actually I did. We were on this weekend. I spent most of the night talking with her family and friends. Big shocker to everyone, to tell you the truth."

"What's it looking like?"

"A head-scratcher, for sure." Jack thought he could hear Troy literally scratching the shortly-cropped hair on his scalp on the other end of the line. "Sure looks like suicide, but every single person I talked to said, 'No way.' They couldn't buy it."

"Any note or anything?" Jack asked, then wondered to himself if that voicemail could be interpreted as her suicide note in some way.

"Nope. Nothing. She had been seeing a therapist for the last year since her separation, but she—the therapist—said that Melissa had never been suicidal. In fact, she always denied any suicidal thoughts."

"Huh." Jack felt like scratching his own head. "Well I wanted to let you know that she called me on Friday."

"Really?"

"Yeah. It was pretty weird. I hadn't seen her since Melvin Young's sentencing, and we hadn't spoken since even before that."

"Really?" Troy repeated. Jack could hear him shuffling some papers, likely finding a spot in his tablet to start taking notes. "What did she say?"

"Something... well... weird. We didn't speak; she just left me a voicemail."

"Uh-huh. Do you still have it?"

"I do."

"Uh-huh. And what time was this?"

"A little before ten. I can tell you exactly..." Jack scrolled through the menu on his phone to missed calls. "9:46 am."

"Uh-huh. And did you call her back?"

"I didn't listen to the message until late afternoon, around four o'clock, I think. I did try to call her back, several times, but it kept going straight to her voicemail."

"Huh." Troy didn't say anything for several seconds. Scratching his head again, perhaps. "Do you think you could come in and play that message for me?"

"Yeah, gladly. That's why I called," Jack said.

"OK. How about eleven? I guess the easiest place to meet would be at my office."

"That's the main headquarters, right? On Indiana Avenue?"

"No. We're on M Street, 101 Southwest," Troy confirmed. "I guess they don't want us Homicide boys scaring off John Q. Public at Main Headquarters."

"OK," Jack said, essentially ignoring the comment. "I'll see you at eleven."

"Great. Glad you called, Jack."

Jack wasn't so sure yet, but he agreed with Troy anyway before signing off.

52

Worth going to see D Coulters family?

Reilly looked down at his phone, considering how to respond to Corinne's text. He sat in the front corner of the conference room in the Warren County Sheriff's Office. He and Camilla had planned a debriefing and strategy-planning session with Hank Hanley, county deputies, and nearly two dozen members of the local police officers from around the county, many of whom volunteered their time on this Sunday morning to help find Danielle Coulter's killer. Only a few of the planned attendees, including Camilla, had arrived yet. He tapped out a response on his iPhone.

Prob not. Pretty upset & bitter. Give it 1-2 days.

He closed his text program and opened up his e-mail, finding no response yet from Terry Friesz. Not long after arriving at the county office building, Reilly went to the morgue to retrieve the message the Predator had left inside Danielle Coulter's sock. Keeping it inside the clear plastic bag, he had taken a photo of it with his phone and e-mailed it to Friesz, copying himself, Harringer, and Camilla as well. This one looked nothing like the previous two, though Reilly recognized it surely as some kind of foreign language, probably Middle Eastern. Reilly opened up the photo again on his phone to take another look at it.

He studied the lines, the curves, the dots placed at seemingly random locations. He had trouble imagining how someone could derive meaning from this.

His phone vibrated briefly; a new text message—again from Corinne— had come in:

OK Thx. This sucks for them, but sorry you had to deal with that this morning.

Reilly smiled subtly. He appreciated her empathy, more so for him than for the Coulter family. He got the sense that she really cared.

Another vibration; another text from Corinne.

BTW, OK to use Playground Predator, now that its out there?

Reilly contemplated her inquiry for a moment. His initial instinct told him to first discuss it with Harringer— probably the prudent thing to do. He knew, though, that Harringer didn't want to micromanage stuff like this. To demonstrate his ability to serve as a lead investigator, Reilly decided to make this call himself. He considered the possibility that their derisive, somewhat disparaging approach in her article on Friday may have, in fact, provoked the Playground Predator to kill again so quickly. Perhaps throwing their un-sub a proverbial bone in the media wasn't such a bad idea. He

278

thought that it couldn't turn out too much worse than the previous strategy.

OK. But not in headline, and only once.

Reilly hit send and felt good about it, confident he had made the right decision. Before he could bask in his own glow too much, his phone vibrated again. He had received an e-mail. He exited out of the text program and anxiously opened up his e-mail inbox. The lone unopened message residing at the top of the list had arrived from Terry Friesz.

Reilly opened the e-mail, which contained just one sentence. Not even a sentence, actually. Just six words.

Arabic. The man of the hour.

53

Corinne sat on the edge of the bed in her hotel room, planning out her day in her head. She had put on her bra and underwear, but hadn't dressed any further, as her agenda would influence what clothes she wore. Going to see the Coulters: a professional but unassuming business suit. Stopping by police headquarters: business casual. Pounding the local pavement to try to ferret out a witness or two: jeans and a light sweatshirt.

Her hair still hung wet down her shoulders, an infrequent drop of water falling from the end of one of her red coils onto the bedspread. She looked down at her phone, reading over the last text from Reilly. It reminded her that she needed to get in touch with her friend Meredith today. She had to send a thank you.

She scrolled through her phone menu, contemplating whether to send a text or an e-mail. E-mail would probably be better; she could say a little more. She eschewed her phone for her laptop, tossing the handheld onto the bed beside her and hopping to the other bed in the room, on which lay her laptop. She opened up Outlook and began writing a new message before a thought occurred to her: *I probably shouldn't lay down an electronic trail.*

She hadn't done anything illegal, per se. At least she didn't think so. Still, perhaps a phone call would be best.

Corinne had met Meredith Rivas back in college. Both had been journalism majors at American University, so they shared several classes throughout their four years. Meredith possessed a natural beauty which made many other females envious; it made it difficult for her to make friends at times. Girls often assumed that she found herself too pretty, too special, or too important to be a good friend. Corinne always found that kind of approach to interpersonal relationships foolish— "horseshit" in her lexicon. She and Meredith shared a healthy competitive friendship in their classes, but this never permeated into their personal life. Even when Meredith landed her first TV job straight out of college, it didn't bother Corinne. She figured Meredith would find herself at home in front of a TV camera, whereas Corinne had always wanted to pursue work in print. Her skills and ambition as a writer far surpassed her desire to put on make-up, go out on assignment, and talk about the latest pseudo-tragedy at the local animal shelter. Not unexpectedly, Meredith quickly ascended the ranks at her local station and recently moved on to one of the major networks. She currently worked as a field reporter for ABC. (Within three more years she would land a spot as a weekend anchor, one step closer to her lifelong dream—supplanting the evening daytime anchor.)

Corinne got up off the bed and grabbed her phone from the other bed. Meredith answered after the third ring.

"Hey, girlfriend!" Meredith answered.

"Hey," Corinne responded.

"Long time no talk." Meredith always seemed to slip this into the early part of one of their conversations, whether in truth or facetiously, like now.

"Yeah. Hey, I can't talk long, but I wanted to thank you for your beautiful work yesterday."

"No sweat. Thank you for the tip. We were the only network to run it at six. Everybody else played second fiddle at eleven," Meredith remarked.

Corinne smiled. "Nice. I will put the finder's fee on your tab. But I'll subtract twenty bucks as a tip for the subtlety with which you threw it out there."

"Subtle? Hardly. I punched that shit as best I could with shouting it. 'The Playground Predator has struck again, and he remains at large'." Meredith's voice changed with that last sentence, coming through a little deeper and with added inflection. Corinne recognized it as her Reporter Voice.

Corinne laughed. "At any rate, you hit it out of the park. It got back to my contact, and he said today that I can start using it. So I won't get credit for it, but…"

"But mission accomplished," Meredith finished.

"Mission accomplished," Corinne agreed.

54

Jack parked across the street from the MPDC Homicide Headquarters shortly before 11:00 am. His Nav system had confirmed the address, but the brick building in front of Jack looked to him more like a residential home than a branch of the MPDC. He walked up the sidewalk to the bright blue front door. Before he could knock, Troy Scharf opened it from inside.

"Hey, Jack, come on in," Troy said, turning his shoulder so Jack could walk past him in the small foyer. They did not shake hands. "Any trouble finding it?"

"Nope," Jack replied, trying to act casually.

Troy moved quickly down a hallway directly across from the door, assuming Jack would follow behind, which he did. "Good, good…" Troy said over his shoulder, his voice trailing off. Troy acted differently from any of their previous meetings. More tense, perhaps. His voice didn't sound shaky or quivering, but… tight. *Maybe this is just how he is at work*, Jack thought.

Troy stopped in front of an open office door on their right and turned back to face Jack. He extended his hand into the room, suggesting that Jack enter. Jack walked in to see another officer, wearing a button down shirt without a tie, standing up behind a desk.

"This is my partner on this one, Jacob Sednick," Troy announced.

"Hi, Jacob," Jack said.

Jacob came out from behind his desk and extended his hand, which Jack accepted. "Hi, Jack. It's really a pleasure to meet you. We always tease Troy," he lightly smacked Troy's abdomen with the back of his hand. "'Cause he says that he knows you, and we say he's just making it up!"

"Yeah, no, it's true. Our wives have been friends since college," Jack confirmed with a hint of a smile.

Despite the lighter mood in the room, Troy seemed to remain somber. "Jack, sorry to do this, but something's come up and I have to be on the phone for a little bit on a separate matter. Is it OK with you if you talk with Jacob for a little bit?"

Jack shrugged. "Sure, that's fine."

"Great," Jacob said, almost gleefully. He pulled back an upholstered chair with a metal frame for Jack to sit in before he moved back behind his desk.

"Thanks. I'll catch up with you two in just a little bit." Troy closed the door behind him as he left. Jack thought to himself that possibly the tension that he detected in Troy stemmed from this other matter that came up, a matter that had to pull him away from this. Perhaps he felt bad about ditching Jack with this sycophant. Jack sat down in his assigned chair.

"So... Jackson Byrne," Jacob said.

Jack wondered if he detected a hint of sarcasm, but he decided not to play into it either way. He raised his eyebrows. "Yeah."

"Troy told me that you got a voicemail from Melissa Hollows the other day."

Jack reached to his side and got his Blackberry off his belt. "Yeah..." He began navigating through the welcome screen to retrieve the message.

Jacob grabbed a pen that had been lying on his desk. He flipped to a fresh page on a legal pad in front of him and began taking notes. "What time did you receive the call?"

Jack scrolled through his missed call log. "9:46 am."

"OK," Jacob responded, scrawling notes. "And I take it you did not answer the call, since she ended up leaving a voice mail."

"Yeah," Jack affirmed. He resisted the urge to add a sardonic "That's right, Sherlock" to his response.

Still writing, not making eye contact, Jacob asked, "And when had you last spoken to Mrs. Hollows?"

Jack took a deep breath, trying to answer as precisely as possible. "Last fall. Mid- September, I believe. At Melvin Young's sentencing."

Jacob looked up from his legal pad. "Who?"

Jack paused, looking straight back at the detective. Jacob's initial impression led Jack to believe that Jacob had been a fan, of sorts. That he had followed his work. Yet, he didn't know the name Melvin Young? It struck Jack as quite odd.

He began to reconsider his rationalization for Troy's stiff demeanor. Something else was going on here.

"Melvin Young, the man who killed Melissa's daughter," Jack answered finally, still not averting his eyes.

Jacob raised his head in an exaggerated nod before looking back down at his legal pad. "Oh, right, of course." He scribbled a few more before dropping his pen dramatically. "All right, let's hear this bad boy."

Jack dialed his voice mail and listened for the menu. He then hit the speaker function and lay the phone down face-up on top of Jacob's desk.

A quiet, stifled sob from Melissa, the first sound on the recording, sent a chill down Jack's spine. She inhaled through a snotty nose. "We were made for each other, Jack." Quick sob. "You and me." A brief pause, followed by the hurried, "Me and you! Me and you." The first "Me" came out abruptly, as if rooted in a startle. Then silence. The end of the message.

Jack looked across the desk at Jacob, who stared wide-eyed at the phone. He continued to avoid eye contact with Jack. "Whoa," the detective finally said. He picked his pen back up, tapped it on his pad a couple of times, thinking about his next question. Pointedly he suddenly looked Jack straight in the eye. "What do you make of that?" The calm, conversational lilt in his voice contrasted the intensity of his gaze.

"I'm not sure," Jack responded honestly, fixed on Jacob's eyes. It felt unnatural to keep gawking at each other like this, but, given Jack's competitive nature, he resolved not to lose this weird impromptu staring contest. "I've been racking my brain about that for the last two days. Something about it feels familiar, as if she were reciting something, but I can't place it for the life of me."

Jacob looked down at his legal pad to jot something, leaving Jack the victor of the staring contest. "She never said anything like this to you before?"

Jack shook his head. "No."

"And what was the nature of your relationship with Melissa Hollows?" Jacob asked. He nonchalantly grabbed his coffee mug and took a drink.

Jack opened his mouth to answer, but then paused for a beat. Now he understood why Troy had passed this conversation onto his partner: he didn't want to have to ask these questions. These questions that—Jack knew for the integrity of the investigation— needed asking. "Professional, lasting through the investigation of her daughter's murder. I came to like her and respect her on a personal level, but never saw her in any capacity outside of the investigation." Jack had thought this lie in his head so many times that he almost believed it. He felt extremely confident that it came out convincing to Jacob in this moment.

"OK. You said that you last spoke in September. Did you keep in touch by any other means? E-mail? Texts?"

"No."

"Had you seen her, even from a distance, during that time?"

Jack thought for a brief moment. "No."

"And what did you do after you heard the voicemail?"

Jack scratched his ear and thought back to the events of Friday afternoon. "I didn't listen to it until I was leaving work, a little after four, I guess. I tried to call her right back, but it went straight to voicemail."

"Uh-huh." Jacob continued writing his notes.

"I tried several more times, with the same result."

"Did you leave a voicemail?"

"No."

"Uh-huh. And were all of these calls from your cell?"

"Yes." Jack began to feel uncomfortable. As part of his FBI training, he had to undergo interrogations. Even these simulated questioning sessions had made him feel uneasy, as they should when conducted by a skilled inquisitor. Gradually over the last few moments, he sensed that kind of tension rising. He found himself the subject of an interrogation. *Why?* he wondered. *Because Melissa killed herself?* It didn't make sense. *Unless...Was this on behalf of Vicki? Had Brenda found an opportunity to have her husband—or one of his associates—interrogate Jack about his affair with Melissa?*

"OK. And then what did you do?"

"I—"

Before he could begin his response, Troy burst into the room. He walked around Jack to the side of Jacob's desk, triangulating the two of them so that they all could see each other. "I just got a call from the coroner," Troy proclaimed. "Melissa Hollows' death has been ruled a homicide."

Jack's eyebrows rose instinctively. "Holy shit," he said quietly. He looked at Troy, who kept his attention towards Jacob, as if he only cared about informing him of this revelation. Jack looked down at Jacob, who kept his eyes trained right back at Jack. Jack now sensed that Jacob had been looking at him the entire time since Troy entered the room, watching for his reaction to the news.

With that observation, Jack came to the realization that Troy and Jacob had staged this revelation for that sole purpose. He suddenly understood why this had felt so much like an interrogation—because it was one. Troy and Jacob had known about the autopsy report before Jack arrived that morning. Naturally, given his prior tabloid "relationship" with Melissa and his receiving her ostensibly final phone call, Jack became a "person of interest," if not an actual suspect.

Jack looked back up at Troy, trying to get a read out of him: his face, his posture, his breathing pattern. Troy gave away nothing. Had Jack thought about this for a while, he may have decided to let this all slide, to not let on that he recognized the rouse. His initial instinct, however, forced him to prove that they hadn't tricked him. Jackson Byrne couldn't just walk away from such an intellectual battle.

"Troy," Jack said. Troy turned his head to look at Jack for the first time since he re-entered the room. "Did you know that when I spoke with you this morning?"

Troy tried to look perplexed. "No, I just got off the phone."

Jack gave him a disappointed look. "Troy? Come on, man. This felt like The Spanish Inquisition since I sat down here."

"Jack," Troy began, but Jack cut him off by putting his hands in the air.

"No hard feelings, Troy. I probably would have done the same thing if the roles were reversed."

Troy's shoulders began to slump, as if this were the first time he had allowed himself to relax in a week.

"Except I would have asked the questions myself," Jack added. "But Torquemada here did a bang-up job."

"Sorry, Jack, I just…" Troy began to trail off.

"Seriously, don't think twice about it," Jack reassured. "For the record, I know nothing about her death other than what I told you—the voicemail, and that's it."

289

"While we're on the record, Jack, I got the phone call from the coroner's office about ten minutes before you got here," Troy confessed. "I didn't know about it when we first spoke this morning."

Jacob dropped his pen and rubbed his eyes. "Do you wanna hear it?" he asked Troy.

"Yeah. Let's have you play it one more time, and then—if it's OK with you—we'll have you take it over to our forensics guys so they can record it."

"Sure," Jack obliged. He played the message aloud again.

"She sounds terrified," Troy observed.

Pinching the bridge of his nose between his thumb and forefinger, his eyes closed tightly, Jacob offered, "The killer made her say it."

Jack and Troy exchanged a glance, tacitly displaying their agreement. In the context of a murder, the message seemed to make a lot more sense.

"That's why it sounds like she's reciting something," Jacob continued. He opened his eyes and looked at Jack. "Because she is. And it would seem—this being your voicemail, and all—it would seem that the killer had her recite it for *you*."

55

Randall lay on the grey, black, and tan plaid couch in his above-the-garage apartment, his office, his sanctuary. He had just put a new album on the turntable—James Taylor's breakthrough album, his 1970 masterpiece *Sweet Baby James*. Randall always found JT's pure, soulful voice—the original and best JT, by the way, not the modern-day pop icon Justin Timberlake—uplifting, and this particular album showcased it better than any other. Though he had experienced pain and torment, and these emotions shone through in his performances, JT never let them eclipse hope, the hope of something better, the phoenix rising from the ashes. This record perfectly matched Randall's current mood.

For the first time in weeks, Randall felt tired. He hadn't slept more than four hours a day in probably two months, and most nights he didn't sleep at all during this stretch. He knew this would eventually creep up on him and bring him crashing down, but he had hoped that he could complete his Work first. He would have plenty of time to rest once he finished his Work. Thankfully, he didn't feel sleepy yet. Just tired, worn down.

He knew he should spend this time on the next phase of his Work, but, for right now, he preferred to reflect. He wanted to spend a little time recounting his accomplishments thus far.

The Prozac enabled him—or at least helped him substantially, gave him the necessary nudge—to keep propelling himself on little to no sleep these past months. He had learned this lesson—unintentionally, unfortunately—back in college. During his sophomore year, when he began to delve deeply into the core coursework of his major, Randall suffered a "nervous breakdown," to use a lay term.

Many people assume this kind of event happens abruptly. The word "breakdown" probably invites this presupposition, as if a person's psyche behaved like a '77 Chevy, smoke billowing from under the hood as it sits idly along the side of the highway. In reality, for the majority of cases of incapacitating depression, the symptoms come on gradually.

That fall Randall's cousin died in a car accident. By Thanksgiving break, his girlfriend since the second month of freshman year broke up with him. (He had always considered this the main impetus for his emotional decline. Yet, had he listened to his nineteen-year-old girlfriend two decades ago, he would have learned that his depression was the major force behind the dissolution of their relationship.) When the ever-important finals week came in early December, Randall found it increasingly difficult to focus on his work. He couldn't sleep well. His appetite diminished. He had no energy. He performed quite poorly on every exam, bringing his semester grades down to one B and four Cs, a horrible underachievement by his standards.

When he got home for the holiday break, his mother quickly realized that her son was depressed. She set up an appointment for him with her therapist, Dr. Beatrice Joust, an insightful and delightfully optimistic psychiatrist from Sweden. Even her name— pronounced "Yoost"—seemed to have an uplifting quality. At the end of their first session, Dr. Joust prescribed Prozac for Randall, as this medication had worked so well for his mother over the past year. Prozac, a selective serotonin reuptake inhibitor, or SSRI, had first appeared on the market about two years earlier and had gained notoriety as a miracle drug for sufferers of major depression. He had one more session with Dr. Joust before going back to school for the spring semester, and he began to feel better already.

Once the drug reached a steady state in mid-January, Randall felt wonderful. Better than he had every felt in his life, in fact. He had more energy than he had ever had before. He experienced one epiphany after another, making huge strides towards completing his senior thesis in electrical engineering—and he was just barely past halfway in his sophomore year!

Amazingly, he also taught himself how to play the guitar that winter. He began writing songs, and in less than two weeks he had enough material for what he guessed would generate two entire albums, one of them a concept album.

One night a hall mate in his dorm knocked on Randall's door at 3:30 in the morning. Apparently, while he could endure it the past five nights, this student didn't appreciate Randall's guitar playing all night long, as he had a big exam the next day. He politely asked Randall to stop playing, or at least play only into his own headphones. Randall dismissed him and closed the door, going back to his music. The neighbor knocked again, this time wording his request more as an ultimatum. Randall did not reply. Instead, without warning, he punched the student square in the nose, knocking him to the ground. He shut the door again and tried to further refine the third act of his concept album. Campus police called his family later that morning to let them know that they had detained Randall since the incident, and someone would need to come down to the university to claim him.

Randall went home with his parents that day and never returned to that university. Clearly recognizing his mental state of disrepair, his parents took Randall straight to Dr. Joust's office. An astute psychiatrist, she easily recognized Randall's manic condition. Also an honest psychiatrist, she admitted to Randall's family that she had previously misdiagnosed him. Randall did not suffer from major depression; rather, he suffered from bipolar disorder, known commonly as manic depression. She decided to initiate lithium therapy along with the Prozac.

In the next decade, mental health research would demonstrate that SSRIs such as Prozac can precipitate manic episodes when used alone to treat bipolar disorder. They should instead be used in conjunction with a mood stabilizer, such as lithium.

Though Randall hated taking the lithium, due to the relatively constant side effects of nausea and fatigue, he took it religiously. It worked beautifully to help control his mood for over a dozen years. In 2004, Dr. Joust—still Randall's primary psychiatrist—switched him from lithium to Zyprexa, a drug previously used to treat schizophrenia that had also recently been approved for the treatment of bipolar disorder. Randall's side effects mostly went away, yet he still maintained adequate control of his mood disorder.

Until nine months ago. When his world ended.

No amount or type of medication created by God or man could stave off the awful grief and depression that ensued.

Finally, though, while staring at the television one night, Randall found a way out, a path to salvage him from his hell, a purpose to make life worth living.

His Work.

A BUSTLE IN THE HEDGEROW

That was the last day he took his Zyprexa.

But not the Prozac, though. The Prozac he took every day.

56

"What do you mean, the message was meant for you? I don't... I don't know what you mean?" Vicki asked.

They sat on opposite sides of their bed, each with one bent leg on top of the mattress and the other dangling over the side, facing each other. Jack had just finished telling her about his meeting with Troy Scharf and his partner in DC. He left out some of the details, of course, especially the ones known only to him. He also omitted that when he volunteered to go help investigate the crime scene with Troy and Jacob Sednick, they denied his help. They both thought it best that Jack, as a possible witness due to the phone call, not muddle the investigation in any way with his presence at the crime scene. Troy assured Jack that he did not consider him a person of interest, yet it still left Jack with an unsettling feeling.

"I think it was a message, directly from the killer to me, read by Melissa Hollows before he killed her," Jack explained.

"What did Troy think? Did he agree?"

Jack nodded. "Yeah."

"What does it mean? Play it for me again," she requested.

Listening to Melissa Hollows' quivering, sobbing voice induced nausea, but Jack played it one more time for Vicki. He tried to remove all emotion—sadness, guilt, remorse—and pay close attention to any subtlety, any background sounds, anything that might provide an additional clue. To devoid himself of emotion usually came easily, given his years of experience in investigating violent crimes, yet no previous investigation had hit quite this close to home before. At the conclusion of the voicemail, he looked up at Vicki expectantly. "Anything?"

She shrugged. "I don't even know what to listen for. She sounds... miserable. Terrified."

Jack nodded. He tossed his phone onto the bed beside him. "I made a side trip after my meeting with Troy. That's why I didn't get home until late." He had arrived at dusk, just in time for dinner. He didn't discuss his day until now, after they had put Jonah to bed. "My first thought was about Melvin Young."

Vicki gasped involuntarily and put her hand to her mouth. She normally possessed a very composed demeanor, though certainly not stoic, so her demonstratively shocked reaction struck Jack as oddly stereotypical.

"Yeah." Jack said, agreeing with the enormity of the concept that Melvin Yong could have somehow gotten out of jail to begin to exact his revenge on Jack and the Hollows family. "I tried to think of who would want to hurt her and involve me at the same time. Any way I stack this up, it keeps coming back to him. So I went to Jessup."

Located about halfway between Washington, DC, and Baltimore, the Jessup Correctional Institution had a maximum security division where Melvin Young currently resided. Jack had called ahead and spoke to a man named Steve Kurwood, the Chief of Security and the highest in command at the institution on a Sunday afternoon. Kurwood welcomed Jack at the main entrance and led him to his office. From there they went to the nearby video surveillance room. Kurwood leaned over the main console, shooing away a seated security guard. He used a mouse to click through a small menu on a screen on the right.

"There." Kurwood pointed at a black and white screen in front of Jack. "He's right there."

Rumor had it that Melvin Young had a rough go of his first year in prison, not uncommon for pedophiles, especially a pedophile incarcerated in the state of Maryland who kidnapped and murdered the child of a Redskins superstar. Sure enough, when Jack focused on the image in front of him, he recognized Young, lying in a cot in the infirmary.

"Got the shit beat out of him again two nights ago," Kurwood explained. "Broken nose—second or third one since he got here, I think—broken arm, bruised nuts."

"Bruised nuts?" Jack asked.

"Got kicked in the nuts so hard that they bled a little."

Jack scowled, an involuntary response for most any man when presented with such a story. Kurwood noticed the expression and agreed. "Yep. He's still in the infirmary for pain control. And to protect him a little while his buddies cool down a little."

Jack studied the man on the video screen in front of him. Though Young's cot sat at least twenty feet from the closed circuit camera mounted in the corner of the infirmary ward, Jack recognized Melvin Young without a doubt. He looked quite different, at least forty pounds lighter and with an uneven, scruffy beard, but the mannerisms and those cold, menacing eyes were unmistakable. He felt a twinge of relief, knowing that Young had not somehow murdered Melissa.

"That's him, all right," Jack confirmed. "Can we go look at his visitor's log?"

Kurwood nodded. "Sure." He tilted his head to the right abruptly, signaling for Jack to follow him in that direction. They exited the closed circuit surveillance room and went back to Kurwood's office. "It's all computerized now," he said as he sat down at his desk.

Jack looked around but could not find any other places to sit in the small office. He crossed his arms and stood in place, waiting for Kurwood to search the database in his desktop computer. Neither said anything for several minutes, the only sound in the office Kurwood's pecking on his keyboard.

"None," Kurwood finally said.

"None?"

Kurwood pursed his lips, raised his eyebrows, and shook his head slowly. "Not a one. He's been here since the day after his sentencing. Not one visitor in nearly a year."

When Jack finished retelling this part of his day to Vicki, he added the comment: "Can't say I'm surprised."

"No," Vicki agreed. "So you were worried that he might have hired someone to kill Melissa?"

"Something like that. I called Troy as I left, suggesting that they look more into Young and his activities from inside Jessup, especially any correspondence, cell mates, anything like that. But, I needed to see him with my own eyes, you know?"

Vicki nodded. "So now what?"

Jack shrugged, looking down at the empty space on the comforter between them. "I don't know. I'll help Troy any way I can, but it's really outside my jurisdiction."

Vicki leaned in, trying to catch his eye. "Plus...?"

"Plus?" Jack met her eyes, not understanding the question.

"Plus, it's not really your line of work anymore, right? Don't you have a meeting with Philip tomorrow?"

"Yeah, plus that. More importantly, that." He leaned over and kissed Vicki on the forehead. "Which reminds me that I need to go prepare. I got kind of sidetracked today."

"I'll say. You can take the agent out of the FBI..." She smiled.

Jack rolled his eyes good-naturedly. "But you can't take the FBI out of the agent."

Vicki's smile began to fade. "You probably can't, can you?"

"I don't know," Jack smirked. "That's a little too deep for me right now."

"OK, Senator." Vicki got off the bed and walked around to kiss Jack on the cheek. "I'm going to get a glass of water from downstairs. You want one?"

Jack put his arms around her waist. "That sounds great."

A few minutes later, Vicki arrived in the study, glass of ice water in hand as promised. Jack sat in front of his computer, but he focused on the front cover of his copy of *Class Dismissed*. "We've got to fix this," Jack said to her, tapping the book in his hands. "Seeing Melvin Young today reminds me of what a poor system we have in place right now. We can do better, I know it."

"I know it too. And you're just the man for the job," she said before she dipped down to kiss him. "Goodnight, honey."

"Goodnight," Jack echoed. She left him alone in the study. He looked back down at the book. He thought that rereading chapter nine would serve as a good starting point in preparation for his talk with Philip Prince tomorrow. He thumbed quickly from the back of the book to the penultimate chapter, the one that discussed how Melvin Young, a convicted child molester, came to work as a teacher at an elementary school.

CHAPTER 9
MELVIN YOUNG, AND HOW THE SYSTEM FAILED

Over the last two decades, several federal and state laws have been enacted to help protect the general public, and children in particular, from sexual predators. Though these laws were created with the best intentions, they are inherently flawed. No fewer than four such gaps in this system designed to protect children led to the abduction and murder of Lamaya Hollows by the convicted sexual offender Melvin Young.

Before dissecting these flaws, it is important to note that it is entirely possible that a predator like Melvin Young could have attacked another child regardless of any state or federal regulations. It is also noteworthy that every individual involved in this case who had been entrusted to carry out the current state and federal laws acted in accord with their duties to the best of their abilities. This chapter is not meant to indict any one person, but rather the current legal infrastructure that is in place.

Melvin Andrew Young was born February 18, 1978, in Dixonville, Tennessee, a small town about 25 miles north of Memphis. His mother, Geraldine "Gerri" Wesley, was twenty years old at the time of his birth. She had been dating his father, Patrick Young, a twenty-nine year-old mechanic, for about six months when she got pregnant. They moved in together and tried to raise Melvin as an unmarried couple, but, after only four months, they realized that they could not co-exist under the same roof. Gerri moved out to her parents' house and took Melvin with her. Patrick remained involved peripherally, seeing his son on the occasional holiday. Public records cite no infractions against Patrick Young for failing to pay child support.

By all accounts, including Melvin's, Gerri Wesley had been a loving mother. Her parents pitched in to help take care of Melvin so that she could go back to work as a secretary at a local real estate company. In that office in the summer of 1981, she met Porter Upton, a forty-two year old retired army officer, once divorced, who moved to Dixonville to start a riverboat fishing expedition business. (Dixonville is only a few miles from the Mississippi River, and the region draws thousands of vacationing fishermen annually in search of legendary big blue catfish.) Upton courted her for over a year before she agreed to date him, telling him that her duties as a single mother took priority over dating.

They dated for three years before marrying in February, 1985. They had two children together, both girls—Harriet born in January, 1986, and Faith in August, 1987. There were never any official or unofficial reports of inappropriate activity between Melvin and his two younger half-sisters. In fact, Melvin led a seemingly normal childhood. Despite the lack of a meaningful connection with his biological father, Melvin did not want for a father figure. Porter Upton served this role well. Once Melvin was old enough, he worked part-time in Upton's business, eventually working his way up to fishing guide during the summer after he finished high school.

In school Melvin neither was an outcast nor a member of the in-crowd. He got along well with almost everyone, but had no real close friends. He dated a few girls from his class minimally. He earned decent grades. He participated on the track and field team as a hurdler. In August 1996, he matriculated to Middle Tennessee State in Mufreesboro, Tennessee, about four and a half hours from home. His half-sisters were ten and nine years old at the time.

Melvin seemed to have difficulty adjusting to life away from home. He did not make friends. He wrote frequent letters home to his mother, and occasionally wrote to his younger sisters Harriet and Faith. He called home weekly during the first semester. Though he requested to come home many weekends, his mother refused to come to Murfreesboro to get him. Her letters (which Melvin kept) declined lovingly, saying that she knew it would be "best for him to enjoy a college life," a life she herself never got to experience. This must have created a schism in the relationship, because he stopped writing letters to his mother (though continued writing to his sisters), and the phone calls were much less frequent.

Despite his social shortcomings, Melvin continued to perform adequately in his academic work. The summer between his freshman and sophomore year he got a job as a research assistant in a pharmacology lab. After graduation in 2000 with a Bachelor's of Science in chemistry, Melvin took a full-time job in the lab of Ghorge Mihalac, a doctor of pharmacology with the University. Melvin's duties included working on preservatives for various chemicals and drug components. According to interviews with members of the research staff, Melvin never contributed any original work in the lab, but he performed his assigned tasks without difficulty. He was initially considered a valued member of the research team.

Dr. Mihalac was known throughout his department, and even in far corners of the University, as an admired leader and generous man. He frequently held social gatherings for his staff, from hosting an open tab at a local bar during happy hour to pool parties at his family's home. It was at a pool party in 2004 that Melvin met Mihalac's then eight-year-old daughter Natasha. Colleagues remember Melvin and Natasha having a brief conversation in the shallow end of the pool during that party, but nothing else. However, at each successive gathering over the next year, party-goers recall only in retrospect that Melvin seemed to seek out more and more interactions with Natasha. Dr. and Mrs. Mihalac do not have the same recollection, citing their focus on hosting parties as the reason they did not notice Melvin spending time with their daughter.

The Mihalacs held another pool party over Labor Day weekend 2005. It was there that Melvin sexually assaulted Natasha. He followed her upstairs to her bedroom when she invited him up to see her newly acquired goldfish. After a failed attempt to force her to perform oral sex on him, he convinced her to take off her bathing suit while he masturbated. After he finished he told Natasha never to mention this incident to anyone. They returned to the pool party separately, as per his instructions. Shortly afterward Melvin excused himself and went home.

Natasha did not mention anything to her parents or anyone else for three months, though her parents noticed a distinct difference in her demeanor over that time. Her grades in school dropped from straight As to Bs and Cs. She did not want to spend time with any of her friends. When her goldfish died in late September due to starvation, she did not ask her parents to replace them.

Her unusually withdrawn behavior rapidly escalated the day before the Mihalacs were due to host a holiday party for Dr. Mihalac's office staff in December. She finally confessed to her parents about the incident at the pool party over Labor Day. Livid, Ghorge Mihalac called Melvin directly and berated him over the phone. His wife had to restrain him from getting in his car to go after him. She called the local police to report the incident.

An officer came to the Mihalac home and interviewed the family. As a father of a young girl himself, the officer was outraged toward Melvin Young and extremely empathetic to Natasha. While being very sensitive to her understandable fear of a strange man, he asked her several questions to clarify the information that her parents had provided. He then called his station to be connected to detectives involved in sexual crimes. One detective was dispatched to the Mihalac home, while another detective, accompanied by two uniformed officers, went to Melvin's apartment and brought him to the police station for questioning.

306

A BUSTLE IN THE HEDGEROW

When the detective from the sexual crimes division arrived at the Mihalac home, the first thing he did was to ask the responding officer if he had asked Natasha any specific questions about the alleged assault. He affirmed that he had. Unfortunately, the officer did not know that this was a breach of protocol. Children under such stressful circumstances can be highly suggestible, a fact known to every good criminal defense lawyer. In order for a child's testimony regarding sexual crimes to stand up in court, the child needs to be questioned in what is known as a forensic interview. Such an interview process follows a prescribed set of questions designed to not lead children in any direction when retelling their experiences as possible victims of sexual crimes. These interviews are conducting by trained professionals in an observed, designated setting. The fact that the responding officer asked pointed questioned directly to Natasha could provide ample ammunition to a defense lawyer if the case were to go to trial.

The protocol for interviewing children who are potential victims of sexual crimes was taught to all students enrolled in police academies in the State of Tennessee beginning in 1998. However, this particular officer had graduated years earlier, before this information had been added into the curriculum. He should have participated in an in-service program as part of ongoing education, but there was no record of that having taken place. One could argue that this officer himself should be held accountable for his ignorance of best practice. A reasonable counterargument is that he simply acted as most caring human beings would in such a situation, having either missed or forgotten some of his necessary training. In either case, had the interview of Natasha Mihalac been conducted appropriately, perhaps she could have been a viable witness to take the case of her sexual assault to trial.

As it turned out, the case never did go to trial. Melvin Young denied all of the accusations from the Mihalacs. No evidence of the crime existed, despite the efforts of the forensics team that scoured Natasha's bedroom looking for traces of semen. A search of Melvin's apartment revealed dozens of photographs of young girls on his computer, most of them naked. His files also included several photos he had taken with his own camera of Natasha Mihalac, fully clothed. Melvin's possession of these types of photos surely seemed incriminating. However, without a reliable witness, the charge of sexual assault still amounted to a circumstantial case. As a result, the District Attorney of Rutherford County, Tennessee, an honorable man named Ward Valker, offered a plea deal to Melvin Young. According to the deal, the County would drop the felony charges of Use of a Child in a Sexual Performance and Promoting a Sexual Performance by a Child, and Melvin would plead guilty to Sexual Misconduct and Possession of Child Pornography, both misdemeanors. He would serve a twelve-month sentence, but likely receive parole in nine to ten months. Young's attorney, knowing well the conservative juries in Tennessee, advised his client to take the deal. Melvin Young accepted the plea deal and, on November 29, 2006, he was incarcerated at South Central Correctional Facility in Clifton, Tennessee.

Melvin served just under ten months of his twelve-month sentence. He was released on September 26, 2007 into parole. He would need to remain in Tennessee to complete his parole term, which was a total of three years from conviction. He completed his parole term while residing in Clifton, where he had found a job working as a truck driver for a dry cleaning business. His family back home had cut off all communication, presumably out of embarrassment, which further isolated Melvin.

During this time he opened an account with a popular online social network, through which he reconnected with an acquaintance from high school, Gregory Trumbull, who lived in North Kensington, Maryland. They became close friends via their internet connection, closer than they had been in high school. Once Melvin's parole term was complete, he moved to North Kensington in December, 2009, presumably to be closer to his good—and only—friend in his time of need. Trumbull had recently been diagnosed with Stage IV Hodgkin's Lymphoma, which offered a poor prognosis.

As a convicted sexual offender, under the Wetterling Act of 1994 and the so-called Megan's Law of 1996, Melvin Young would need to register himself with his local community as such, regardless of location. Prior to 2006, each state had to maintain its own registry and its own method of organizing and maintaining it. Very little consistency or communication existed between states regarding the practices of their sexual offender registries. In an attempt to rectify this situation, in 2006, President George W. Bush signed the Adam Walsh Child

Protection and Safety Act, named after the boy who was abducted and killed in Hollywood, Florida, in 1981, and whose father, John Walsh, went on to become host of TV's America's Most Wanted and a strong advocate for victims' rights. One provision of this act is the Sexual Offender Registration and Notification Act, commonly referred to as SORNA.

The main purpose of SORNA was to standardize sexual offender registration and community notification practices in individual states. SORNA famously uses a three-tiered system to stratify offenders on their risk of recidivism (repeat offenses). The basis for placing a sexual offender in a particular tier comes solely from his or her crime of conviction. Presumably, an offender from Tier 1, which is composed of seemingly less heinous crimes, is less at risk for recidivism than an offender from Tier 3, the harshest and most violent crimes. Therefore, under SORNA, Melvin fell into the Tier 1 classification, as he had only been convicted of a misdemeanor. This meant that he would need to register with the national database registry annually for 15 years, and with any change of address. His registration would include his address, photograph, phone number, e-mail address, and place of employment. In contrast, someone convicted of a Tier 2 felony needs to register every six months for 25 years, and someone convicted of a felony that falls into the Tier 3 classification must register quarterly for the duration of his or her life. Both Tier 2 and Tier 3 offenses also carry longer parole terms with higher levels of monitoring.

Unfortunately, recent research has shown that this three-tiered system does not work. In fact, a study conducted by the State of New York Department of Corrections published in 2009 showed that Tier 1 offenders were actually more likely to be arrested for repeat offenses—both sexual and non-sexual—than Tier 2 or Tier 3 offenders. In addition, on average Tier 1 offenders were also arrested sooner after their release than offenders from the other two tiers. Therefore, monitoring these criminals less vigorously and less often does not seem to make any sense.

Instead, profiling tools have been developed that seem to hold up to scrutiny much better that SORNA's three-tiered system. Two such systems developed in the late 1990's – Static-99 and the Minnesota Sex Offender Risk Screening Tool, Revised, or MnSOST-R—had been implemented in several states prior to the signing of The Adam Walsh Act. However, once SONRA came into effect, these states had to abandon those systems due to cost issues; no state could afford to carry out two separate screening and risk stratification tools.

An economic paradox exists in this situation as well, sadly typical in our current political climate. It is estimated that each state would need to spend around $30,000,000 annually to implement and maintain the SORNA Tier system. Failing to do so would result in the forfeiture of 10% of that states' annual financial support from a specific federal fund known as the Byrne fund (no association with this author). In 2009, this amount totaled $1,127,984. In theory, then, a state could save itself nearly $29,000,000 annually by deliberately disobeying the federal Adam Walsh Child Protection and Safety Act.

Had Rutherford County DA Valker pursued and obtained a conviction for Melvin Young of a felony in 2006, Young would have fallen into Tier 2 status, which would have required closer and more frequent monitoring. In addition, not surprisingly, had he been evaluated by one of the more effective screening tools, Melvin Young would have scored sufficiently high on either the Static-99 or MnSOST-R to warrant closer scrutiny as a high risk for re-offense. This illustrates yet further ways in which the current system failed to help protect people like Lamaya Hollows.

Finally, Melvin Young found a way to exploit one more hole in our current system of trying to protect children from sexual predators. Six months after Melvin moved to North Kensington, Gregory Trumbull stopped working at his current job due to his illness. Trumbull had been a middle school chemistry teacher at North Catholic School in nearby Silver Springs. Having completed the academic year in June, 2010, Trumbull had asked for a year's sabbatical to deal with his illness, which the school granted. He never returned to teach at North Catholic, however.

Miraculously, over the next year, Gregory Trumbull recovered from his ostensibly terminal illness. He applied for a new teaching job in the Middle School at Washington Country Day School. School officials from Washington Country Day contacted administrators from North Catholic, who vouched for Trumbull as a conscientious and attentive teacher. He had all of his necessary paperwork, including his Federal Act 33 Clearance papers and state documents citing no history of offenses against children. He had previously undergone FBI fingerprint clearance for his previous teaching job. Washington Country Day School hired him without reservation, and in September, 2011, Gregory Trumbull began teaching third grade.

In May 2012, the man named Gregory Trumbull, like every other teacher at Washington Country Day, participated in interviews by police and federal investigators regarding the disappearance of Lamaya Hollows. He claimed no knowledge of her case. In May, Melvin Young's DNA was found in gum recovered from the stomach of Lamaya Hollows. Photographs of Melvin Young revealed that he had assumed the identity of Gregory Trumbull sometime between June, 2010, and September, 2011, presumably to be hired as a school teacher and have easy access to young girls.

Melvin Young has revealed nothing about those 15 months between Trumbull's last days at North Catholic School and Young's first appearance in Trumbull's guise at Washington Country Day. Trumbull's cancer-riddled body was found in a large meat freezer in the garage of his own home. An autopsy could not accurately determine how long Trumbull had been dead, due to the significant delay in decomposition while in the freezer. The cause of death was determined to be his lymphoma, so, while eventually convicted of numerous crimes, Young was never charged with Trumbull's murder.

Young had seemingly taken up residence at Trumbull's home. His official residence that he registered with the Sexual Offender Database was the apartment he had originally occupied upon his arrival in North Kensington. This had never been verified by any government agency. He also listed his occupation as a freelance telemarketer working from home, which a telemarketing corporation later confirmed, but only from March through November 2010.

After the discovery that Young had been masquerading as Trumbull to obtain employment in an elementary school, initial blame fell hard upon administrators at Washington Country Day School. However, it is important to point out that they followed all due diligence and regulations as stipulated by state and federal governments. Any individual working with children (e.g. school employees, day care workers, hospital volunteers) must first receive clearance to do so by both state and federal governments. This usually consists of three phases: a criminal record check and child abuse clearance, which are conducted by the state, and a fingerprinting check conducted by the FBI. Interestingly, in most states, including Maryland, none of these steps require direct contact with a full-time government official. The child abuse clearance requires that the applicant sign the document in the presence of a notary public. While notary publics ostensibly serve as extensions of government, in reality many of them— including the one who signed off on Melvin Young's false paperwork—receive their notary designation through a five- to ten-minute online process. In addition, results from the FBI fingerprinting clearance are sent directly to the individual, not his or her place of employment. The document also has no photographic or other form of identification on it. Melvin Young simply found Gregory

Trumbull's copy of his FBI clearance and dropped it off at Washington Country Day. In fact, in a matter of a few weeks, this child molester received his clearance to work as a school teacher and had earned a job at Washington Country Day School.

Given his history of escalating violence and seemingly insatiable hunger for young girls, it is very likely that Melvin Young would eventually have attempted another attack on an innocent child. However, if numerous points within our system or protecting citizens from people like Young were changed—like SORNA's three-tier stratification, or properly enforcing all police officers to follow protocols when dealing with underage victims of alleged sexual abuse, or insisting that state or clearances involve direct contact and scrutiny by a trained government employee—perhaps Lamaya Hollows would still be alive today.

DAY EIGHT: MONDAY

58

Heath Reilly had lain awake most of the night, staring at his bedroom ceiling, thinking about the Playground Predator, with several thoughts about Corinne O'Loughlin sprinkled throughout. When he looked at his alarm clock and it read 5:00, he admitted to himself the futility of lying there any longer. He got out of bed, contemplated a jog, declined, got a shower, dressed, and left for the office in Quantico without eating breakfast.

Harringer had called for a task force meeting at 8:00 am on the Playground Predator case. Reilly had come back to Quantico for it, but Camilla remained in Front Royal to continue CASMIRC's involvement in that investigation. She would join the meeting via video conference as before.

By 6:55 Reilly sat in the conference room looking at the dry-erase board in front. It contained the timeline of events in the case, as well as the text—both original and the English translation—from the notes left on each victim by the Predator. A bulletin board on the front wall had numerous photos tacked to it, each with a typed label pinned beneath it: two photos each—a posed school portrait and a forensic crime scene photo—of Stephanie McBurney, Adrianna Cottrell, and Danielle Coulter; the school playground in York; the bushes behind the playground in Frederick; the woods adjacent to the soccer fields in Front Royal; and the only identifying piece of the killer, the muddy shoeprint.

Reilly tried to clear all conscious thought, tried to open himself up to an epiphany. He thought his subconscious might connect dots that his consciousness could not. He had heard that this worked for some people. So he stared at the photos. He closed his eyes, imagining the scenes live, in three dimensions, during the times of each killing. He tried to focus on the gentle lilting of the leaves in the spring breezes. Tried to feel it, not just think about it. He saw the little girls playing, walking, weaving the fabric of their own young lives, not knowing how abruptly it would end.

But he couldn't see the main event, the middle steps. His vision skipped to the end photos, of the dead bodies lying in the weeds. He just couldn't see it, and it pissed him off.

59

The tiny spider stood motionless on the cream-colored ceiling, defying the laws of gravity as spiders are wont to do. It hadn't moved in nearly an hour. *Is it sleeping?* Randall wondered. *Do spiders even sleep?*

Randall lay on the couch in his apartment. He had been here all night. He hadn't slept, but he had rested. Over the last hour, as he kept watch over the miniscule arachnid, he felt increasingly more energy. This rest would suffice.

Muddy Waters wailed—both vocally and through his guitar—from the turntable through the speakers. Randall had put on *At Newport 1960*, Waters' breakthrough live album. He often found that this album helped him to transition from a restful state to a more active, wakeful one.

He hadn't bothered to tell his wife that he would be staying out here tonight. He had spent so many nights out here the last several months that it had become the norm; he assumed his wife stopped wondering, and likely even stopped caring. Just as she had stopped caring about everything else.

As his vitality continued to surge, his thoughts turned to his Work. The end drew near. He felt that he had sufficiently completed the preliminary tasks that set up the climax, but time would tell. Before venturing off the prescribed path of his Work, he would wait to see how things developed in the next few days. He would have to stay on top of the news, follow every footstep as best he could.

Spiders must sleep, he concluded. *All living things need to sleep, at least at some point.*

A BUSTLE IN THE HEDGEROW

The next step would prove the hardest, of that he felt certain. As much as his life and his passions had changed in the last six months or so, he knew that the penultimate act of his Work would be difficult, possibly even excruciating. But necessary. He knew it was necessary.

Necessary and sufficient.

This phrase popped into his consciousness, reminding him of a Logic class he had taken in college. He recalled his professor, in a thick Italian accent—*What was his name?*—teaching the language of logic, with its various symbols and phrases. Randall could not remember ninety-nine percent of what he had learned in that class, but he could remember the diminutive lecturer using "necessary and sufficient" several times during each lecture to drive home one point or another.

His eyes had wandered, scanning the familiar room. All in its place, as always. He stared back up at the ceiling. The spider remained a black speck against the pale background. Had it moved? Randall couldn't be sure.

Not all living things need sleep, he reminded himself. *Plants don't need sleep. Fungi don't sleep. Why would arthropods have to sleep?*

He could feel the spider staring back at him. He sensed a kinship, and he knew the spider would sense it too, if spiders could sense such a thing. And if spiders could read or even just comprehend language, then this spider could have a deep understanding of Randall's Work, as long as he had been creeping around this apartment long enough. Randall hoped that he had. And he hoped the

319

spider would stick around for a while, maybe a few days, at least long enough to see the conclusion of his Work.

Because Randall knew it would end soon.

60

Jack tapped the radio power button on his steering wheel to silence the stereo. For the first time in a very long time, he did not want to listen to any music while he drove to his office at CASMIRC. While he often found that music relaxed him and allowed his mind to work more effectively, right now he required silence.

He told Vicki that he needed to pick up some of his research files from *Class Dismissed* so he could review them again before his late morning meeting with Philip Prince, which was true. He also needed to make sure—even though he knew he had at least twice before—that nothing in the official or unofficial files from the Lamaya Hollows case could make any connection between Melissa Hollows and him, beyond the obvious professional relationship. They had never exchanged text messages, e-mails, or other forms of electronic communication. The very few phone calls they shared—prior to Friday—had been during reasonable, daylight hours in order to set up interview times or pass along any new information on the case.

In addition, he hoped that reviewing the files could spark something, point him in some direction to help discover who had killed her. And why. And why this person felt it necessary to get Jack involved.

He arrived at the FBI complex in Quantico at 7:35 am. When he got off the elevator, he did not see anyone else in the office. He noticed the conference room door standing open; the lights from inside it cast a soft pale-yellow glow over most of the cubicles on the floor. Outside remained dark and dreary, accentuating the illumination from the conference room. Jack began walking towards his desk, but then he diverted his path to walk by the conference room.

Jack got to the doorway and peered in. Jack could see Reilly in semi-profile, his back mostly to the door. Reilly sat in the second row, leaning forward with his elbows on his knees, staring straight ahead intensely. His eyes did not waver but remained focused on the bulletin board in the front of the room. Jack got the impression that Reilly studied the photos like someone might study one of those three-dimensional computer-generated pictures, waiting for a clearer image to pop out from the obscure colored dots.

"Heath."

Reilly blinked once but did not startle. He slowly turned his head to the door, but his eyes did not leave the collage in front of him. Jack thought that Reilly felt on the brink of an epiphany and didn't want to miss it. Once his head had turned nearly over his shoulder, Reilly's gaze shifted to the door. His face, initially completely expressionless, displayed a modicum of surprise a few deliberate blinks later.

"Jack. What brings you in?"

Jack shrugged. He moved into the room and sat down a row behind Reilly, a few chairs to his side. A fatherly sense came over him, instructing him to provide some comfort and reassurance to Reilly. Had he spent more time and energy looking introspectively, he would have realized that he also did this out of guilt about abandoning the CASMIRC team in the middle of a big investigation to pursue his own political ambitions. "I needed to go over some stuff from the Hollows files."

Reilly's eyes lit up with recognition. "Oh, yeah. I heard about Melissa Hollows. How bizarre. And sad. You'd think that family had been through enough."

Jack was taken aback by this last statement. In Jack's experience Reilly had never expressed much emotion about victims or their families. *Perhaps acting as a lead investigator has provided him with a different perspective*, Jack thought.

"Yeah," Jack agreed. He opened his mouth to say more— about the voice mail, or the coroner's report, or an equally empathic statement—but stopped himself. Best not to get into any detailed discussion about that case right now. Moreover, Reilly presently seemed much more interested in his Playground Predator case.

Jack looked up at the front of the room. He took in the images on the photographs. Unlike Reilly, Jack focused more on the school photos of the girls, smiling, vibrant, and still alive. He consciously tried not to focus on the crime scene photos, not because he felt squeamish in any way, but because he didn't want to let himself get engaged in the process. His attention passed to the messages neatly written on the dry-erase board:

JA донт 'стварно мрзим вас -- SERBIAN
I DON'T REALLY HATE YOU

ฉันต้องการใคร -- THAI
I WANT TO BE SOMEBODY

الساعة رجل -- ARABIC
THE MAN OF THE HOUR

"Another message came with the third victim, huh?" Jack asked, mostly rhetorically.

"Yep," Reilly replied.

"The man of the hour," Jack read aloud.

"Yep."

Jack couldn't remember ever seeing Reilly so taciturn. *Either he's so engrossed in this case that he doesn't want to talk much, or he already feels defeated,* Jack thought, hoping it was the former rather than the latter. While his paternal instincts suggested that he stay, Jack began to get up to leave, thinking he would leave Reilly alone with his thoughts.

Before he could fully stand up, Reilly asked, "What do you think it means?"

Jack looked down at him, then back to the dry-erase board. He didn't say anything for several seconds. As much as he didn't want to get involved in this case, for his own sake, he couldn't allow himself to ignore Reilly's reaching out for help. "Well, I think the obvious thing is that he is out for attention."

"Yeah," Reilly agreed. "What else? I feel like there's something else here, and I just can't see it."

Jack sat back down. Both men leaned forward. "The focus changes," Jack noticed. Reilly looked at him quizzically. "The first statement is all about the victim. 'I don't really hate you.' The last one is all about him, 'the man of the hour.'"

Reilly nodded. "And the middle one is what he wants to be, but he's not there yet. By the third one, he's attained what he wants? He's now the Man of the Hour?"

"Maybe." Jack began to see where this might go. His paternal instinct grabbed his tongue before he could announce his suspicion; he wanted Reilly to feel like he could figure it out for himself. "So what happened between the second victim and the third victim? What allowed him to achieve his desired status?"

Reilly's eyes widened. "The article. The article in *The Post*."

Jack's eyes widened too, though not as dramatically, as if he had not already considered this. "Yes."

"But we were so disparaging to him in that article. Why would that help him? How could that build him up?" Reilly asked.

Jack shrugged. "What is it they say in Hollywood—there's no such thing as bad publicity?"

Reilly sighed. "I guess." He placed his head into his hands and rubbed his eyes. "Christ, I really hope we didn't set him off with that article."

From behind both of them, an ever-confident voice answered, "We didn't." Reilly and Jack turned to see Dylan Harringer, standing in the doorway. "He had done too much recon. He knew those soccer fields and those trails way too well to have put it together in two days."

"Right," Reilly remembered, breathing an inner sign of relief.

Harringer moved toward the front of the room. "This continues to be all part of his master plan. We just have to figure out the next step before it happens." Without a pause in his cadence, Harringer asked, "What are you doing here, Jack?"

Jack looked up, somewhat startled by the abrupt change in topic. "I came to look over a couple more old files."

"Melissa Hollows?" Harringer surmised. Jack nodded. Harringer looked down at his watch. "We're meeting to discuss this—" He tapped the top of the dry-erase board, where it said **THE PLAYGROUND PREDATOR**, with an almost imperceptible roll of his eyes. "—in five minutes. You're welcome to sit in if you'd like."

Jack shook his head. "No, thanks, I need to get going soon."

Harringer nodded as he looked down at the front podium. "Right." Jack detected a hint of disdain in his voice, and, while he may have understood the reason behind it, he did not care for it. Jack kept looking at Harringer, but Harringer kept his focus on the podium, as if he couldn't muster enough respect for Jack to look him in the eye.

The growing tension broke when the computer in the front podium beeped with the characteristic tones of an incoming video call. Harringer moved the mouse and clicked. "Hello, Camilla," he said into the computer.

"Hi, Dylan," they could all hear through the computer's speakers. Harringer grabbed a remote control from a small drawer in the podium and turned on the overhead projector. He made a slight adjustment to the camera on top of the podium that faced out to the rest of the conference room. Before the projector had warmed up enough for Camilla's image to appear in front of them, Camilla said, "Hi, Heath."

Reilly, who had been staring down at the floor the last few minutes, looked up to the camera. "Hey, Camilla."

"Is that Jack?" she asked.

"Hey, CC, how are you?" Jack responded.

"Good, are you back on this case?"

326

"No, I just needed to stop by for a minute and saw Happy Pants here sitting by himself," he thumbed toward Reilly, "so I thought I'd try to cheer him up."

"You should have seen him the other night," Camilla cajoled. Her faint image began to appear on the front screen as the bulb in the projector warmed up. "He really was Happy Pants."

Reilly looked up at her, confused at first. He then rolled his eyes. "Christ."

Jack looked at Reilly. "What's this?"

Reilly shrugged, trying to act nonchalant. "It's nothing. She's being ridiculous."

"He had drinks with your reporter friend, Corinne O'Loughlin," Camilla explained, a widening smirk on her face. While it came across as a tease, she genuinely appreciated the opportunity to imbue some humanity into Reilly, the erstwhile just-the-facts-ma'am Special Agent. She hoped others could see him a little more like she had, with a little more depth to him.

"Wartime?" Jack asked, turning toward Reilly.

Reilly looked up at him, no longer hiding any emotion. He looked offended. "Yeah, Wartime. What's that all about?"

Jack smiled warmly. "It doesn't mean anything, Heath. I know it sounds pejorative, but it's not meant to. It refers to lyrics from a song she reminded me of, and then it seemed to fit her personality." He could tell that this did not make Reilly feel much better, so he tried to retreat. "A little bit, just a little bit."

"Well, I still don't think it's right and I still don't think…" He trailed off when his eyes met Jack. Jack stared straight ahead. The intense expression on Jack's face brought a pit immediately into

327

Reilly's stomach. Reilly felt scared, as if something unexpected had just happened; he wondered if the abrupt change in Jack's countenance signaled that he had suffered a mini-stroke. "Jack?" he said, almost whispering through tightened vocal cords, his voice cracking a little.

Jack stood up, walked to the end of the row of chairs, and up to the front of the room beside the dry-erase board, his eyes never leaving the text upon it. "Lyrics," Jack said softly. He turned to face the rest of the room. Harringer and Reilly both watched him intently, their eyes tracking his every movement. "They're song lyrics," he repeated.

"What?" Camilla blurted through the video screen. She could see Reilly and Harringer and their puzzled expressions, but she could no longer see Jack nor hear him well. "What did you say, Jack?"

Harringer turned toward the computer. "He said they're song lyrics." He turned to face Jack and took a few steps towards him, centering himself in front of the dry-erase board. "What song, Jack?"

Jack's focus stayed on the dry-erase board, his head cocked to the side. He read over the lines one-by-one, trying to find the melody from the recesses of his mind. He knew he had heard this song before. He thought he had known it well, at one point in his life. At the moment, though, he couldn't find it.

Reilly pulled out his laptop from the bag beside his chair. "I'll Google it," he announced. He opened his laptop and began booting it up.

Saxophone. Jack could hear the saxophone around the phrase, *I don't really hate you.* He found the melody. The next line came to him, flowing freely now. All of a sudden the entire song popped into his brain. He knew the title and the artist. He had the original vinyl at home, somewhere in his attic. His facial expression changed, signaling his enlightenment. Harringer caught this and became excited himself. Before Jack could give voice to his epiphany, his mind played the next full line of the song. It had continued to play in his head, even though his conscious thought had nearly moved on.

We were made for each other, me and you.

"Oh, fuck," Jack whispered.

"What?" Harringer pleaded. Reilly had stopped his internet search and joined Harringer in staring at Jack, waiting for the answer.

Melissa. The Playground Predator had killed Melissa. His message for that slaying had been the voicemail to Jack.

Jack took a short breath to collect himself, blew it out in a spurt. He focused on Harringer's face. He would serve Harringer's needs first, before delving into the Melissa Hollows connection.

"It's Peter Gabriel. It's called 'Family Snapshot.'"

Reilly typed furiously on his laptop, plugging the title into Google's search field.

Harringer honed his focus on Jack. "Are you sure?"

"Positive."

"OK, well, what does it mean?" Harringer demanded.

Jack shook his head and lifted his shoulders in a muted shrug. He turned his gaze back to the dry-erase board. He needed to work out a few things in his head before he could offer any further speculation out loud.

Harringer spun towards the back of the room. "Reilly?"

"I'm on it," Reilly replied, not lifting his eyes from the computer screen. "Here," he looked up. "I found the song lyrics."

"Project them," Harringer ordered.

Reilly lifted the computer from his lap and carried it down the row of chairs and to the front of the room. At the podium he unplugged the projector connection from the embedded computer and plugged it into his laptop. Within seconds a web page with the lyrics from the song shone on the screen in the front of the room.

"Turn the camera around," a now disembodied Camilla requested, still linked to the room via the connection between her laptop in Front Royal and the podium computer. Reilly grabbed the mounted camera and turned it toward the front screen. Reilly and Harringer read the lyrics silently to themselves. Jack did not need to read them; he sat down in the front row, running the lyrics over in his head.

"Shit, I can't read them," Camilla complained. If anyone in the conference room happened to look at the podium computer, he would have seen Camilla using her Blackberry to search the internet to find the lyrics for herself.

"What does it mean?" Harringer asked, clearly not having completely finished reading all of the lyrics.

"This involves me," Jack said quietly.

Harringer's face twisted in incomprehension. "What?!"

Jack did not make eye contact and spoke very deliberately. "Melissa Hollows called me the day she was killed. I didn't pick up, but she left me a voice mail. She said, 'We were made for each other, you and me,' but then corrected herself. 'Me and you,' she said." He pointed to the screen. "She was quoting this song. There—just two lines below the line quoted in that first message from the killer."

Reilly had turned to face Jack, also with a puzzled expression. "I don't get it. You think Melissa Hollows was wrapped up in this shit?" he asked, pointing to the photos on the bulletin board.

Jack looked up at him, still pacing his words, choosing them carefully. "No. Not like that. I think your Playground Predator killed Melissa Hollows. And instead of leaving a message behind with the body, he made her call me, give it to me directly."

Harringer narrowed his eyes, studying Jack as he would an interrogated suspect on the other side of a one-way mirror. A thousand questions circled in his head, but he couldn't decide on which one to ask first. So he just stared.

"I don't get it. What does Melissa Hollows have to do with this? Why would the Predator want to get you involved?" Reilly queried.

"I don't... know," Jack said. He rubbed his temples with his first two fingers. Perhaps if he squeezed them hard enough, the answer might pop out. Or he might magically turn back time, go back forty-eight hours, before all of this holy shitstorm.

"I might," Camilla said from the ether.

Harringer and Reilly turned toward the computer in the podium. "Go, Camilla," Harringer commanded. Reilly quickly moved over to the podium so he could see Camilla; Harringer kept his attention on the screen in front of him, reading over the lyrics again.

"This song seems to be about someone seeking fame. He's so desperate for it, in fact, that he shoots someone. I—"

Jack interrupted. "It's actually—"

"Uh," Harringer stopped Jack, sticking his open palm a foot from Jack's face without turning to face him. "Let her finish."

331

Jack could sense the irritation and suspicion in Harringer's voice. *With good reason,* Jack thought. *Maybe he should suspect me. Maybe I am going to pay for my sins.* Suddenly Jack felt as if he stood on top of a mortar-less brick wall, swaying back and forth, waiting for the inevitable crumble of his foothold and the horrific crash that would follow. Out of nowhere he thought of Vicki, and of Jonah, and he wanted more than anything else to see them, to try to protect them from this impending downfall.

Camilla continued. "If the Predator wants to be famous, he would want the most famous lawman in the country to be on his tail, right? That's Jack. He wants Jack."

Harringer completed reading the lyrics as Camilla finished speaking. "Ok, I'm buying so far." He turned to face Jack. "But how does this involve Melissa Hollows?"

Jack shrugged, not yet sure what to say.

"She symbolized his most important accomplishment, what made him famous—solving the Lamaya Hollows case," Reilly exalted, proud of making the link.

"Maybe… maybe," Harringer conceded. "Jack?" His tone relaxed, became less interrogatory and more collegial.

Jack sighed, shrugged again. *Sounds pretty good to me. And maybe it's right. Maybe this has nothing to do with sleeping with her,* he hoped. "I suppose it makes sense."

Harringer nodded. He looked back to the screen, to the lyrics. "What were you going to say earlier?"

Things had been moving so fast, Jack had to stop to think for a moment. He remembered what he had intended to say a few moments ago, but it didn't seem that significant. In reality, he mostly had been trying to change the subject. "Oh. I was going to say that specifically the song is about the Kennedy assassination from the perspective of Lee Harvey Oswald. That is his motivation—his destiny, even. To be famous, like JFK."

Harringer and Reilly turned back to the screen; in her hotel room in Front Royal, Camilla went back to studying the web browser on her phone. "Huh," Reilly uttered, agreeing with Jack's interpretation of the lyrics.

Jack stood up abruptly, his hand pointing to the screen. "That's it." Only those who knew him as well as Harringer, Reilly, and Camilla could sense the trembling in his voice.

"What?" Harringer asked.

"He doesn't want to be famous *like* Lee Harvey Oswald. He wants to be as famous *as* Oswald."

"How do you get as famous as Oswald?" Reilly asked without taking any time to think about it.

Camilla nearly shouted through the computer. "You assassinate the President."

Jack glared at his compatriots in the conference room. "Or the President's daughters."

61

The young girl looked out the car window from the back seat. She watched the buildings pass by, but she didn't recognize most of them. Even the small sapling trees lining the road didn't look familiar. *This isn't the way home*, she thought. She sat up a little higher, trying to get a better view of the landscape whirring by. Nothing rang a bell.

She hesitated to say anything to the man driving the car. Surely he knew where he was going. She looked to her left, to the other side of the backseat. Her older sister sat there silently, her thumbs working wildly on the cell phone in her lap. Apparently she hadn't noticed anything unusual. Even leaving school early hadn't fazed her. And not just early—*super* early. The day had just begun, really. But her sister didn't seem to care in the least.

She looked into the front seat. Neither the driver nor the man in the passenger seat acted as if anything were awry. But she didn't think she could trust their reaction, or lack thereof. They had been trained to remain calm.

Her parents had always taught her to speak her mind, that her opinion mattered just as much as anyone else's. She reminded herself of this, and decided to ask aloud, "Where are we going?"

The man in the passenger seat, Dan, turned his head over his left shoulder. "We're going home early today, like we said."

The girl looked out the window again, just to confirm her original thought. *Nope, still not familiar.* "But this isn't the way home."

Dan turned more fully this time, so he could make eye contact with her. At the same time, the conversation had broken her older

334

sister out of her texting trance. She looked up from her phone and tried to get a sense of her surroundings. She felt a bolt of adrenaline surge through her, as if suddenly realizing something scary. Dan said, now to both of them, "We're taking a slightly different way home today. But it's the way home, trust me."

"It's the way home," Paul, the driver, echoed, without taking his eyes off the road.

The older sister looked back out the window. Though she had known both of these men for a few years, and had no reason to doubt them, she couldn't shake the tingle of that fresh epinephrine coursing through her veins. "Is something wrong? Is it Dad?"

"Nothing's wrong. Your dad's fine, and your mom is too. We are just going to get you home for the day. OK?"

"OK," they each said in turn, neither sounding thoroughly convinced. The little sister went back to looking out the window, as did the older one. Without looking down, she folded her phone up and put it in her jacket pocket.

62

Jack sat with his elbows on his knees, hands clasped in front of him, staring at the intricate pattern on the rug beneath him. His eyes followed the swooping patterns of dark and light. The design somehow projected both a classical and contemporary feel at the same time. It added warmth to the otherwise light—and, quite frankly, drab—color scheme of the rest of the room.

Though partially enamored by the rug, Jack's mind focused mostly on the boggling mystery at hand. He tried to connect the playground murders, Melissa Hollows, himself, and "Family Snapshot" in some fashion that made sense, but the logic continued to elude him. Occasionally his thoughts oscillated back to his original stressor of the day: his meeting with Philip Prince to discuss his campaign paradigm and to plan a schedule of upcoming events. He had called Philip as he left the office to tell him that he would need to reschedule the meeting. Philip tried to interrupt, asking Jack to explain in better detail, but Jack deferred. He didn't offer a reason. Prince would hear soon enough through the media—or, more likely, his far-reaching web of insiders—about the recent happenings in the Playground Predator case and its probable link to the Melissa Hollows murder. And to Jackson Byrne.

"I can't believe we're in the Oval Office," Reilly whispered, sitting beside Jack on the cream-colored couch.

Jack looked up from the carpet toward Reilly, whose neck craned upward to appreciate the elaborate molding and painted icons on the ceiling. Jack nodded, which Reilly sensed through his peripheral vision, but he did not say anything.

Reilly looked over at Jack, who turned his focus back to the carpet between his knees. Despite the fact that they sat alone in the room, Reilly kept his voice low. "Do you really think our un-sub is targeting the President's kids?"

Jack shrugged. "I think we have to assume that it's a very real possibility."

Opposite them a door swung inward, opened with authority by the man walking through it. He left the door open behind him as he walked straight across the room toward Jack and Reilly. When he got within two steps his right hand shot out at waist height, open-palmed for a handshake.

"Devin Nicholas," he announced. Jack and Reilly each stood up, introduced themselves, and shook his hand. "I'm the Director of the Secret Service."

He needed no introduction for Jack. He knew of Devin Nicholas and had never heard anything less than glowing remarks about him. Jack also knew that he and Reilly need not introduce themselves; Nicholas surely knew any and all pertinent details about them already.

"I'm Special Agent Heath Reilly and this is Special Agent Jackson Byrne, FBI, Child Abduction and Serial Murder Investigative Resource Center," Reilly introduced unnecessarily.

Nicholas nodded. "Pleasure to meet you. Please sit." He gestured to their couch, and backed himself into the couch opposite them.

Just as they all entered their individual crouches, President Sullivan walked through the open door opposite them. He closed the door behind him as all three of the other men in the room promptly stood back up straight. "Hello, Jack," he said and he walked over and shook his hand.

"Hello, Mr. President," Jack replied. The memory of using "awesome" in his previous meeting with The Most Powerful Man in the World jolted him, and he had to restrain a shudder from coming over him.

"Special Agent Heath Reilly," Reilly said as the two shook. "It's an honor sir."

The President nodded as he turned and sat on the couch beside Nicholas. "I have to be honest, I didn't expect to see you again so soon, Jack."

"No, sir, I imagine you didn't. Nor did I."

"So please tell me why I had to take my daughters out of school this morning."

Reilly, silent, looked at Jack, apparently awaiting the answer just as eagerly as The President. Jack understood the message in this gesture: Reilly came along today to project his assumption of the leadership role of this investigation, but the theory of the President's family's involvement belonged primarily to Jack. *Smart move*, Jack thought. *If I'm right, it looks like you supported me. If I'm wrong, you can quickly separate yourself from the idea by laying it all back on me.*

"Have you heard of the so-called Playground Predator?" Jack began.

"I have, a little, but enlighten me," The President replied.

Jack briefly recounted the events of the past several weeks in York, Frederick, and Front Royal. He described the notes planted on the bodies, likely novel information to The President, as it had not yet been released to the press. Finally he discussed his theory of the link to "Family Snapshot," and the possibility of The President and his family as targets. He left out the link between this case and Melissa Hollows' murder.

"I am a fan of Peter Gabriel, but I have to admit I'm not familiar with this song," said The President.

Reilly pulled a manila folder out of his leather satchel and extended it to Jack, all without saying a word. Jack glared at Reilly, trying hard to hide his incredulity. *Since when am I your errand boy?* he telepathically asked Reilly. Before waiting for Reilly to intuit the question and send a mind message back his way, Jack decided that this wasn't the time for a swinging dick contest. He grabbed the folder and walked it the few feet across to the two gentlemen opposite them.

The President took the folder and opened it up, revealing one sheet of paper inside: the complete lyrics to "Family Snapshot" by Peter Gabriel.

63

Before leaving the morning meeting about the Playground Predator to attend another meeting regarding a possible child abduction in the Pacific Northwest, Dylan Harringer had put Amanda Lundquist on the assignment of working on the song angle. She had contacted Peter Gabriel's management team in the UK to see if they had received any unusual requests, contacts, fan mail, etc. The individual with whom she had spoken, Lonny White, expressed genuine concern. He said he had not heard of anything, but he would ask around the office to the rest of the team and let her know if anything came up. Mr. Gabriel had started a music publishing company several years ago, so his "team" had actually grown quite large.

Amanda then conducted internet searches, trying to find any recent references to that song. She learned that the book *An Assassin's Diary* written by Arthur Bremer, the man convicted of the assassination attempt of the Democratic Presidential candidate George Wallace in 1972, had actually served as the initial inspiration for Peter Gabriel to write the lyrics. Whether Gabriel intended to create a parallel to Lee Harvey Oswald's assassination of JFK seemed to remain open to interpretation.

A handful of blogs made reference to the decades-old tune. After spending nearly four hours and going through dozens of results, she singled out four blog entries that seemed odd, ominous, or in any way suspicious. The author's complete information, including address and phone number, had been listed on two of the four blogs. While she made notes on both, she felt confident in eliminating them based on location: one blogger lived in Lake Tahoe, Nevada, and the other in Chelmsford, England.

The other two bloggers did not have any identifiable markers on their blogs, at least not that Amanda could find. She called one of her colleagues in CASMIRC's internet crime division, a skilled IT specialist named Matt. She either couldn't remember his last name, or had never actually learned it. Or he had only one name—one could never know with some of these hackers who spent more time in virtual reality than in *reality* reality. Matt promised her that he would carve out a few minutes later in the afternoon to take a look at her request.

Not long after Amanda had hung up with Matt, Lonny White called back. After speaking with nearly everyone at Peter Gabriel's management team and his publishing company, including Mr. Gabriel himself, he could confirm that they had not received anything suspicious. Amanda thanked him for his efforts and reminded him to call back if anything arose.

64

Vicki studied her husband's face, taking in all the information he had just shared. "You think this is about you." It clearly came out as a declaration, not a question.

Jack looked back at her. "Yeah," he admitted. They had put Jonah to bed a little bit ago. As she often did—and did well—Vicki offered to serve as a sounding board for Jack as he worked through various angles and theories on a case. Also as per usual, after an especially stressful day, they each had a bottle of beer in hand. "I mean, is there any other way to see it?"

Vicki sat back in her dinette chair. After a pensive moment, she set her beer down on the dinette in front of her so she could count on her hands. Her right index finger pushed on the pad of her left pinky. "The foreign language messages, meant to get FBI—and CASMIRC—involved…" Her pointer finger moved over to depress her left ring finger. "…Involving a public figure from your biggest case…" Her left middle finger. "…The personal phone call to you, with another message…" Index finger, followed by a pause. "…What else?"

"The song," Jack answered. "It's kind of an obscure song, but it's a song that I knew."

"How could this guy possibly know that?"

Jack shook his head. "I don't know. I know it doesn't entirely make sense."

"Did you recently buy the CD, or download it, or something? Maybe this guy hacked into your computer at some point to find your MP3s?"

"No. It's an old song. I'm pretty sure I don't even have a digital copy of that song. I haven't heard it in...forever. Fifteen, twenty years."

They sat silently for several minutes, each mulling over the facts and circumstances. "Poor Melissa Hollows," Vicki sighed. "As if that poor woman hadn't been through enough."

Jack nodded. Vicki didn't know half of the real story. Jack could not expend the mental or emotional energy to deal with his guilt at this time, so he let this pass quickly. Luckily Vicki changed the subject for him. "What did Philip say when you canceled the meeting? Was he upset?"

Jack shook his head as he took a swig of his beer. "I didn't give him a chance to be the first time. I just told him I had to postpone our meeting then kind of hung up." He had felt the carbonation from the beer accumulate in his stomach until it bubbled up and he let it out in a silent burp. "I called him back later this afternoon to tell him a little more, without going into too much detail. He seemed a little... disappointed that I was working on an active case, even after I explained to him that I got pulled into it unexpectedly. But he did love that I had a meeting with The President. We're going to try to meet again tomorrow afternoon."

They sat in silence for a few minutes, each looking down at the beers in their hands. Vicki began peeling back the top label, a habit that had stuck with her since she first started drinking beer in college. Her thumb worked at the tiny balls of adhesive that remained on the tinted glass, slowly stripping them away into a larger conglomeration of glue. "How does it feel?"

Her voice nearly startled Jack, who had settled comfortably into their moment of silence. He looked up at her. "How does what feel?"

She examined his face, trying to find the answer to her question in his countenance. Like a soothsayer and her crystal ball, Vicki thought she knew her husband well enough to discern sufficient information from looking deeply into his eyes. Even though she thought she knew the answer, she elucidated her original question. "This. Being a lawman. Not a politician."

"Well, I wouldn't call myself a politician yet," Jack responded in an attempt to avoid the question.

"OK, fine. But you haven't been this involved in an investigation in... what?... a year?"

Jack nodded.

"So how does it feel? Are you making the right choice by leaving the Bureau for politics?"

Jack scratched his head. So caught up in the happenings of the day, he hadn't stopped to think about that at all. Thank God for Vicki, who helped keep him grounded and offered him these avenues to reflect, avenues he would have trouble finding on his own. After a moment, he answered, "Stressful."

Vicki tilted her head; "stressful" was not the answer she had expected, not the answer she had read in his eyes. But she chose not to call him on it, at least not right now. "Then maybe we should get to bed and get you some rest." Jack nodded. They each swallowed down the last drops of beer, took turns rinsing out the bottles in the sink before placing them in the recycling bin in the cabinet underneath, and went upstairs.

65

Caleb Goodnight, buzzing with excitement, walked down the brightly lit hallway toward his office. He had just come out of the production meeting for tonight's show: a chat with George Lucas, the auteur of the *Star Wars* film saga. Caleb's ever-calm demeanor belied his enthusiasm for doing his show; he still got butterflies in his stomach almost every night. He felt a special twinge of delight to speak with a filmmaker who revolutionized digital effects and forever changed the landscape of science fiction.

As he approached the office door, his cell phone vibrated in his breast pocket. He looked at the display— Unknown number. He had received a call from an unknown number on Friday night too, right around the same time. He had let that one go to voice mail, but the caller had not left a message. He thought about answering this time, but again decided against it. He noted the time: 9:18 pm. After six vibratory surges, his phone stopped. He stood there in the hallway, staring at the display, waiting to see if the voice mail icon appeared on his screen. After over a minute, it did not appear. Again apparently the mystery caller did not feel the necessity to leave a message.

Caleb entered his office, lay the phone down face-up on his desk—where it would remain for the duration of his show, as always— and sat down. If he got another call from the unknown number, he thought he might answer it next time. For now, he reassured himself that it couldn't be too important if the caller waited three days between attempts and chose not to leave a message either time. He turned his focus back to his notes for tonight's show, and the titillation over interviewing an icon returned.

66

Jack lay in bed on his side, his eyes open. The bathroom door ajar, a slim triangle of light spread across the floor beside the bed. The fine buzz of Vicki's electric toothbrush emanated from inside the bathroom. Though his thoughts remained with the Playground Predator case, he could feel his focus fading, less sharp than earlier. Still baffled by the case, but even more fatigued by it, he hoped sleep could soon creep in. Vicki's toothbrush stopped with a final soft pair of beeps. After gargling with mouthwash and turning off the bathroom light, she walked around the bed to her traditional side and crawled under the covers. She hugged Jack from behind and kissed his ear.

"Are you feeling tired? Do you think you're going to be able to get some sleep?" she whispered.

"Yeah, I think so." He rolled onto his back and kissed her lips. She then rolled away and laid her head on her own pillow. Jack stayed on his back, looking up at the ceiling, an all-too familiar vista on many previous sleepless nights. Fortunately, his eyes felt heavy. He let them close.

"Oh, I almost forgot," Vicki said, a little too loudly given the quiet ambience in the room. She rolled toward Jack. "I scheduled a session with that photographer for Thursday afternoon, from four to five. Is that OK?"

"What photographer?" Jack asked. "For what, now?" He hadn't yet fallen asleep, but the question seemed so out-of-left-field that she might as well have asked it straight from a deep dream at 3:00 am.

"That photographer in the strip mall beside Dr. Franklin's office. We talked about this last week, remember?"

Jack's mind worked backwards, back to their conversation in the kitchen days earlier. He remembered the conversation with Vicki. A vision of the photographer's brochure came into his head. He looked at Vicki wide-eyed and slowly sat straight up in bed. "What's the name of that place?" he asked her deliberately. He knew that he already knew the answer; he needed confirmation.

The name initially eluded her. She thought about it for a second, and after a few seconds she remembered. "Family Snapshot," she said. "Why?"

"The song. That's the title of the song," Jack replied in monotone. His mind tried to work fast, but it still needed to shake off the previously imminent sleep.

"What?!" Vicki said in a whispered shout. "That... do you think that's a coincidence?"

"I don't know." Jack's voice still lacked any inflection. He looked at his wife, both sharing an expression of disbelief. "It can't be, can it?"

DAY NINE:
TUESDAY

67

Faint drops of rain settled onto the windshield, much lighter than the downpour that had lasted most of the last twelve hours. The temperature had begun to warm up, but it still seemed like an especially wet spring so far. Thanks to a recent waxing, small beads of water formed on the hood, sometimes coalescing into a larger pool. Once the pools on the far sides of the hood got large enough, they slipped off onto the parking lot below.

Jack looked at the storefront in the strip mall about thirty yards away. He had parked in the middle of the lot, close enough to keep an eye on the front door of the photography studio, but far enough away that passersby going to other businesses wouldn't pay much heed to the man sitting in the front seat of his car for the last forty-five minutes. He looked down at his watch. 11:54. The brochure said that Family Snapshot opened at noon on Tuesdays, or sooner by appointment. He had tried calling several times earlier this morning, but no one answered.

He had spent the morning at the office, but he hadn't said a word to anyone about his suspicion over the photography studio. It still seemed like too much of a coincidence to have much significance. The rest of the office had enough going on without this distraction, anyway. Mr. and Mrs. Vance Cottrell, Amy and Carl Coulter, and Jennifer and Mario Cugino had all appeared on *Good Morning America* to talk about their daughters' deaths and to plead with anyone to offer information. Harringer had received advanced notice of this from *GMA*'s producers—along with an invitation to appear for an interview himself. While he declined the interview—and purposefully failed to offer it to anyone else, knowing full well that Heath Reilly would have jumped at the chance—he did offer to help staff a tip line that *GMA* could disperse to the general public. The phones actually rang in a call center in another building in their complex in Quantico, staffed by FBI employees. Harringer had assigned Reilly and Lundquist to supervise and delve further into any tips that had merit.

So Jack he had spent his time at his computer, going through public records and FBI databases to learn more about the proprietor of Family Snapshot. According to the lease, the business belonged to Shawn Toussant, a thirty-five year-old married father of two. He lived in a modest home less than ten minutes from the photography studio. (Jack had driven by there on his way here but saw no activity. This did not disappoint him, as he would rather visit him at his place of business.) Toussant had bought the house eight months ago, around the same time that he got the lease on the studio. He had a mortgage on the house, but otherwise no significant debt. He paid his bills on time. He had no criminal record. He did not fit any criminal profile, let alone that of a serial killer of children. Yet Jack could not shake the feeling that Toussant somehow played a role in this.

Something flashed out of the corner of Jack's eye. He looked back at the storefront, concentrating. The sign in the front window had been flipped; it now read "OPEN." Jack got out of the car and trotted briskly to the sidewalk, jumping over several puddles in the parking lot along the way. He acted casually as he peered through the large plate glass window into the store. Other than two large easels displaying a variety of professional photographs—weddings, landscapes, high school senior pictures—he couldn't see much, only that no one stood within a few feet of the door. He walked up to the front door and entered.

He did not notice the small black plexi-glass bubble embedded in the ceiling, concealing a security camera inside, its focus on the front door.

68

Heath Reilly stood, arms folded, in the corner of the call-center room. He had the strong and strange urge to bite his nails, a habit in which he had never previously partaken. He couldn't understand it, it bothered him, and he couldn't shake it.

The phones rang consistently, such that the three FBI employees manning the phones stayed relatively busy. They took copious notes on laptops as they spoke on the phone with citizens calling in tips. When they finished and the call ended, they automatically sent the notes to Amanda Lundquist's computer. Sitting at a table right in front of Reilly, she scanned each note, looking for anything that seemed helpful. If she found a hit, she would notify Reilly right away, as he knew much more about the case and should serve as the final gatekeeper before the team acted on any tip.

Reilly's iPhone vibrated on his hip. He took it out of its clip: Corinne. He hadn't spoken to her since Sunday, since the case seemed to have blown up. He immediately felt guilty, felt that he had kept a secret from her. He quickly contemplated not answering, but, he knew that he wanted to speak with her. He stepped out of the room into the adjacent hallway and answered his phone. "Hey," he said with an air of familiarity that surprised even him.

"Hey, it's Corinne," she said on the other end.

He liked hearing her voice. "Hey, what's up?"

"Our story is blowing up, that's what's up. Way up," she replied.

"Really?" Now he truly was surprised. "You mean because of the *Good Morning America* piece?"

"Yeah. It's all over CNN. All of the major networks are planning stories tonight for the evening news. I think Nancy Grace is having the Coulters on her show tonight."

"Wow. How do you know all this?"

"I'm a reporter," she answered, with more than a hint of "duh!" in her voice. "It's kind of what I do."

"Right," Reilly said.

"So… any news for me?" Corinne asked.

Reilly, feeling torn, paused. Discerning which facts to share with the media and which to withhold still did not come naturally to him. In addition, he recognized that he might be in the early stages of developing feelings for Corinne, and this added pressure to disclose things to her. Even though no one stood within earshot, he lowered his voice. "We might be in the middle of a big break," he whispered.

"No shit!" Corinne reflexively whispered too, even though she sat in the relatively private comforts of her cubicle at work. "What?"

"It's too soon and too… cloudy… to say yet," Reilly answered.

Corinne didn't respond.

Several seconds of silence elapsed. Reilly sensed that she waited for him to say more, but he decided he wouldn't cave. "I will let you know when things become clearer," he said. He would wait until later to cave.

Corinne sighed, her last ditched effort to induce guilt. "OK. Call me later then, OK?"

"Will do," Reilly said, preparing to hang up.

"Now I have a proposal for you," she announced.

Reilly's face lit up. "Oh, yeah? I like the sound of that."

"*The Today Show* called me. They want me to come on tomorrow morning to talk about The Playground Predator."

"Oh. Good for you." Reilly could sense the excitement in her voice.

"Why don't you come on with me?" Corinne offered.

Reilly's heart raced, stoked by such an opportunity. He could make the world—or at least Dylan Harringer and the muckety-mucks in the Bureau—forget about Jackson Byrne sooner than they otherwise would. He could be their new Golden Boy, the media darling from CASMIRC. But he knew he had to exercise caution; he couldn't break the chain of command. He would need Harringer's blessing, which would require some cajoling. "I need to talk to my superior first," he finally responded, trying to hide the excitement in his voice. "Let me call you a little later and we'll talk about all of this."

"Sounds good," Corinne said with a smile. "Talk to you then."

They hung up. Reilly decided to take some time to think about the correct wording of his proposition before going straight to Harringer.

69

Shawn Toussant stood behind a chest-high counter on the right side of the room. Dozens of framed photographs peppered the ecru-colored walls. Jack pretended to gaze at them in appreciation as he worked his way toward the counter.

"Hi, there," Toussant greeted, smiling.

Jack turned his focus to Toussant and returned the smile. "Hi. Are you the store owner?"

Toussant smiled proudly. "Owner and photographer."

Jack nodded. "Then you must be Shawn Toussant," he announced confidently, his smile fading.

Toussant appeared surprised. "Yes," he said with a lift in his voice, almost like a question.

Just as represented in Hollywood, Jack reached into the inside pocket of his suit jacket and brought out his badge, flipping it open in one agile move. "I'm Special Agent Jackson Byrne of the FBI." Toussant looked at the badge, actually taking a moment to inspect it. *Like you would be able to spot a fake*, Jack thought, but did not say aloud. Toussant turned his attention back to Jack, who flipped his badge closed and placed it back into his pocket. He didn't speak for a few seconds, hoping Toussant might say or do something the least bit incriminating.

"OK…" Toussant said unsteadily. "What can I do for you, Special Agent…sir." Jack thought that he wanted to complete the phrase, but had forgotten his name. It happened all the time.

"Byrne. Is it OK if I ask you a few questions?" Jack let his stiff demeanor soften a bit.

"Sure," Toussant replied.

"Are you expecting any clients?"

Toussant looked down at his appointment book in front of him. "Not until 3:30 today."

"Oh, I don't plan on taking that long," Jack said, his smile returning.

"OK. Should we sit down?" Toussant gestured toward the area behind Jack, a section of the room opposite the counter. This area obviously served as Toussant's studio. Two beautifully upholstered arm chairs sat at an obtuse angle to one another, a warm lavender backdrop behind them. Opposite the chairs stood a tripod, barren at the top—Jack assumed that Toussant chose to not leave his (likely expensive) camera out in the open—and several light stands, none of which were currently turned on. Neatly leaning against the opposite wall lay a stack of screens of various shapes and sizes.

"Sure," Jack replied. He turned his back on Toussant and walked over to take his seat in the far chair, positioned with its back toward the corner of the entire room, so that he could see the whole room from his vantage point. He shifted his position in the chair a couple of times, trying to find a comfortable spot in the lumpy cushion. For such a fine-looking chair, Jack found it surprisingly uncomfortable. Toussant sat himself in the other chair and looked at Jack expectantly. Jack noticed Toussant's calm demeanor, hardly that of a criminal sitting down to talk with the FBI.

"I am investigating a series of crimes over the last several weeks, and I'm hoping that you can help me," Jack began.

"Um, OK. I'm happy to help if I can." Toussant remained upbeat, as if he felt excitement over assisting the FBI in an investigation.

"Can I ask… Where were you on Saturday?"

"This past Saturday?"

"Yes," Jack confirmed.

"I had a wedding. I spent the morning at the bride's house, taking photos of her getting ready with her bridesmaids. The ceremony was at St. Luke's, just over in Montclair, and the reception was at a hotel downtown."

Montclair was about ten miles southwest of Lake Ridge, and a good sixty miles east of Front Royal. "So what time did you get to the bride's house, and what time did you leave the reception?"

Toussant tilted his head back and looked at the ceiling. Apparently this position helped his memory function. "I got to the bride's house around…10:30 that morning, and I left the reception around 8:30 or 8:45 that night."

"Were there any breaks during the day, a gap between the ceremony and the reception?" Jack knew it would take at least two hours round trip to get from Montclair to Front Royal. His suspicion that Toussant had direct involvement with Danielle Coulter's murder on Saturday began to fade quickly.

"Yeah, but I was working the whole time. We had about an hour and a half between the ceremony and the reception, and that's when I took the formal wedding photos."

Jack nodded. Toussant had not been in Front Royal on Saturday. He would later make sure to obtain more information to verify this alibi, but he knew that too many people could confirm it to make it false. No one makes up a fake alibi that involves a couple hundred people.

"What happened on Saturday?" Toussant asked.

Jack found this a very reasonable question, but he did not want to answer it yet. "I'm sorry, I'll get to that. Tell me a little more about your business. When did you open?"

Toussant seemed a little annoyed that Jack evaded his previous question, but he remained cool. "Uh… I got the lease on this place about eight months ago, in October last year. It needed some renovations, which I mostly did myself. I opened in January."

"Uh-huh. And what had you done before that?"

"I've been a professional photographer for the last thirteen years, but I just worked out of my home. Business had been pretty good, but I wanted it to grow more, to include some studio work."

"And do you have any employees here, or any business partners?"

Toussant shook his head. "No. My wife helps out on the weekends with big events. She worked the wedding with me this past Saturday. She's never had any formal training, but she's a pretty great photographer in her own right. But as far as employees, none. And no investors or partners. Just me."

Jack nodded again. For the first time, he began to think that this Family Snapshot angle might turn out to be a dead end. However, he felt that he had developed enough rapport with Toussant to ask a couple more questions. "How did you come up with the name for your studio?"

Toussant opened his mouth reflexively to answer, and then shut it. He had not expected this question. "Uh… It was actually my neighbor's idea. I was going to call it 'Toussant Photography,' you know, something real straight-forward."

"Your neighbor?" Jack had driven by Toussant's house this morning. Had he driven by the home of the Playground Predator as well?

"Yeah. I was in here working on my renovations one afternoon—I hadn't been in more than a few weeks—when one of the docs from next door stopped in to welcome me to the neighborhood."

A light went off in Jack's head, but he didn't yet know what it illuminated. "Your neighbor *here*?" He jerked his thumb toward the wall behind him, the wall separating Family Snapshot from the doctors' office next door. "One of the allergists?"

"Yeah. To be honest I'm not sure which one. He came over, we chatted for a while, and he asked me about the name of my place. When I told him, he didn't like it. I mean, I couldn't care less what he thought, you know? But when he suggested Family Snapshot, I kind of loved it. So, I used it."

"Did he say why? Why he liked that name better?" Jack's speech became pressured.

"No. He left shortly after that. But every time I ran into him during the renovation, he would just look at me, point, and say 'Family Snapshot. Think about it.' When I put the sign in, he came by and looked at me with this... pride, like he had accomplished something. He didn't say anything, he just smiled. Proudly. It seemed a little weird at the time, actually."

Jack stood up quickly. "Thank you for your time, Mr. Toussant," he said, then began moving quickly toward the front door.

"Sure. Are you going to tell me what this is about?" Toussant asked, but Jack did not answer. He had already passed through the front door.

70

"Yep," Dante McClendon said aloud, despite sitting alone in the small dark room. He spent so much time alone on the job that he didn't feel the need to defend the fact that he sometimes talked to himself. He held the photo up to the video screen in front of him, comparing the two one final time. "Yep, that's him."

Dante had worked as the security guard for the Hilltop Shopping plaza—a misnomer in his mind, as it sat on a mere swell on an otherwise flat stretch of road—for the past three years. He had never taken his job too seriously—just seriously enough, his father would have said—until two months ago. That's when the man who introduced himself as Randall approached him with an odd proposition. Randall said that he worked at one of the shops in Hilltop—Dante couldn't remember which one—and he needed help finding some former customers who owed him money. Debt collection agencies would only waste his time and money, he said. He offered Dante a deal almost too good to be true: man the security cameras at Hilltop during all business hours, even on the days that Dante wasn't scheduled to work. Randall would supply Dante with five numbered photographs of these offenders. If he ever saw any of these five people, Dante needed to call Randall right away. In return, Randall paid him $500 per week, plus a bonus of $5000 if he ever fingered one of the debtors. If he identified all five in the next year, Randall offered an additional "job-completion bonus" of $10,000. Seeing that the weekly $500 cash—under the table, no taxes—would basically double Dante's current earnings, not to mention the bonuses—up to $35,000, Dante had done the math!— he jumped on the deal right away.

Since then he devoted himself to this task. Every Friday Randall dropped off an envelope filled with $500 cash, just as promised. Then last week Dante spotted a woman in one of the photographs. He called Randall right away, but he didn't answer. He left a voicemail, as instructed, along with the time, exact location, and the number "2," which identified the woman from the numbered photographs. He didn't receive a return phone call from Randall, but the next day an envelope awaited him at work with $5000 in it. Since then Dante set himself to Randall's task with even more diligence.

"Yep, yep, yep," Dante said aloud again. "That's number one, comin' out the photographer's place." He grabbed his cell phone and dialed Randall's number. Had he had any idea about the chain of events that phone call would spark, he probably would not have dialed. *Probably* not. It was $5000, after all.

71

Jack pushed through the glass door with "Lake Ridge Pediatric Allergy Specialists" painted neatly across the top. Underneath it read, it italics: "Specializing in Asthma, Allergies, and Immunology. J.R. Franklin, MD and F.A. Panigrahy, MD." When the door opened, Jack heard a pleasant two-tone chime go off from inside the office. He let the door swing closed behind him as he approached the front desk.

"Good afternoon!" The bubbly receptionist April greeted Jack from behind the desk. Her enthusiasm for sitting in a swivel chair all day took Jack aback.

"Hi." Jack put both of his palms on top of the reception counter and looked the receptionist square in the eye. "Is Dr. Franklin in?"

April shook her head demonstratively. "He's not in today. If you tell me your name and the nature of your business, I can pass on a message. I will tell you, though, that we do not accept solicitors, and Dr. Franklin frowns upon meeting with pharmaceutical reps. Now, Dr. Panigrahy, on the other hand…"

Jack interrupted her by pulling his badge out of his suit pocket. "I'm Jack Byrne, FBI. Do you know where Dr. Franklin is?"

April looked at his badge and then up at Jack's face with a ray of recognition. "You're Jonah's father!"

"Yes." Jack forced a smile. He realized that, despite his enormous sense of urgency, he may need to utilize some patience with this pleasant but seemingly somewhat ditzy young woman. "Is Dr. Panigrahy in?"

"He is, but he's with a patient right now. Would you like to wait for him?"

Jack thought for a second. "I would. Do you know where Dr. Franklin is?" he repeated.

April shook her head. "He's off this week. He called in yesterday morning and said he was taking the week off. Made for a lot of work for me, having to call all of his patients to reschedule. I'm not sure where he is." She leaned forward in her chair, lowered her voice a little. "He's been calling off a lot lately, to be honest with you, Mr. Byrne."

Jack could feel the puzzle pieces coming together. He could begin to see the image. His gut knew what it would show, but it remained a bit fuzzy in his mind. "Is that right?" he replied, looking around the room.

"Yep," April answered. "You can have a seat right here and I'll let Dr. Panigrahy's nurse know that you're waiting to see him." April spun around in her chair and got up, proceeding through a door to the hallway on the right.

Jack nodded, but didn't move. He continued to survey the room, thinking that within those four walls he might find the right lens to sharpen his focus on his mental image. Several framed posters hung on the wall around the waiting room and reception area. Jack could easily divide them into two categories: about half of them depicted beautifully painted landscapes, the other half offered information about various disease processes, such as a poster with "ASTHMA" printed across the top and an artist's rendering of the inside of an asthmatic's lungs. On the wall behind April hung various certificates in plain black frames. A few personal photographs also joined the decorations on this wall. Jack recognized J.R. with a handsome Indian man—presumably Dr. Panigrahy—their arms over each other's shoulders, each holding an end of a plaque in the middle of them. To the left was a photo of a large Indian family, with the same Indian man in the middle with an attractive Indian woman. On the right was a photo of J.R. with a woman and two small girls, all wearing Mickey Mouse ears and standing in front of the Magic Kingdom. Their beaming smiles exuded glee, an emotion Jack never saw in J.R. back in high school.

April came back from the exam room hallway. "Dr. Panigrahy will be with you in a few moments. Again, you're welcome to take a seat over here." She indicated the waiting room with her hand as she walked back behind the desk and sat in her chair.

Again Jack ignored her offer. He pointed to that photo on the far right. "Is that Dr. Franklin? And his family?"

April looked over her shoulder at the photo, then back at Jack. Her bottom lip curled out in an obvious frown. "Yeah."

Her response surprised Jack. "Why the sad face?"

"Aw." April took in a deep breath and blew it up into her face, as if trying to dry her eyes. She spun around in her chair and pointed at the photo, to the younger of the two girls. "She... um... passed away recently."

All of the blood drained out of Jack's face. "What? When?"

"Oh... about eight months ago now. She had a sudden asthma attack and just stopped breathing. Dr. Franklin tried to resuscitate her, and they tried for hours at the hospital, but... she died. It was horrible." April's voice began to crack with that last sentence. "What an awful, tragic irony, huh? The asthma specialist's daughter dies from an asthma attack."

Jack nodded, speechless.

April shook her head as she grabbed a tissue from the cardboard dispenser on her desk. She dabbed the moist corners of her eyes. "Poor little Lily..."

72

Reilly broke into a light jog from his previous brisk walk. Harringer had called him moments before: Jack had broken the case. He had a very strong suspicion on a suspect. He had a home address. Reilly ran across the Quantico complex to get to his car. Harringer would call local police in Lake Ridge and Prince William County to organize local support. Jack was en route to the suspect's house. Harringer wanted Reilly to assist in the local inspection of the suspect's house, hopefully leading to an apprehension.

Assist.

He knew he didn't have time to get upset. But Fucking Jack Byrne! Or Jackson Fucking Byrne, in the words of Amy Coulter. Reilly has lived and breathed this case for the last ten days; Jack jumps on it for thirty hours and he's got it solved. While he wanted nothing more than to catch this killer, *he* wanted to solve the case. Not Jack the fucking superstar, who days earlier had gracefully bowed out of his job in the Bureau to become a fucking politician. What the fuck.

In his haste to get to the scene, and distracted by his anger, Reilly didn't call Corinne to update her on the information. When it briefly crossed his mind as he climbed into the driver's seat, he decided against it. A part of him wanted to hold out hope that Jack had made a mistake, that his lead would turn into nothing. Another part of him, perhaps the more prudent part, didn't want Corinne to see him so spiteful. Little did he know at the time—but would later find out—that, if he did express his feelings to Corinne, she would share his disdain for the thunder-stealing Jackson Byrne.

73

Jack rolled two small pieces of stone around in the palm of his hand. He crouched on the curb beside his car, parked across the street from J.R Franklin's house. Harringer had told him to wait for Reilly and the local PD to show up before proceeding into the house. He had tried to sit in his car but couldn't; he had too much energy. He wanted to pace, but he didn't want Franklin to spot him, to tip him off in any way. So he crouched, sifting loose pieces of gravel in his hands.

James, he thought, recalling his difficulty in remembering Franklin's first name last week when he and Vicki talked about him. "James Randall Franklin" his medical school diploma had read on the office wall. He never remembered calling him James. All he could remember was J.R. *Had he always been a sociopath?* Jack didn't know. Jack always found him weird and a little aloof, but not crazy. Perhaps the death of a child can break someone, just totally shatter them into something else entirely.

He didn't know the answer, but he became acutely aware that the escalating tension in his body wouldn't allow him to crouch here any longer. He stood up and strode across the street. He placed his right hand on his hip, checking to ensure that his sidearm still rested there, though he clearly remembered putting it there moments before. Force of habit.

The Franklin home, a large, two-story wood-framed Colonial replete with columns in the front porch and a clichéd white picket fence across the front, sat about twenty yards back from the street. The yard and landscaping held promise, but it appeared in a state of disrepair: the grass looked as if it hadn't been mowed all spring, the hedges had shabby green haphazard sprouts in all directions, weeds outnumbered the flowers in the mulch-less flower beds inside the fence. A detached garage sat at the end of the driveway to the right of the house. Jack peered back the driveway and did not see any cars there. In order to gather information about possible escape modes for Franklin, he wanted to go back and look inside the garage, to see if any cars sat in there. If he did, though, he would risk getting spotted from the house, perhaps tipping off Franklin to go running out the front door. He decided to approach the front door, but keep his eyes peeled and ears pricked for any car engines starting up. He thought he could move fast enough off of the front porch to stop a car coming down the driveway.

Two segments of sidewalk led to the front door: one from the main sidewalk along the street, running parallel to the driveway, and the other coming at a right angle from the driveway right along the front of the house. He walked the twenty yards along the driveway and turned to his left, moving along the front of the house toward the front door. He peeked into the large windows in the front as he passed by. No lights were on. The dismal day outside did not illuminate much inside the home either. As a result he could not see much other than the sheer curtains that curved down either side of each window.

He got to the front door and paused a beat. He looked behind him. The local cavalry had not yet arrived. He had gone too far to turn back at this point. He grabbed the dull brass knocker at eye-level on the large wooden door and rapped three times. He could hear it echo off the hardwood floors inside the foyer just on the other side of the door. But he heard nothing else. No one running to the door—or, perhaps more reassuring, running away from it. After waiting several seconds, he knocked again, first with the knocker and then with his own knuckles. To the left of the door he noticed the small plastic doorbell ringer embedded in the wood siding. He reached over and depressed it, subsequently hearing the melodic chimes from inside. He rang it again. Then again once more.

Having already come from the right, he walked to his left toward the front windows on that side of the house. He cupped his hands and peered inside. He looked into what looked like a formal living room: a fireplace in the center of the wall to the left, a richly upholstered sofa opposite with a thick, intricately designed afghan hung over the back, a matching love seat in front of him, just below the windows. A cherry wood coffee table sat in the center of the room, a few knickknacks on its surface. He couldn't make out much past this room, but it looked like the kitchen lay beyond. To the right— on the other side of the front door— he could see the first few steps going to the second level.

The lack of movement was the most striking thing on the other side of the glass. At this point Jack had every reason to believe no one was home.

Jack walked back to the front door. Again he looked over his shoulder, and again he did not see anything resembling police presence. He thought at least the local PD would have arrived by now. He made an executive decision. He put his left hand on the front door handle, his thumb settling into the curvature of the thumb piece above the grip. His right hand went to his waistband, resting on the butt of his magnum. He listened carefully one more time, but again only perceived silence. His thumb pressed down and did not meet resistance. The door was unlocked.

370

He pushed forward slowly at first, moving the door through the threshold. Suddenly he heard a high-pitched beeping from inside. He had set off the alarm system. He threw the door open and drew his gun, all in one reflexive motion. "FBI," he shouted, gripping his firearm at shoulder level with both hands, arms nearly in full extension. The incessant beeping disoriented him. It greatly impaired his ability to hear footsteps, the inner working of a cocking firearm, or any other sounds. He suddenly felt out of place, at a significant disadvantage.

He moved quickly through the door, leaving it open behind him. The keypad for the security system identified itself by the green LED glow from its display across the foyer on the right. He turned to his right and looked into what appeared to be the TV room. He took a quick step into it, surveyed the room with a sweep of his handgun, and found no one. He turned back and performed the same action in the living room to the left of the foyer, again revealing nothing. He walked across the foyer and took his left hand off his gun, letting it fall down to his right side. He opened up the plastic security keypad, unsure what exactly to do. He knew that most such systems had no way to disable them from inside the home without the proper code. He hoped that this particular system had intercom capabilities. If so, the monitoring company would soon call into the home, and Jack could identify himself and ask the system operator to turn off the alarm. That's if the BEEP-BEEP-BEEP didn't drive him mad first.

He moved down the hallway beside the stairs, moving away from the front door. He entered the kitchen, the back door of the home directly opposite him on the other side of a small mud room. He approached it to inspect the back yard. He saw a dilapidated swing set directly behind the house, sitting in the middle of a yard equally as ignored as the front. The detached garage sat off to his right, still without any activity.

A head appeared in the window of the door directly in front of Jack, making him jump back.

"Lake Ridge police!" an officer shouted from behind Jack.

Jack whirled around, putting his back toward a small laundry room so that he could face both the officer that had come through the front door and the one about to come through the back. The officer in the front wore full riot gear and stood with his legs spread wide, his handgun aimed straight at Jack. Jack put his hands in the air, his gun pointed at the ceiling. "I'm FBI!" he shouted. "Jack Byrne!"

Heath Reilly appeared behind the officer and placed a hand on his shoulder. "Stand down. He's with us," Reilly instructed. The officer nodded and turned his attention to the TV room on his right.

"Those front rooms are clear!" Jack shouted, trying to be heard over the alarm. The beeping stopped for a split second, allowing Jack a brief moment to feel thankful. A fleeting moment, though, as an ear-piercing, high-pitched constant screech then emanated from the central alarm control in the basement. The previous beeping seemed like pleasant dinner music compared to this.

"Holy shit!" Jack yelled, putting his fingers over his ears. Reilly did the same. Another officer came through the front door, seemingly unaffected by the electronic shriek. Jack turned to face the back door, where the officer stood calmly looking at him from the other side. He pointed down, indicating the door handle. Jack twisted the deadbolt and opened the back door. This officer came in, mouthing "thank you" to Jack as he passed by and entered the laundry room.

Though he felt paralyzed by the squeal of the alarm, Jack knew he needed to keep moving. They had to rip this house apart, looking for any clue where Franklin would go. Just then the telephone rang. Jack surmised that Franklin's system did not have an intercom; this call would come from the security monitoring center. He found the cordless phone sitting on its base on the kitchen counter. He grabbed the handset and ran outside the house, hoping that he could find enough quietness out there to hear the phone call.

"Hello," he shouted into the phone.

"This is Adam with Century Home Security. Do you—"

Jack cut him off. He did not have time for Adam to go through his protocol. "This is Jack Byrne of the FBI. We set off the alarm. We have tons of cops here, but you can call more in if you don't believe me. You need to turn off the alarm."

"Uh…" Clearly Adam had never encountered such a situation. "We can't turn off the alarm until we hear the code from the policy owner or the police."

"Listen, Adam—" Jack began. One of the police officers, the first one through the front door, approached Jack.

"Is that the security company?" the officer asked. Jack nodded. The officer indicated for Jack to give him the phone, which he did. "This is Sergeant Rick Kensington of the Lake Ridge PD. The code is 'syphilis.'"

"Syphilis?" Jack repeated.

Sergeant Kensington shrugged.

Suddenly the screeching stopped. The silence seemed like the most beautiful sound in the world. Jack could think straight for the first time in what seemed like hours.

"Thank you," Sergeant Kensington said into the phone, and then he hung up.

"How did you know the code?" Jack asked loudly, trying to overcome the remaining din in his ears.

"It's a generic code," Kensington answered, using a more acceptable volume. "We have one with every local home security agency." Carrying the phone with him, he went back inside the home. Jack followed.

Reilly stood over a small kitchen table in the far corner of the kitchen. "Jack, look at this."

Jack walked over to the table, purposefully opening and closing his jaw, hoping it might get the ringing out of his ears. Reilly pointed to a piece of note paper in the middle of the table. Jack leaned over it, careful not to touch the table as to avoid contaminating it.

See you at the cabin.
---Randall

Jack stood up straight and looked at Reilly.

"What do you think?" Reilly asked.

"I think we're going to Franklin's cabin," Jack replied without missing a beat.

"How do you know it's not a set-up—a trap or something?"

"I don't," Jack answered. "But we're going to find out."

374

74

Randall sat in silence in his idle car, his gloved hands folded in his lap. He realized that he no longer needed the gloves to prevent leaving fingerprints. However, he had become so accustomed to donning gloves before performing his Work that they had become a necessary component of it.

As he looked through his windshield at the street before him, he wondered if Jack and his team had ever alerted the President about Randall's Work. The song he had chosen—or had it chosen him?—offered a delicious red herring about the President as a target, based on the thinly veiled JFK reference in its lyrics. He had hoped that Jack would waste some time down that path, but not too much time. While flexible in some respects, his Work did not allow much time for deviation. Based on the message Randall received earlier today from that security guard at his office, if Jack had pursued the President-as-potential-victim route, he had since gotten back on track.

From the passenger seat beside him, Randall's phone rang. Before he looked over, a smile covered his face. The timing fit; he knew who had to be calling. He picked up his phone and looked at the display. His phone showed the digits, which Randall recognized: Century Security, his home security monitoring company, who only called in the event that someone had triggered his home alarm. The FBI had found him.

Right on time.

Even though he knew his Work constituted pure genius, it still could astound him how closely the events that actually transpired matched his plan. His smile broadened and he shook his head, feigning disbelief without any audience to deceive.

He turned his phone off, removed the battery, and placed both in the glove compartment. He had no further need for either one, and he didn't want the FBI tracking his location from the GPS device embedded in the phone, which remains active as long as the battery is engaged. He laced his fingers together, tightening the gloves over his hands. He grabbed the door handle, took a deep breath, and got out of the car. The wheels of his Work had been set into motion. He just needed to continue along for the ride.

75

Dylan Harringer did not consider himself a list maker. Seldom did he find the need to write out an agenda or a to-do list. He focused more on the big picture, the gestalt. His mind naturally worked better in broad strokes rather than fine detail. It was part of what made him a good leader. However, while on the phone with Jack earlier, he found himself taking copious notes, which, by the end of the phone call, had turned into a list.

By now he had placed a mark to the left of everything on his list, meaning it had been assigned to someone. He had called Amanda Lundquist and Charlie Shaver into his office after hanging up with Jack. Amanda had come back to the CASMIRC headquarters from the call center when Reilly had gone to Lake Ridge. He split the list up among the three of them.

Upon completion of a task on his list, Harringer would strike a line through it. At this point, almost an hour after his call with Jack, only two items, both assigned to Harringer, had hashes through them: contacting Randall Franklin's mobile carrier to trace all of his calls and track its location, and finding the location of Franklin's "cabin." His bank records showed a mortgage on a home on Belmont Bay, just outside of Woodbridge, Virginia.

Harringer had called Jack immediately to give him the address. In the interim since their last conversation, Jack and Reilly had supervised the investigation of Franklin's home in Lake Ridge. Jack reported finding nothing of obvious significance. Harringer gave them the address of the cabin. Jack and Reilly embarked for the cabin urgently. Harringer then alerted local police in Woodbridge as well as

Virginia State Troopers. As before in Lake Ridge, Harringer ordered that no one approach the property until all law enforcement parties had arrived. He hadn't yet found out that Jack had broken that protocol at the Franklin residence. If he had he may have changed his mind about putting Jack in charge of the cabin investigation.

Harringer now got up from his desk and walked out to Amanda's cubicle. She reported no luck in getting in touch with Franklin's wife, Sheila. She had called several family members, but could only get in touch with Sheila's brother Sheldon, who had not spoken to her in a couple of weeks. Amanda had also called Mary Beth Franklin's school. Franklin's daughter had not shown up for her third grade class yesterday or today. The school had also been unsuccessful in getting in touch with the Franklins the last two days.

Harringer and Amanda went into the conference room, where Shaver had taken his laptop and spread his work out on the front table. He had printed Franklin's last several credit card statements and highlighted any charge outside of Lake Ridge. Many of them had been internet purchases without much description, which they ignored for now. They focused on the charges from gas stations.

Shaver had used the map on the front bulletin board—the one that already had large red thumbtacks planted on the three previous murder sites— to start placing pins near every gas station outside of Lake Ridge where Franklin had made a purchase in the last four months. He had five tacks in place when Amanda and Harringer arrived. Within ten minutes the three of them had completed the task. When they stood back to appreciate their work, an obvious pattern developed: three lines in the shape of a wide, bisected "V," resembling an overweight bird's footprint. Moving from left to right, or west to

378

east, each line connected the central point, Lake Ridge, to Front Royal, Virginia; Frederick, Maryland; and York, Pennsylvania respectively.

If Harringer still possessed any doubt about Jack's suspicion of Franklin, it evaporated in that instant. They had found their Playground Predator.

76

"Are there any questions?" Jack looked around at the faces surrounding him in the back of the SWAT van. All ten officers had donned their riot gear, the visors on their helmets flipped up for this tactical planning session. Most of the men shook their head subtly; all had the seriousness of death upon their countenance. "OK," Jack summarized. He looked down at his watch— 3:23—and then over at Sergeant Gino Curlew, the officer who identified himself as the SWAT leader shortly after they had all arrived in Woodbridge. Sergeant Curlew nodded. Jack looked over his shoulder at Heath Reilly, who crouched behind him in the crowded van. Reilly offered a single-shouldered acquiescent shrug and nodded as well. Jack finally peered back at the men in front of him.

"Let's go," Sergeant Curlew said. With that the men lowered their visors in unison and the back of the van flew open, officers pouring out in tandem, splitting off to their specific assignments.

They had parked the unmarked SWAT van about eighty yards down the street from Franklin's vacation home, a lovely Cape Cod that sat about twenty yards back from the small street, and about forty yards off the bay on the other side. Because it sat on the outside of a slight bend in the road, and a twenty-to-thirty yard strip of white gravel, bushes, and crab grass separated it from the neighboring house on either side, it seemed relatively isolated. Curlew had obtained a copy of the basic blueprint of the house from the county assessment department, so every officer had an understanding of what to expect once inside.

A BUSTLE IN THE HEDGEROW

Only Jack and Reilly remained in the back of the SWAT van, still crouching next to each other. Jack looked at Reilly, hoping to catch a sense of optimism. Instead he saw... disappointment. Or dismay, perhaps? "What?" Jack asked.

"What?" Reilly returned serve.

"You all right?" Jack rephrased.

"Yeah. Let's do this," Reilly replied. He got off his haunches and walked, bent at the waist, to the end of the van and out. Jack followed him.

They went around the right side of the van, opposite from the house. The driver had picked a perfect spot to view the front of the home clearly yet still keep a safe distance to elude obvious detection. Jack and Reilly would remain in this location until the local police and SWAT teams had secured the home.

The drizzle that covered the morning had stopped and the day had brightened, though the sun still had yet to show itself. Jack would have preferred a nighttime approach, but no one felt safe wasting any more time. As he and Reilly looked upon the scene, they noticed intermittent bursts of tiny movements in the trees and bushes around the home. Finally, like a band of beautifully synchronized swimmers, the eight of the ten SWAT members closed in on the home, positioned at various equidistant points around all four sides. The other two members kept themselves at a distance, the sites of their rifles kept on the front and back doors, respectively.

With that Jack pulled a two-way radio off his hip, depressed the button on the side, and said "OK, now" into the plastic grill in the front. He put the device back in its place. Within seconds a marked Woodbridge Police car slowly meandered down the lane and then

381

swung into the gravel driveway beside Franklin's vacation home. Two uniformed police officers got out of the car and walked shoulder-to-shoulder up to the front door. Jack and Reilly saw one officer knock on the front door, and they could even hear the sound faintly from this distance. After several seconds, the door hadn't opened. The knocking officer looked at his partner, then knocked again.

"Dr. Franklin?" he said. "Mrs. Franklin?" Jack and Reilly could clearly hear the officer, but they could not hear any response. Given the lack of movement or recognition from the officers on the front stoop, Jack guessed that they hadn't received one. He could see a lamp lit in the front right room of the house casting a glow on the closed curtains, but he could not perceive any motion around it or from within the home.

The officer reached up and knocked once more and repeated his call for the Franklins, a little louder this time. He and his partner waited another thirty seconds, and then walked off the stoop back to their car, exactly as instructed if they received no response. They got back into the car, reversed out of the driveway, and drove slowly down the road from where they came, towards Jack and Reilly.

Jack reached down for the radio on his hip again. Before he got his hand around it, he felt a vibration on the other side of his belt. His cell phone. He quickly reached over and pressed the top button to silence the phone and he removed it from its clip in one fluid motion. He looked at the display: Vicki. He let out a sigh. He had expected Harringer with some breaking news on the case. But it was just his wife. He put the phone back on its clip and pulled the two-way radio off his hip.

"OK. Plan B. Now," he said calmly into the radio, which instantaneously sparked a well-choreographed chain of events. All eight SWAT officers moved nimbly into place, three at the front door and two at the back. One remained on each side of the building. The eighth member had positioned himself at the back corner of the house where the electric meter and phone lines entered the home. He had already removed bolt cutters from his gear and, with Jack's most recent signal, he cut the power and phone service to the home. The lamp in the front room went dim, and the officers in the front and back simultaneously broke through the entryway doors.

"Police!" they each shouted several times, clearly audible to Jack. He and Reilly had drawn their firearms and waited several beats. Once all three officers had entered the front of the home without incident, Jack said, "Go!" They broke into a full sprint heading straight for the front door. Even though they covered the ground between the van and the house in less than fifteen seconds, they couldn't immediately see any SWAT members when they got to the front door. But they could still hear them, shouting "Police" each time they entered a room or opened a closet door. Jack moved to his left, into a rec room with a bumper pool table in the middle. Reilly moved to the right, into the TV room. A SWAT officer remained on each half of the first floor and at the base of the stairs as the other three (the bolt-cutting man had joined his compatriots inside the house) ascended the stairs to the second floor.

A few more incantations of "Police" echoed down the stairwell before a new, more intense shout came raining from the second floor. "POLICE! FREEZE! DON'T MOVE!"

Then silence. No response.

Jack still breathed heavily from his sprint less than a minute ago. He tried to control his breathing so he could focus on the sounds from above, but he could not stop his heart from thumping, drumming in his own ears. He heard a creak in a floor board above his head, startling him. He looked up at the cream-colored ceiling above him. A bead of sweat that had settled in his eyebrow dropped into his eye, causing him to blink repeatedly until his hand could wipe it away. Another creak, this time a couple of feet closer to the far wall. He walked along under the sounds, tracking them from one floor below. Then the creaks stopped; the person above him stood still. More silence. Jack looked at the SWAT officer standing a few feet away him in the rec room, but the officer did not return the glance. He kept his focus—and the aim of his assault rifle—on the ceiling above them.

Then the voice, the same one who had demanded a freeze, came down from above, this time talking more than shouting. "We're gonna need a bus. We got two bodies up here."

Jack's breathing involuntarily stopped, his heart sank, his eyes fluttered, his head dipped down. They had failed. They had failed to stop Franklin before he killed again.

77

Jack stood motionless in the threshold of the small bedroom, gazing upon the scene within. The light pink walls had a darker pink wallpaper border that ran along the top, assimilating crown molding, adorned with a pattern of white and red hearts. Twin beds with matching white quilts sat in the two far corners of the room, a shelf of knickknacks on the wall above each one. The bed on the right seemed untouched, completely empty. Two lifeless bodies, a woman's and a young girl's, lay nestled next to each other face up on the other bed. Their arms at their sides and their eyes closed, they looked as though they could be sleeping soundly, save their pale, bloodless complexion and their lack of chest wall motion. Even without the suntans and the smiles, Jack recognized them from the photo on the wall in the doctor's office earlier: J.R. Franklin's wife Sheila and his younger daughter Mary Beth. He had murdered the remaining members of his own family.

The SWAT team had cleared the rest of the house, including the small crawl space above the second floor: No sign of J.R Franklin. They awaited the arrival of the local coroner and crime scene investigation team; Reilly had called Quantico to inform Harringer of their findings and to request an FBI team on the scene as well. A quick survey revealed a pristine home without sign of forced entry or even the slightest struggle. It would seem that Sheila and Mary Beth Franklin had died peacefully.

Jack crept forward into the girls' bedroom to get a closer look at the bodies. He crouched down next to the bed, careful not to touch the quilt or even the floor below as he had yet to don any gloves. He

385

looked at the expressionless faces of the two victims. He wondered if they fully realized at the moment of their death what a terrible monster their husband and father had turned into. Or perhaps they knew full well. Perhaps he had always been a monster, but he waited until the last two months to unleash it on the rest of the world. Jack did not want to try to imagine the horror these two people suffered.

He leaned in closer to examine the skin on Mary Beth's face, her hair, the quilt behind her head. His eyes worked over her outfit— a collared knit shirt with a plaid skirt, strongly resembling an elementary school uniform—for any blemishes, any tears or stains. He studied the skin on her exposed arms and legs. He could not find any obvious outward signs of trauma. To him the cause of death remained a mystery at this point.

"Sick fuck," Reilly said from the doorway, staring down at the corpses with his hands on his hips.

Jack looked sideways at Reilly as he stood up. He nodded in response. "You don't know the half of it." His voice felt foreign, quiet, as if he had consciously to push the words through his vocal cords and out of his mouth.

Reilly's eyes narrowed. "What does that mean?"

Jack looked at him and sensed that he had upset him. "No offense. It's just... you don't have a family. Yet, I mean." Jack looked back down at the dead woman and her little girl. "How anyone could do this... to their own family... It's unspeakable. Unimaginable."

Reilly nodded in agreement. "Super sick fuck."

Jack let a smile crack on his lips, in spite of himself. "Super sick fuck," he repeated.

Jack's phone vibrated on his hip. He pulled it off to look at it, suddenly remembering that he would need to call Vicki back soon. "Harringer," he announced to Reilly. He pressed the Send button and put the phone up to his ear. "Jack Byrne."

"Get Reilly and put me on speaker," Harringer instructed from the other end of the phone line. Jack and Reilly went downstairs and each grabbed a pair of disposable gloves out of a box on a lamp stand by the front door. They walked into the rec room, where Jack placed the phone face-up on top of the bumper pool table.

"OK, we're both here," Jack said towards his Blackberry.

"You have anything there? Any clue as to where Franklin might go?" Harringer asked.

"Not yet," Reilly answered. "But we're really just getting started."

"Move fast," Harringer commanded. "You both know as well as I do that an event like this usually signals the beginning of the end. We need to find Franklin before he continues this killing spree."

"Definitely," Jack concurred. "Anything with cell signals?"

"No. Franklin's phone has been off since we started to trace it. Same with the wife's. Both had what would seem like normal activity yesterday. Neither of them made or accepted any calls today. Any guess on COD?"

Reilly looked at Jack, who answered. "No obvious signs of trauma. I'm gonna guess poisoning or intoxication of some kind. He's a doctor—he could have access to all kinds of stuff."

"Right." Harringer seemed resigned. "We'll keep you posted; you do the same."

"Yep," Jack said, while Reilly responded with a "Roger."

Jack picked his phone up off the table and went to put it back on his belt clip when he remembered that Vicki had called. He looked at his display to find that she had not left a voice mail, nor had she texted him. He decided that she must not have needed anything dire, so he could wait a little later to call her back. He wrote her a text instead:

Big break in case today with crazy developments. Will call soon.

78

The coroner arrived just before 4:15. Jack met him in the front entryway of the house. A short, stout, balding man with an overgrown, unkempt beard, Dr. Grayson Battle had served as the Prince William County Coroner for almost two decades. Jack found him surprisingly spry and cheerful given the horrific situation.

"Hey, Jack Byrne, pleasure to meet you!" he said as he vigorously shook Jack's hand. "Let's get a look at this crime scene!"

Jack pointed up the stairs. "First room on the left…" He couldn't finish his sentence, as Dr. Battle bounded up the stairs two-at-a-time, an impressive feat given his size and stature. Jack followed him up at a slightly slower, steady pace. He saw Dr. Battle march into the middle of the bedroom, where he set down a kit that resembled a large tackle box. Dr. Battle flipped open the top and strapped on two large latex gloves. He then spun around to look at the corpses on the bed. He pulled a handheld digital audio recorder from his front pants pocket, depressed record, and began speaking, spewing out the time, date, and location.

Jack went back downstairs and returned to his task of going through items in table drawers, chests, cupboards, etc. Franklin had led them all down this path so far with his variety of clues; Jack felt certain that another such message awaited them somewhere in this house to send them to their next stop on this wild goose chase. He leafed through a stack of magazines in a basket in the corner of the TV room, finding nothing. *Where would he leave a message?* Jack wondered to himself. He thought of the link between the song and the previous messages. He suddenly wished that he were back at

Franklin's house in Lake Ridge, closely perusing the album collection they had found in the apartment above the garage.

"They got the door off of the little boat house."

Jack looked up from the magazines to see Reilly, who had come into the house through the back door and taken a few steps towards the TV room. Without saying anything, Jack got up to follow Reilly, who turned and jogged back outside.

A small structure— more of a boat *shack* than a boat *house*— stood at the edge of the back yard. A small wooden dock extended from beside it to about fifteen yards into the bay. If the Franklins owned a boat to dock there, it had spent the winter in storage and hadn't made it out yet. The shack had both a padlock and a deadbolt on the only door. They had cut the padlock off a while ago, but they couldn't get the deadbolt easily. No one found any keys in a quick survey of the house. The SWAT officers had decided to remove the door from its hinges, as this might take less time than getting a lock expert to pick the deadbolt. The door had been pulled back to reveal a meager shed. Life vests hung on a short two-by-four nailed perpendicularly into the frame of the shed on one side. Small spikes nailed into the frame at about shoulder height supported two unused oars. In the corner sat a set of bocce balls, horseshoes, and some Frisbees. On the right a large fiberglass chest took up nearly a third of the floor space in the small enclosure. It too had a padlock on the front of it.

For reasons he didn't fully understand, Jack felt a chill run down his spine when his eyes fell upon that chest. As he regarded the large size of it, his first thought was that it could easily fit a dead body. Or even a few dead bodies, if they were small enough. He knelt down and examined the floor around the chest. He didn't know what he'd expected to find, but he couldn't see anything abnormal, such as any drainage from inside the chest or damage to the floor below.

Jack stood back up and looked around him, noticing that everyone's eyes had fixed upon the chest. He sensed that they shared his apprehension about what lay inside it. He looked at the officer who still held the bolt cutters from before, the one who had severed the power supply and the padlock on the shed door. "Could you cut that, please?" He pointed to the padlock on the front of the chest.

The Bolt Cutting Man nodded and stepped forward. He opened up his trusted device and placed the blades on either side of the semicircular arch running through the loop on the chest. He took a deep breath, flexed his arms, and snapped them together, letting out a short but clearly audible grunt. The padlock cracked and fell loudly to the floor, followed by a lighter clang of the now displaced piece of the loop. Bolt Cutting Man then stepped back and out of the shed. He had completed his job; he wanted nothing to do with actually opening the chest.

Jack looked at him out of the corner of his eye with a hint of disdain. He stepped forward into the shed. Daylight, which hadn't surfaced to any impressive degree all day, had begun to fade, making it a little difficult to see clearly inside the shack. Jack didn't have the patience to wait for someone to retrieve a free-standing light, though. He reached down and grabbed the now free metal plank that had been locked under the metal loop in front of the chest and threw it back on top of the lid. He placed each hand on a corner of the chest, having to crouch slightly to expand his arms out that far. He paused for a brief but palpable second before lifting up on the lid to open the chest.

"Special Agent Byrne!" The shout came from behind them all, from someone running out of the house. Startled, Jack let the lid slip, crashing back down at he turned around. The officer came running straight to him, stopping less than a yard in front of Jack's face. "We need you inside. We've found something."

79

Following the young officer, Jack jogged into the vacation home through the back door. The officer led him to the base of the stairs. He grabbed the top of the post at the bottom of the railing and used it to center himself as he pivoted the corner.

"Whoa!" The officer stopped at the base of the steps and backed away. Two uniformed officers descended the stairs with one of the bodies on a gurney. By the size of the form encased in the black bag, Jack guessed it contained Sheila Franklin's remains. When the officers got to the bottom of the stairs, the wheels of the gurney flopped down and began rolling along the ground as the officers pushed it out the front door. The young officer leading Jack leaned forward to peer up the stairs. "The coast is clear," he announced as he began ascending the stairs. Jack following closely behind, two steps at-a-time.

They turned and entered the girls' bedroom, where Dr. Battle crouched in the center of the room near his tackle box, peeling his latex gloves from his fingers. The officer walked to the back of the room as Jack approached Dr. Battle.

"Obviously I still need to do the autopsies, but I have a prelim on COD. I found small needle marks in the antecubital fossae of each of their right arms." He pointed to the inside of his right elbow with his left hand, indicating where he had found the injection sites on the bodies. "I think some toxic agent was injected there, likely after the victims had been sedated, as there were absolutely no other signs of trauma. They did not object to getting a needle in their arms."

Dr. Battle shifted his weight on his haunches, turning back towards the bed. "And, after we removed the bodies, we found that." Jack followed Dr. Battle's gaze to the bed. On it laid a standard size white envelope. Even from this distance, Jack could read the handwriting on the envelope:

FOR JACKSON BYRNE

Jack's gaze darted back to Dr. Battle, who broke his trance from the envelope to look back at Jack. "I didn't move it. It's been there since we removed the bodies."

Jack had found his message from Franklin. He walked over to the bed and leaned over to closely examine the envelope. It sat idly, unsuspectingly on the quilt, with a few wrinkles around its edges from the weight of the bodies that had sat upon it. Jack reached out with a gloved hand and picked up the envelope. He half-expected some alarm to sound, some booby trap to go off, but nothing happened. He stood up and held the envelope in front of his face, between his eyes and the portable halogen that the coroner's team had brought it. Light passed easily through the edges, but not so much through the rest.

"It's just paper," Jack surmised aloud. He held the envelope with both hands by the top corners as he walked out of the room and down the stairs. Reilly had just come in from outside and met him there.

"What is it?" Reilly asked.

Jack shot him a sardonic glance as he held up the envelope, hoping the paper would speak for itself. He rounded the corner and walked into the rec room, placing the envelope on top of the bumper pool table. He swallowed hard, audibly.

Reilly stood alongside him at the table. "That chest in the boat house was full of boating and fishing equipment: electronic depth finders, fishing rods, stuff like that. Nothing else."

Jack nodded.

"Are you gonna open that?"

Without averting his eyes from the envelope, Jack answered, "Yeah." He walked into the kitchen, pulled a knife out of the block on the counter, and brought it back into the rec room. He picked up the envelope and slid the knife into the corner, carefully cut along the top. He set the knife down on the table and pulled apart the slit he had made, revealing a folded up piece of paper inside. He extracted it from the envelope and set the empty envelope back on the table. The unlined paper had been folded into thirds, much like any traditional letter. He unfolded it. In contrast to all of Franklin's previous messages for them, which had been printed on a computer printer in a foreign language, this message was hand-written in plain English. Only a few words appeared on the first page, written on one line across the top:

If you don't get given...

Jack looked carefully down the rest of the page, but could not find any other markings on it. He flipped to the second page:

you learn to take...

Again, the rest of the paper was blank. He pulled it down to the look at the third and final page, which only had an ellipse across the top:

...

Jack's mind raced. He knew what this meant, but it hadn't surfaced into his consciousness yet.

"If you don't get given, you learn to take…?" Reilly read aloud, his intonation indicating that he didn't yet understand.

Hearing it aloud actually helped Jack. Suddenly the ellipse on the last page made sense. In fact the ellipse held the crux of the message. Jack reached down and flipped the envelope over so the front faced up toward him, confirming what he already knew.

FOR JACKSON BYRNE

Jack quickly grabbed his phone off his hip. "Oh fuck." He unlocked his phone and held down the "V." "Fuck, fuck, fuck, fuck," he repeated under his breath. He held the phone up to his ear and looked at Reilly, who stared back at him dumbfounded.

The phone rang once on the other end. "The song," Jack said hurriedly to Reilly.

A second ring. No answer.

Reilly pulled out his phone and opened the web browser. He had bookmarked the website with the lyrics to "Family Snapshot."

In Jack's ear the phone rang a third time.

Reilly waited for the website to load then began scrolling down the page.

A fourth.

Jack felt the urge to swallow, but he couldn't. His mouth had gone completely dry.

Voicemail. Jack brought his phone down and hung up. He looked at Reilly, who had never seen Jack look so helpless, so lost. "If you don't get given you learn to take," Jack began, reciting the song lyrics. "And I will take you."

"You?" Reilly asked, pointing at Jack.

Jack looked back at Reilly. Life began to come back into his face, but it came from an evil place. Rage filled Jack's being, so much so that he almost slurred his words as they came out. "My family."

"Oh, shit," Reilly replied. He tapped his phone a couple of times to speed-dial Harringer, who picked up on the second ring. "Dylan, this is Reilly," he said into his phone. "Get a black and white out to Jack's house in Lake Ridge." To Jack, he asked, "Should they be home?"

Jack had hit the "H" on his Blackberry, speed-dialing his home. He tried to clear his thoughts for a second, to focus on Reilly's question. He thought about Vicki's normal schedule on a Tuesday as he looked at his wristwatch: 5:48 pm. "Should be," Jack replied to Reilly. His phone began to ring in his ear as he got connected to his home phone.

Jack could hear a muffled Harringer on the other end of Reilly's phone. Then Reilly said, "We have reason to believe that Jack's family might be the next target."

After the standard four rings, the home line also went to voice mail. Jack hung up that line, as he decided he would try Vicki's cell again. Before he could dial the outgoing number, though, his phone began to ring. He had to do a double-take on the display to make sure it actually displayed the current incoming call: Vicki.

Thank God, he thought. *She's OK.*

He hit the Send button and held the phone up to his ear, breathing a huge sigh of relief. Like a wave in the ocean, he could feel the rage that had built up fall down upon him, splashing around his feet and washing away.

"Hey," he said into the phone.

"Hey," a nonchalant voice on the other end said. A man's voice. Not Vicki. A man.

Jack hadn't heard the voice in years, but he knew whose voice it was. Like a second wave coming rhythmically behind the first, the rage filled back up, but this time the wave did not break. And this wave stood much higher and stronger, and sheer terror accompanied it.

80

"It's been a long time, Jack," Randall said into Vicki's phone.

"Yes it has, James." Jack tried to remain calm. Though J.R. Franklin had clearly gone insane, he still possessed great intelligence. Jack would need all of his faculties to outwit this foe.

Randall chuckled on the other end, almost gleefully. "I go by Randall now. Have for years. Sure beats J.R."

Jack could detect the contempt in his voice. *Has he done this to me because I used to call him J.R.?* Still having difficulty finding any saliva, Jack cleared his throat in a quick burst. "OK, Randall. Where are you?"

"At your house, with your wife and your son."

Jack bit his lip, holding in his anger. "What do you want?"

Again Randall chuckled. "You know what I want, Jack. You've followed me this far."

"Well, I guess you must have us all fooled, because I'm not exactly clear on that point."

"Oh, you know. And you know you know. You just need to go back to the beginning, go back to where we started. It will come to you."

"What have you done with my family?" Jack kept trying to redirect Randall, get him back on Jack's task.

"Jack, Jack," Randall said, adding a "tssk, tssk" with his tongue. "They're fine. You need to refocus."

"Let me talk to Vicki," Jack requested calmly.

"You have to be asking yourself a question right now, Jack," Randall responded, ignoring Jack's appeal. "You're asking a lot of questions, but not the right one."

Jack did not respond. *What does he want? What does he want me to say?*

Randall continued. "You've followed along. You tried not to, actually, but I pulled you back in. I made you follow." The jovial, almost playful quality fell out of his voice; it became menacing. "You've seen what I've done. You saw what I did to those little girls, Jack. You saw what I did to those two in that house. The question you should be asking yourself—the question I would be asking myself, if I were in your shoes—is..." His voice finished with a lilt, waiting for Jack to finish his thought.

Jack did not respond right away, waiting for Randall to continue. Randall had a script in his mind, and, at this point at least, Jack thought it best to allow him to continue with his own monologue. Perhaps Randall would inadvertently reveal something he'd hoped to keep secret; perhaps Jack could pick up a clue.

But Randall did not continue. His script called for Jack to deliver the next line. So Jack obliged, but surely not with the line Randall wanted. "Let me talk to my wife," Jack demanded more strongly, imperatively.

"The question you should be asking is...," Randall repeated, agitated, his voice louder, his cadence slower, more forceful. "...If I did that to my own family... just imagine what I'm going to do to yours."

Then he hung up.

81

"The black-and-white is reporting no visible activity at your house," Harringer reported to Jack over the phone. "All the lights are off and they can't detect any motion inside."

"OK." Jack sat in the passenger seat of his car as Reilly drove. Marked police cars from Woodbridge escorted them as they raced along I-95 on their way from Franklin's vacation home back to Jack's home in Lake Ridge.

"More local PD and Bureau support is en route, and Amanda and I are on our way there too," Harringer said reassuringly.

"No one does anything until I get there," Jack commanded.

"Of course," Harringer appeased.

They hung up. Neither Jack nor Reilly said another word for the remainder of their drive to Jack's house, which took almost another twenty minutes despite their high speed of travel.

Jack had tried to call Vicki's cell phone again several times after Randall had hung up on him earlier, but Randall never picked up. After the third time, Jack's call went straight to voice mail. Randall had turned the phone off. Jack never decided what he would say if Randall did pick up. He just felt the need to continue to maintain the connection, the last remaining life line with his wife and his son. His loving, devoted wife and his sweet little boy. Jack thought back to the call he'd received from Vicki right before the raid on Franklin's vacation home. He missed a chance to talk to her, and he hated himself for it. Or had that even been Vicki? Was that Randall, calling from her phone?

The digital clock on the dashboard read 6:32 when they pulled onto Jack's street. The day's meager light had begun to fade. Reilly parked Jack's car behind the marked police car that sat about four houses down from Jack's. He waved a hand out the window to the Woodbridge officers who had accompanied them. They turned around in a nearby driveway and took off.

Jack got out of the car at the same time as Harringer got out of his across the street from them. "It looks empty, Jack," Harringer stated. "We've got men with infrared on all sides. No one is picking up any heat signals inside."

"Empty? Or nothing alive inside?" Jack asked, as he began jogging toward the house.

Harringer followed him. "Empty," he said in a loud voice, clearly audible to most of the neighbors on this otherwise quiet street. "Bodies don't stop giving off heat until hours after death." It didn't do much good—Jack now reached a full sprint. "Jack!" Harringer shouted, trying to stop him, or at least slow him down. Harringer couldn't keep up.

Jack didn't stop. Rather, he sped up. He couldn't remember the last time he ran this fast. The toes of his shoes barely skimmed the sidewalk with each bounding step; it felt like flying low to the ground. When he got to his driveway and turned into it, he could perceive two officers hiding in bushes to his right. They rose up instinctively, as if to stop him, but, unsure, they hesitated. Jack blew by them and up the sidewalk to the front door. His hand darted into his pants pocket to get his keys, which, he recalled at that instant, sat in the ignition of his car half a block away.

"Keys! Shit!" he scolded himself. He nearly skidded on the sidewalk as he stopped and turned around. Surely one of the local cops in the bushes would corral him this time, not let him burst into his own home and contaminate what surely had become a crime scene. Regardless, he bent his knees to start his sprint back towards his car.

Before his first running foot hit the ground, Reilly barreled around the corner of the bushes. "Here," Reilly called out, accompanied by the familiar jingle of a set of keys. He underhand tossed the key ring to Jack, who caught it with both hands at his waist. Jack looked up at Reilly, who pulled out his firearm as he continued past Jack. "I'm going around to the back," Reilly shouted as he passed by.

Without saying a word, Jack turned to his front door and withdrew his gun as well. He inserted the key into the deadbolt on the door—an act he had done less than a handful of times in the past, as he almost always came in through the garage. He threw open the door.

"Vicki!" he screamed, echoing off the ceramic tiles on the floor. "Vicki! Jonah!" He moved quickly into the kitchen. He could hear officers filing in the front door behind him. He flicked on every light he could access easily on his way to the back door off of the kitchen. Reilly stood on their deck on the other side of the door. Jack flipped over the deadbolt before whirling around, continuing his survey of his home. Reilly came through the back door swiftly, joining the officers inside to search the home.

Keeping a wide-based stance and his gun in front of him, Jack moved throughout every room on the first floor. No sign of Vicki or Jonah. Or Randall. Suddenly he had a vision of Sheila and Mary

Beth Franklin, lying peacefully side by side on top of Mary Beth's twin bed, her beloved dead sister's bed left empty.

Jonah's room.

Yet again Jack disregarded his training in securing a potentially hostile location when he leapt up the stairs, going straight to Jonah's bedroom. The door stood slightly ajar. He stopped in the hallway outside, bracing himself for what awaited him inside that room. He slowly pushed back the door, reached along the adjacent wall, and flicked the light switch. In the middle of the room was Jonah's empty bed, the comforter thrown lazily over his crumpled sheets, as usual. Jack sidled over to the corner of the room where he knelt down to check under the bed. Also empty. He grabbed the closet door and threw it back. Empty. Just like the rest of the house.

Randall remained one step ahead of him. And now he had Vicki and Jonah, captive.

82

Harringer hung up his phone and walked into Jack and Vicki's bedroom. Jack knelt beside the bed, an open lock box on the comforter in front of him. Jack's gaze arose from the stack of papers in front of him. His eyes met Harringer's with an intensity Harringer had never before seen, in Jack's or anyone else's eyes. "The clue is here somewhere," Jack told him. "We just need to find it."

Harringer nodded. "We are monitoring Vicki's phone now too. It's also off right now, but as soon as he…" Harringer caught himself and decided to rephrase. "As soon as it is turned on, it will ping off a tower and we'll know where she is."

Jack nodded and returned to sifting through files that he and Vicki had considered important enough to store in a fireproof lockbox that they kept on the floor of their walk-in closet. "We'll know," he said confidently. "It's gonna be here somewhere." Having peeled back every document in the box, he dumped them back inside and put the box on the floor. He stood up, regarding the bed. He reached down and pulled back the comforter, followed in turn by the blanket and the sheet underneath. "He's left a clue for us everywhere he's been. He wants to be found." Nothing revealed itself within the bed. Jack bent at the waist and wedged his hands between the mattress and the box springs. He lifted the mattress up and shoved it away from him. It slid off the box springs onto the floor on the far side of the bed, coming to rest at Harringer's feet. Only the white dust ruffle lay on top of the box springs. Jack lifted that up and threw it aside, but he found nothing underneath there either.

Harringer watched this scene with pity, though he made sure not to show it. He could not imagine how he would react if some madman had taken his family away from him. Harringer recognized the impossibility of remaining impartial in this manhunt, yet still he tried to focus on the case at hand. "He didn't leave a clue everywhere," Harringer commented.

Jack looked at him, an annoyed if not mildly angry snarl on his face. "Yes, he did." He whirled and exploded into the closet, where he began rifling through the hanging clothes. Clearly he had begun deviating from rational thought, as he didn't even know himself what he thought he'd find on the hanging rod. "Every body we found, his family…"

Harringer cut him off. "Not with Melissa Hollows."

Jack stopped, each hand with a firm grasp on one of his dress shirts. He looked at Harringer. "The phone message."

"Yep," Harringer agreed.

Jack hurriedly took his phone off his belt clip and looked at the display, affirming that no voice mail had been left for him today. Strike one. He looked back up at Harringer, then launched into a sprint out of the bedroom and down the stairs, into the kitchen. Harringer followed him. He found Jack standing over their answering machine mounted on the wall above the kitchen counter. The LED display showed a zero—no unheard messages. Strike two. Jack hung his head. Harringer sighed disappointedly. Suddenly Jack picked his head up, having found some new hope. He hit a button on the top of the console on the answering machine, which played back the outgoing message.

406

"Hi, you've reached the Byrne Family. We can't get to the phone so please leave a message."

Swing and a miss, strike three.

Jack pivoted to face Harringer and leaned against the counter, his arms crossed over his chest. "What am I going to do, Dylan?"

Harringer had never seen Jack so sad, so despondent. He wanted to say something reassuring, something optimistic, but nothing came. He opened his mouth in a likely feeble attempt to provide comfort, but, before he could say anything, Heath Reilly burst into the kitchen.

"We've located Vicki's cell signal," Reilly told them. "It came back on just a few minutes ago."

Jack and Harringer exchanged a glance. Harringer recognized a glimmer of hope in Jack's eyes, which transferred to him as well. He found the optimism that had eluded him just seconds before.

Reilly, oblivious to this non-verbal communication between the other two, continued. "And it's on the move."

83

Jack stood on the driver's side of the unmarked car, his elbows on the roof of the car and his hands up by his face. He ran the smooth surface of his thumbnails back and forth along his bottom lip, his eyes fixed on the highway in front of him. Dusk had come and gone; night had officially fallen. The flashing strips on top of the half-dozen police cars forming the road block thirty yards in front of him provided pulsating illumination to the darkness.

They had tracked the movements of Vicki's phone signal along interstate 270 North, heading away from Washington, D.C. When they quickly consulted a map, the destination seemed clear: I-270 headed toward Frederick, Maryland, the site of Franklin's first murder. In his brief phone conversation with Jack, Franklin emphasized going back to "the beginning," which now made more sense. For reasons that still eluded Jack, Franklin planned on taking Jack's captive wife and child to the scene of his first crime.

Jack, Reilly, and Harringer had boarded an FBI helicopter in Quantico and flown to Frederick, where they met local FBI agents and police support. They quickly drove down I-270 South to set up a road block on the northbound side of I-270, just south of the route 85 exit for the Francis Scott Key Mall. When they had received information from their IT agents back in Quantico that Vicki's cell signal had come within a half mile of their location, the FBI and police team initiated the road block. Heavy traffic filled the causeway. Surely they had pissed off hundreds of commuters this evening, but Jack couldn't care less about that right now.

Still, something felt off. Jack couldn't put his finger on it, but this just didn't feel... right. He thought that they had missed something, an important yet subtle clue, but he didn't know what. He knew he should feel anxious, nervous, excited—*something*—because they would capture Franklin soon, and hopefully he would see his family well again. But instead he stood there empty, emotionless, his mind searching for that crucial piece of the puzzle that might still be missing.

From the haze of lights in front of Jack, Harringer emerged, walking back towards Jack. He stopped on the other side of the car and put his hands on the roof. Though only a few feet separated them, Harringer had to shout to Jack due to the din of the fast-moving traffic on the open southbound side of the highway. "Now that traffic has slowed, we've triangulated the signal more precisely."

Jack gave a nod of understanding.

"It's the bus." Harringer turned to point to the top of a Greyhound Bus sticking out above the rest of the traffic. "We're going in, but I need you to stay here." Jack opened his mouth to protest, but Harringer cut him off. "Jack, you broke protocol— badly— back at your house. I need to control this scene. We will have civilians around, and I need to keep things under control."

Jack exhaled, displeased, but still confused. "A bus?"

Harringer nodded, turning and pointing again. "That bus."

"It doesn't make any sense," Jack said. "How is he getting them on a bus?"

Harringer ignored him. "Stay put, Jack, please. I will call you as soon as I have any news, OK? Just... stay here." He put his hands out, palm down, pushing the air between them in Jack's direction, like he just told his dog to "stay." Harringer then spun around and jogged back toward the lights.

Jack looked after him, squinting into the lights. Nothing fit. He knew Vicki would never voluntarily get on a vehicle of public transportation without making some kind of scene, something to indicate wrong-doing. He just couldn't imagine that Franklin held Vicki and Jonah on that bus. He must be on there by himself, and Vicki and Jonah remained captive somewhere else. *But why a bus?*

84

She could feel beads of sweat on her forehead, soaking into her bandana. Her cheeks felt moist too. She looked down at her lap, where her arms rested on top of her tattered backpack. She held the small cell phone with both hands tightly, though it became more and more slippery with each passing moment as the salty sweat poured out of her palms.

So stupid, Mary Weardon thought to herself. *When something seems too good to be true, it's because it is, you dumbass!*

She looked back out the window of the bus, trying to peer past the line of cars beside and in front of the bus to the flashing police lights ahead. Movement below the window frightened her: a uniformed cop, walking along the bus toward the front. And a few other cops followed him, all cautiously creeping toward the door of the bus. They were coming onto the bus.

She tried to remain calm, but it didn't work too well. *Maybe this ain't got nothin' to do with me?* she hoped. *Maybe that guy was on the up-and-up.*

She looked around her. Most of the other passengers had fallen asleep. The awake ones either listened to their MP3 players or played games on their portable gaming devices. No one else seemed to notice the road block or the policemen about to board their bus.

She looked down at the cell phone in her lap, lightening her grip on it. The man had paid her $3000 to get on this bus in Bethesda and get off in Frederick. All she had to do was take the cell with her—keeping the power on the entire time— and drop it off with some guy named Heath in Frederick, and Heath would pay her an additional

$5000. *Cash!* The man, who introduced himself as Randall, seemed so nice. Of course she was skeptical at first, but when he whipped out that wad of cash, she put her skepticism aside. Easy money, he had told her. And nothing illegal, he reassured.

Bullshit, she thought to herself now.

She startled when the phone began to vibrate in her hands. She looked at it. "Jack" the display said. *That's it. Fuck this!* She made a snap decision. She stood up and went to the back of the bus. Thankfully no one occupied the bathroom. She opened the door and walked inside, not taking the time to lock the door behind her. She tossed the phone into the toilet and hit the flush button. She opened the door and quickly returned to her seat. Sweat soaked her bandana around her forehead.

She looked around. No one glared back. Perhaps no one noticed. She looked to the front of the bus, where she could see the characteristic blue hat of the police officer rise on an angle as he ascended the stairs to board the bus.

85

Jack regarded the Blackberry in his hand. No one had answered Vicki's phone when he called.

Why had her phone signal gone silent for two hours, then miraculously come back on? Randall knew they would track the phone signal. Suddenly, Jack felt so stupid. Randall had sent them on a wild goose chase. He had never intended to go on that bus. When the police searched that bus, they would find Vicki's phone and nothing else.

So where had Randall gone? Jack felt sure that Randall's reference to "the beginning" had some meaning. Randall rambled a bit during their phone conversation, but he spoke so clearly and carefully when he talked of "the beginning." "Back where we started," he had said.

We.

What did that mean? Did Randall have someone working with him? Had this been a partnership from the beginning? If so, with whom?

Again, it didn't make sense, didn't fit with any of their thinking about this case. Jack's sea of confusion that he swam in suddenly seemed deeper, murkier. It engulfed him. He put his head down on his forearms on top of the car. He refused to admit defeat, but he just felt so... hopeless.

In his mind he heard Vicki's voice—a beacon, an arm reaching into the abyss to rescue him from his bewilderment. "This is about you," she had said last night in their kitchen, after he had told her about the details of the case. What if she were right? What if the "we" meant him—Jack? Jack and Randall?

Pieces fell into place quickly in Jack's mind, as if someone had opened the box of the jigsaw puzzle, dumped the pieces onto the floor, and they fell in a miraculously organized fashion into their designated spots to form the intended picture. For the first time today—perhaps the first time in a very long time—Jack could see clearly.

He opened the car door and sat in the driver's seat. The keys swung from the ignition. He glanced at the phone in his hand and quickly decided that he would call Harringer and Reilly later, en route. He needed to get going. He turned the keys in the ignition, put the car in drive, and drove off I-270 North. He ran the red light at the bottom of the exit ramp after quickly looking both ways, went under the overpass, and drove onto the on ramp for I-270 South. He had to get to Chevy Chase. Back where he and Randall had started.

86

Caleb Goodnight sat in the cushioned armchair in his dressing room. Even though he had spent the last hour in a production meeting for tonight's show—an interview with legendary TV producer Lorne Michaels—he still basked in the glow of his phenomenal show with George Lucas last night. He had garnered some of his highest ratings ever and walked away with the personal satisfaction of a very successful, informative, and entertaining interview with one of his childhood idols. Sitting here now, he felt sure that last night's show would go down as one of his best ever.

His cell phone rang, shattering his daydream. He looked down at the display: Unknown caller. He looked at the time on his phone: 9:18 pm. Same time as the call the last several nights. Intrigue overcame him— he had to know who was on the other end. He answered.

"Hello," Caleb said cautiously into the phone.

"Hello. Caleb Goodnight?"

"Yes," Caleb confirmed.

"Hello, Caleb. My name is Randall Franklin. You don't know me, but you will soon."

"OK," Caleb replied. He really had no idea what to say. He couldn't explain why, but he felt a chill of fright.

"I have some instructions for you. If you follow them, you will have a highly successful show tonight."

Caleb relaxed. Just another crack pot with some shitty advice or scheme to "help" him with his career. He received notes or calls like this a lot when he first started out. Sufficed to say, none had ever been all that helpful.

"OK," Caleb responded with condescension. "Sure, buddy. Can I refer you to my fan line?"

"No," Randall said imperatively. "Because you haven't heard the other end of the deal yet, Caleb." He paused. Something in his voice made that chill come back to Caleb's spine. "Do exactly as I say, and you will have an exclusive on one of the biggest news stories of the year, maybe the decade. Deviate from them, and I kill your friend Jackson Byrne and his entire family."

87

Jack stared at the rock near his feet. He nearly couldn't believe it was the same one. The large black smear of long-ago dried paint gave it away; he knew it had to be the same stone from two decades ago.

The Rock had earned its simple but infamous moniker about five years before Jack entered high school. Two swim team members had used the stone to prop open the back door to the boys' locker room, thus providing access to the school late at night, after security guards had locked up all the other doors to the building. These highly motivated athletes wanted to come get in an extra swim a couple of nights per week; both went on to win state championships in their events. Within a couple of years, however, other members of the swim team would plant The Rock in its place with less ambitious goals: to get high, get drunk, and have a pool party. "Party at The Rock Tonight" became a popular slogan among the in-crowd at Chevy Chase High School. Amazingly, no school official ever discovered their clandestine pool parties, as the participants kept meticulous care of their refuse. These were a rather rare breed of rambunctious but responsible teenagers.

In his high school career, Jack took part in both types of activities: he swam an extra session several times throughout the season and regularly in the off-season, and he drank his share of shitty beer while frolicking with some coeds.

Now, looking at the old stone on the ground, propping open the familiar locker room door, Jack racked his brain to try to

417

remember if he had even seen J.R. Franklin at those parties. He thought not.

Regardless, J.R.—now Randall—had led him here. Back where they began, where he and Jack had first met.

Jack pulled his Magnum from its holster on his hip and grabbed the edge of the door. No light emanated through the thin slit between the door and the outside wall of the school, so when he pulled back the door, he expected to stare into the darkness of the locker room. As long as no one had done any significant remodeling, he thought he could find his way around in there well enough, given the amount of time he had spent there in his youth. His main concern was trying to figure out how Randall planned to ambush him.

He yanked on the door quickly and planted his feet wide, holding his gun with both hands in front of him at eye level, his elbows bent slightly to brace for any recoil should he need to fire. The street light from the school driveway behind him threw illumination into the hallway in front of him, save his long shadow cast along the back of the locker room. He could not see anyone or any movement. Without taking his eyes from the hallway in front of him, he used his feet to shuffle The Rock to his right, leaning against the door to keep it fully open, hoping to pour as much light into the locker room as possible.

He walked slowly into the back hallway, his gun remaining at the ready. "Randall," he yelled out. His own voice echoed off the myriad reverberating lockers in the cavernous room. When he reached the end of the short hallway and entered the locker room proper, he strafed further along, keeping his back sliding along the wall behind him. "Randall," he called out again, and again he got no reply. He held his breath for a moment, trying to hear another's breathing within the room. He heard nothing.

As his eyes adjusted to the darkness of the large room, he could discern some light entering from the middle of the room along the far wall. He immediately knew its source: the light came from the door that connected the locker room to the swimming pool. Jack assumed that Randall wanted to direct Jack's attention to that light, so he tried to ignore it. He knew he needed to clear the rest of the locker room first, lest he get ambushed as he entered the swimming pool.

Luckily each locker didn't have the width necessary to fit a grown person, so Jack felt certain that he did not have to open each one of them. Of course, Jonah was small enough to fit in one. Jack considered this momentarily, but then he decided that Randall would most likely keep both of his hostages together rather than split them up.

They are hostages, Jack reassured himself before moving on. He would not entertain any thoughts that those hostages had already become victims.

He checked the bank of lockers to his right and found nothing. He worked his way past the next bank, crouching to look under the wooden bench bolted to the floor in the middle. He quickly slid past the banks that provided the walkway to the door into the pool. His rapid flash into the pool revealed nothing as well. He cleared the last three banks of lockers in the same fashion, without any sign of Randall, Vicki, or Jonah.

The pool.

He doubled back to the middle set of lockers and turned to face the open doorway. With this full, head-on view, he had to squint

419

to let his eyes adjust. Every light around the swimming pool had been turned on. "Randall," he yelled one last time, his voice revealing a hint of frustration and fear. He slowly advanced forward. As he neared the door, more and more of the room beyond came into his field of view. His eyes scanned back and forth, looking for any clue, any hint of where his potential attacker lay.

As he got within a few yards of the door, he could begin to see the diving boards on the far end of the pool. At first he could just see the middle two, then the next two. When he got within arm's reach of the door, his heart racing, knowing with complete certainty that Randall waited for him somewhere on the other side, he could see the final two, outward-most diving boards. Each had a form on top of it, the weight of which made each board sag closer to the water than their empty counterparts. Jack thought that the one on the far left sagged a little lower than the one on the far right. Jack squinted again, trying to make out more details of those lumps on the diving boards. They didn't move.

He arrived at the threshold, the toes of his left shoe bumping up against the tiled step that separated the locker room from the swimming pool. Nothing but tiled floor existed to his left once he would enter the pool area. Therefore, he assumed that Randall would be somewhere to his right, somewhere on, near, or under the six rows of bleachers. *But what about those figures on the diving boards?*

With his gun still raised, preceding him into the room, he stepped up onto the threshold. He planned on turning to his right as soon as he entered to scan the bleachers, but, with the six inches of height the step added to his vantage point, he could now recognize with certainty the forms on top of the diving boards: people, one on each board. Surely that was Vicki on the left and Jonah on the far right.

In retrospect, Jack would later say that one of the greatest challenges in his career was fighting the urge to sprint to the other end of the pool. He recalled Harringer chastising him for breaking protocol to rush into his own home earlier that day. He let his tensed arms sag only a little and only briefly before regaining his resolve. He burst into the room and turned to his right.

"Hello, Jack." Randall sat on the front row of the bleachers about a quarter of the way down the room, less than twenty yards away from Jack.

"Freeze, Randall!" Jack screamed, extending his arms almost completely to fix the small sight of his Magnum on Randall's chest.

Randall, relaxed and acquiescent, shook his head. "I'm not going anywhere, Jack. You can relax."

Jack began sidestepping to his left, closer to the pool, but he didn't let his eyes leave Randall. "Vicki!"

"She can't hear you," Randall informed him.

Jack ignored him. He continued walking sideways to the left side of the pool, opposite Randall and the bleachers. A four-foot strip of tiled floor ran the length of the pool. He started to shuffle down it, his back to the wall, facing Randall. "Vicki! Jonah!" He briefly looked out of the corner of his eye. Neither form on top of the diving boards moved.

"Jack, stop!" Randall raised his voice now showing urgency.

Jack looked back at Randall. "Fuck you! Don't fucking move!"

Randall rolled his wrist and opened up his arm, revealing to Jack a plastic device in the palm of his hand. "If you don't stop then they'll die."

Jack stopped. He tried to see what Randall held in his hand, but he couldn't tell for sure from this distance. "What is that?"

"Come back here," Randall replied, his voice returning to its usual calm.

Jack looked back at Vicki and Jonah, allowing them his full attention for the first time since entering the room. He could see that each had been strapped to the diving board face up. He could not see any blood or any other trauma to either of them. The grisly image of Sheila and Mary Beth Franklin, lying dead on that twin bed without any overt evidence of bodily harm, popped into his mind. Behind each one of them on the tile sat a small machine with a blinking light and a red LED display, each showing a number. Vicki's machine read "98." He couldn't quite see Jonah's well, but he thought it read "98" as well. In addition to these little machines, Jack could see a thick black wire running from each diving board to a rectangular shape in the middle of the opposite end of the pool. The box looked like a home gaming console.

Jack looked back at Randall, who waved him to come back toward him. Randall pointed to a metal-framed folding chair that sat on the tile less than ten feet in front of Randall; Jack hadn't noticed it when he had first entered the room. "Have a seat," Randall offered.

Jack did not let his weapon waiver, but he slowly walked back to the locker room end of the pool, facing Randall head on. He took a few steps forward, stopping about two paces short of the folding chair. "What is that?" Jack asked again.

Randall held his right palm up, revealing the device to Jack. He splayed out his middle, ring, and pinky finger, but kept his thumb and forefinger wrapped tightly around it. "This?" he asked, almost playfully.

Jack nodded.

"Oh, this... this is what is allowing your wife and son to continue breathing."

Jack himself stopped breathing. He wanted to ask Randall to expound on that comment, but he couldn't seem to push the air out of his chest to ask.

"Can you see the little monitors at the end of each diving board?" Randall asked.

Jack could feel some wind coming back into his lungs, but he still didn't speak. He assumed that Randall referred to the machines with the LED displays, so he nodded.

"Those are called pulse oximeters. Do you know what a pulse oximeter is, Jack?"

Jack shook his head.

"A pulse oximeter is a machine designed to read the percentage of oxygenated hemoglobin coursing through peripheral arteries. Your wife and your son each have a lead—a little sticker— on their fingers. Light passes through from one end of the sensor to the other and it can tell how much oxygen their little red blood cells are carrying around."

Jack thought he understood and regained his voice. "So they're breathing?"

Randall smiled, as a math teacher would when his pupil finally understood long division. "Yes. In fact, quite well. One

423

hundred percent is the best one could hope for, and they're both
satting at ninety-eight percent. They received propofol, a powerful
sedative. They're in a sort of twilight state right now, in a very deep
sleep. But still alive.

"Now, do you see that little box on the far end?" Randall
asked.

Jack again nodded. "Yeah."

"That is, of all things, a Wii console. Nintendo Wii. Have
you heard of it?"

"Yeah." Jack began to sense that Randall intended to confuse
him with this discourse on modern technology. He knew he needed to
concentrate, stay focused, maintain his edge, for he recognized that his
family lying in peril at the other end of this room would cloud his
judgment, impair his negotiating skills.

"Good. It's not a regular Nintendo Wii, though, but I'll come
back to that. This..." He pointed with his left hand to his right, and
then he shifted his weight a little, turning slightly to his left. He
looked to the left, then quickly back at Jack. "This is a Wii controller.
My finger is holding down the trigger on the back side of this
controller on purpose. If I release this trigger, it sends a signal to the
game console—kind of the whole purpose of these remote, wireless
game controllers, you know, to send signals to their consoles.
Anyway, when that happens—or if, I guess I should say 'if'—then the
console will respond by sending out a signal along those little black
wires towards the diving boards, detonating small charges at the base
of each diving board. Simultaneously. See, that's the genius of it,
Jack. They would both go off *simultaneously*."

He paused to place emphasis on this word. As Randall continued his smile broadened, gleeful over the ingenuity of this whole situation. "You see, the charges at the base are not nearly powerful enough to kill them. Actually, if it goes as planned—and, well, everything for me goes as planned—the explosion wouldn't even injure either of them. But it would cause the diving board to shatter at the base. And both your wife and your son would fall into the pool." He studied Jack's face and could not yet perceive terror. He didn't even see fear. Jack just focused on the other end of the pool, looking at Randall's electrical handiwork.

Apparently Randall needed to explain it further. "Jack, your unconscious wife and your unconscious son would fall into the water, at opposite sides of the pool, *simultaneously*. Within seconds their lungs fill with water, their bodies weighed down by the diving boards themselves. Now you could jump in and try to save them. But you'd never get them both. In fact, I'd put money down against your even saving one of them."

Jack turned back to face Randall. He couldn't believe this far-fetched scenario. Clearly Randall's delusions of grandeur had led him astray. He stared dead into Randall's eyes.

"Do you remember what Sarah said, Jack?"

What? Who the fuck is Sarah? Jack tried to not let the confusion in his mind seep into his facial expression. He tried to think about women he knew named Sarah. None of the victims in this case, or their family members. None of his friends or family members. An old acquaintance from high school? Someone Randall knew?

"Loving someone means you're willing to watch them die." Apparently, Randall had given up on the chance that Jack would reply, so he answered his own question. "I'm paraphrasing here, of course." He rapidly cocked his head to the left, as if avoiding some unseen flying insect. "Copyright laws..." he whispered, his face curling into a wince as he shrugged.

Jack had no idea what this meant. It seemed to reference some irrelevant piece of pop-culture, but he could not place it. Jack had a sudden irrational fear that, if he continued to talk to Randall in this meandering manner long enough, Randall's insanity might rub off on him, start to invade his brain like an infection, make it impossible for him to follow a linear thought.

"So, the next question would be, Jack, when I release—sorry, if, *IF*—if I release this trigger, which one do you love more?"

What was Randall getting at? *Loving someone means you're willing to watch them die?* So, would Jack save the one he loved more, or would he watch the one die who he loved more? None of this made any sense to Jack. He teetered on the edge of delirium. He suddenly found himself back in that tent on that camping trip with Uncle Ned, drowning in terrifying uncertainty. He had to shift the conversation; he needed to take some control.

"You're bluffing," Jack accused, still boring holes into Randall's retinas with his stare.

Randall's smile evaporated as he leaned forward and stared right back, deadly serious, for several seconds. As if he had just lost a middle school staring contest, Randall's serious countenance suddenly broke, back into his animated demeanor. "Maybe," he shrugged. He then began to nod, his expression becoming a little more serious again. "Maybe," he repeated. "Do you know what I did after high school, Jack?"

Another diversion in the conversation. Jack's frustration with the lack of contiguity in this conversation began to boil over. He needed to throw a wrench in Randall's plans, an improvisation into his script. "You mean before you started killing little kids?"

"Oh, yes, long before that," Randall replied with a wave of his hand, completely unfazed. "In college. I majored in mechanical and electrical engineering. I actually worked on a couple of projects that later went on to form the basis for much of modern day home gaming devices. But, silly me, I left that field to go on to medical school, 'cause I thought I could make a difference in the world. I thought I could improve people's quality of life. But, no, you're right, I'm probably bluffing about my silly little system down there. Probably." He nodded several times in succession, his bottom lip jutting out, as if agreeing with Jack's earlier notion. Suddenly, though, he stopped nodding and glared at Jack. His voice changed abruptly as well, became more menacing, much like it had over the phone earlier. "Or maybe I've been working on this for the last several months, I've tested it on two separate occasions, and I know exactly what I'm fucking talking about."

Randall held his right hand up in the air again, palm out. "Why don't we find out, huh?" He extended his forefinger straight but kept it bent at the first knuckle, keeping it in contact with the trigger.

"No!" Jack screamed and took a step forward. For the first time since entering the pool, he took his left hand off of his gun put both hands in the air, removing his aim from Randall. "No," he repeated, this time a little more calmly.

Randall smiled. He finally had instilled fear in The Great Jackson Byrne. "Good." He returned a full grip to the controller and brought it back to a neutral position in front of him.

Of course, Randall could be bluffing. His whole Wii Bomb thing could be a total load of horseshit. But Jack could not risk his wife's and his son's lives to take that chance. He admitted to himself that he held an inferior position. He now needed to focus on negotiating. "What do you want?" Jack asked.

Randall's already broad smile widened even further. "Ah, now you're starting to ask the right kinds of questions. I like this!" He slapped his knee with his left hand. "Well, since you asked, I think the first thing—the most polite thing, I suppose—would be to say hello to all the folks watching at home!"

88

Caleb Goodnight stared at the screen in front of him through tears that had welled in his lower eyelids. His terror from the scene before him outweighed the countless other emotions he experienced—guilt, devastation, helplessness. There stood Jack Byrne—more than just an acquaintance, someone he would consider a friend—facing every man's greatest fear: the potential loss of his family. Somehow Jack seemed to keep himself together better than Caleb, though Caleb knew that one should not judge a book by its cover, so to speak.

Randall Franklin had revealed his identity as The Playground Predator to Caleb over the phone less than an hour ago. Franklin then curtly described his current situation, possessing Vicki and Jonah Byrne as hostages, awaiting Jack Byrne to come rescue them. He provided Caleb with a URL which led to a website that Franklin had set up to provide a live feed of the chilling event inside the swimming pool of Chevy Chase High School. Billing it as "the entertainment opportunity of a lifetime," Franklin instructed Caleb to run this streaming footage live during his show. He offered Caleb and his production crew creative control over the editing process, as his website provided two simultaneous views of the pool from which to choose. He promised adequate but not high sound quality, noting that it may go out from time to time. "Beyond my control," Franklin had explained, though, given the intricacy of the entire set-up, Caleb found this hard to believe. Before hanging up Franklin assured Caleb that he would monitor the cable news channel to insure that his broadcast went through as instructed. If Franklin saw anything else on CNN that night, he promised to swiftly execute the Byrne family.

Caleb had immediately tried to call Jack Byrne, but it went straight to voicemail. He did not leave a message, not knowing how he could possibly convey his sentiments in such a medium. After a discussion with his co-producers and the network head, in which Caleb had detailed his conversation with Franklin, including the consequences for failing to comply, they had collectively agreed not to discuss the topic with any police officials. They knew the FBI's policy on reacting to terroristic threats like this one. Even if authorities forbade them from airing the footage, Caleb and his cohorts all felt the moral obligation to follow through with Franklin's demands; they could not bear the thought of owning responsibility for anyone's death. Thus, Caleb had gone on camera at the top of the hour.

During the segment in which he usually provides a flattering introduction of his nightly guest, Caleb Goodnight looked directly at the camera with the seriousness unmatched previously in the history of his TV persona. A memory of President George W. Bush addressing the country from the Oval Office on the evening of September 11, 2011 came to his mind.

"Our normal show has been pre-empted tonight by a terrorist," he began. "A man by the name of Dr. Randall Franklin has identified himself at the so-called Playground Predator that has taken the lives of three small children over the last several weeks throughout the mid-Atlantic. He currently has kidnapped the wife and young son of famed FBI agent, and former guest of this show, Jackson Byrne. He is holding them hostage and filming the entire event, as Special Agent Byrne is expected to negotiate for their safe return.

"I implore you to use extreme caution in watching this show. I assure you that this is very real and, quite frankly, very terrifying. Nothing has been staged. A madman is in control, and we are simply complying with his demands in hopes of savings innocent lives." The show then flipped to the streaming footage from inside the high school.

Now, several minutes later, Caleb, feeling defeated, leaned forward in a chair in the production control room as he watched the events unfold before him. The tears slowly began to stream down his cheeks. He wanted to leap through the screen, to somehow help his friend Jack.

In this sentiment, Caleb was not alone. Over 60 million other viewers at home wanted to do the same thing.

89

Randall pointed off to his left. Jack followed his finger to the end of the first row of the bleachers. A small but clearly recognizable video camera, its red light aglow on its façade, sat on a small tripod which rested its legs on the second bleacher from the bottom. Jack couldn't believe he hadn't noticed it before now. Though Jack remained utterly bewildered, suddenly some of Randall's previous gestures-- those made in the direction of the camera— made more sense.

Randall then pointed to his right. "And there's another one." All the way at the other end of the bleacher sat another camera on another tiny tripod. This one tilted downward, its focus clearly on Jonah and Vicki strapped to the diving boards.

"Your good buddy Caleb Goodnight is doing me the favor of broadcasting our little tete-a-tete on his show tonight," Randall explained.

Jack tried to comprehend this, tried to understand how and why Randall could achieve such an accomplishment. Whether or not it held any truth. Another bluff, perhaps? What kinds of ploys would Randall have used to try to convince Caleb to display this horror show? Quickly, though, Jack became aware that he could not let his thoughts of safely retrieving his wife and son get derailed. He needed to maintain focus. He needed to negotiate.

"You know that's where this all started for me," Randall stated, back in a friendly, conversational manner. "On The Goodnight Hour. I watched you on that show, talking about your heroic and insightful solving of the Lamond Hollows case, and it inspired me."

"Yeah," Jack said, just trying to keep the monologue going. His mind worked on a strategy to turn this monologue into more of a dialogue, but he hadn't arrived at the proper method yet.

Randall continued. "I was in a pretty... dark place, I guess."

Jack noticed a chink in the armor, so he took a shot. "Because of Lily?"

Randall stared at Jack through his eyebrows, doing his best impersonation of Jack Nicholson in *The Shining*. Another terrifying chill passed down Jack's spine, but he didn't let it show in his face. Randall then lifted his head, a satisfied smirk on his face. He waved a finger with his free left hand in front of his face. "We're not going to go there, Jack. Not tonight. Tonight is not for that."

Jack nodded. "OK. Then what is it for, Randall? What do you want with me?"

"What do I want with you?" Randall repeated. "What I want is what you have."

Jack scowled, not understanding. "What I have? My family? You had a family, and you destroyed them."

Randall shook his head in disagreement. "No, not that. And my family was already destroyed. I just put them out of their misery. Their past, present, and future misery."

"Misery that you brought upon them." Jack continued to fire at Randall's perceived weakness, hoping to distract him long enough to take a chance to overcome him, to get that goddamned controller away from him. "Your own daughter, Randall? And you, a doctor, and you couldn't—"

"No!" Randall shouted. "That was out of my control! There was nothing I could do! She stopped breathing! She was dead before

433

I even laid my hands on her!" Shades of despair began to creep into Randall's face, which gave Jack hope. He needed to find the exact right moment to make his move. He concentrated on every expression in Randall's face, on the tension in his grip, the muscle tone in his entire right arm.

But that relaxed, insane smile came back to Randall's face, and Jack's hope faded once more. "Oh, you're good, Jack." Randall pointed at him, like a teammate would after a brilliant pass to set up a go-ahead goal. "I may have under-estimated you. You are a worthy adversary. But seriously, don't go there again or your family is dead, OK?

"What I want," Randall continued, raising the volume in his voice to indicate his bringing the conversation back to where he wanted it, "is your fame. To be remembered, talked about. To go down in the annals of time. You knew that. You figured it out with the messages I left behind, with the song. Oh, that beautiful song. I deserve that, Jack. Not you. You were the star athlete in school, getting all the headlines, all the notice. But I was smarter than you. I was going to do great things in my life. I went to medical school, Jack. I save lives every single day. I deserve to be recognized. Not you."

"So that's… that's what this is all about?" Jack tried to hide his incredulity. In this moment his brain could not conceive how someone could take lives just to get famous.

"Yes," Randall affirmed matter-of-factly. "This has been my way. My way out of my rut. My rotten, rotting, miserable life. My Work."

434

"Why not, I don't know, write a book? Cure cancer? Do something, anything else? Why this?" Jack raised both palms to his sides—his magnum still in his right—illustrating the horrific scene surrounding them.

"I know it seems cruel, but sometimes we have to be cruel to for the greater good. One step backward and two steps forward, you know? Sometimes cruelty is what people need, but they may not know it. Do you know how to break an infant out of SVT?"

Jack's brow furrowed in confusion. Before he could try to respond, Randall continued.

"Of course you don't. Why would you? When I was a resident in pediatrics covering the cardiology floor, we used to do it all the time. Babies who have certain abnormal heart rhythms, like SVT, need interventions to put them back into sinus rhythm. Now, we could give them medications that often work, but they have side effects, and it can take several minutes to draw them up and infuse them. So, instead, you know what we do? We put a bag of ice on their face. We hold it on there, shoving it into their face, until they break out of it. It induces fright, causes them to gasp, to Valsalva, sending a nerve signal to their heart to jump back into a regular rhythm. Talk about cruel, Jack! But it's for their own good, you see?"

Jack slowly nodded. Of course he didn't see. The rationale, the comparison, was completely insane. This verified for Jack that Randall had moved beyond rational thought. The ability to reason likely lay well behind Randall in his current state. Jack would need to tread carefully in this negotiation.

Randall nodded in return. "Good. You know, now's a good time. Now's a good time to look behind you."

Jack quickly turned ninety degrees, opening himself so he could see behind him without losing sight of Randall, frightened about what lay behind him. He now realized that he hadn't searched the entire room as he should have when he had entered. Despite his enormous effort to remain focused, the sight of his family tied to those diving boards on the other end of the pool had sufficiently distracted him that he forgot standard procedures. Now, for the first time, he examined the back corner of the large room. Nothing scary lie there, just a stack of two empty milk crates, likely from the gym supply room, turned upside down. On top sat an envelope.

"Go. Go ahead," Randall instructed. "You'll walk off-camera for a minute, but it's OK."

Jack looked back at Randall, who shooed him forward with a wave of the back of his hand. Jack shuffled toward the milk crates, making sure not to turn his back on Randall. As he approached, he could see his name had been written on the front of the envelope. "Jack," in true Randall Franklin fashion. He reached out and picked up the envelope with his left hand, still holding his Magnum in his right. He would need both hands to open the envelope, so, after a pause, he placed the gun on top of the crate. He scowled back at Randall, who shrugged. It seemed that both understood how useless that gun was at this point. Jack wouldn't dare shoot Randall, knowing that—or at least fearful that—causing Randall to drop the controller would result in Jack's family spilling into the water.

He opened the envelope, which contained one page, folded into thirds. He unfolded it. A copy of a photograph occupied the majority of the page. It turned Jack's stomach, as he suddenly learned more about his position in relation to Randall's.

90

Dylan Harringer and Heath Reilly watched on the small monitor in front of them as Jack walked off-screen. They sat in the back of an FBI van in the parking lot of Chevy Chase High School, where they had pulled in minutes earlier from northern Maryland. They needed to devise a plan for entering the school and trying to save the Byrne family, but, for the last several moments, they couldn't take their eyes from the screen.

From their perspective Jack maintained sufficient control of the situation so far. They both got the impression that Randall wanted to talk more than anything else. He had achieved his moment in the sun, and he wanted to shine and make the most of it for as long as he could. They all knew that, as the name well implies, The Goodnight Hour lasted sixty minutes. So far Randall and Jack had taken just over half of them. As time approached the top of the hour, Harringer and Reilly feared that they may be thrust into action. For now they awaited a sign from Jack to help determine their course of action.

Now that Jack had walked off-screen, for reasons they could not discern, Harringer and Reilly took the opportunity to begin planning. Placing SWAT officers around the perimeter of the school was their obvious first step. How to invade that swimming pool while maximizing the chances of retrieving all three Byrnes alive presented a much more difficult challenge.

91

The stark contrast in the expression of the two faces in the photograph stood out the most at first. On the right Randall's face beamed. His eyes aglow and his smile flashing both rows of teeth, he looked like a nine-year old who has just heard that his family planned to vacation at Disney World. The positioning probably exaggerated this, as his face appeared much closer to the camera that the other person; Jack assumed that Randall had held the camera—likely a cell phone, judging by the photo quality—in his left hand to take this portrait.

It took Jack several milliseconds to recognize the other person in the photo. Her normally natural beauty had washed away. Black streaks of mascara ran down each side of Melissa Hollows' face. Even in this poor copy of the grainy photo, Jack could see the sheer terror in her eyes.

Jack's focus then went to the bottom center of the photo. In her hands, obviously bound at the wrists, Melissa held a book with a flowery green and yellow cover. Jack squinted to try to read the fancy script font in the lower left corner of the book: "My Journal"

Randall had typed a message across the bottom of the page, which he had surely printed off the same computer as all of his previous messages. It read:

THIS JOURNAL DETAILS EVENTS OF JUNE 28 AND JULY 2, 2012. IT WILL REMAIN IN A SAFE PLACE AS LONG AS WE CONTINUE TO HAVE AN UNDERSTANDING. DO NOT DEVEATE FROM OUR

A BUSTLE IN THE HEDGEROW
UNDERSTANDING, OR THIS WILL BECOME
PUBLIC KNOWLEDGE.

Jack looked up at Randall from the page in front of him. Randall smiled back at him. Not only had Randall killed several innocent people and kidnapped his family, but now he also attempted to blackmail Jack. Jack's fury boiled, overtaking his fear for a brief second, but his sense of reason took control, trying to keep him from erupting. Randall still held all of the cards—even more cards now than Jack had previously suspected.

Randall's smile dissipated and he looked at Jack seriously. "You shouldn't run for public office, Jack."

Jack folded the page back up and put it in his inside breast pocket. "No?"

"No," Randall replied. He pointed to a spot on the tile floor where Jack had previously stood. "Come on back over here."

Jack slowly walked back over, forgetting his gun on the milk crates. "Any reason?"

"It doesn't… become you, for one. And, second, you need to continue doing what you do. You do it well." Randall paused and bent forward, the Cheshire grin coming over his face again. "But you can do it better, and I can help you."

"How's that?" All of the inflection had gone out of Jack's voice. He tried not to feel utterly defeated, but it required more and more effort with each passing moment and each demented twist that Randall threw his way.

"You will consult with me on your cases." Randall leaned back again. "I have an intimate understanding of the criminal mind,

439

right? You come tell me about your cases, I will provide insight. I will be the Hannibal Lector to your Clarice Starling. Or you can be Will Graham, if that makes you feel better—more manly. Though I will say that Jodie Foster is pretty butch, so..." Randall looked for Jack to appreciate his humor, or at least a glimpse of recognition of these Thomas Harris characters in Jack's face, but it remained expressionless. "Will Graham was the lead in the first Hannibal Lector book, *Red Dragon*. Edward Norton played him in the film version, which was actually not the original. Michael Mann made an earlier version called *Manhunter*, with William L. Peterson in the role of Will Graham. Far superior, too. I mean, let's face it, Michael Mann versus Brett Ratner? No contest. No one in their right mind would say Ratner could do better than Mann."

The phrase "no one in their right mind" resonated in Jack's ears. How could this fucking lunatic comment on others' judgment about anything? He was reminded briefly of something one of his partners had told him back in his days as a prosecutor: the truly insane don't know that they are insane. Everything makes sense to them in their version of the world.

"So, you can create any mental imagery that you want, but the bottom line is that you will use me as a consultant on your cases." Randall paused briefly, bending forward, adding emphasis to his next question. "Do we have an understanding?"

Ah, Jack thought, *part of the blackmail agreement. I can do that. Or at least promise to do that, if it means getting Vicki and Jonah back.* "Yes," he said.

"Great!" Randall responded. "And then, of course, you should write a book about this case. About me. Do the talk show circuit, the book signings, the lectures. The whole nine yards. The whole shebang. You can call it whatever you like, but I like the moniker Miss O'Loughlin planted: The Playground Predator. It's got a great ring, and I think it's caught on.

"Tell me, Jack. Can you do that? Do we have... our understanding?"

Jack stared at Randall Franklin, the sad, disgusting, demented creature in front of him. His mind flipped through all the details of this scenario, now that it had all been laid out before him. He tried to find options, alternatives to Franklin's proposal. A counter-proposal, perhaps. But he couldn't. And, if it got his family back in one piece, the items listed in Franklin's understanding didn't seem all that bad.

"We can have an understanding."

A knowing smile slowly formed on Randall's lips. "Good. Glad to hear it. I'd offer to share a hug, but I sense I would be rejected."

"You're gonna die," Jack droned, purposely remaining in his monotone voice. While before he couldn't seem to muster any inflection, now he let his affect remain flat intentionally. He wanted to sound ominous.

Randall paused, tilting his head. He didn't seem to know how to respond.

For the first time, Jack felt that he had sufficiently thrown Randall off of his script. He took inner pride in this small victory. "You're going to fry. You'll get the death penalty for this. And with this little dog and pony show you just put on TV, you just signed your own execution papers."

"Wow," Randall replied, his face expressionless. "I'm disappointed, Jack."

"Disappointed?" Jack's face screwed into a question mark. "Disappointed" didn't quite match the retort he had expected.

Randall studied Jack, with a glare of disdain. "I thought you would have grasped this better by now. I don't care about the fucking death penalty. Look what happened to Bundy; he got more and more famous during his time on death row. He reached his height of infamy the day he died. And the trial? Forget about the trial!" Randall started beaming again, and it nauseated Jack. "My trial will blow O.J. Simpson's out of the water. And that cunt from Florida? Casey Anthony? Nothing! She killed one little kid. No comparison."

Jack did not respond to this; he had nothing left to say. He just wanted—and needed—this all to be over. "Now how do I get my family back."

Randall thought for a moment, going back over their conversation in his head, to the extent that he could. After he felt comfortable with their understanding, he nodded. "Yes. Yes you can, thank you for asking. I think we're about done here."

He pointed to the other end of the pool, to the game console behind the diving boards. "Behind the console there's a power strip that's plugged into an extension cord from the coaches' office. Just turn the power strip off. That goes to the console. Without power to the console, my little controller here is useless."

Once again Jack looked at Randall incredulously. "That's it? The charges won't go off once the power supply is cut"

"No. That's it. Then you'll have to arrest me, of course. And no funny business, Jack. Remember…" He pointed to the camera to his left and the other one to his right. "…The world is watching."

92

Vicki opened her eyes, and Jack thought he witnessed a miracle. The paramedics had placed an oxygen mask over her mouth and nose after untying her from the diving board and pulling her back onto the dry, safe tiles. She looked dazed and confused at first, until her gaze focused on Jack's face. She smiled weakly, then her eyes closed again heavily.

"She'll be more awake in the next several minutes," a short, curly-haired female paramedic said to Jack. "Now that we've stopped the propofol infusion, it won't take too long for it to wear off."

"Is everything else OK?" Jack asked.

"Seems so. Good heart rate, blood pressure. Good sats."

Jack breathed a sigh of relief. He met the paramedic's kind eyes. "Thank you," he said earnestly.

He then crawled over to Jonah, who still lay fast asleep, also with an oxygen mask over the lower half of his face. Jack looked at the baby-faced paramedic who had just connected a bag of saline to the IV in Jonah's left arm. "How is he?"

"Stable," the young man said. Jack thought the EMT couldn't be more than seventeen years old. "We need to get him on the bus and get him to a hospital."

Jack nodded to convey understanding. He looked back at Jonah's sweet, innocent face. He looked so peaceful. His eyelids fluttered and he looked at Jack. "Hi, daddy," he said weakly before he closed his eyes again. Tears began to fall down Jack's cheeks.

"Ok, let's get them loaded up," the young paramedic announced. Based on the paramedic's age, Jack assumed that he did not have command of this group, though he thought for sure that he would receive the opposite answer if he were to ask the young paramedic himself.

"They're fine, aren't they, Jack." Randall shouted from the other end of the pool, stating it more than asking. Heath Reilly held on to the handcuffs around Randall's wrists, pulled together behind his back, as he led Randall out of the pool. "I held up my end of the deal, Jack."

"Shut up," Reilly instructed and he yanked down on the shackles, pulling Randall's shoulders back uncomfortably.

Just as Randall had promised earlier, the game console had shut down when Jack turned off the power strip. No booby-traps. No explosions. Randall made a deliberate gesture to the camera beside him of placing the game controller down on the bench beside him and slowly raising his hand away from it. He kept both arms aloft in a classic surrendering gesture, knowing that reinforcements would not take long to arrive.

True to Randall's prediction— much like almost everything over the preceding weeks— a team of officers burst into the room less than fifteen seconds later, led by Harringer and Reilly. Two pairs of paramedics followed shortly afterwards and made beelines to the diving boards and the victims that lay upon them.

Now Jack followed the two stretchers carrying his wife and son out through the locker room and the back door, past The Rock, toward the ambulances parked nearby. The silence awaiting them outside struck Jack as odd. He hadn't thought about it before, but, based on his experiences with a plethora of other crimes scenes, he half-expected a media swarm when they emerged from the school.

445

But no TV cameras or flash bulbs blinded him as they emerged into the back parking lot; no paparazzi scrambled to get a photo of his family on gurneys. He assumed—incorrectly— that enough people could have viewed the entire scene from the comfort of their own homes that the reporters didn't feel the need to come straight down to the scene. In fact, though the public had a front row seat to the proceedings inside that high school swimming pool, no one in the media knew which school housed the event.

Almost no one.

Jack stood by as the EMTs put Jonah in the back of the first ambulance; he decided to ride in the back of the second ambulance with Vicki. As the doors shut on Jonah's, Jack looked up to walk over to the back of Vicki's. Across the blacktop lane he saw a familiar face, flashing him a respectable, sympathetic smile, bordered by curly red hair hanging in her face. "Hi, Corinne," Jack said.

Corinne pushed herself forward from her position leaning against her car. "How are you doing, Jack?"

"Been better."

"You were amazing in there. You did the right thing."

Jack nodded. He knew it would take him a long time to process the happenings of tonight, and even longer to come to judgment in his own mind about his actions.

Corinne swung her head to the side, trying to shake some of the curls from her eyes. "I know you have so much going on, so I don't want to be a bother... but would it be OK if I followed along to the hospital? Maybe we could talk for a few minutes if you have any down time?"

446

Jack put his feet up on the running board along the back of the ambulance. "Not tonight. OK?"

"Of course," Corinne replied.

Jack lowered his head as he lunged forward into the back of the ambulance. "Call me tomorrow," he said to Corinne. The kind-faced female paramedic closed the door behind him and hopped in the front passenger seat before the ambulance pulled away.

93

PLAYGROUND PREDATOR CAPTURE DRAWS RECORD TV AUDIENCE

by Corinne O Loughlin, Staff Writer

In an odd but not unpredictable twist, an alleged serial killer fulfilled his wish of attaining widespread notoriety prior to being apprehended by federal authorities. Over 62 million people tuned in two nights ago during CNN's "The Goodnight Hour" to observe the tension-filled showdown between FBI Special Agent Jackson Byrne and alleged child serial killer Dr. J. Randall Franklin, known better as The Playground Predator. It is the largest audience in cable TV history, and the largest audience ever of a live non-sporting event.

Franklin has been accused of killing three young girls in three different states over the last few weeks, as well as the murders of his wife and young daughter earlier this week. He then allegedly kidnapped the wife and young son of FBI Agent Byrne, holding them captive in a swimming pool while he made demands from Byrne to insure their safe return.

Byrne heroically complied in order to save his family. Due to some intermittent difficulty with the audio of the broadcast, which Franklin himself orchestrated via closed circuit web video and cell phone threats to the show's host Caleb Goodnight, complete details of the negotiation were not evident to the viewing public. At this point, Special Agent Byrne has refused to comment on this aspect of the interaction.

At this point both Byrne's wife and young son are recovering well without any major injuries. They have been discharged to their home after a brief observation period in Suburban Hospital. "Physically they are fine," Special Agent Byrne said in a private, exclusive interview. "Emotionally, I think we'll all need time to heal."

"We are all obviously very relieved at the safe return of the Byrne family," said Special Agent Heath Reilly, who helmed the majority of the Playground Predator investigation for the FBI's child abuse branch CASMIRC. "We also take solace in the successful apprehension of Dr. Franklin. Within hours of his capture, Dr. Franklin signed a written confession to all three killings. While this does not approach compensation for the McBurney, Cottrell, and Coulter families, we hope that his capture may allow them to find some quantum of peace."

Despite Franklin's apparent confession during the broadcast to the murders of his own wife and child, Reilly further said that Franklin has yet to offer any comment on their deaths. Franklin's family and the family of his deceased wife have declined any comment at this time.

Reilly himself declined to comment on whether Franklin's case would be tried in court in order to seek the death penalty. "That's up to the attorneys," he said. All three states in which Franklin allegedly committed murders—Maryland, Pennsylvania, and Virginia—currently offer the death penalty.

Arthur B. Lange, the Attorney General for the State of Maryland, announced at a press conference yesterday that, "Though our discussions with the State's Attorneys' offices in PA and Virginia are preliminary, it is our understanding that we will have the first opportunity to try Dr. Franklin, as the first murder happened in Maryland. And we fully intend to seek and obtain the death penalty."

Another interesting development will be the decision of Franklin's fitness to stand trial. Anonymous sources suggest that Franklin suffered from Bipolar Disorder, also known as Manic Depression. He allegedly was currently under medication therapy for this condition.

Dr. Stanley Christner, Professor of Psychiatry at George Washington School of Medicine, viewed the tape of the broadcast, though he has never met or interviewed Franklin. "Dr. Franklin clearly seemed to be suffering from acute or sub-acute mania," Dr. Christner said. "His pressured speech and constant flight of ideas support that diagnosis."

Dr. Christner further explained that "launching into a psychotic state, characterized by things like delusions of grandeur and a loss of touch with reality, is a relatively rare but very real complication of Bipolar Disorder. The risk of psychosis increases the longer that manic periods go untreated."

From the comfort of his home, Byrne reflected on his interaction with Franklin. "I could tell his thought process seemed faulty," he said. "It really helped to make any decision on my part pretty easy. As long as I could get my family back, I was willing to do or agree to just about anything. In my training and experience, I've learned that it's virtually impossible to negotiate with someone who's not thinking rationally."

Byrne stated that he will continue a brief leave of absence from the FBI, but he plans to return soon. He declined to comment on the recent rumors about his pursuing a career in politics. When asked if he would write a book about his experiences in this case, like he did with the Lamaya Hollows case, Byrne did not initially respond. After a long, pensive pause, and without making direct eye contact, he finally affirmed what many already assumed.

"I suppose."

ACKNOWLEDGEMENTS

Even though this novel is "self-published," a number of people provided significant contributions to this work. Without their help and support, much of this would not have been possible.

First and foremost I want to thank my family. The support and inspiration from my wife Julie and our two amazing daughters are immeasurable. They are the center of my world. Also, photo credits from my website (*www.benmillerbooks.com*) go to my wife Julie Byrne.

I am lucky to have such great family and friends who volunteered as my test-readers early on, so I want to extend special thanks to Marsha Miller, Nate Miller, Bob Miller, Casey Hancox, Andy Findlan, and Nicole Verdecchia. Despite their busy lives, they all took time not only to read my novel, but also to provide critiques and editorial comments. Their feedback and encouragement have been invaluable. I also leaned on sage advice from Thomas Kavanaugh. I appreciate his counsel and, as always, his unfettered exuberance.

I also want to thank best-selling novelist Elin Hilderbrand. A family friend (more thanks to Dolores Fennell) connected us, and Elin offered advice and assistance with extreme grace and impressive punctuality. I have been very touched by her kindness and insight.

Another inspirational force who deserves gratitude in perpetuity is Peter Gabriel. Not only have his songs and lyrics had a huge influence on this work, but he has also been extraordinarily generous in allowing me reprint permission for "Family Snapshot." This novel in this iteration simply would not have worked without it. Also special thanks to Rob Bozas from Real World Publishing for helping to coordinate our interactions.

Thanks also to Dr. Rachel Berger, who initially raised my awareness about the short-comings of child protection laws. She is a nationally recognized specialist in child abuse medicine, and I am fortunate to have her as a colleague and professional reference in my day job. A conversation with her a few years ago sparked the construct of the Melvin Young case and prompted me to delve deeper into some criminal justice literature.

Finally, I want to thank those in law enforcement, child care, education, and pediatric medical care who have dedicated their professional lives to protecting and improving the welfare of children. Though people like Randall Franklin and Melvin Young exist in the world, the evil that they present is and should always be outweighed by the good deeds that you all do.

--*BGM*
March 2010 – September 2013

Opening two chapters from

THE PIPER

Available in paperback and e-book on June 26, 2017!

DAY ONE:
WEDNESDAY

1

Sara Gardner yawned. She knew why her eyelids felt coated in lead, but that knowledge didn't make them any less heavy. Theodore spent nearly the entire night crying—his third night in a row. The sweet little angel she brought home from the hospital four weeks ago had turned into a screaming banshee in the span of a few days. She couldn't figure out what the little bastard was so upset about or why he had turned on her: his belly was full, his diaper dry, and he had a clean binky at the ready all the time. She imagined she shouldn't take it personally, but since it was just the two of them in this one-bedroom apartment, she couldn't help it. There was no one else for him to be pissed at.

She felt like going to the WIC office about as much as she felt like jamming a hot poker down her throat. But she was low on formula, and, if she didn't show, those assholes at WIC would be calling her with threats of Child Protective Services. She'd heard that story too many times from her friends. Granted, she wouldn't trust those deadbeat friends to watch Theodore alone for five minutes, but she still didn't want to take any chances.

Of course, Theodore lay fast asleep in his bassinette. She had splashed water on her face, gotten dressed in relatively clean clothes—no visible spit-up, a near miracle—and packed everything she would need in the diaper bag. She couldn't kill any more time. She knew they had to leave now to make it to the appointment on time, but she relished this precious silence so much that she didn't think she could bear to wake him. Could she make the magical transfer? Gently slip her arms underneath him, lift him lightly, and place him securely but softly into his car seat? It seemed like a long shot, the stuff of legend, but she knew she had to try.

She tiptoed to the crib along the carpeted floor. She put the backs of her hands on the small mattress, depressing it to slip under his back more easily. She bent at the waist and slowly inched her hands under her sleeping baby. He didn't stir. She nimbly raised him out of the bassinette and put him in the car seat on the floor. He barely moved a muscle. He must have completely wiped himself out with the wailing all night. She encircled his arms in the straps and clicked home the buckle, which he miraculously tolerated without opening his eyes. She breathed for the first time in what seemed like minutes. She scooped up the car seat and the diaper bag and left the apartment.

Her piece-of-shit 1997 Accord was parked only two spaces from the door to her apartment building. The temperature had already reached 80 even though the clock hadn't hit 10:00 yet—pretty unusual for late September in Boston. Indian summer must have arrived. Still tiptoeing, she moved from the building's entryway door to the car and put the car seat on the pavement while she put the key in the lock on the door. She never knew if her car was made before automatic door locks, or if hers had been just too cheap to have them.

"Hey," she heard from behind her. She didn't recognize the man's voice. Even though she hadn't seen anyone else out here in the parking lot, she assumed he must have been talking to someone other than her. Besides, she didn't have the time or the interest to talk to anyone right now. She opened the passenger door and began to pull the front seat forward, preparing to lock Theodore's car seat into its base in the back seat.

"Hey." The voice was much closer this time. She put Theodore's car seat back down on the ground and began to turn around. She didn't want to be a bitch, but she was going to tell this guy to get lost.

As she pivoted, she could see the guy walking toward her. Fast.

"What the hell?" she wanted to say, but she never got a chance. As she opened her mouth, the guy pulled his right hand out of his jacket pocket and thrust it into her left side. An intense tingling exploded from her torso throughout her entire body. She stiffened and fell to the ground, every muscle fiber in her body firing at once. She landed on her back, looking straight up at the sky. The guy leaned over her. Sunglasses, a baseball cap, and a fake mustache obscured his features. He blackened her world with a black silk hood over her head. Though she still couldn't move, he hit her again with the Taser, this time in the neck. Her body jerked again and the pain surged. She tried to scream, to speak, to gasp, anything; all that came out was a pathetic gurgle.

She heard the bottom of the car seat scrape against the concrete as the man lifted it up. She heard his rapid footsteps as he hustled away. But she never heard Theodore.

He slept through the whole thing.

2

Jackson Byrne's ass hurt. He shifted in the chair, gave it a few seconds, and concluded that his predicament had not improved. He spread his legs a little as he looked down at the chair. The dull gray hue, the glossy surface, and its composition—not quite ceramic, not quite plastic, but some bastardized amalgam of the two—reminded him of the chairs in his high school classrooms. He understood why those chairs had to be so uncomfortable: to keep students awake during the day. (God forbid the teachers should bear that responsibility.) But why here? Sure, it was prison, but did things have to be so dreadful even for the visitors?

Before he let his mind wander too far, Jack focused on why he was here. He came because he had made a deal, one witnessed by over 60 million people on national TV. Even though the deal was made under duress, and with a madman, he had held up his end of the bargain. But integrity wasn't the reason for his presence here today. He sat in this ass-agonizing chair because of his indiscretions, and he showed up every month to keep his infidelity from reaching the masses.

Not that he cared about the masses necessarily. He once had, and his father's dear friend Philip Prince certainly would, even now. Jack cared about his family.

Every time he sat in one of these chairs, Jack thought about his wonderful wife Vicki and his adorable son Jonah. Coming here was his penance for protecting them from the truth. He conjured further justification by preserving the incarceration of the pedophilic murderer Melvin Young, as a news release of Jack's previous affair would bring Young's conviction into question. Jack had just enough insight to know that his efforts served to protect himself just as much—if not more—than anyone else, but thinking about his family and the innocent children he protected made it easier to tolerate these visits to Coffeewood Correctional.

Jack yawned, his mouth agape like a capuchin monkey fending off an enemy. He really needed a good night's sleep, but deep slumber had evaded him for weeks now.

On the other side of the thick glass in front of Jack, a large metal door opened at the opposite end of a narrow room. With a guard at his flank, Randall Franklin shuffled through the door. Surely he knew that Jack was today's visitor—Jack was one of only three people to visit since his incarceration, and his lawyer was not due to come back until tomorrow— yet he looked pleasantly surprised when he saw Jack. The corner of the left side of his mouth lifted in a half-smirk. It turned Jack's stomach.

Jack had seen Randall three times since his capture more than four months ago. Each time he experienced a fleeting moment of rage. He hated the man on the other side of the glass. He hated him for what Randall did to those three little girls, for what he did to his own devastated family, for making Jack come here every month. (For that Jack also loathed himself, knowing how much responsibility he took for it.) Most of all, though, he hated Randall for what he had done to Vicki and Jonah. The kidnapping had left Vicki with a near-crippling case of agoraphobia; at present she would only leave the house for her scheduled psychiatry appointments. Thankfully Jonah seemed to be better recently; he hadn't woken up from horrible nightmares in almost two months. But even this harbinger of sustainable improvement could not quell Jack's acrimony for Randall.

Jack's pride would not allow him to show his rage to Randall, however. He would not give this stack of shit the satisfaction of even a glimpse at how he had altered Jack's life. It was bad enough that he dragged his ass—his inordinately and excruciatingly flattened ass— here every month. So he swallowed down his anger and shook his head at Randall's smirk.

He would never admit it aloud, but Jack had fantasized on more than one occasion about killing Randall—or hiring someone else to murder him. He replayed that night in May in his head countless times, wondering if he could have found a way to kill Randall on those swimming pool bleachers and still save his family. He had yet to come up with a viable scenario. He realized that this exercise was nothing more than mental masturbation, and that his fantasy would never become reality. This didn't stop him from letting his imagination wander episodically.

Randall sat down in a chair opposite Jack. The guard yelled "Ten minutes," as he turned to walk out of the room.

"Thanks, Boss Edgecomb," Randall said over his shoulder. He called every guard Boss Edgecomb, after the lead character in Stephen

King's *The Green Mile*. The guard did not pause but shook his head as he left the room and shut the door.

Randall brought his shackled wrists up to his chest, opened up his right palm to face Jack, and rapidly oscillated his hand left and right, giving an overly enthusiastic wave, that sick smile still stuck on his face. The gesture reminded Jack of another character (also portrayed by Tom Hanks): the simple-minded Forest Gump. Jack couldn't be fooled, though; Randall Franklin was anything but simple-minded.

Jack picked up the telephone from its hook to his left. Randall grabbed his too, though it required slightly more effort because of his handcuffs. Jack was pretty sure that the handcuffs were not part of protocol; he surmised that the guards cuffed Randall during these visits as a small act of retribution for what an annoying prick he was.

"Hello, Randall," Jack said flatly.

Randall did not reply at first, his face frozen in that smile. He stared at Jack as a teenager ogled his classroom crush. Finally, he pursed his lips, presenting a façade of seriousness. "How's the book coming?"

"Slowly," Jack answered. "But we're making progress."

"Good! That's good... good news, that. What news have you on the Whalen kidnapping?" Every so often Randall used this faux-British sentence structure. It irritated the shit out of Jack.

Jack's end of his deal with Randall entailed coming to these monthly meetings and bringing the details of an active case from his FBI division. Randall wanted a part in Jack's work, a role to play in Jack's investigations. As he had suggested during their negotiation (if one could call it that), Randall would play Hannibal Lector to Jack's Clarice Starling.

The last time Jack visited Randall he gave him the case of the Whalen kidnapping. Dustin Whalen, the 2-year-old son of financial planner Darren and chiropractor Elizabeth, had been taken from his home in Central California in the middle of the night. Within hours, Jack's FBI division CASMIRC (the Child Abduction and Serial Murder Investigative Resource Center) had been called in at the request of the family. Less than two days later, the local authorities apprehended the culprit: Darren's jilted lover who took Dustin in an act of revenge. The story hit the California news circuit heavily, but national coverage was scant.

"Right again," Jack said. "Darren, the father, was involved. In a sense. Just like you predicted."

"A shorted business associate?"

"Pissed-off mistress."

"Ah. Yes, yes." Randall nodded several times, soaking in this information. "Anything new for me?"

Jack glared at him. Heretofore, Jack had not been fully honest with Randall about these cases. He had no real intention of informing Randall of the inside details of an active investigation. Instead, he had pulled files of older cases on his way out of the office. He held no reservations about spilling data to Randall from a closed case that would soon be part of public record, if it weren't already. He had to choose relatively low-profile cases, though, to insure that Randall had not heard of them before.

Randall's record now stood at 3-0: his interpretation of the investigative information Jack provided had yielded a correct analysis every time. He didn't always nail the exact culprit precisely, but his intuition pointed in the right direction. Applying Randall's input in retrospect, Jack concluded that Randall's contribution would have eventually led to the perpetrator, perhaps faster than the existing authorities had.

Given this, Jack had decided to divulge some information to Randall about an active case, one that had just come into CASMIRC this morning. Now, sitting across from the target of his most fiery enmity, he second-guessed his earlier decision. Other than inflating Randall's already unparalleled ego, sharing this intelligence with him bore no risk or downside. Yet Jack abhorred the thought of colluding with him.

It's for the case, he reminded himself. *If he can help, we could potentially save lives.* He would put his personal vendetta—one he had every right to bear—aside.

Jack leaned forward, talking a little more quietly and pointedly. "This morning an infant was abducted in Massachusetts, just south of Boston."

Demonstrating that his interest had been piqued, Randall also leaned forward, his face less than a foot from Jack's—two inches of which were glass. His smile had faded. Amazingly, he said nothing.

"It's the second such abduction in the last month. Same MO."

Randall leaned back in his chair, his face remaining expressionless. "You've got two babies go missing in Southie?"

"Not Southie, technically. But near there. You know the area?"

"Not outside of Matt Damon movies, no." Unlike previous interactions, Randall didn't even crack a smile when using a pop culture reference.

Jack knew he had his full attention. So far he didn't regret disclosing this case to Randall.

"What happened to the first baby?" Randall asked.

"The first infant has not been found. She's still missing."

ABOUT THE AUTHOR

Ben Miller was born in Franklin, Pennsylvania. He earned his Bachelor's Degree in Psychology from Yale University and his Medical Doctorate from the University of Pittsburgh. Since completing residency training in pediatrics, he has worked as a Pediatric Hospitalist and Diagnostic Specialist.

In addition to *A Bustle in the Hedgerow,* Ben is the author of *The Piper*, the second book in the CASMIRC series. He resides with his wife and three daughters in a suburb of Pittsburgh, PA, where he continues to work on his next novel while practicing and teaching pediatrics.

73097936R00260

Made in the USA
Columbia, SC
05 July 2017